Dear Reader,

Welcome to Whitehorse, Montana. It is so nice for me to be back, since I live in a town so much like Whitehorse that locals think they see themselves in my books.

It's a Western town with lots of cowboys, pickup trucks, one grocery and no stoplight. But most of us have everything we need here. If we feel adventurous, we can drive five hundred miles round-trip to the closest big-box store. Except in the winter, when the roads are sometimes closed.

But that's why I set the Whitehorse series here. I love the wild, open spaces where there are more cows than people and more dirt roads than paved ones. This is cowboy country and always has been.

In my new book, *Rough Rider*, the McGraw family has found one of the missing twins kidnapped from their cribs twenty-five years ago. But Jesse Rose is still missing and it's up to Boone McGraw to find her and bring her home. It's going to take the help of a very determined female PI. C.J. West has no idea what she'd gotten herself into with the handsome cowboy.

As a bonus, you get *Matchmaking with a Mission*, an older Whitehorse book. I love old houses and their history, and there are a lot of them in this part of Montana. A few are haunted, as McKenna Bailey will find out. Cowboy Nat Dempsey only knows about some of the ghosts, but once they start digging...

I hope you enjoy these Whitehorse, Montana books as there are now twenty-seven of them in the series—and more to come next year!

B.J. Daniels

B.J. Daniels is a *New York Times* and *USA TODAY* bestselling author. She wrote her first book after a career as an award-winning newspaper journalist and author of thirty-seven published short stories. She lives in Montana with her husband, Parker, and three springer spaniels. When not writing, she quilts, boats and plays tennis. Contact her at bjdaniels.com, on Facebook or on Twitter, @bjdanielsauthor.

B.J.

NEW YORK TIMES **BESTSELLING AUTHOR**

DANIELS

ROUGH RIDER &
MATCHMAKING WITH
A MISSION

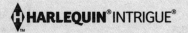
HARLEQUIN® INTRIGUE®

ISBN-13: 978-0-373-83905-6

Rough Rider & Matchmaking with a Mission

Copyright © 2017 by Harlequin Books S.A.

The publisher acknowledges the copyright holder of the individual works as follows:

Rough Rider
Copyright © 2017 by Barbara Heinlein

Matchmaking with a Mission
Copyright © 2008 by Barbara Heinlein

Recycling programs for this product may not exist in your area.

This edition published by arrangement with Harlequin Books S.A.

For questions and comments about the quality of this book, please contact us at CustomerService@Harlequin.com.

Printed in U.S.A.

www.Harlequin.com

CONTENTS

This book is for Anita Green, who opened a quilt shop in our little town. There is nothing like sitting in her shop after a long day writing and dreaming of new projects—both writing and quilting.

ROUGH RIDER

Chapter One

Boone McGraw parked the pickup at the edge of the dark, deserted city street and checked the address again. One look around at the boarded-up old buildings in Butte's uptown and he feared his suspicions had been warranted.

Christmas lights glowed in the valley below. But uptown on what had once been known as the richest hill on earth, there was no sign of the approaching holiday. Shoving back his Stetson, he let out a long sigh. He feared the information the family attorney had allegedly received was either wrong or an attempted con job. It wouldn't be the first time someone had tried to cash in on the family's tragedy.

But he'd promised his father, Travers McGraw, that he would follow up on the lead. Not that he believed for a moment that it was going to help him find Jesse Rose, his sister, who'd been kidnapped from her crib twenty-five years ago.

Boone glanced toward the dilapidated building that reportedly housed Knight Investigations. According to the family's former lawyer, Jim Waters, he'd spoken to a private investigator by the name of Hank Knight a few times on the phone. Knight had asked questions that supposedly had Waters suspecting that the PI knew something more than he was saying. But Waters had never met with the man. All he'd had for Boone to go on was a phone number and an address.

The phone had recently been disconnected and the century-old brick building looked completely abandoned with dusty for-lease signs in most of the windows and just dust in others. No lights burned in the building—not that he'd expected anyone to be working this late.

Boone told himself that he might as well get a motel for the night and come back tomorrow. Not that he expected to find anything here. He was convinced this long trip from Whitehorse to Butte had been a wild-goose chase.

His father had been easy prey for twenty-five years. Desperate to find the missing twins who'd been kidnapped, Travers had appealed to every news outlet. Anyone who'd watched the news or picked up a newspaper over the past twenty-five years knew how desperate he was since each year, the amount of the reward for information had grown.

Boone, suspicious by nature, had been skeptical from the get-go. The family attorney had proven he couldn't be trusted. So why trust information he said he'd gotten? His father hadn't trusted the lawyer for some time—with good reason. He swore under his breath. All he could think about was how disappointed his father was going to be—and not for the first time.

But he'd promised he would track down the PI and follow up on the information no matter what it took. And damn if he wouldn't, he thought as he started his pickup. But before he could pull away, he caught movement out of the corner of his eye. A dark figure had just come around the block and was now moving quickly down the sidewalk. The figure slowed at the building that housed Knight Investigations. He watched as the person slipped in through the only door at the front.

Across the street, Boone shut off the truck's engine and waited. He told himself the person he'd seen could be homeless and merely looking for a place to sleep. It was late and the fall night was clear and cold at this high altitude. Butte sat at 5,538 feet above sea level and often had snow on the ground a good portion of the year.

Boone hunkered in the dark, watching the building until he began to lose patience with himself. This was a waste of his time. The cab of the truck was getting cold. What he needed was a warm bed. A warm meal didn't sound bad, either. He could come back in the morning and—

A light flickered on behind one of the windows on the top floor and began to bob around the room. Someone was up there with a flashlight. He squinted, able to finally make out the lettering on the warbled old glass: Knight Investigations.

He felt his pulse thrum under his skin. It appeared he wasn't the only one interested in Hank Knight.

Chapter Two

After climbing out and locking the rig, Boone headed for the door where he'd seen the figure disappear inside. A sliver of moon hung over the mountains that ringed Butte. Stars twinkled like ice crystals in the midnight blue sky overhead. Boone could see his breath as he crossed the street.

The moment he opened the door, he was hit with the musky scent of the old building. He stopped just inside to listen, but heard nothing. Seeing the out-of-order sign on the ancient elevator, he turned to the door marked Stairs, opened it and saw that a naked bulb dangled from the ceiling giving off dim light. He began to climb, taking three steps at a time.

As he neared the top floor, he slowed and quieted the sound of his boot soles as best he could on the wooden stairs. Pushing open the door marked Fifth Floor, he listened for a moment, then stepped out. A single bulb glowed faintly overhead, another halfway down the long empty hallway.

The building was eerily quiet. No lights shone under any of the doors to his right. To his left, toward the front of the building, he saw that there were four doors.

The last door, where he estimated Knight Investigations should be, was ajar. A faint light glowed from within.

As quietly as possible, he moved down the hall, telling himself maybe Hank had come back for something. Or someone else was looking for something in the detective's office.

He was almost to the doorway when he stopped to listen. Someone was in there banging around, opening and closing metal file cabinet drawers. Definitely searching for something.

Boone leaned around the edge of the doorjamb to look into the office. In the ambient light of the intruder's flashlight, he saw nothing but an old large oak desk, a worn leather chair behind it and a couple of equally worn chairs in front of it. Along the wall were a half dozen file cabinets, most of them open. There seemed to be files strewn everywhere.

With Knight Investigations' phone disconnected, he had assumed Hank had closed down the business. Possibly taken off in a hurry. Now, seeing that the man had even left behind his office furniture as well as file cabinets full of cases, that seemed like a viable explanation. Hank Knight was on the lam.

His pulse jumped at the thought. Was it possible he did know something about Jesse Rose and the kidnapping? Is that why he'd taken off like he apparently had?

Boone couldn't see the intruder—only the flashlight beam low on the other side of the desk. He could hear movement. It sounded as if the intruder was rustling through papers on the floor behind the desk. Looking for something in particular? Or a homeless person just piling up papers to make a fire in the chilly office?

Stepping closer, Boone slowly pushed the door open

a little wider. The door creaked. The intruder didn't seem to hear it, but he froze for a moment anyway. For all he knew, the person going through papers on the floor behind the desk could be armed and dangerous— if not crazy and drugged up.

Pushing the door all the way open, he carefully stepped in. He took in the crowded office in the ambient light of the intruder's flashlight beam. The office had clearly been ransacked. Files were all over the floor and desk.

He realized that this intruder hadn't had enough time to make this much of a mess. Someone had already been here. Which meant this new intruder was probably too late for whatever he was searching for. If that's what he was doing hidden on the other side of the desk.

The line of old metal file cabinets along the wall all had their drawers hanging open. In the middle of all this mess, the large old oak desk was almost indistinguishable because of piles of papers, dirty coffee cups and stacks of files.

He moved closer, still unable to see the intruder, who appeared to be busy on the floor behind the large worn leather office chair on the other side of the cluttered desk.

The flashlight beam suddenly stilled. Had the intruder heard him?

Boone reached into his pocket, found his cell phone, but stopped short of calling 911. His family had been in the news for years. If the cops came, so would the media. He swore under his breath and withdrew his hand sans the cell phone.

Boone had a bad feeling that anchored itself in the pit of his stomach. He reminded himself that the person behind that desk might be someone more dangerous than he was in the mood to take on tonight.

He looked around for something he could use as a weapon. He had no desire to play hero. He'd always been smart enough to pick and choose his battles. This wasn't one he wanted to lose for a wild-goose chase. Seeing nothing worthy of being a weapon, he took a step back.

The person on the other side of the desk had stopped making a sound. The beam of the flashlight hadn't moved for a full minute.

He took another step back. The floorboards groaned under his weight. He swore under his breath as suddenly the flashlight beam swooped across the ceiling. The figure shot up from behind the office chair. All he caught was a flash of wild copper-colored hair—and the dull shine of a handgun—before the light blinded him.

Instinctively, he took another step backward. One more and he could dive out into the hallway—

"Take another step and you're a dead man."

He froze at the sound of a woman's voice—and the imminent threat in it. Not to mention the laser dot that had appeared over his heart.

C.J. STARED AT the cowboy standing just inside the door. The gun in her hand never wavered. Nor did the red laser dot pointed at his heart move a fraction of an inch. He was a big man, broad-shouldered, slim-hipped and rugged-looking. He wore Western attire, including a Stetson as if straight off the ranch.

"Easy," he said, his voice deep and soft, but nonetheless threatening. "I'm just here looking for Hank Knight."

"Why?"

He frowned, holding up one hand to shield his eyes from the flashlight she also had on him. "That's between him and me. How about I call the cops so they can ask you why you're ransacking his office." He started to reach into his pocket.

She lowered the flashlight so she was no longer blinding him and shook her head. "I wouldn't do that if I were you," she said, motioning with the gun. "Who are you and why do you want to see Hank?"

"Why should I tell *you*?" She could see that he was taking her measure. He could overpower her easily enough given his size—and hers. But then again, there was that "equalizer" in her hand.

"You should tell me because I have a gun pointed at your heart—and I'm Hank's partner. C.J. West."

He seemed to chew on that for a moment before he said, "Boone McGraw."

She took in the name. "Kidnapping case," she said, more to herself than to him. Fraternal twins, six months old, taken from their cribs over twenty-five years ago. A ransom was paid but the twins were never returned. That was the extent of what she knew and even that was vague. The only reason she knew this was because of something she'd recently seen on television. There'd been an update. One of the kidnappers had been found dead.

"Your partner was looking into the case."

"That's not possible."

"Our lawyer spoke with him on two different occasions, so I'm afraid it definitely happened. So how about lowering the gun?"

Frowning, she considered what he'd said, still skeptical. She and Hank talked about all their cases. It wouldn't have been like him to keep a possible case like this from her.

But she did lower the gun, tucking it into the waistband of her jeans—just in case.

"Thanks. Now, if you could please tell me where I can find him..."

"Day after tomorrow he will be in Rosemont Cemetery."

He'd been looking around the office, but now his gaze shot back to her. *"Cemetery?"*

"He was killed by a hit-and-run driver three days ago." Her voice cracked. It still didn't seem real, but it always came with a wave of grief and pain.

"A *hit-and-run*?"

She wondered if he planned to keep echoing everything she said. She really didn't have time for this.

"Clearly you're too late. Not that Hank could have known anything about the kidnapping case." Picking up one of Hank's files, she shone the flashlight on it and then began to thumb through the yellow notebook pages inside.

Not that she didn't watch Boone McGraw—if that was really his name—out of the corner of her eye. She'd learned never to take anything at face value. Hank had taught her that and a lot more.

The cowboy swore as he looked around the destroyed office. His expression said he wasn't ready to give up. "If you're his partner then why is the Knight Investigations phone disconnected and this office without electricity?"

"Hank was in the process of retiring. I have my own office in my home. I was taking over the business."

"So you hadn't spoken for a while?" He was guessing, but he'd guessed right.

"We were in transition."

"So you can't be sure he didn't know something about the kidnapping case."

She gritted her teeth. This cowboy was impossible. "Hank would have told me if he knew something about the case. I'm sorry you've wasted your time." She just wanted him to leave so she could get back to what she was doing.

Since Hank's so-called accident, she'd been hard-pressed to hold it together. All that kept her going was her anger and determination to find his killer. She was convinced that one of his cases had gotten him murdered. All she had to do was figure out which one.

The cowboy moved, but only to step deeper into the room. "You said he was killed three days ago? Is that when he returned from his trip?"

"His trip?" Now she was starting to sound like him.

He frowned and jammed his hands on his hips as he looked at her. "My father's lawyer talked to him over two weeks ago. Your partner told him that he was going to be away and would get back to us. When we didn't hear from him…"

She shook her head. "He didn't go anywhere."

"Then why did he lie to our lawyer? Unless he had something to hide?"

C.J. threw down the files in her hands with impatience. "Mr. McGraw—"

"Boone."

"Boone, you didn't know Hank, but I did. He wouldn't have lied."

"Then how do you explain what he told our lawyer?"

She couldn't and that bothered her. She studied the cowboy for a minute. Had Hank gone on a trip—just as he'd told the McGraw lawyer? C.J. thought of how distracted Hank had been the last time she'd seen him. He hadn't mentioned talking to anyone connected to the McGraw kidnapping and for a man who loved to talk about his cases, that was more than unusual.

A case like that didn't come along every day, especially given Knight Investigations' clients. But it also wasn't the kind of case Hank would be interested in. If it was true and he'd called the McGraw lawyer, he must have merely out of curiosity.

She said as much and picked up more files.

"It wasn't idle curiosity." Boone stepped closer until only the large cluttered desk stood between them. He loomed over it. His presence alone could have sucked all the air out of the room. Fortunately, all he did was make her too aware of just how male he was. He didn't intimidate her, not even for a moment. At least that's what she told herself.

"I guess we'll never know, will we?" she said, meeting his steely gaze with one of her hard blue ones.

"If there is even a chance that he knew the whereabouts of my sister, Jesse Rose, then I'm not leaving town until I find out the truth. Starting with whether or not Hank Knight recently left town. It should be easy enough to find out. How much?"

C.J. stared at him. "How much what?"

"How much *money*? I want to hire you."

Chapter Three

Boone was surprised by the young woman's reaction.

"Sorry, but I'm not available." She actually sounded offended.

"Because you're too busy going through dusty old files?"

She looked up from where she was leafing through one and slowly put it down. "The reason my partner is dead is in one of these files. I need to find his killer."

"Wait, I thought it was an accident?"

"That's what the police say, but they're wrong."

He shook his head. He'd run into his share of stubborn women, but this one took the cake. "You seem pretty sure of yourself about a lot of things."

She put her hands on her hips and looked like she could chew nails. "Hank was murdered. I'd stake my life on it."

"If you're right, then there is probably a good chance that's what you're doing."

"He would have done the same for me. Hank… Everyone loved him."

Well, not everyone, but he knew now wasn't the time to point that out. He could see how hard this was on her and told himself to cut her some slack. But if he had any hope of finding out if Hank Knight had known where his kidnapped sister was, then he needed this woman's help.

"I'm sorry. Apparently the two of you were close," he said, which surprised him since Waters had said Hank Knight was elderly. She'd just said the man was in the process of retiring.

Hank's advancing age could be the reason he had such a young partner. In the ambient glow of the flashlight C.J. didn't even look thirty, though given her confidence, she could have been older. Her long curly hair was the deep, rich color of copper, framing a face flecked with freckles. Both made her brown eyes look wider and more innocent. She had her unruly hair pulled back into a ponytail and wore an old Cubs baseball cap. His father had always been a huge Cubs fan. Boone wondered if Hank had been.

C.J. West was a slight woman but one he knew better than to underestimate. He needed her help because the more he thought about it, the more he felt the answers were here in Butte, here in this office.

"I've known Hank since I was a child playing in this building," she said. "My mother had a job on another floor. I used to hang out with him. He taught me everything I know about the investigative business plus much more. He was like a father to me."

Boone nodded. "I can't imagine how hard this is for you. I hate that I have to add to your problems at a time like this, but let's say you're right and your partner was murdered. Why an old case? Why not the McGraw kidnapping? One of the kidnappers is still at large. If your partner knew something and made inquiries that alerted the kidnapper..."

He was winging it, but he saw that at least she was considering it. Of course, there was also the chance that Hank Knight's death was just an accident. That the man had merely been curious about the McGraw kidnapping case. That all of this was a waste of time.

But Boone had always gone on instinct and right now his instincts told him he had to get this woman to help him. If Hank had been telling the truth and he'd left town, then maybe where he'd gone would lead them to Jesse Rose—and her partner's killer.

ACROSS THE STREET from the Knight Investigations office, Cecil Marks slumped down in his vehicle to watch the office of Knight Investigations. He'd been worried when he'd heard that there might be a break in the kidnapping case. That some private investigator in Butte might know not just where Jesse Rose was, but might also know who was the second kidnapper—the one who'd handed the babies out the window to the man on the ladder.

After twenty-five years, he'd thought for sure that the truth would never come out. Now he wasn't so sure. He'd known that Boone McGraw was like a dog with a bone when it came to not letting go of something. The moment he'd heard about Hank Knight and Knight Investigations, he'd known he had to take care of it.

Once he came to Butte and found out that Hank Knight was retiring, he'd told himself that no one would tie the kidnapping to the old PI.

But unfortunately, he hadn't known about the man's partner. It was her up there now with Boone McGraw. He doubted they would find anything. He hadn't when he'd searched the office, and he'd been thorough. He'd left the place in such a mess, even if he had missed something, he doubted it would turn up now.

It was cold in his truck without the motor running, but he didn't want to call attention to himself. As badly as he wanted to go back to the motel where he was staying, he had to be sure they didn't find anything. Once Boone went back to Whitehorse, he figured he wouldn't have to worry anymore.

He told himself that the little gal partner, C.J. West, wouldn't be searching the office if she knew anything. Also if she knew, he would have heard by now.

She suspected the hit-and-run hadn't been an accident. But there was no proof. Nor did he think the cops were even looking all that hard. He'd seen something on the news and only a footnote in the newspaper. Hank Knight had been a two-bit PI nobody. Look at that heap of an office he worked out of.

He tried to reassure himself that he was in the clear. That nothing would come of any of this. He'd done what he'd had to do and he would do it again. His hands began to shake at the thought, though, of being forced to kill yet another person, especially a woman.

But if she and Boone didn't stop, he'd have no choice.

C.J. HATED TO admit that the cowboy might be right. Before Boone McGraw had walked into this office, she'd been sure Hank's death had something to do with one of his older cases. All of his newer cases that he'd told her about were nothing that could get a man killed—at least she didn't think so.

Now she had to adjust her thinking. Could this be about the kidnapping? Her mind balked because Hank loved nothing better than to talk about his cases. He wouldn't have been able *not* to talk about this one unless... Unless he did know something, something that he thought could put her in danger...

"Why do you think the hit-and-run wasn't an accident?" the cowboy asked.

It took her a moment to get her thoughts together. "This ransacked office for one. Clearly someone was looking for something in the old files."

"You're that sure it involved a case?"

She waved a hand through the air. "Why tear up the office unless the killer is looking for the case file—and whatever incriminating evidence might be in it?"

He nodded as if that made sense to him. "But if it was here, don't you think that whoever did this took the file with him?"

"Actually, I don't. Look at this place. I'd say the person got frustrated when he didn't find it. Otherwise, why trash the place?"

"You have a point. But let's say the file you're looking for is about the McGraw kidnapping. It wouldn't be an old file since he called only a few weeks ago. When did he turn off his phone and electricity here at the office?"

C.J. hated to admit that she didn't know. "We've both been busy on separate cases. But he would have told me if he knew anything about the case." He wouldn't have kept something like that from her, she kept telling herself. And yet he hadn't mentioned talking to the McGraw lawyer and her instincts told her that Boone McGraw wasn't lying about that.

That Hank now wouldn't have the opportunity to tell her hit her hard. Hank had been like family, her only family, and now he was gone. And she was only starting to realize how much Hank had been keeping from her.

She had to look away, not wanting Boone to see the shine of tears that burned her eyes. She wouldn't break down. Especially in front of this cowboy.

"If Hank did know something about the case, would he have started a file?" the cowboy asked as he picked up a stack of files from the floor, straightened them and then stacked them on the edge of the desk.

"He would have written something down, I suppose."

"But wouldn't have started a file."

C.J. sighed. "No, but you're assuming a twenty-five-year-old kidnapping is what got him killed. It wasn't the kind of case he worked. Not to mention that Butte is miles from Whitehorse, Montana. The chances that Hank knew anything about the kidnapping or the whereabouts of your sister, Jesse Rose—"

"Are slim. I agree. But I can't discount it. He called our attorney. He knew something or he wouldn't have done that. I don't think he was curious and I don't think you do, either."

She wanted to argue. The cowboy brought that out in her. But she couldn't. "Fine, let's say he did know something."

"So where are his notes?"

C.J. shot him a disbelieving glance as she raised her hands to take in the ransacked room. "Let me just grab them for you."

"I'd be happy to help you look."

"I don't need your help," she said. "For all I know, you're the one who tore the place apart."

"And then came back to confront you and pretend to look for my own file? How clever of me. If I couldn't find it when this place wasn't a mess, why would I think you could now?"

She saw the logic, but hated to admit it. "Or maybe you didn't find what you were looking for and hope that I'll find it for you."

He grinned. "I admire the way your mind works, though I find it a little disturbing."

C.J. bristled. Was he flirting with her?

"You really think I'm the killer cozying up to the partner? Pretty darned gutsy of me." He shook his head. "Hit-and-run is a coward's way of killing. Your killer wouldn't have the guts to come waltzing in here and face you." He had a point. "But don't you want to call the cops and report the break-in before you destroy any more evidence?"

"I already called them."

Boone heard the anger in her voice as he noticed the old photographs framed on the walls. "They weren't helpful?" he asked as he got up to inspect them with the flashlight on his cell phone. The snapshots were of the same man, Hank Knight, no doubt, with a variety of prominent men and women and even a couple of celebrities. From the looks of the photos they were old. Which meant Hank Knight had been doing this for years.

"The local cops, helpful?" C.J. let out a laugh. "They don't believe the hit-and-run was murder because we normally don't take those kinds of cases."

"I would think any kind of case could turn violent under the wrong circumstances," he said, turning from the photographs on the wall. "Look, I'm not leaving town until I get some answers. So what do you say? Let me at least help you look through the files. Other than one on the McGraw kidnapping, what are we looking for?"

She glanced up at him and her gaze softened a little toward him as he took off his coat and rolled up the sleeves of his Western shirt. "Fine. While you're looking for something on the kidnapping, keep an eye out for any recent entries, even in the old files." She showed him what to look for on one of the files. "Hank had his own way of doing things."

"I can see that," Boone said as he scooped up more folders.

"We did work closely. Until recently. I did a lot of the legwork. I have to admit, the last few weeks...I hadn't seen much of Hank."

So, just as he'd guessed, she was looking for a needle in a haystack and had no idea what had gotten her partner killed. He dropped the folders on the desk next to the others and began going through them quickly. "I suppose you know from the news. One of the kidnappers was found. Dead, unfortunately, so one is still out there. But it's put the kidnapping back in the news. More information was released. That's why I assume your partner called. Also my brother Oakley's been found, although that information hasn't been released."

She looked up in obvious surprise. "I thought the man who came forward proved to be a fraud?"

Boone nodded. "Vance Elliot was an impostor, but surprisingly he helped flush out my real biological brother. The news media doesn't know about it because he doesn't want the publicity, which I can't blame him for. In fact, he wants nothing to do with my family. Another reason why I need to find Jesse Rose. Hopefully, *she* won't break our father's heart."

THE NEWS TOOK C.J. by surprise. A son who wanted nothing to do with his family? The subject, though, appeared to be closed as he went back to work. Not that she wasn't curious, but right now she had to find out who had wanted Hank dead.

Sometimes she forgot he was gone. She'd spent so many hours in this office with him growing up… She swallowed the sudden lump in her throat. Hank had meant everything to her. The thought of him being gone… She pushed it away, telling herself she owed it to him to find his killer. That's what she had to focus on right now. Later she would have time for grief, for regrets, for the pain that lay just beneath the surface.

She reached for more files from the floor, her fingers trembling. She stopped to squeeze her hands into fists for a moment. If there was one thing C.J. hated to show, it was any kind of weakness. Maybe especially to a man like Boone McGraw. She could look at the set of his jaw or gaze into those frosty blue eyes and she knew what kind of man he was. Stubbornly strong, like a tree that had lived through everything thrown at it for all its years. Just like Hank.

"It's not here," Boone said after an hour had passed. "Unless your partner didn't write it down. Or if he did, whoever tore up this place took the information with him."

With a sigh, C.J. carried a handful of case files over to one of the cabinets and set them inside just to get them out of the way. Files were everywhere. Then again, this was pretty normal for Hank's office. He'd never been organized. It was one reason they'd never been able to share an office.

She took a moment before she turned to look at

Boone McGraw. The cowboy took up a lot of space. The broad shoulders, the towering height—all that maleness culminated into one handsome, cocky cowboy. She bet most women swooned at his feet and was glad she wasn't one of them.

"So we're back to square one," she said, sounding as discouraged as she felt. She'd looked through all of the files, including those that Boone had also looked through. Not only hadn't she found anything about the McGraw kidnapping, she hadn't seen any old case that might have gotten Hank killed.

"Not necessarily," Boone said as he put both palms on the desk and leaned toward her. "Your partner knew something about the kidnapping. Hank Knight asked questions about Jesse Rose and an item that was taken from her crib the night she was kidnapped. His questions led our lawyer to believe Hank had knowledge about the crime and possibly where Jesse Rose is now. I think he got too close to the truth. Too close to the kidnapper's accomplice. And if I'm right then you can help me prove it."

Chapter Four

C.J. pulled up Hank's old leather chair and dropped into it. She was too tired, too wrung out, too filled with grief to take on this cowboy. Nor could she see how she would be able to prove anything.

She pushed a stack of old files out of the way and dropped her elbows to the top of the scarred desk to rest her chin in her hands. She watched Boone McGraw pick up files and put them back into the filing cabinets. He was actually cleaning up the office. The sight would have made her laugh, if she'd had the energy.

What she needed was sleep. She hadn't had a good night's sleep since Hank's death. She doubted she would tonight, but sitting here wasn't helping. As she started to get up, she pushed off the desk only to have the worn top shift under her hands.

With a start she remembered something she'd seen Hank do when he was interrupted by a walk-in. Sitting back, she felt into the crack between the old oak desktop and the even older one beneath it. Hank had loved this desk and hadn't been able to part with it even after one of his cigars had burned the original top badly. Rather than replace it, he'd simply covered it up.

She'd seen files disappear from view only to be retrieved later after a client left. Her fingers brushed against something that felt like the edge of a file folder. She worked it out, her heart leaping up into her throat as she saw the name printed on it in Hank's neat script: McGraw.

"Did you find something?" Boone asked, stopping his organizing to step closer.

She looked up, having forgotten about him for a moment. When had Hank shoved this file into the crack? Who would have walked in that he didn't want them to see it? Her heart began to pound. Until that moment, she had refused to believe that Hank would have taken the McGraw kidnapping case—let alone that it could have anything to do with getting him killed.

C.J. tried to remember the last time she'd stopped by Hank's office. The thousands of times all melted together. Had he ever furtively hidden a file when *she'd* walked in? Had he the last time she saw him alive, just hours before he was struck down and killed?

Her fingers were trembling as she opened the file and saw that there was only one sheet of yellow lined notebook paper—the kind Hank always used. There were also only a few words written on it, several phone numbers and some doodling off to one side. She read the words: "Travers McGraw, Sundown Stallion Station, Whitehorse, Montana. Oakley, Jesse Rose, six months old. Stuffed toy horse. Pink ribbon. Pink grosgrain ribbon."

BOONE HAD SEEN her expression when she'd pulled the manila file folder out from what appeared to be a crack between the new desktop and the old warped one. She'd found something that had made her pale.

"May I?" he asked again.

Silently, C.J. handed over the file, crossed her arms and watched as Boone opened it as if she'd known he was going to be disappointed.

"Where's the rest of it?" he said after looking at the words written on the yellow sheet of paper inside.

"That's all there is."

He could see that she was shaken by what she'd found. Not only had Hank started a file, he'd hidden it. That had to mean something given how the color had drained from her face and how shaken she still looked.

She started around the desk, bumped into him as she stumbled into an unstable stack of files. He caught her, his hands going around her slim waist as she clutched at him for a moment before she got her balance and pulled free. She headed toward a small door he hadn't noticed before. As she opened it, he saw it was a compact bathroom.

Boone turned his attention back to the file as she closed the door. So Hank Knight *had* started a file. But if he'd found out anything, there was no indication of it. Maybe the man didn't know anything about Jesse Rose. Maybe he *was* just curious.

Or maybe not, he realized as he stared at the notes the PI had taken. He'd known about the stuffed toy horse. But he'd also known about the pink ribbon around its neck—something that hadn't been released to the press.

He studied the doodling on the side of the page. Hank had drawn a little girl with chin-length hair. His depiction of Jesse Rose from his imagination? Or his memory? Beside the girl, Hank had drawn what looked like a little dog.

A few moments later, he heard the toilet flush. C.J.

came out drying her hands on a paper towel. He studied her for a moment. She seemed different somehow. She looked stronger, more assured. He realized she'd probably used the bathroom to get over the shock of finding the hidden file. But what about it had shaken her? The realization that he could be right?

"Did you ever have a dog?"

She blinked. "I beg your pardon?"

He motioned to the file and the doodle on the side.

"You think that means something? Doesn't every little girl have a dog?"

"Did you?" Boone waited patiently for her to answer.

"No, all right? If you must know, we lived in a building much like this one. The landlord didn't allow dogs."

"Hank doodled a dog. A girl with a dog. So there must be more than this," he said, indicating the file.

She shook her head. "Talk about jumping to wild conclusions." She picked up the flashlight from where she'd left it lying on the desk, the beam lighting most of the room, and shone it on the single sheet in the file.

"Hank had his own system. He numbered the pages in each file, keeping a running tally. It was his idea of organization. If you look on the back of the file, it shows how many papers are in each file. That way you can tell if anything is missing."

"Your partner got his office broken into a lot?" Boone quipped.

"It's the nature of the business," she said offhandedly.

He turned the folder over. There was a one on the back. One sheet of paper inside. He looked up to see her headed for the door. "Wait a minute, where are you going?"

"Home to bed," she said, after picking up three file folders from the desk where she'd stacked them earlier.

"That's all you're taking? Aren't you even going to lock the office door?"

"What's the point?" she said over her shoulder. "If there was anything in here worth stealing, it's long gone now."

Taking the McGraw file, he went after her, catching up to her at the stairs. "Look, Ms. West—"

"C.J." She met his gaze. In the dim light of the naked bulb over the stairs, he noticed her eyes were a rich, warm brown, the same color as his favorite horse. "Yes?"

He realized he'd been staring. At least he had the sense not to voice his thoughts. He doubted she would appreciate her eye color being compared to that of his horse's hide even if it was his favorite. "You should at least have my phone number, don't you think?"

He started to reach for his wallet and his business card, but stopped when she smiled, a rather lopsided smile that showed definite amusement. "I already have it." Reaching into her pocket, she brought out his wallet.

"You picked my pocket?" He couldn't help the indignation in his tone. "What kind of private investigator are you?" he demanded, checking his wallet. His money and credit cards were still there. Now he knew what she'd been doing in the bathroom. All she'd apparently taken was his business card.

When he looked up, he saw pride glittering like fireworks in the rich brown of her eyes. "I'm the kind of PI who doesn't take anything at face value. I'm also the kind who doesn't work with amateurs, so this is where we part company. I'll call if I find out anything about your sister or the kidnapping." With that she turned and disappeared down the stairs.

He caught up with her at the street. "I'm not leaving town. If I have to, I'll dog your every footstep."

"As entertaining as that sounds—"

"I'm serious. I'll stay out of your way, but you can't keep me out of this."

She smiled as if she could and would and climbed into an older-model yellow-and-white VW van. The engine revved. He thought about following her to see where she lived. But he wasn't going to sit outside her residence all night to make sure she didn't give him the slip in the morning. He couldn't force her to help him anymore than he could make her keep him in the loop.

The woman was impossible, he thought as he climbed into his pickup and watched C.J. West drive away. A car a few vehicles away started up and left, as well. He glanced at it as it passed but didn't notice the driver. His mind was on C.J. West.

He knew nothing about her. She, he feared, knew everything about him, or would soon. The entire story of his family's lives for the past twenty-five years was on the internet.

Swearing, he reminded himself what was at stake. He couldn't go home without good news for his father. Hank Knight had started a file. He thought of the brief file now lying on the seat next to him. "Pink ribbon. Pink grosgrain ribbon."

It didn't take much of a mental leap to come up with a pink ribbon since Oakley's horse had a blue ribbon on it. If that information had gotten out, then... But pink grosgrain? Had their attorney, Jim Waters, released that information to the PI? Or had Hank already known about the toy stuffed horse and the key bit of information about the pink ribbon?

Now more than ever, Boone believed that Hank Knight had known something about the kidnapping. Had maybe even known where Jesse Rose was. Or at least suspected. And it might have gotten him killed.

One way or the other, Boone had no choice. He was staying in Butte and throwing in with this woman whether she liked it or not. He just hoped he wouldn't live to regret it.

Chapter Five

C.J. closed her apartment door and leaned against it for a moment. Tonight, being in Hank's office, she'd felt him as if he was there watching her, urging her on.

Tell me who killed you! she'd wanted to scream.

She hadn't been able to shake the feeling that he'd left behind a clue. Some lead for her to follow that even whoever had ransacked the office wouldn't get, but she would because she and Hank had been so close they could almost read each other's mind.

Until recently. Lately he'd been secretive.

But did it have something to do with the McGraw kidnapping? Just because she'd found the file in Hank's hiding place, it didn't mean it was the last case he was working on. While she and Boone had found a couple of recent case files, neither of them had seemed like something that could get Hank killed. Then again, like Boone had said, any case could turn violent.

She'd tossed the three file folders from fairly recent cases of Hank's on the kitchen table as she'd come into the apartment. Now she moved to them. Other than the McGraw file, there was one labeled Mabel Cross. Inside, she found a quick abbreviated version of Mabel's problem. The woman suspected that her niece had taken an antique brooch of hers. But she also thought her daughter's husband might have taken it. She had wanted Hank to find it and get it back.

The second file folder was labeled Fred Hanson. His pickup had been vandalized. He was pretty sure it was one of his neighbors since they'd been in a disagreement. He wanted to know which one of them was guilty.

The third case, Susan Roth Turner, suspected her husband might be having an affair.

C.J. sighed. None of those seemed likely to have gotten Hank killed. But she knew better than to rule them out since other than the McGraw file, they were his most recent cases and three of his last ones before he was to retire.

Moving to the refrigerator, she poured herself a glass of red wine and headed for the couch. This was the hardest part of her day. As long as she was busy taking care of all the arrangements for Hank's funeral, tying up loose ends with their business dealings and looking for his killer, she could keep the grief away.

But it was moments like this that it hit her like a tidal wave, drowning her in the pain and regret. Hank had taught her everything about the private eye business from the time she was old enough to see over the top of his big desk. Her mother had worked in the building back in those days and C.J. used to wander the halls, always ending up in Hank's office.

He'd pretended that her visits were a bother, but she'd known he hadn't meant it. He'd started bringing her a treat, an apple, a banana or an orange, saying she should have something healthy. He'd always join her, pushing aside a case file to sit down and talk with her. Even extinguishing his cigar so the smoke didn't bother her.

From the time she was little, she loved listening to him talk about the cases he was working on. He never mentioned names. But he loved discussing them with her. She had seen how much he loved his job, how much he loved helping people. He'd hooked her on the PI business. All she'd ever wanted was to be just like him.

Hank had loved it all, especially solving mysteries that seemed impossible to solve. He was good at his job and often worked for little or nothing, depending on how much his clients could afford.

Sometimes we're all a person has, he used to tell her. *They need help and everyone else has turned them down.*

So how was it that he'd gotten himself killed?

Exhausted, still grief stricken and feeling as if she was in over her head, she wandered into the bedroom to drop onto the bed. She desperately needed sleep, but she picked up her laptop because she had a feeling she hadn't seen the last of Boone McGraw.

Within minutes she was caught up on the latest information that had been released to the press about the twenty-five-year-old kidnapping as well as what she could find out about Boone. The more she read about the kidnapping, the more she worried that he was right and Hank had discovered something about the case that had gotten him killed.

She didn't want to believe it. What could he have found out that had put him in such danger? She recalled something Boone had said and dug her cell phone out of the back pocket of her jeans.

"Can't sleep?" Boone said in answer to her call.

"You said something earlier about this Vance Elliot turning out not to be Oakley McGraw. He must have had some kind of proof to make you think he was the missing son."

"He had my little brother's stuffed horse."

She lay back on the bed. "What made you think it was the same horse?"

"It had a blue ribbon tied around it and some of the stitching was missing. Oakley never slept without it in his crib."

"So how did he just happen to have this horse, if he wasn't the real Oakley McGraw?"

"It's a long story, but basically, someone had picked up the horse as a souvenir at the crime scene and later decided to use it to get money out of my father."

"So you have no idea who in the house helped the kidnapper take the twins? What about the nanny who became your stepmother? She seems the perfect suspect. I just read that she might be released from jail until her trial for attempted murder."

"Suspect, yes. But for trying to kill my father, not for the kidnapping."

Exhaustion pulled at her. She could hardly keep her eyes open. "So they were fraternal twins, right? Six months old." She was thinking of what Hank had written in the file. "I'm assuming your sister also had a stuffed horse toy in her crib that was taken that night? One with a pink ribbon."

"Yes."

She closed her eyes, seeing the yellow lined paper and the words *pink ribbon* written in Hank's even script. *Pink grosgrain ribbon.* "Was there anything about the ribbon around its neck released to the media?"

"No. There was nothing about it being a pink *grosgrain* ribbon."

"That's the kind that has the ridges, right? The lawyer must have mentioned it to Hank—"

"I'm sure he provided information about the kidnapping to Knight Investigations, but not that," Boone said. "Hank knew something before he made the call. Otherwise why would he have contacted our family lawyer with questions about Jesse Rose?"

Good question. Unfortunately, C.J. had no idea. But her gut instinct told her that Boone was right. Hank had already known all about the kidnapping twenty-five years ago. For some reason, he had followed the case closely all these years.

But if he'd kept anything in writing, she hadn't found it. Yet.

"I'm going to the police station in the morning to find out more about Hank's death," Boone said.

"Good luck with that." She hung up and rolled over, too tired to get undressed. And yet her thoughts refused to let her sleep.

Was there more information Hank had hidden somewhere? Why wasn't the information in the file? Because he knew enough to know he was in danger?

If this was about the McGraw kidnapping, had Hank gotten too close to the truth? But wouldn't that mean that he had inside knowledge? Wasn't the fear that Hank had inside information and that was what had her running scared now?

She rolled over on her back and stared up at the ceiling, her mind racing. Had Hank already known about the pink ribbon? Or had the attorney told him? Either way, Hank had written it down. He'd also told the attorney that he had to go out of town. But he hadn't. Or had he?

She thought of Boone McGraw. He'd seen the words *pink grosgrain ribbon* in Hank's scrawl. He'd known then that Hank knew more than he had told the lawyer. Why hadn't the cowboy said something then?

Because he was holding out on her. Just like she was on him.

She felt a shiver and pulled the quilt over her. If Hank had known where to find Jesse Rose, then he would have told the McGraw lawyer, she told herself. Unless…unless he had something to hide.

Her eyes felt as if someone had kicked sand into them. She closed them and dropped like a stone into a bottomless well of dark, troubled sleep.

THE NEXT MORNING, Boone stopped by the police station and after waiting twenty minutes, was led to a Detective Branson's desk. The man sitting behind it could have been a banker. He wore a suit, tie and wire-rimmed glasses. He looked nothing like a cop, let alone a detective.

As Boone took a seat, he said, "I'm Boone—"

"McGraw. Son of Travers McGraw. I know. You told my desk clerk. That's why you're sitting where you are when I'm so busy."

He was used to his father's name opening doors. "I'm inquiring about a private investigator by the name of—"

"Hank Knight. He's dead." He looked back at the stack of papers on his desk, then up again. He seemed surprised Boone was still sitting there.

"Can you tell me under what circumstance—"

"Hit-and-run. Given the time of night, not that surprising, and in front of a bar." The cop shrugged as if it happened all the time.

Boone could see why C.J. hadn't been happy after talking to the cops. "So you think it was an accident?"

Branson leaned back in his chair, his expression one of tired impatience even this early in the morning. "What else?"

"Murder."

The detective laughed. "Obviously you didn't know Hank or you wouldn't even ask that question. Hit-and-run accident. Case closed."

"Surely you're investigating it."

"Of course," Branson said. "Right along with all the other crimes that go on in this city. Why the interest?"

Boone could see that the hit-and-run was low priority. He thought about mentioning the kidnapping case. For twenty-five years anyone who heard the name would instantly tie it to the kidnapping. It had been a noose around his neck from the age of five.

"His partner believes it was murder."

"C.J. West?" He sneered as if that also answered his earlier question. The detective thought this was about him and the private eye?

"She has reason to believe it wasn't an accident," he said.

"PIs," Branson said and shook his head. "They just want to be cops. Trust me, it was an accident. So unless you know different, I have to be in court in twenty minutes…"

The detective went back to his paperwork. Boone rose. On his way out the door, he called C.J. on the number she'd called him from last night. "You were right about the cops."

"You doubted me?"

"My mistake." He could hear traffic sounds in the background on her end of the line.

"Think you can find the Greasy Spoon Café around the corner from the cop shop?" she asked.

Chapter Six

"You call this breakfast?" Boone McGraw said as he looked down at his plate thirty minutes later.

He'd had no trouble finding the small hole-in-the-wall café. This part of uptown Butte hung onto the side of a mountain with steep streets and over-hundred-year-old brick buildings, many of them empty. The town's heyday had been in the early 1920s when it was the largest city west of the Mississippi. It had rivaled New York and Chicago. But those days were only a distant memory except for the ornate architecture.

"They're pasties," C.J. said of the meat turnover smothered with gravy congealing on his plate. "Butte is famous for them." She took another bite, chewing with obvious enjoyment. "Back when Butte mining was booming, workers came from around the world. Immigrants from Cornwall needed something easy to eat in the mines." She pointed at the pasty with her fork. "The other delicacy Butte takes credit for is the boneless deep-fat-fried pork chop sandwich."

"Butte residents don't live long, I would imagine," he quipped. "When in Butte, Montana…" He poked at the pasty lying under the gravy. It appeared to have meat and small pieces of potato inside. He took a tentative bite. It wasn't bad. It just wasn't what he considered breakfast.

He watched her put away hers. The woman had a good appetite, not that it showed on her figure. She was slightly built and slim but nicely rounded in all the right places, he couldn't help but notice. She ate with enthusiasm, something he found refreshing.

As he took another bite of his pasty, he studied her, trying to get a handle on who he was dealing with. There was something completely unpretentious about her, from her lack of makeup to the simple jean skirt, leggings, sweater and calf-high boots she wore. Her copper-red hair was pulled back in a loose braid that trailed down her back.

She looked more like an elementary school teacher than a private investigator. Because she was so slight in stature it was almost deceiving. But her confidence and determination would have made any man think twice before taking her on. Not to mention the gun he suspected was weighing down the shoulder bag she had on the chair next to her.

"What does the 'C.J.' stand for?" he asked between bites.

She wrinkled her nose and, for a moment, he thought she wasn't going to tell him. "Calamity Jane," she said with a sigh. "My father was a huge fan of Western history apparently."

"You never knew him?"

With a shake of her head, she said, "He died when I was two."

"Is your mother still…?"

"She passed away years ago."

"I'm sorry."

"Hank was my family." Her voice broke. Eyes shiny with tears, she looked away for a moment before returning to her breakfast. He did the same.

A few minutes later, she scraped the last bite of gravy and crust up, ate it and pushed her plate away. Elbows on the table, she leaned toward him and dropped her voice, even though the café was so noisy, he doubted anyone could hear their conversation where they sat near the doorway.

Her brown eyes, he noticed, were wide and flecked with gold. A faint sprinkling of freckles dotted her nose and her cheekbones. He had the urge to count them for no good reason other than to avoid the intensity of those brown eyes. It was as if she could see into him a lot deeper than he let anyone go, especially a woman.

"Tell me more about the kidnapping case," she said, giving him her full attention. "Don't leave anything out."

He took a drink of his coffee to collect his errant thoughts and carefully set down the mug. Last night she'd been so sure that the kidnapping case couldn't be what had gotten her partner killed. He wondered what had changed her mind—if that was the case.

"We all lived on the Sundown Stallion Station ranch, where my father raised horses. I was five. My older brother, Cull, was seven, Ledger was three. We had a nanny—"

"Patricia Owen, later McGraw after she became your father's second wife and allegedly tried to kill him," she said.

He nodded. "Patty stayed across the hall from the nursery. She heard a noise or something woke her. Anyway, according to her, she went to check on the twins and found them missing. When she saw the window open and a ladder leaning against the outside of the house, she started screaming and woke everyone up. The sheriff was called, then the FBI. A day later there was a ransom demand made. My father sold our prized colt to raise the money."

"Why wasn't the kidnapper caught when the ransom was paid?" she asked.

"The drop was made in a public place, but a fire broke out in a building close by. Suddenly the street was filled with fire trucks. In the confusion, somehow the kidnapper got away with the money without being seen."

She shook her head. "Who made the drop?"

"The family attorney, Jim Waters."

C.J. raised a brow. "Isn't he the one who was also arrested trying to leave the country with a bunch of money and has also been implicated in your father's poisoning?"

Boone nodded, seeing that she knew a lot more than she was letting on. "But so far no charges have been filed against him in the poisoning and there is no proof he was involved in the kidnapping. We now know that Harold Cline, a boyfriend of our cook, climbed the ladder that night and got away with the twins. The person who hasn't been found is the one who it is believed administered codeine cough syrup to the twins to keep them quiet during the ordeal and passed them out the window to the first kidnapper."

"What about the broken rung on the ladder?" she asked.

"It was speculated that the kidnapper might have fallen or dropped the babies, but we now know that didn't happen. The babies were alive and fine when they were found by our family cook and taken to—"

"The Whitehorse Sewing Circle member Pearl Cavanaugh. Wasn't she or her mother the one who started the illegal adoptions through this quilt group years ago?"

C.J. had definitely done her homework. He figured she must have been up before daylight. Either that or she had known more about the case than she'd led him to believe last night.

"That's right. Unfortunately, they're pretty much all dead, including Pearl."

"So there is no record of what happened to the twins," she said and picked up her coffee mug, holding it in both hands as she slowly took a sip.

"In light of what we learned from our family cook before she died, the babies probably went to parents who couldn't have children and were desperate," he said.

"I can't imagine how they couldn't have known about the kidnapping. So in their desperation, they pretended not to know that the child they were adopting was a McGraw baby? Didn't Oakley's and Jesse Rose's photos run nationally? So no one could have missed seeing them."

He nodded. "It makes sense that whoever got each of the twins knew. We've been led to believe that the adoptive parents were told the twins weren't safe in our house."

She put down her cup, her brown-eyed gaze lifting to his. "Because of your mother's condition."

He thought of his mother in the mental ward, the vacant stare in her green eyes as she rocked with two dolls clutched in her arms. "We now believe that her condition was the result of arsenic poisoning. It causes—"

"Confusion, memory loss, depression… The same symptoms your father was experiencing before his heart attack. Patty's doing is the assumption? So you're saying your mother probably wasn't involved."

He met her gaze and shrugged. "In her state of mind at the time of the kidnapping, who knows? But she definitely didn't run down your partner. She's still in the mental ward. And neither did Patty, who is still behind bars."

C.J. bit at her lower lip for a moment. He couldn't help noticing her mouth, the full bow-shaped lips, the even white teeth, just the teasing tip of her pink tongue before he dragged his gaze away. This snip of a woman could be damned distracting.

"You said Oakley has been found?"

That wasn't information she could have found on the internet. "He has refused to take a DNA test, but my father is convinced that the cowboy is Oakley. He owns a ranch in the area. Apparently he's known the truth for years, but didn't want to get his folks into trouble. They've passed now, but he still isn't interested in coming out as the infamous missing twin. Nor does he have an interest in being a McGraw."

She raised a brow. "That must be both surprising and disappointing if it's true and he's your brother."

"It's harder on my father than the rest of us. He's been through so much. All he wants is his family together."

She said nothing, but her eyes filled before she looked down as the waitress came over to refill their coffee cups.

C.J. STUDIED BOONE while he was distracted with the waitress refilling his cup. She'd known her share of cowboys since this was Montana—Butte to be exact. Cowboys were always wandering in off the range—and usually getting into trouble and needing either a private investigator or a bail bondsman. She and Hank had been both.

But this cowboy seemed different. He'd been through a lot because of the kidnapping. He wasn't the kind of man a person could get close to. Last night she'd noticed that he didn't wear a wedding ring. This morning online, she'd discovered that only one of the McGraw sons, Ledger, the youngest one, had made the walk to the altar.

"You drove a long way yesterday," she said after a few moments. "Seems strange if all you had to go on was Hank asking a few questions about the kidnapping and Jesse Rose."

He pushed away his plate, his pasty only half-eaten. "I quizzed the attorney when he told me about the private investigator calling. Truthfully, I figured this whole trip would turn out to be a wild-goose chase."

"So why are you here?"

"Because my father asked me and because our attorney said that Hank Knight sounded…worried."

Her pulse quickened. *"Worried?"*

Boone met her gaze with his ice-blue one. "I think he knew something. I think that's why he's dead." When she didn't argue the point, he continued. "From what you found last night, we know that he knew more about the ribbon on the stuffed toy horse than has been released."

"Why would he keep that information to himself?" she asked more to herself than to him.

"Good question. He told our attorney that he had to

take a trip and would be out of town," Boone reminded her. "Makes sense he'd want to verify what he was worried about, doesn't it?"

It did. "Except I don't think he left town."

"Or maybe he had a good reason not to want me following up on it."

She bristled. "Hank was the most honest man I've ever known. If he knew where Jesse Rose was, he would have told your family."

"Maybe. Unless someone stopped him first."

Chapter Seven

After he paid the bill, they stepped outside the café. The morning air had a bite to it although the sky was a cloudless blue overhead. He was glad he'd grabbed his sheepskin-lined leather coat before he'd left home. Plowed dirty snow melted in the gutters from the last storm. Christmas wasn't that far off. There was no way Butte wouldn't have a white Christmas.

"What do you know about Butte?" C.J. asked as she started to walk up the steep sidewalk.

He shook his head as he followed her, wondering why she'd called him. Was she going to help him find out the truth? Or was she just stringing him along?

"What most Montanans know, I guess. It's an old copper mining boomtown and we're standing on what became known as the Richest Hill on Earth," he said. "It is now home to the Berkeley Pit, the most costly of the largest Superfund sites and a huge hole full of deadly water."

He saw that she didn't like him talking negatively about her hometown and realized he would have taken exception if she'd said anything negative about Whitehorse, too.

"Why are you asking me about Butte? What does this have to do with Hank or—"

"Butte was one of the largest and most notorious copper boomtowns in the West with hundreds of saloons and a famous red-light district."

Butte hadn't lived down its reputation as a rough, wide-open town. He'd heard stories about the city's famous red-light and saloon district called the Copper Block on Mercury Street. Many of the buildings that had once housed the elegant bordellos still stood.

"The first mines here were gold and silver—and underground," she continued. "They say there is a network of old mine tunnels like a honeycomb under the city."

"Where are you going with this, C.J.?"

"Hank loved this town and he knew it like the back of his hand."

Boone often wondered how many people actually knew the back of their hand well, but he didn't say so. "Your point?"

"He believed in helping people. Often those people couldn't pay for his services, but that never stopped him. You've seen his office. He wouldn't have been interested in your family kidnapping case. It wasn't something he would have taken on."

"Then how do you explain the fact that he knew about the ribbon?"

"Maybe the attorney told him. Look, there was only one sheet of paper in the file. Hank might have been curious given the latest information that's come out about the kidnapping. But he wouldn't have pursued it. Which means if not an older case, then one of his more recent ones has to be what got him killed. I need to investigate those. I'm sure you have better things to do—"

He didn't believe her. All his instincts told him that she wanted him to believe Hank hadn't known anything about the kidnapping. She was scared that he had. And maybe even more afraid because he hadn't told her.

So she was going to chase a few of Hank's last cases? He'd seen her take three files last night. "Fine, but you aren't getting rid of me, because once you exhaust your theory, we're going to get serious and find out what Hank knew about the McGraw kidnapping and Jesse Rose."

"Fine, suit yourself. I'm going to visit Mabel Cross and see if her brooch has turned up."

Boone shook his head. "Seriously?"

"As Hank used to say, there are no unimportant cases." She headed for her VW van. He cursed under his breath, but followed and climbed in on the passenger side. She was wasting her time and his. But he needed her help and antagonizing her wasn't going to get him anywhere, he told himself as he climbed into the passenger seat of her van.

"So we're going to pay a visit to these people?" he asked, picking up the three case files she'd taken from Hank's office last night as she slid behind the wheel. "Tell me we aren't going underground." He didn't want to admit that one of his fears was being trapped underground. The idea of some old mine shaft turned his blood to ice.

She laughed. "I'm afraid we are. So to speak," C.J. said and started the engine.

The buildings they passed were old, most of them made of brick or stone with lots of gingerbread ornamentation. He recalled that German bricklayers had rushed to Butte during its heyday from the late 1800s to the early 1920s.

Nothing about Butte, Montana, let you forget it had been a famous mining town—and still was, he thought as they passed streets with names like Granite, Quartz, Aluminum, Copper—and Caledonia.

As she drove, C.J. waved or nodded to people they passed. He couldn't tell if she was just friendly or knew everyone in town. On Iron Street, she pulled to the curb, cut the engine and climbed out. As she headed for an old pink-and-purple Victorian, he decided he might as well go with her.

Glancing around the neighborhood, he took in the historical homes and tried to imagine this city back in 1920. From photos he'd seen, the streets had swarmed with elegantly dressed residents. Quite a contrast to the homeless he'd seen now in doorways.

C.J. was already to the door and had knocked by the time he climbed the steps to the porch. The door opened and he looked up to find an elderly woman leaning on a cane. "Mrs. Cross," C.J. said. "I'm Hank Knight's associate."

"Hank." The woman's free hand went to her mouth. "So tragic. If you're here about his funeral—"

"No, I'm inquiring about your brooch. I wanted to be sure Hank had found it before—"

"Oh yes, dear," she said and touched an ugly lion studded with rhinestones pinned to her sweater. "Silly me. I feel so badly now to have thought my niece or my daughter's husband might have taken it and all the time it was on this sweater in the closet. I told Hank. I suppose he didn't get a chance to tell you before… He was so loved." She sniffed. "You'll be at his funeral, I assume."

"Of course. I'm just glad you found your brooch." C.J. turned and headed for the van.

Boone wanted to point out what a waste of time that had been, but one look at her face when she climbed behind the wheel and he bit his tongue. "When is the funeral?"

"Tomorrow afternoon." She started the van, biting at her lower lip as if to stanch the tears that brimmed in her eyes.

As she pulled out on the street, he saw her glance in the rearview mirror and then make a quick turn down a side street. "So do we check on these other two cases?" he asked picking up the file folders.

"I already called Fred Hanson this morning. Hank got the neighbor to admit he did it and pay restitution."

Boone couldn't help being impressed. Who had this Hank Knight been to have such a devoted following, including C.J. herself?

"I also drove by the Turner house earlier this morning."

"The cheating husband case," he said.

"The husband's clothing was in the yard."

"Another case solved by Hank Knight. So are you ready to accept that he might have been involved in my family's case?"

She said nothing. On Mercury Street, she stopped in front of a large redbrick building and, cutting the engine, climbed out.

"The Dumas Brothel?" he asked, seeing the visitor sign in the window as he hurried after her.

"One of Hank's best friends works here," she said as she opened the door and stepped in.

He followed, wondering if she wasn't leading him on a wild-goose chase this morning, hoping he'd give up and leave town.

It was cool and dimly lit inside the brothel museum. The older woman who appeared took one look at C.J. and disappeared into the back. Surely C.J. didn't plan on taking him on a tour.

But before he could ask, she turned and went to the front window. He could see her pain just below the surface and reminded himself that her partner had been killed only days ago. He didn't kid himself when it came to her priorities. She was looking for Hank's murderer—not Jesse Rose.

But if he was right, then it would lead them to the same place.

As he studied her, he couldn't help but wonder what she would do when she found the murderer.

An elderly man came into the room and C.J. turned and said, "Can we go out the back?"

Without a word, the man led them through the building and the next thing Boone knew, he was standing in a narrow alley surrounded by tall old brick buildings.

"What was that all about?" he demanded. He had expected her to at least ask the man about her partner or his death.

"Someone's following us," she said as she led him into another building, this one apparently abandoned. A few moments later, they spilled out into a dark, narrow alley. "This way."

Boone followed her through the alley between two towering old brick buildings before she dropped down some short stairs and ducked into a doorway. He stopped to look back and saw no one.

"Come on," she called impatiently to him.

He hurried down the steps as she opened a door with a key and he followed her inside another musty building. "Calamity—"

"C.J.," she snapped over her shoulder as she took a set of stairs that led upward. Only a little light filtered through the warbled old dust-coated windows as they climbed.

Four floors up, she stopped. He noticed that she wasn't even breathing hard although she'd scaled the stairs two at a time as if they really were being chased. Now, though, she moved across the landing to a door marked Fourth Floor. Motioning for him to be quiet, she opened it a crack and looked out.

Boone couldn't help but think she was putting him on. All this cloak-and-dagger stuff. Was it really necessary?

She motioned for him to follow her as she finally pushed open the door and headed down the long hallway, stopping short at the last door. From her bag, she pulled out a set of keys, pushed one into the lock and then seemed to hesitate.

"What?" he whispered, even though all the doors along the hallway were closed and he could hear nothing but the beat of his own heart.

C.J. shook her head, turned the key and pushed open the door. It didn't connect until that moment where they were and why she'd been hesitant to enter.

Past her he could see what appeared by the decor to be a man's apartment. There was a photo on one wall of a middle-aged Hank Knight and C.J. when she was about eight and had pigtails. Both Hank and C.J. were smiling at the camera. "You haven't been here since he was killed."

"No." She stepped in and, after a furtive glance down the hall, he followed, closing and locking the door behind them.

Chapter Eight

The first thing that hit her in Hank's apartment was the scent of cigar smoke. It lingered even though he'd quit smoking them some years ago. At work, he had taken up sucking on lemon drops. She'd often wondered if he'd done that for her because of how often she would end up at his office visiting with him about their cases.

Tears stung her eyes. She drew on her strength as she looked around the room. The door opened to a small kitchen and dining room. Past it was the living room, a dark curtain drawn over the only window. Beyond that was the bedroom and bath.

She'd only been here one other time. "I doubt there is anything here to find, but we can look." She hated that she'd brought Boone. But if the McGraw kidnapping had gotten Hank killed…

"I would think this is the logical place for your partner to keep information he possibly didn't want you or anyone else to see," Boone said, stepping past her and deeper into the apartment. "I meant to ask you last night. He didn't use a computer?"

"No." She glanced toward the kitchen sink. One lone cup sat on the faded porcelain. An old-fashioned brew coffeepot sat on one of the four burners on the stove. A half-eaten loaf of bread perched on an ancient toaster.

She moved to the refrigerator and opened the door to peer inside. A plate with a quarter stick of butter sat next to a half-empty jar of peach jam, Hank's favorite. The jam and butter shared space with two Great Falls Select cans of beer. Other than containers of mustard, ketchup and mayonnaise, there was a jar of dill pickles and one of green olives.

Closing the door, she felt Boone's impatient gaze on her.

"What are you looking for? Don't tell me you're hungry again," he said. Out of the corner of her eye, she saw him reach down to go through some magazines on the coffee table in front of the worn couch.

She didn't answer as she checked the garbage. Empty except for a clean bag. The Hank she knew was far from neat. The other time she'd been here, the garbage had been near full and there'd been toast crumbs on the counter, the butter dish next to them. Was Boone right about Hank either just coming back from somewhere— or getting ready to go somewhere?

"I think you'd better come see this," Boone called from the bedroom.

C.J. headed in that direction, half-afraid of what he'd found. When she looked through the door, she saw a beat-up brown suitcase open on the bed half-full of clothing. Stepping closer, she saw that Hank had packed two pairs of slacks and his best shirts.

She quickly glanced toward the closet, suddenly worried that he had planned to be gone longer than a few days. But most of his clothing was still hanging in the closet.

"What do you make of this?" Boone asked, eyeing her openly.

"He was either leaving or had just come back. His refrigerator is nearly empty and everything is cleaned up."

"So what he told my family lawyer might be true. He'd gone somewhere. To visit family?"

She shook her head. "He didn't have any family that I knew of." On top of that, Hank had hated to travel. In all the time she'd known him he'd left Butte only a couple times a year and always on a case—or so he had led her to believe. That she doubted his honesty now made her feel sick to her stomach.

She stepped to the suitcase to run her fingers along the fabric of one of the shirts. It was a gray-and-white-striped one she'd bought him for Christmas last year. He only wore it for special occasions. So what was the special occasion?

And why had he kept it from her?

BOONE COULD SEE C.J.'s confusion and hurt. Whatever her partner had been up to, he hadn't shared it with her. "I don't see a phone and he'd had the one at his office disconnected. I can see living off the grid, but..."

C.J. seemed to stir. Before that, she'd been staring into the suitcase, her thoughts dark from the frown that marred her girl-next-door-adorable face. "He recently bought a cell phone." Her frown deepened. "It wasn't found on his body."

Boone's pulse kicked up. "Was it possible someone took it off his body?"

Her brown eyes widened. "You mean someone in the crowd that must have gathered outside the bar?"

"We should search the rest of the apartment," Boone

said, seeing how hard it was for her to keep her emotions at bay. He looked through drawers in the bedroom while she searched the bathroom and the living room.

"Something else is bothering me," he said when he found her going through a pile of old mail. "How was he planning to travel? I went through the suitcase but there wasn't a plane ticket in there. I suppose it could be an e-ticket on his phone."

She shook her head. "Hank wouldn't have flown. He always said that if God had wanted us to fly, He would have given us wings. He must have driven or been planning to."

"Where's his car?"

C.J. HAD BEEN so upset and busy with funeral arrangements and everything else that she hadn't been thinking clearly. It explained why she hadn't sent this cowboy packing. Like she'd told him last night, she didn't need or want his help. At least the latter was true.

"I hadn't even thought about his car. I just assumed that he'd walked down to the bar from here," she said. "He was hit in front of the bar. Now that I think about it, I didn't see his car parked where he usually leaves it."

"I think we should find it. What does he drive?" Boone asked as they left the apartment via the fire escape and ended up in another alley. The wind had picked up and now blew between the buildings, icy cold. A weak December sun did little to chase away the chill.

"A '77 Olds 88, blue with a white top."

"So where is this bar?"

"Not far." She thought of the bar owner and realized she should have gone to see him before this. Natty would be as upset by all this as her. But then Hank had had so many friends.

A few blocks later, they entered the rear of the bar and she braced herself. This had been Hank's favorite bar. When he'd walk in the door, there would be a roar of greetings. Everyone had wanted to shake his hand and buy him a drink. But, never one to overindulge, he'd merely thank them and say he wasn't staying long.

As she started toward the front of the bar, C.J. half expected to see Hank on one of the stools. She thought of his face lighting up when he saw her and had to swallow back the lump in her throat and surreptitiously wipe her tears.

BOONE CAUGHT THE smell of stale beer and floor cleaner—like every Montana bar he'd ever been in. He'd grown to love the feel of them in college, but had been too busy on the ranch to spend much time on a barstool.

They went down a short hallway that opened into a dark room with a pool table. Ahead of them, he spotted a row of mostly empty stools pulled up to a thick slab of a bar. Only a little light filtered in through a stained-glass window, illuminating a scarred linoleum floor and a half dozen tables with empty chairs pulled up to them.

Following the sound of clinking glasses and the drone of a television, they reached the bar.

"What do you have against front doors?" Boone asked as C.J. headed for the bearlike man washing glasses behind the bar. When the grizzly bartender saw her, he quickly dried his hands and hurried around to draw her into a hug.

"How ya doin', sweetheart?" the man asked in a gravelly voice.

"Okay," C.J. answered. "I do have some questions, though, Natty."

The man called to one of the customers at the bar to hold down the fort and ushered them into an office down the hallway where they'd come in. Natty shot Boone a look, but C.J. didn't introduce either of them. On the wall, though, was a liquor license in the name of Nathaniel Blake.

"Did you see what happened or did anyone else we know?" she asked.

The man shook his head. "We just heard it. A couple of fellas went out to see what was going on." He looked as if he might cry. "I couldn't believe it."

"Did you talk to him before that?" she asked, her voice cracking a little. "I thought he might have mentioned where he was going."

Natty nodded. "I was surprised he was leaving again. He'd just gotten back. But he said he'd be gone for a few days and I knew what to do."

Boone saw her surprise and wondered at the man's words—*and I knew what to do*.

"Natty, he didn't tell me he'd left or that he was leaving again." She sounded close to tears and he wasn't the only one who heard it.

The big man put a hand on her shoulder. "He didn't tell me anything about it. But he hadn't looked happy about either trip. I wish I knew more. Whatever was going on with him, he wasn't saying."

She nodded. "You haven't seen his car, have you?"

"Matter of fact, it was parked across the street. I didn't think anything about it until I saw it being hauled off by the city. I would imagine it's down at the yard.

Sorry, I should have called you, but I figured you had your hands full as it was."

She nodded. More sorry than the man could know, Boone thought. Everyone thought Hank's hit-and-run had been an accident. Everyone but his partner.

"I knew it was just a matter of time before you came by." He reached behind him, dug in a drawer for a moment and came out with an envelope. "I've been hanging on to this for you. Hank left it and said if anything should happen to him… I just thought it was because he was flying somewhere. You know how he felt about flying."

So he'd taken a flight. Boone could see that the news had astonished C.J.

"This last time, he said he was leaving town for a while and didn't know when he'd be back, but I got the feeling he didn't think he was coming back. You think he knew?"

Knew that someone might try to kill him? Maybe, since he'd been in so much trouble that he hadn't wanted to share it with his partner, Boone thought.

Natty handed her the envelope. Even from where he stood, Boone could see that all it seemed to hold was a key. She undid the flap and took out the key. He saw that her fingers were trembling. There was a number printed on the key. 1171. He felt his pulse jump. Was this where Hank had hidden the information Boone desperately needed?

"You have any idea what that key opens?" Boone asked, worried that she might not.

Actually she did know, as it turned out. "It's to one of the lockers at the bus station."

His cell phone rang. He saw it was his brother Cull calling. "I need to take this. You won't—"

"I'll wait for you," she said, clearly upset from the news Natty had given her—and maybe the key, as well?

He stepped out of the office, but stayed where he could watch in case she tried to give him the slip. It wasn't that he didn't trust her... Oh, who was he kidding?

"Hello?"

"I was hoping we'd hear from you by now," his brother Cull said on the other end of the line.

"Afraid I haven't had much to report. It's been...interesting," Boone said.

"I know you didn't think much of Jim Waters's tip—"

"Actually, I'm beginning to think that there was something to it." He quickly told his brother about Hank Knight having been killed by a hit-and-run driver. "I'm hoping he left behind some information. It's why I'm working with Hank's partner to try to find it. What's that noise in the background?"

"Tilly vacuuming," Cull said, raising his voice to be heard. "Let me step into Dad's office."

"*Tilly?* I saw her the other day as I was leaving, but I thought she'd just come by to visit. Didn't she quit when Patty was arrested?"

"Yep," Cull said, the sound of the vacuum dying in the distance as his brother closed the office door. "Dad gave her a nice severance package for all the years she was our housekeeper, but apparently either it didn't last or she missed us."

"More than likely it's the new house," Boone said. "She always thought that the old one was haunted. I'm not surprised Dad took her back, though. I just hope she didn't let her ex get hold of her severance money. He kept her broke all the time. It was one thing after another with that guy."

"I doubt Tilly would want anything to do with him. When she needed him the most he ended up in the hospital after getting drunk and wrecking their car."

"Poor Tilly. I hope you're right about her being back because of the new ghost-less house."

"No ghosts yet anyway," Boone said under his breath.

"So what is this partner like? Does he think Hank's death had something to do with the kidnapping and Jesse Rose?"

"Not exactly. She's been skeptical at best but—"

"She?"

Just then C.J. came out of Natty's office saying her goodbyes.

"Is that her? She sounds *young.*"

Boone wasn't about to take the bait. "I'll call you as soon as I know something." He disconnected and followed C.J. out the back way of the bar again.

THEY WALKED THE few blocks to the bus station. A cold wind blew between the buildings. They passed a homeless man playing a pink kid's guitar. C.J. dropped a few dollars into the man's worn cowboy hat and he promised to play a song just for her.

After a few chords, they moved on, only to pass other homeless people, who C.J. called by name. Each time, she gave them a few dollars and wished them well. Boone found himself enchanted with her generous spirit. Whitehorse didn't have homeless. Sure, a few passed through, spending a night in one of the churches, being fed by locals, but then they were on the road again.

The bus station was empty. Not even any buses in the enclosed cavernous parking area. The lobby had a dozen empty chairs. Past it were the restrooms and finally a hallway filled with old metal lockers.

"Why would Hank leave something here for you?" Boone asked. She had recognized the key so she'd either been here before or—

"When I was a girl, it was a game we played," she said as she pulled the key from her pocket. "He would hide things for me to find and give me clues. He said it was a good way for me to train if I really wanted to be a private investigator like him. I think he did it just to keep me busy and out of his hair and my mother's."

He watched her insert the key and turn it. The locker door groaned open. For a moment, he thought the space was empty. But C.J. reached into the very back and brought out another key, this one to a safety-deposit box.

Boone shook his head. "Are you sure he isn't just keeping you busy again?"

She cupped the key in her hand, her fingers closing over it. "The bank is only a few blocks away," she said, closing the locker and leaving the first key still in the door.

Back out in the fall sunlight, Boone took a breath. He was trying his best not to be irritated by all this cloak-and-dagger secrecy. He kept asking himself, what if Hank Knight's death *had* been nothing more than an accident?

Inside the bank, they were led to the back. C.J. had to sign to get into Hank's safety-deposit box. Apparently her name had always been on the list since they were quickly led into a room full of gold-fronted boxes. The bank clerk put her key into one, then took C.J.'s key and inserted it before she stepped away.

The moment they were alone, C.J. turned her key and pulled out the box. She carried it over to a table and simply stared at it.

"Aren't you going to open it?" he asked.

"I have a bad feeling I don't want to know what's in there."

"Want me to do it?"

She looked up at him with those big brown eyes and nodded.

He stepped closer and slowly lifted the lid, also worried that whatever was in there might devastate C.J. If Hank had been involved in the kidnapping in any way, he feared it would break her heart. Hank Knight was a saint in her eyes. What would happen if she learned he was just a man—a man with a possibly fatal flaw?

Chapter Nine

C.J. wasn't sure how much more she could take. Hank had known he was in trouble. Otherwise he wouldn't have left the keys for her. Why hadn't he let her help him? Maybe he would still be alive if—

She heard Boone open the safety-deposit box, heard him make a surprised sound. Before that, she'd turned away, fighting for the strength she needed to face whatever Hank had left her. A confession? Something he needed her to hide?

"What is it?" she demanded now as she turned to Boone again.

He reached into the box and brought out the contents. He fanned some documents in front of her face.

"What are those?"

"Stocks and bonds, a whole hell of a lot of them. It appears he left you a small fortune."

She shook her head. "How is that possible? He barely made enough money to keep a roof over his head and what he did make, he gave away."

Boone laid the certificates on the table. "C.J., these are pretty impressive. Either he had a good stockbroker or he made more money than anyone thought he did or…" His gaze came up to meet hers. He lifted an eyebrow.

"He wasn't into anything illegal." She picked up one of the stock certificates and quickly put it down to look into the safety-deposit box. It was empty. No note. No explanation. Just a whole lot of questions she didn't want to ask herself.

"It appears that you were his sole beneficiary."

BOONE COULD TELL that C.J. was shaken. She put all the stock certificates back into the safety-deposit box and returned it, pocketing the key. He wanted to say something that might make her feel better. Hank Knight had left her a small fortune. She was rich. But clearly she wasn't happy about any of it.

Probably because it brought up the question of where Hank had gotten his money. On the surface, his life made it appear that he didn't care about money.

But the safety-deposit box proved that was a lie. Had Hank Knight been leading a double life? Had he been involved in something illegal? Not the kidnapping, since that money had been found before the first kidnapper had been able to split it with his accomplice. At least that was the theory.

But there still could have been a payoff. It's possible whoever had Jesse Rose had been forced to pay for her. It still didn't explain the amount of money Hank had left C.J., unless selling babies had been his real ongoing business.

Boone was half-afraid what else they would find. All he could hope was that this runaround would eventually lead to Jesse Rose.

He watched C.J. call the city on her cell. She hung

up after apparently only reaching a recorded message. "They're closed today. I can't get his car out until tomorrow."

"What now?" Boone asked.

"There's someplace I need to go," she told him. She still looked pale. As strong as she appeared, he could tell that all of this was taking its toll on her.

Again she took to the alleys, working her way through the maze of old buildings overlooking the valley.

He couldn't help thinking of her as a child racing around this tired old city to find the clues Hank had left her. He'd trained her well. So why hadn't he told her what was going on? Wouldn't he know that his holding out on her would hurt her? Clearly he'd been trying to protect her. But protect her from what?

All Boone could figure was if Hank had been half the man C.J. thought he'd been, then he'd been in trouble and didn't want to bring her into it. He felt his heart drop at the thought that Hank had known where Jesse Rose was and had now taken that information to his grave.

Ducking into a tiny café stuck between two old brick buildings, Boone followed C.J. inside. She headed for a table, sitting down with her back to the wall as if wanting to watch the door. Were they really being followed? If so, she hadn't mentioned it again since this morning.

C.J. WATCHED BOONE glance behind him before the door closed. She could tell that he hadn't believed her about someone tailing them earlier. He thought she was putting him on, leading him around just to wear him out. She smiled to herself, thinking that might have been partly true earlier.

"What are we doing?" he demanded.

"*I'm* having lunch," she said glancing past him at the large window that looked out onto the street. She saw movement in the deep shadows next to one of the buildings. But who or whatever it had been was gone now.

"If your plan is just to try my patience or wear me down…"

"You know my plan. It's to find out who killed Hank. If it is because of your kidnapping case…" She didn't need to finish since Boone was smart. He'd hang in as long as he thought she might lead him to his kidnapped sister. Even if it was the last place she hoped Hank's trail would lead them.

Not that she didn't want him to find his sister and reunite his family, but not at the expense of Hank's reputation. If Hank was involved, she wouldn't be able to protect him. Whatever happened now, she had no choice but to do her best to find out the truth. Wasn't that what Hank had taught her?

With obvious reluctance, Boone took a seat across from her. What choice did he have? She was his only hope of finding out why Hank had contacted Jim Waters and they both knew it. Boone had said that he couldn't go home until he had answers. Even if it meant putting up with her. And vice versa.

A waitress appeared and, without even looking at a menu, C.J. ordered "the usual" for them both.

"A little presumptuous," he said. "Tell me we aren't having more of those pasty things."

She ignored him as she looked past his shoulder. He turned to follow her gaze to the street but like her seemed to see nothing of interest.

"Still pretending we're being followed?" he asked, turning back to her.

Her gaze shifted to him. In the light coming through the window, his eyes were a brilliant blue. The cowboy was too handsome for his own good. Not that he seemed to realize it, though. She wondered how many women had flirted with him to no avail.

"Why don't you have a girlfriend?" she asked.

Those blue eyes blinked in surprise. "Who says I don't?"

She chuckled at that.

"I've had girlfriends," he said defensively. "I also have a horse ranch to run with my brothers. My father—"

"Had a heart attack. I understand he's better."

"He is. What about you?"

"I'm fine."

"You know what I mean. You have a steady beau?" He didn't wait for her to answer. "I didn't think so. So what's *your* excuse?"

She shook her head to keep herself from telling him the usual line—too busy, not interested in the men who were interested in her, hadn't met the right one yet and all the other things she'd told Hank when he'd asked the same question.

"I'd think you'd have a string of girlfriends," she said, knowing she was only trying to distract herself from what they'd found in the safety-deposit box.

"And you'd be wrong."

"Why is that? Some girl break your heart? Make you swear off women?"

"No. Is that what happened to you? The quarterback in high school or some studious young man at college?"

Fortunately she was saved as the waitress came back with two overflowing plates. Fried pork chops hung over the buns next to heaping piles of french fries. "I didn't want you to leave Butte without a pork chop sandwich and this place makes the best ones," she said.

He locked eyes with her. "I'm not leaving until I find out what your partner knew about Jesse Rose and the kidnapping."

C.J. was the first to look away. "Like I think I've mentioned before, I'd have a better chance of finding out the truth without you tagging along."

"Too bad. You're stuck with me."

She glanced out the window again. "Is there any reason someone would be following *you*?"

He laughed. "Seriously? *If* someone really is following us, why would they be after me?"

"I don't know," she said, holding his gaze for a moment before she picked up one of her french fries.

"Well?" He apparently wasn't letting her off the hook.

She took a bite, chewed, swallowed and said, "It's none of your business."

"Aha! There *was* some boy." He laughed again. "I would think it's hard to find a man willing to date a woman who carries a gun in her purse."

C.J. smiled at that, seeing that he was trying to get a rise out of her. "You know so little about women—and men—it seems." She picked up her pork chop sandwich and took a bite. No simple task given the size of it.

He sighed, picked up his and took a big bite. She saw his expression and hurriedly swallowed before she laughed.

"You like, huh?"

HE LIKED, BOONE thought as their gazes met and held for a long moment. He liked the sandwich. He liked her—a lot. The more he was around her... He looked away first.

They'd just finished their lunch when his cell phone rang. He stepped outside the door to take the call. But he stayed where he could see C.J. He suspected she wanted him around now even less. The things they were finding out about her deceased partner weren't things she wanted anyone else to know—maybe especially him.

"One of those strings of women after you?" C.J. asked when he returned to the table after assuring his father he'd call as soon as he knew something.

"My father. After my brother Cull told him about your partner being killed in a hit-and-run, he was worried about me."

"He should be," she said. "Someone has been following us all day."

WHEN THEY LEFT the café, C.J. took them out the back door. Boone's father was worried about him. She was, too. She didn't want to get Travers McGraw's son killed. That's why she knew she should stop this now.

She knew she could get rid of this cowboy without much effort. He didn't know Butte and she did. But she had to admit, there were moments when she didn't want to be alone. Sometimes, she thought, remembering the way he'd devoured his pork chop sandwich, she enjoyed his company. He kept her mind off Hank and the pain of his death.

But the more she learned about Hank, the more worried she was becoming. Where had he gotten all that money for the stocks and bonds? Had he known something about the kidnapping? About Jesse Rose?

She was still shocked and shaken by what she'd discovered at the bank. It was one thing for Hank to be going somewhere without telling her, but all that money… It was as if she'd never known the man. Like the clothes in the suitcase.

Hank hated dressing up. She hadn't even known that he owned a suit. He was as bad as she was when it came to dressing casually for their work. Most of the people they saw couldn't afford to hire a private investigator. They dressed so they fit in with the community since Hank had never been interested in taking what he called highbrow cases.

Let some other PI take care of the rich, he'd always said. *We'll take care of the little guys, the ones who need us the most.* And she'd felt the same way.

It's called giving back to the community, Hank told her the first time she realized he didn't make much money. *People need help. If I can help, I do. This job isn't about the money.*

She'd seen right away how kindhearted the man was. He'd taken her on to raise, hadn't he? The only way C.J. had kept a roof over their heads once she'd become his partner was by taking insurance fraud cases while Hank continued to help those who couldn't help themselves.

That's why she'd been so sure Hank's death couldn't have had anything to do with the McGraws. It wasn't the kind of case that interested him. It was highbrow *and* high profile. A wealthy horse ranch family. And yet, she'd found the file. She knew that Boone wouldn't lie about Hank talking to his family lawyer. But why?

And did the case have anything to do with Hank's hit-and-run? How about all that loot in the safety-deposit box? It made no sense given the way Hank had lived.

As they came out on the street, she glanced back. She hadn't spotted the tail since before lunch. All she'd caught was a shadowy figure lurking not quite out of sight. Why follow her to start with? Because they were afraid she would find out the truth?

"I should have gone to the restroom back at the café," C.J. said. "I'm going to duck in here."

"I'll wait out here for you," he said after glancing into the Chinese restaurant. He watched her go inside and disappear into a door marked Women. The air was brisk this afternoon, especially in the shade. He stomped his feet to keep them warm as he looked up the street toward the Berkeley Pit. What had once been a large natural bowl sitting high in the Rockies straddling the Continental Divide was now an open pit that stretched over a mile wide. It had become a tourist attraction, he thought with a shake of his head.

He glanced inside the restaurant. The door to the women's restroom was ajar. There was no sign of C.J. Even before he went inside and saw the rear entrance, he knew she'd given him the slip.

Chapter Ten

C.J. couldn't believe that she felt guilty about losing Boone McGraw. There was someplace she needed to go without him. When she was a girl and Hank was teaching her the PI business from the ground floor up, as he liked to call it, he would leave her messages in an old building uptown. She had looked back on those days, thinking it was charming, the cute things he came up with to keep her busy and out of his hair.

It had been years since he'd left anything for her at this particular place, but after everything that had happened, she felt she needed to check it.

And check it without Boone. He'd already learned too much about her and Hank. She was sure by now that he thought Hank had been dirty—how else could all those stocks and bonds at the bank be explained? That he'd saved that much from his PI practice? Not a chance.

She couldn't stand the thought of an investigation into Hank because of her. Boone swore that all he was interested in was finding his sister. She prayed that was true. Still, she thought as she walked the last block to the old building, she couldn't have Boone tagging along. Not right now. Hank had been in trouble or he wouldn't be dead right now, no matter what the police thought.

The building was abandoned like so many in Butte. She was just glad to see it still standing. One of these days it would either crumble and fall down or someone would come along and tear it down. Her heart ached at the thought of the memories that would go with it—not to mention the beautiful structure it had once been.

She climbed the steps to the wide double doors, now chained and padlocked, then stepped into the alcove to the right. At one time, there had been a fountain with water sprouting from the mouth of the ancient-looking stone face. But that had been years before C.J. herself. For as long as she could remember, the mouth had been dry like the bowl shape under it.

Today there were leaves and garbage in the bowl that used to catch the fresh water. She wished she'd brought a bag so she could clean it out, then reminded herself why she was there. She couldn't save this place. She wasn't even sure she could save herself if Boone was right and she was Hank's beneficiary. If her partner in business had gotten all that money from something illegal…

Reaching into the mouth, she felt grit and nothing else. Then her fingers brushed something cold. She touched it tentatively before she pulled out the small package. It was wrapped in plastic.

Seeing it, she began to cry. Hank knew her so well and vice versa. With trembling fingers, she saw the thumb drive protected inside the plastic cover and stuffed it into her pocket, her heart in her throat.

AFTER CUSSING AND carrying on for a while, Boone drove down random streets looking for her. Clearly there was someplace she'd wanted to go without him. Or maybe she'd just wanted to be alone.

That thought struck him hard. He'd seen how upset she'd been after finding the stocks and bonds at the bank. Didn't it make more sense to give her some space? He pulled over, parked and spent the next hour learning as much as he could about PI Hank Knight and his partner.

Everywhere he went, he heard nothing but praise about Hank and respect for C.J. The two were well-known around town as do-gooders. People liked them. People had been helped by them.

So where had all that loot come from? Hank had to be into something illegal. Perhaps a baby ring. The thought that Jesse Rose could have been one of the babies set his teeth on edge. C.J. knew more than she was telling him. Once he found her again...

He'd just driven down one of the main streets in uptown Butte, when he spotted her VW van and went roaring after her, riding her bumper. He cursed himself as C.J. whipped across two lanes of traffic on Montana Avenue and came to a tire-screaming stop at the curb. Before he could pull in behind her, she was already out of her van and storming toward him.

"What do you think you're doing?" she demanded.

He wished he knew. He wanted to throttle this woman or kiss her. Right now, he wasn't sure which and that said a lot about his frustration.

"I have no idea what I hope to accomplish by hanging around Butte—let alone tailing a junior PI who can't investigate her way out of a paper bag."

Hands on her hips, she glared at him. "What did you

just call me? A junior PI who can't investigate her way out of a paper bag?" she demanded indignantly.

"Prove me wrong. Help me find my sister."

She glared at him for a full minute. "I told you what I'm doing. Trying to find my partner's killer."

"How are you doing on that?"

C.J. narrowed her eyes at him. "There is one more place I need to look. I'm assuming you plan to come along?"

"You're assuming right. We walking or taking my truck?"

She looked as if she could spit nails. "We're taking my van since you don't know where we're going." With that, she spun on her heel and headed for her van. He took a few deep breaths himself before following her.

Once behind the wheel with the van engine revved, she peeled out into the street and roared down the hill. Uptown Butte was a rollercoaster of steep streets. After a few blocks, she swung into a parking spot in front of one of Butte's historic buildings.

He climbed out after her and headed for the front door. C.J., he realized belatedly, was headed down the alley between the two buildings. The alley was just wide enough to walk down. It was cool and dark.

"Where—"

"If you're determined to tag along," she said over her shoulder, "then no questions."

Halfway down the long alley, she stopped at an old weathered padlocked door. Pulling out a set of keys, she opened the padlock and swung the door open.

Boone peered down a dark narrow concrete hallway, a musty, dank smell wafting out. He didn't like the looks of this.

"Close the door behind you," she ordered and stepped in.

He hesitated but only a moment before following her. Their footsteps echoed on the damp concrete. The smell got much worse as the passage became more tunnel-like.

She made a sharp right, then a left, then another right. He tried to keep track, telling himself he might need directions to get out of here. It crossed his mind that she might be leading him into a trap. If she and her partner were in league…

Boone realized that he'd lost track of the twists and turns. He was screwed if he had to get out of here by himself. If he was that lucky.

C.J. stopped and he almost crashed into her in the dim light. He heard the jingle of keys again. "Hold this," she ordered as she dug a flashlight from her shoulder bag and handed it to him.

He held the light on another padlock and a few seconds later, she was entering yet another narrow passage.

"Where the—" He didn't get the rest of the words out as she turned on him.

"Shh," she snapped and was off again.

He had no choice but to go with her. If he thought she'd been leading him on a wild-goose chase earlier, he'd been wrong. But this definitely felt like she was fooling with him.

The next padlock opened into a room filled with file cabinets. She flipped on a light switch and for a moment he was blinded by the overhead bulb.

C.J. had stopped just inside the door.

"What?" he asked.

"Hank didn't leave anything in here."

He stared at her. "You haven't even looked."

"Come on," she said, turning and starting for the door.

"No, wait, we came all this way, why not—"

"The dust."

"What?"

"Didn't you notice the dust on the floor?"

He couldn't say he had.

"Hank hasn't been in that room in months."

"Based on a little dust."

She glared at him in the ambient glow of the flashlight. "I'm just a junior PI who can't investigate my way out of a paper bag, but yes, that's my conclusion. I don't just jump to conclusions without facts."

"Really? And why all this subterfuge? What was it your partner did that he not only had to hide his files, but that he made a ton of money from?"

She gave him an impatient look before turning and heading down a different tunnel than the one they'd come in from. She had the flashlight. He had no choice but to follow her.

They came to a narrow stairway that wound up a couple of stories and the next thing he knew they were standing outside in the sunlight.

He glanced around, trying to get his bearings. The tall brick buildings that had rivaled New York City now just looked sad, so many of them empty. They had come out not that far from the Berkeley Pit, a huge hole that was now full of bad water. Butte was now the butt of jokes, a decaying relic of better times.

"I don't know where else to look," she said, sounding

disheartened. "I need a hot shower. You aren't going to insist on coming along for that, are you?"

It was late afternoon. The sun had sunk behind the mountains to the west. Dark shadows fell across the streets and a cold wind whipped between the buildings. Butte had fallen on hard times, especially the old uptown, and yet there was a quiet elegance to it. He wished he had seen it during its heyday. He was feeling a little nostalgic and disheartened himself.

"I'm sure it is all going to make sense at some point," he said.

Her smile was sad. She looked close to tears. He wanted to take her in his arms. But if he did, he knew he'd kiss her. He realized looking at her now that she had a bow-shaped mouth that just begged to be kissed.

"A hot shower sounds great. Back at my motel," he added, thinking a cold one might even be called for. "If you wouldn't mind dropping me at my truck."

BACK AT HER HOUSE, C.J. closed and locked the door behind her. She kept thinking of Boone. For a moment back there on the sidewalk, the sun slanting down through the buildings, she'd thought he was going to kiss her.

She shook her head now, telling herself she was tired and discouraged and scared. Boone wanted just one thing from her: answers.

Her hand went to her pocket and closed around the thumb drive Hank had left for her. She feared he'd left her answers—and she wasn't going to like them.

Taking off her jacket, she tossed it aside and picked up her laptop. Popping it open, she slid in the thumb drive, all the time praying she wasn't about to read Hank's confession.

What came up was even more shocking.

The photo was of a beautiful young dark-haired woman with the greenest eyes C.J. had ever seen. She was much prettier than the digitally enhanced photos that had run in the news showing what Jesse Rose McGraw would look like now. The young woman was smiling at the camera, eyes bright, as if whoever was taking the photo had said something funny.

She looked quickly to see what else was on the thumb drive, but there was only the one photo. She stared at Jesse Rose McGraw, her heart pounding. Hank had definitely known something about Jesse Rose.

But did it mean he'd been involved in the kidnapping? Or had he found out about Jesse Rose only recently? That was the question, wasn't it? The fact that he'd inquired with the McGraw family attorney gave her hope that he'd only recently stumbled onto the truth.

So why hadn't he told the attorney? Or at least called Travers McGraw and told him where he could find his daughter? It wasn't like Hank to keep a secret like that. So what had held him back?

It was the thought of what had stopped Hank from telling the McGraws the truth that had her running scared. Hank had been hiding something, there was no doubt about that. But what had kept him from doing the right thing?

C.J. closed the file, pulled out the thumb drive and pocketed it, her hands shaking. Hank had kept this from her and now she was about to do the same thing with Boone McGraw.

But she couldn't throw Hank under the bus. She had to know how he was involved—if he was. She had to find out where he fit into all of this. And then she would turn over this thumb drive. But until then...

AFTER A HOT SHOWER, followed by a cold one, Boone had gone over everything that had happened that day. None of it made any sense. The only conclusion he'd reached—and one he figured C.J. had, too—was that Hank was dirty.

That made him sad for C.J. Everything he'd learned about the two private investigators, though, was at odds with that conclusion. He'd seen C.J.'s reaction to the stocks and bonds in the safety-deposit box. She'd been dumbfounded. Which meant she had to be devastated by what they'd discovered today.

The question was, though, how did it tie in with the kidnapping and Jesse Rose? If it did at all.

He pulled out his cell phone and called C.J. "I need a drink after a day spent with you. What do you say to joining me?"

"A drink?"

He heard something in her tone. "Look, I don't have to get you drunk to hit on you, which I'm not, but if I was, I'd just back you up against a wall and—"

"Until you felt my gun in your ribs."

He laughed at the image. "Yes. Just so there is no misunderstanding, let's have dinner. We both have to eat. Or you don't even have to eat. You can just watch me."

She sighed and he thought for sure she was going to turn him down. To his surprise, she said, "There's a steakhouse close to your motel. I'll meet you there. Order me a steak, medium rare."

"Wait, you don't know where I'm stay—" He realized she'd already hung up. Of course she knew where he was staying. He could only guess how she knew. She'd probably followed him last night. He'd been too distracted to notice. He regretted what he'd said to her earlier about not being able to investigate her way out of a paper bag.

BOONE HADN'T BEEN waiting long when C.J entered the steakhouse. She looked a little out of breath as she slid into the opposite side of the booth. She'd told him to order for her and he had.

"I guessed baked potato loaded and salad with ranch dressing," he said.

She cocked a brow as she slid into the booth across from him. "I can live with that. What did you order?"

"The same." There was something different about her, he thought as he studied her. He got the impression that she'd walked here. Which meant she must not live far away. Either that or she'd needed the walk in the cold air.

She'd changed clothes and now wore a blouse and slacks, and her hair was tied at the nape of her neck. It cascaded down her back in a fiery river against the light-colored blouse. Silver earrings dangled from each ear and it appeared she'd applied lip gloss.

Something told him that none of this was about him. She seemed to wear all of it like armor as if she were going to war, reminding him that she was a private investigator first and foremost—and a woman on a mission. That they might not be on the same mission was still a possibility he had to accept.

He studied her, feeling a pull stronger than gravity. "I'm sorry about what I said to you earlier, you know, about the paper bag."

She smiled. "I'm sorry about dumping you earlier."

"It gave me time to do some investigating on my own," he told her, making her raise a brow. "I found out a lot about you and your partner."

"Really?" She seemed intrigued by that—and maybe a little worried. "All bad?"

"Actually, all good. The two of you are considered saints in this town."

She shook her head, almost blushing as she picked up her napkin and dumped her silverware noisily on the table. There was a tenseness to her tonight that he also didn't think had anything to do with him. After what they'd discovered at the bank, he'd seen how thrown she'd been. Had she found out even more to shake her faith in her partner?

"How was your time without me?" he asked.

"Pleasantly quiet." She smiled, though.

"I thought you might have missed me," he said.

She chuckled at that and carefully straightened her silverware. As the waitress brought their salads, C.J. looked eternally grateful for something to do with her hands.

It surprised him to see her so nervous. Was it because she was having dinner with him, almost like a date? Or had something happened this afternoon after she'd dumped him that had her even more upset?

"So you talked to people about Hank?"

"And about you. Both of you are highly respected around town," he said when she didn't ask.

"That's nice. Anything else?"

"No one confessed to killing him, if that's what you're asking."

She nodded and dived into her salad as if she hadn't eaten in a week.

"So what *did* you do without me?" he asked, studying her.

"Just tying up loose ends," she said without looking up.

"You're sure that's all?"

She glanced at him, those warm, honey-brown eyes meeting his. He saw defiance along with something that made his chest ache—fear. C.J. was running scared. He got the feeling that didn't happen often.

"Do we have to talk business?" she asked.

"Is that what I was doing?" He took a bite of his salad. What the devil had C.J. found out? And why meet him tonight if she wasn't going to tell him?

Their steaks came as they finished their salads. They ate without talking. He was hungry and quickly put away his steak and potato. Considering everything he'd eaten today, it seemed impossible. Must have been the high altitude of Butte that had him so ravenous. Or maybe it was a different kind of hunger that he was making up for.

As he pushed his plate away, he looked at C.J. She put her last piece of steak in her mouth, closed her eyes and chewed slowly.

"I take it you liked your dinner?" he joked, noticing that she'd eaten everything. "You're welcome to lick the plate."

She opened her eyes and swallowed. "I'm sorry you wasted the trip to Butte. There really isn't any reason for you to stick around tomorrow. I can get a friend to take me down to pick up Hank's car. If something else comes up, I know where to contact you."

There wasn't anything to say except, "Dessert?"

As she devoured a large slice of cheesecake, he had to wonder where she put it. She couldn't eat like this all the time. Then again, she probably had the metabolism of a long-distance runner.

"Thanks for dinner," she said after he'd paid and walked her outside. It was dark with a cold breeze coming out of the mountains.

"I'm taking you home," he said, looking down the street to see several homeless men arguing.

"That isn't necessary."

"I'm afraid it is." He opened the passenger side of his truck and waited. He could see her having a private argument with herself, but she finally relented and climbed in.

He went around and climbed behind the wheel. Whatever she'd considered telling him tonight, she'd apparently changed her mind. Why else have dinner with him? Or maybe she'd just been hungry and he was buying.

"Just tell me where to go," he said as he started the pickup.

"Don't tempt me."

He looked over at her. "I'm going to take a wild guess here. This afternoon you found out something even more upsetting about Hank, but you don't want to tell me. In fact, it's why you gave me the slip earlier today. You're running scared that not only am I right about what got Hank killed, but that he is involved somehow in the kidnapping."

She looked out the side window and for a moment, he thought she might get out of the truck. Finally, she turned back to him. "Isn't it possible I'm just exhausted and have enough to deal with without you?"

He nodded. "But you agreed to have dinner with me. I was watching you while you ate. I could see that you were debating telling me something."

C.J. laughed. "You've never been very good at reading people, have you?" She looked out the windshield. "I live up that way."

He put the truck into gear and started in the direction she indicated. "I'm not leaving tomorrow. I'm going with you to the city car lot to get Hank's vehicle. If you don't want to go together, then I'll simply be waiting there for you."

"Turn left up here," she said. "Then right at the light." They were headed up the mountain to an area he'd been told was called Walkerville. The street went straight up through smaller and smaller, less ornate houses until she told him to turn right.

Her house was the last one on a short street that ended in a deep gully.

"Here," she said and the moment he slowed opened her door to get out.

"What time should I pick you up in the morning?" he asked.

In the cab light that came on as she climbed out, he saw her smile. "Are you always this pigheaded?"

"Always."

"Ten."

"I think you mean nine," he said before she could

close the door. "That is when the city lot opens and when you're planning to be there, isn't it?"

She smiled. "Nine, then," she said, and slammed the door.

THE NEXT MORNING, he was sitting outside C.J.'s house. Walkerville in the daylight looked even more like an old mining community up on the mountain overlooking the city. As she came out of the house, he climbed out of his pickup and went around to open the passenger-side door for her.

"I was hoping you'd left town," she said, clearly not pleased to see him.

"I almost did."

"What stopped you?" she asked as she climbed in.

"You," he said and shut her door.

As he slid behind the wheel, C.J. asked, "Could we make one stop first on the way? It's uptown. The city yard is down in the valley, so it isn't out of your way."

"Not a problem. I'm all yours. So to speak," he added and started the truck. "Sleep well?" he asked as he drove down the steep narrow streets.

"Fine." He glanced over at her. If she'd gotten any sleep, he would have been surprised. There were dark shadows under her eyes.

"I slept fine, too." Not that she'd asked.

She ignored his sarcasm as she gave directions to where she wanted to go. "Right here," she said and the moment he stopped, she was out of the pickup and heading into another large brick building in the seedier part of town.

He cut the engine, parked and got out to follow her. Today she wasn't getting rid of him as easily as yesterday. But the moment he pushed open the door, he saw her in the arms of a large older woman. The two were hugging. He couldn't hear what was being said—no doubt condolences. He reminded himself of C.J.'s recent loss.

Boone felt a stab of guilt. He'd been so wrapped up in finding out what Hank had known about the kidnapping and Jesse Rose that he hadn't given a lot of thought or compassion to C.J. Maybe she was right and Jesse Rose and the kidnapping had nothing to do with Hank's death. Given the amount of money in those stocks and bonds, Hank could have been into something more dangerous than kidnapping.

He heard the older woman say, "I'm sorry, but I hadn't seen Hank in a few weeks. He didn't say anything about leaving town. Not to me."

"And he didn't leave anything for me?" C.J. asked, her voice rough with emotion.

The older woman shook her head. "I'm so sorry."

C.J. brushed at her tears and stiffened her back as the woman looked past her to where Boone was standing. Apparently neither had heard him enter. "Thank you," C.J. said. She turned toward him but she didn't look at him as she made a beeline for the door.

He had only a second to get the door open and follow her out before she was on the curb. "I didn't mean to intrude just now."

Before she could answer, he heard the squeal of tires and the roar of an engine. The car came out of the alley at high speed. He didn't have time to catch more than the general shape and color of the car before it headed straight for C.J.

Chapter Eleven

It happened so fast that C.J. didn't have a chance to react. One moment she was standing at the curb, the next she was shoved aside and knocked to the ground with Boone McGraw crushing her with his body and the thick smell of engine exhaust wafting over them.

"Are you all right?"

She groaned as he rolled off her. The sound of the car engine died off in the distance. She became aware of people on the street huddled around them. "Did anyone get a plate number on that car?" she demanded as she tried to get to her feet.

Boone was on his. "Are you sure you're all right?" he asked, sounding a little breathless as he hunkered down beside her.

She nodded, though her knee was scraped and her wrist was hurt, but wasn't broken. She let him help her to her feet. She was more shaken than she'd thought when she was on the ground. One look at the people huddled around them and she could tell how close a call it had been. They were saying the same thing she was thinking. If it hadn't been for the cowboy...

If it hadn't been for Boone, it would have been another hit-and-run. Immediately, she thought of Hank. He hadn't had anyone to throw him out of the way. Could it have been the same car?

"A license plate number," she said to the small crowd around them again. "Anyone get it or a description of the car?" There was a general shaking of heads. Several said it had happened too fast.

"Kids," one woman said. "They could have killed you."

It hadn't been kids. Her every instinct told her that. It was too much of a coincidence that Hank had been run down and now she had almost been killed by a speeding car, as well.

She finally looked at Boone. He appeared even more shaken than she was. She saw that he'd pulled out his phone. "What are you doing?" she asked as the crowd began to disperse.

"Calling the cops."

"To tell them what? Did you see the car?" She saw that he hadn't gotten a look at it, either, before he'd thrown them both out of the way. "Even if they took it seriously, we don't have any information to give them. They'd just say it was another accident."

He hesitated for a moment before he pocketed his phone. "You're sure you're all right?"

She nodded, although still trembling inside. In all the years she'd been around and in the private investigation business, that was the closest she'd come to being killed. She'd been scared a few times, especially when caught tailing a person in a fraud case. But this was something new.

Which was probably why Hank hadn't seen it coming, either.

Boone opened the passenger side of his pickup and

helped her in. She knew he was just being a gentleman because he felt guilty for still hanging around, but it made her feel weak and fragile—something she abhorred. She'd always had to be strong, for her mother. Now she had to be strong because otherwise she would fall apart. Hank was gone and she was terrified to find out why.

"You still think Hank's death has nothing to do with Jesse Rose and the kidnapping?" he asked as he started the pickup.

She didn't answer, couldn't. Her heart was lodged in her throat. Someone had just tried to kill her and would have taken Boone with her as she realized how close a call that had been. Worse, after looking at what was on that flash drive, there was no doubt. Hank knew something about Jesse Rose—and possibly her kidnapping.

Last night, she hadn't been able to sleep. She'd moved through her small house, restless and scared. At one point she thought she heard a noise outside. She'd never been afraid before living here. She'd always felt safe.

She'd checked all the doors and windows to make sure they were locked. But looking out into the darkness, she'd thought she'd seen the shape of a man in the trees beside the house. As she started to grab her purse and the gun inside, she saw that it was only shadows.

Her fears, she'd told herself, weren't any she could lock out. Hank had known about Jesse Rose. So why hadn't he told the McGraws?

Boone started the car. "Any other stops?"

She shook her head. "Let's go to the city lot and get Hank's car." With luck, he would have left something in it for her, not that she held out much hope. Hank's car always looked as if he was homeless and living in it. Finding a clue in it would literally be like looking for a needle in a haystack.

A FEW BLOCKS AWAY, Cecil pulled over to the side of the road. His hands were shaking so hard he had to lie over the wheel as he tried to catch his breath.

That had been so close. Just a few seconds later and he would have hit them both. Killed them both. He would have killed Boone McGraw. Killing some old PI was one thing. Even killing his young female partner. But if he had killed a McGraw...

The shaking got worse. He held on to the wheel as if the earth under him would throw him off if he didn't. And yet a part of him felt such desperate disappointment. He had to end this. C.J. West wasn't going to stop. He had to kill her. He had no choice.

When had things gotten so complicated? It had started out so simply and then he'd been forced to kill the PI. Now he would have to kill the PI's partner. As long as he didn't kill a McGraw. Travers McGraw would have every cop in the state looking for him if he did.

He began to settle down a little. He wouldn't get another chance, not with a hit-and-run. She would be expecting it now—and so would Boone. No, he'd have to think of something else. He knew where she lived.

An idea began to gel. Kill her and he should be home free.

Wiping the sweat from his face with his sleeve, he pulled himself together. He was steadier now, feeling better. He could do this. He could make up for his past mistakes. His head ached. He felt confused. There wasn't any other way out of this, was there?

He started to pull out, jumped at the sound of a loud car horn. A truck roared past, the driver flipping him the bird as he continued to lean on the horn.

Heart pounding, he checked his side mirror before slowly pulling out. He'd messed up, but he could fix it. He had no choice. But even as he thought it, he wondered how many more people he would have to kill to keep his secret. In for a penny, in for a pound, he thought.

BOONE DROVE TO the city yard and waited while C.J. went in to get Hank's car released. He still hadn't calmed down after their near miss back uptown. He would have loved to have passed it off as nothing but kids driving crazy fast and out of control—if C.J.'s partner hadn't been killed in a hit-and-run.

He would also love to know what C.J. was thinking now. Was she ready to admit that all this had to be about the kidnapping? Was she finally all in? He still couldn't be sure.

She came out shortly, jingling a set of keys. Hank had left his keys in his car? What a trusting soul. It was a miracle the car hadn't been stolen. Not that he ever worried about that in Whitehorse. But this was Butte. He shook his head as he got out and followed her to the blue-and-white Olds.

Unlocking it, she opened the driver's-side door and stopped.

"What is it?" He glanced in expecting to see something awful. But the car looked spotless.

"His car never looks like this. Ever. He cleaned it out." She sounded shocked. And worried.

"So he cleaned his car. Because he was planning to go somewhere in it."

She looked skeptical. "Nowhere I can imagine that he would care."

Boone was disappointed. He'd hoped that they would find something in the car. If the man had cleaned it out, something rare, then he doubted there would be anything to find. "You want me to drive it?"

She shook her head. "I'll take it back to my place. You don't mind following me?"

He'd been following her since he got to town. "Not a problem."

She slid behind the wheel, but before she started the car, she reached up to touch what looked like a new small pine-scented car freshener hanging from the mirror. "This is so not Hank."

Boone went back to his pickup and caught up to her as they headed back to her house. In the distance, he could see the skeletal headframe over one of the old mine shafts, the dark structure silhouetted against the skyline. Another reminder he was in mining country.

Parking, he joined her, looking under the seat to see if Hank had missed anything. The smell of pine was overpowering from the small tree-shaped car freshener hanging from the mirror.

"What do you think he was covering up? A dead body smell?" he asked, only half joking. C.J. hadn't moved from the driver's seat, her hands still on the big steering wheel.

"I don't understand this change in him," she said as if more to herself. "He bought a cell phone, he canceled the landline at his office and had the power turned off.

He packed his best clothes and cleaned out his car. It was almost as if…"

"As if he was leaving for good?"

She slowly swung her head around to look at him. There were tears in her eyes. "I need to get ready for the funeral."

"I'm going with you. Everyone knows that the killer always shows up at the funeral."

C.J. looked as if she wanted to put up a fight but didn't have it in her today after what had already happened.

"The problem is I didn't bring funeral attire."

She snorted. "This is Butte. I can promise you that most of the people there will be wearing street clothes because they're street people." She headed toward the house.

He waited until she went inside before he popped open the glove box. C.J. had already looked in it, but he'd noticed something that had caught his eye.

Like the rest of the car, it had been cleaned out, except for the book on the car. He pulled it out, noticing that it looked as if it had never been opened—except to stick two items into it. One was a boarding pass for a flight to Seattle. He looked at the date and saw that it was from last week—a few days before he was run down in the street.

The other was a train schedule. He flipped it over and recognized Hank's handwriting from the McGraw file the man had started. Hank had written dates and times on the back of the schedule—from Seattle to Whitehorse, Montana.

Chapter Twelve

The funeral was held in an old cemetery on the side of the mountain overlooking the city. C.J. used to come up here with Hank when he visited his long-deceased wife, Margaret. She'd asked him once why he never remarried.

When you have the best, it is hard to settle for anything else, he'd told her. *I didn't have her long, but I'm not complaining. I treasure every day we had together. She's all I need, alive or in my memories.*

The wind whipped through the tall dried grass that grew around the almost abandoned cemetery. But as she and Boone neared Margaret Knight's grave, the weeds had been neatly cleared away and there were recently added new silk flowers in the vase at the base of her headstone. Hank must have added them recently, she realized. Next to the grave site, C.J. saw the dirt peeking out from under a tarp and the dark hole beneath the casket.

C.J. had forgone a church service, deciding that here on this mountainside was where Hank would have liked a few words said over him. He didn't go in for fanfare. In fact he preferred to fly under the radar.

Because he'd had something to hide? That was the question, wasn't it?

She pushed all such thoughts from her mind. She couldn't have been wrong about Hank. Just as all these people couldn't have been either, she told herself.

A crowd had already gathered and more were arriving, most of them walking up from town. A few had caught rides. Many were closer to Hank's age, but still the group appeared to be a cross-section of the city's population. All people whose lives had been touched by Hank Knight.

"Are all these people here for Hank?" Boone asked beside her.

She smiled through her tears and nodded. She saw the mourners through Boone's eyes, a straggly bunch of ne'er-do-wells who'd loved Hank. "These people are his family. They're all he had other than his late wife, Margaret." She frowned. "He once mentioned a sister. I got the impression she'd died when they were both fairly young. He'd once mentioned being an orphan." More and more she realized how little she'd really known about Hank.

As the pastor took his place, C.J. smiled at all the people who'd come to say goodbye to Hank. He would have been so touched by this, she thought as the pastor said a few words and several others chimed in before someone burst out in a gravelly rendition of "Amazing Grace."

C.J. felt as if a warm breeze had brushed past her cheek. Her throat closed with such emotion that she could no longer sing the words. Boone put his arm around her as the coffin was lowered into the ground and she leaned into him, accepting his strength. At least for a little while.

BOONE HAD BEEN to plenty of small-town funerals. Most everyone in town turned up. But he hadn't expected the kind of turnout that Hank Knight got on this cold December day in Butte, Montana. He was impressed and he could see that C.J. was touched by all the people who'd come to pay their respects to her partner. He could tell she was fighting to try to hold it together.

As he listened to the pastor talk, he studied those who were in attendance, wondering if Hank's killer was among them. He spotted one man who'd hung back some. He wore a black baseball cap and kept his head down. Every once in a while, he would sneak a look at C.J.

While the man's face was mostly in shadow, once when he looked up, Boone caught sight of what appeared to be a scar across his right cheek. The scar tissue caught in the sunlight, gleaming white for a moment before the man ducked his head.

Something about the man had caught his eye, but he had to admit there were a dozen others in the crowd who looked suspicious. Hank's clients were a rough-and-tumble bunch, no doubt about it. Anyone of them could have had some kind of grudge against him and done something about it.

But Boone's gaze kept coming back to the man in the black baseball cap. The moment the pastor finished, the man turned to leave. That's when Boone saw the way the man limped as he disappeared over the hill. Boone kept watching, hoping to see what vehicle the man was driving, but he didn't get a chance to see as the crowd suddenly surrounded C.J. to offer condolences.

She'd stood up well during the funeral, but as the

mourners left, some singing hymns as they headed back into town, Boone could see how raw her grief was.

"I'll give you some time alone," he said and walked back toward his pickup. He hadn't gone far when he glanced back to see her, head bowed, body shuddering with sobs. He kept walking, moved by the love and respect Hank Knight had reaped.

When C.J. joined him at the pickup, her eyes were red, but she had that strong, determined set to her shoulders again.

"You must be ready for more food, knowing you," he said. "Where do you suggest we go where we can talk? I found something in Hank's car that I think you need to see."

Just as he suspected, getting back to business was exactly what C.J. needed. He drove to a Chinese food place on the way. It was early enough that the place was nearly empty.

After ordering, he took out the boarding pass and the train schedule. "I found both of these stuck in his vehicle book in a very clean glove box." He pushed the boarding pass across the table. She looked at it and then at him.

"I guess he really did fly to Seattle," she said, sounding sad.

"Who does he know there?"

"I have no idea. He's never mentioned anyone."

"And he's never been before?"

She shook her head, but he could see the wheels turning. "There were a couple times a year when he would take a few days off. I never asked where he went. I just assumed it was for a case. Most of the time he never left Butte. Or at least I thought he hadn't."

Boone nodded. "That's not all." He slid the train schedule across to her. "What do you make of this?"

C.J. studied it for a moment. "This doesn't mean he was planning to take a train," she finally said. "Anyway, no passenger train comes through Butte. The only line is to the north up on the Hi-Line."

He flipped the schedule over. "Look what he had marked. The times for the train from Seattle to Whitehorse, Montana, and the date—day after tomorrow."

Her gaze shot up to his. "I don't understand."

"Your partner was going to meet that train."

She stared at him. "Talk about jumping to conclusions."

"Look at the evidence. He had packed, shut down his office and had this information in the glove box of his car. He flew to Seattle last week. Then he packed and cleaned his car. It seems pretty clear to me that he planned to drive north and meet the train when it came into Whitehorse."

"You're reading a lot into a train schedule and some scribbles."

She wasn't fooling him. He'd seen her expression when she'd recognized Hank's writing, the same way he had. "If you want to find his killer, then I suggest you come with me. Whoever gets off that train is the key."

"Go to Whitehorse?" She raised her eyes to his for a moment. "Let's say you're right. Even if we met this train, how would we know—"

"Whitehorse is just one quick stop for the train. Our depot isn't even manned. Only a few people ever get off there. It shouldn't be that hard to figure out who Hank was meeting. This is about my sister and her kidnapping. Come on, C.J. You aren't going to keep arguing that it's not, are you?"

She met his gaze. He had that urge to gather her up in his arms, kiss her senseless and carry her away. "Whitehorse," she repeated.

He could see she looked scared. "You coming with me?"

BY THE TIME Boone dropped her off at her house to pack for their trip the next day, it was already getting dark. This was why she hated winter hours. Living in Butte, she'd gotten used to the snow and cold. As Hank used to say, *It invigorates a person and makes them really appreciate spring.*

Back in her house, she pulled out her suitcase, but was too antsy to start packing. She made herself a cup of tea and went to sit by the front window. She loved her view of the city below. It had sold her on this house. The view and the small deck off the front. During the warm months, she spent hours sitting out there watching the lights come on. This house had filled her with a contentment—a peace—that she feared she would never feel again.

Hank's death, the revelations he'd left behind, Boone... She thought of the handsome cowboy. Did he really think he was helping her? Just being around him left her feeling...discontent. Certainly no peace. He made her want something she'd told herself she wasn't ready for, didn't need, didn't want.

C.J. shook her head at the memory of being on the street when she'd been so sure he was going to kiss her. He'd been staring at her lips and she'd felt... What had she felt? A tingling in her core. An ache. She'd felt desire.

She groaned. "And now you're really going with him all the way to Whitehorse, Montana, wherever that is? Have you lost your mind?" Her words echoed in the quiet house. She picked up her tea cup and took a sip.

At moments like this she felt the grief over Hank's death more profoundly. She swallowed back a sob as she thought of his funeral and all the people who had shown up. They'd loved him. She'd loved him. He'd saved her when she was a child. Her mother had been struggling just to keep her head above water. Hank had taken up the slack. He'd given C.J. purpose.

So was it possible that he could have been dirty? How else did she explain all that money in those stocks and bonds he'd left her?

Her head ached. None of this made any sense and hadn't since Hank was killed. Exhaustion pulled at her. She'd known the funeral would be hard. She just hadn't realized how hard. But seeing all the people who loved Hank had helped. Just the thought of them brought tears to her eyes again. They couldn't all have been wrong about Hank.

Her mind reeled at the thought of Hank keeping whatever had been going on with him from her. She felt betrayed, adrift. Had he planned to leave town for good and not even mention it to her? Why would he do that?

Because it had something to do with Jesse Rose and her kidnapping. Which meant that Hank either thought it was too dangerous to tell her or… Or he didn't want her to know what he was involved in because he was up to his neck in something illegal.

Either way, there was no more denying it. This was

about Jesse Rose and the McGraw kidnapping case. Hank had been to Seattle, and right before he was killed. She had no idea what that might have to do with the second trip he was apparently planning. Seattle was to the west, while Whitehorse, Montana, was up on the Hi-Line in the middle of the state. What did the two places have to do with each other, except for the fact that the McGraw ranch was outside of Whitehorse?

Nor did she have any idea of who he might be planning to meet on the train from Seattle. The same person he'd visited in Seattle in the days before he was killed?

As if all of this wasn't troubling enough, Hank had a whole bunch of money that he'd left to her and she had no idea where it had come from.

Maybe more upsetting than him not telling her about it was the fact that he'd cleaned his car, packed his best clothing and shut down his office as if…as if he wasn't coming back.

Tears filled her eyes. Had he been running away? Then why the train schedule? Was he meeting someone on that train coming from Seattle to Whitehorse? Someone he planned to abscond with?

A shock rattled through her at the thought. Had she known Hank Knight at all?

But that was just it. She *had* known him. He had been a good man and there was a good explanation for all of this. She just had to find it. That meant going to Whitehorse and meeting that train from Seattle—with Boone.

"You should get some rest," Boone had said when he'd dropped her off. "I'll pick you up in the morning. I hope you'll go with me."

"I—"

"Sleep on it," he had said quickly. And for a moment, he'd gotten that look in his eyes.

She shivered now at the memory and touched her upper lip with the tip of her tongue. She almost wished the man would just kiss her and get it over with. That made her smile.

Wiping at her tears, she turned off the light and started out of the dark living room in the direction of her bedroom. She'd only taken a few steps when she heard the noise and stopped. Her gaze shot to the window. She hadn't realized that the wind had come up. It now whipped the branches of the trees outside.

That must be what she'd heard. One of the branches scraping against the side of the house. Only the noise she'd heard... It had sounded like someone trying to pry open a window. Like a lock breaking?

She reminded herself that last night she'd thought she'd seen a man standing out in her yard and it had turned out to be a shadow and nothing more.

A dark shadow swept past the glass. Her breath caught in her throat as her heart began to pound. Someone was out there trying to get in.

She rushed to the table where she'd dropped her purse when she'd come into the house. As she heard another noise down the hallway in her bedroom, much like the first, she managed to fumble her cell phone from her purse. Her fingers brushed her gun as a louder noise came from the back of the house. It had been one of the old cantankerous windows being forced open.

Her heart pounding, she pulled out the pistol, snapped off the safety and laid it on the table as she turned her attention to her phone. She hit 911, all the time estimating how long it would take for the police to get there. Too long. That's if they even came. Once they knew it was her calling, they'd just think she was being a hysterical woman again. Just like she'd been when she'd told them that Hank's hit-and-run had been murder.

Boone had driven all the way back to his motel but he hadn't pulled in. Something kept nagging at him. He hadn't wanted to leave C.J. alone tonight. After that near so-called accident earlier, he feared she wasn't safe.

Of course, she'd argued that she was fine. She would lock her doors. She had a gun. She could take care of herself.

But still, he didn't like it. He kept thinking about the man he'd seen at the funeral in the black baseball cap. He'd meant to ask C.J. about him. Something still nagged at him about the man. Was it possible he'd been driving the car earlier that had almost run them down?

Reminding himself how exhausted C.J. had looked, he told himself that he could ask her about it tomorrow. She probably wouldn't even know who the man was. Then again, she seemed to know everyone in Butte.

Swearing, he swung the pickup around and went back, knowing it would nag at him until he asked her. Also, it wouldn't hurt to check on her as long as she didn't think that was what he was doing. He told himself that if all the lights were out, he wouldn't bother her. But if she wasn't asleep yet...

As he neared the small house overlooking the city, he saw that the lights were all out. He couldn't help being disappointed. He wasn't good at leaving things undone and for some reason, this seemed too important to wait.

He started to turn around since her house was at the

end of a dead-end street, a deep gully on one side and an empty lot on the other. Walkerville was even older than uptown Butte since this is where much of the original mining had begun. The houses were small and old, but the view was incredible, he noticed as he swung into her driveway to turn around.

The pickup's headlights caught movement at the back of the house.

IN THE DARK living room, C.J. put down the phone as she heard a loud crash at the back of the house—and picked up the gun. She moved slowly down the hallway toward the back of the house and her bedroom, the gun clutched in both hands in firing position.

She spent hours at the shooting range—but she'd never had to use her weapon as a PI. She hoped she wouldn't tonight.

The cold wind that had chilled her at the funeral earlier had picked up even more. She could feel a stiff breeze winding down the hallway from where someone had opened the window.

Stopping to listen, she heard nothing but the wind and the occasional groan of the old house. She knew most of those groans by heart. What she feared she would hear was the creak of old floorboards as some-one moved across them headed her way.

The house was dark, except for the cloud-shrouded moonlight that filtered in through the sheers at the win-dows. Shadows played across the hallway.

As she neared the bedroom where the noise had come from she could make out the glittered remains of her shattered lamp on the floor. What she couldn't see was her intruder. Snaking her hand around the edge of the doorway, she felt for the light switch. She'd just found it when the curtain at the window suddenly snapped as it billowed out on a gust of wind, making her jump.

She found the light switch again and readied herself. Her intruder had either left. Or he was waiting in the pitch-black corners of her bedroom to jump out at her.

BOONE CUT HIS lights and engine and was out of the pickup in a heartbeat. He ran toward the back of the house, realizing belatedly that he should have grabbed something he could use for a weapon.

The dark shadow he'd seen was gone. He was telling himself that the person had taken off when he'd been caught in the beams of the pickup's lights. Then he saw the open window and the large overturned flowerpot someone had used to step on to climb into the house.

His mind whirled. Had C.J. had time to go to bed? He looked around, not sure what was beyond this open window. The person he'd seen could have dropped off into the ravine next to the house and could be long gone. Or he could have gone into the house and was now inside. He could have C.J.

Boone pulled out his phone and quickly keyed in her number. He waited, listening to the wind and his heart, for the phone to ring. And prayed she hadn't turned hers off.

C.J. JUMPED AS her phone rang in the other room. She glanced back down the hallway, distracted for a split second.

At a sound in the bedroom, she turned back, but too late. A large dark figure came busting out of the bedroom. She raised the gun, got off a wild shot, heard a groan. But then she was hit by the man's large, solid body as he crashed into her. He knocked the breath out of her, slamming her back against the wall before she hit the floor hard, gasping for breath.

Her phone was still ringing as she rolled to her stomach, the weapon still clutched in her hand. All her training took over as her intruder pounded toward the front door. "Stop!" she cried, leveling the laser beam on the man's back.

He was fumbling at the door lock.

C.J. pushed herself up to her knees and tried to hold the gun steady. "Stop!" It happened in slow motion, but only took a few seconds. She raised her weapon, the laser jittering in the middle of his back as her mind raced. Pull the trigger? Shoot him in the back? Or let him leave? She'd seen that he was limping. Had she hit him with the first shot she'd fired?

"Don't make me shoot you!" Her voice broke.

He got the door unlocked, flung it open and stumbled out into the night. As her phone stopped ringing, she leaned back against the wall, still holding the gun, her heart thundering in her chest.

BOONE HEARD THE phone ring inside the house just moments before he heard the gunshot and the pounding of feet headed toward the front of the house. He raced in that direction in time to see a large dark figure come running out of the house, leap the porch railing and disappear over the side of the yard and into the ravine. As he did, Boone saw that the man was limping badly.

"C.J.!" he yelled as he ran up onto the porch. "C.J., it's me, Boone. Are you all right?"

"Boone." Her voice sounded distant and weak.

He rushed into the open doorway and fumbled for the light switch. An overhead fixture blinked on, blinding him for a moment. He saw her cell phone on the table next to her open purse.

"I'm all right."

He turned on the hall light and following her voice, he found her sitting at the end of it, the gun resting between her legs. Bright droplets on the wood floor caught his eye. Blood. He rushed down the hall to drop to his knees next to her. "Were you hit?"

She shook her head. "I fired the only shot. I think I caught him in the leg. He was limping."

"Did you get a look at him?" he asked as he pulled out his phone to call the police.

"Don't do that."

He looked up at her in surprise. "But your neighbors…"

"They've heard gunshots before. They won't call it in."

"But—"

"If we hope to meet that train in Whitehorse, we don't want to get involved with the cops, not now. It wouldn't do any good anyway. Nothing was taken. I didn't get a good look at him. And I don't have the best relationship with the cops in this town right now." There was a pleading in her gaze. "I'll just clean up the blood." She pushed herself to her feet.

Boone wanted to argue but he remembered what the detective had said about PIs. Apparently she was right about their relationship. It wasn't one-sided.

He rose with her. He could tell that she was still shocked and off balance. He knew she wasn't thinking clearly. But he couldn't disagree about what would happen if they called the cops. A shooting would mean a lot of explaining. She was right. They had to meet that train if they hoped to find out who had killed her partner and why—and what it might have to do with Jesse Rose and her kidnapping all those years ago.

But what had this been about tonight?

"I'll take care of the window," he said as he moved to the bedroom. The lock had been broken. "I could pick up a new lock at the hardware store in the morning to fix this."

"I don't think he'll be back."

"So you think it was a robbery gone wrong?"

She shrugged, avoiding his gaze. "What else?"

"How about something to do with Hank's death?"

C.J. finally looked at him. "Why would you say that?"

"Because I saw a man at the funeral. He had a scar on his cheek, wore a dark baseball cap pulled low. Ring any bells? He was limping—like the man who just ran out of here."

She frowned. "He doesn't sound familiar. You said he was limping at the funeral?"

"Yes. He kept his face hidden beneath the brim of his baseball cap except when he was looking at you. He seemed to have a lot of interest in you. And unless I'm mistaken, the man you just chased out of here was wearing a dark baseball cap."

SHE'D SHOT HIM! Cecil couldn't believe it. He drove back to his motel room, parked where he couldn't be seen from the office and limped inside. His leg hurt like hell and it was still bleeding. The blood had soaked into his jean pant leg.

He pulled out the motel room key, opened the door and slipped inside. In the bathroom, he pulled down his jeans and looked at his leg. It wasn't as bad as he'd thought it was going to be.

The bullet appeared to have cut a narrow trench through the skin. At least the slug hadn't hit bone. Nor was it still in there. That was something, since that leg had already been injured years ago. He still had the scar, a constant reminder of how badly things had gone that night.

Opening the shopping bag he'd picked up at the convenience mart, he pulled out the alcohol bottle, opened it and, gritting his teeth, stepped into the bathtub and poured the icy liquid over his wound.

He had to hold on to the sink to keep from passing out from the pain. What hurt worst was that he'd failed tonight. He pulled the length of cord from his pocket. It should have been around C.J. West's neck.

His cell phone rang. He checked caller ID. His ex-wife. He'd been trying to get back together with her, because he still loved her. Also he needed her more than she could know. He let it ring another time, before he took her call. As he watched his blood stain the white porcelain of the cheap motel room tub, he said cheerfully, "Tilly, I'm so glad you called. I was just thinking about you."

Chapter Thirteen

Boone rubbed his neck and stretched as best he could as he drove.

"You should have taken the bed last night," C.J. said.

"The recliner was fine." He'd had enough trouble convincing her to come to his motel last night. It was that or the two of them staying in her house. He hadn't liked the idea that the man might be the same one who'd tried to run her down and then broken into her house. He wasn't taking the chance that the man might come back.

"At least at my motel, he won't know where you are."

"I can get my own room."

"Could you possibly just let me take care of you for one night? Two brushes with death in one day? Haven't you been through enough today?" She'd given him a look he couldn't read. "Come on, you need sleep. Right now, it appears that the only thing keeping you on your feet is pure stubbornness."

She'd finally relented. But when they'd gotten to the motel, she'd wanted to argue about who was going to take the bed.

"*You're* taking the bed. You want the bathroom first? Then get in there." When she'd come back out he'd gone right into the bathroom after, giving her a warning look not to argue with him.

Exhaustion had taken her down. When he came out of the bathroom, she was lying on the end of the bed as if she'd been sitting there and had just keeled over for a moment to rest.

Shaking his head, he'd picked her up and carried her around to the side of the bed. He'd never met such a mule-headed woman. She reminded him of... He'd chuckled. She reminded him of himself.

She'd barely stirred but he'd hushed her up as he took off her shoes and tucked her into the bed. Then he'd stood there for a long moment watching her sleep before he'd headed for the recliner.

Not that he'd been able to fall asleep. He kept thinking about C.J. Her loyalty to Hank. Her determination to find his killer at all costs. Her sweet, vulnerable look when she was sleeping. It made him smile.

C.J. West was a complicated young woman who intrigued him more than he wanted to admit.

HIS LEG HURT like hell. Cecil hadn't gotten any sleep. The first thing he'd had to do was put a new bandage on his gunshot wound. Now standing in the bathroom naked, he braced himself for the pain. Pouring more of the rubbing alcohol on the wound, he let out a cry and clutched at the sink.

At least the wound had stopped bleeding, he thought as he covered it with gauze and then a bandage before pulling on his jeans. He hadn't thought to bring more clothing. He hadn't thought out a lot of things, he realized. So many mistakes. And now he couldn't go into a store the way he looked. No, it didn't matter how he was dressed. He needed to finish this.

At the thought of how badly that had gone last night, he wanted to scream. If Boone hadn't come back... Not that he could blame him.

He'd rushed it, just wanting to get it over with instead of waiting until he knew she was asleep. Once inside the house, he'd had a chance to finish it. He'd knocked her down. How much harder would it have been to take the gun away from her, choke the life out of her or use the gun on her?

His first plan had been to wait until she was in bed asleep and then sneak in and put a pillow over her head. He knew he couldn't do it looking at her. But he'd gotten impatient and couldn't wait for her to fall asleep. He had a piece of cord in his pocket. He'd thought that he could get behind her and strangle her as long as he didn't have to see her face.

But things had gone badly. He'd panicked. Isn't that why he hadn't killed her in the hallway last night? It had been so close and personal. Nothing like running someone down in a car.

But he'd even failed at that. His life had been one failure after another. Now if he didn't want to spend the rest of his life in prison...

With a groan, he limped out of the motel bathroom. He had to go back to C.J. West's house. If she wasn't there, maybe he could wait inside for her. Wait and surprise both her and Boone when they came back.

But when he'd gone by her house he'd seen one of her neighbors out in his yard. He'd parked and gotten out, limping over to him.

"I was looking for the woman who lives in that

house," Cecil said, and realized he might be able to pass for a delivery boy even at his age. "She placed an order. I was trying to deliver it."

"Must be some mistake," the man said, eyeing him. "I saw her leave this morning with a suitcase. I got the impression she wouldn't be back for a while. Left with some man. What did you do to your leg?"

"Old war injury," he lied.

"Sorry you came all this way. Is it anything I can take off your hands?"

"No, I don't think so, but thanks for the information." He limped to his vehicle and climbed painfully back in. She'd left with a *suitcase*?

He quickly called Boone McGraw's motel only to be told that he'd checked out. Swearing, he tried his ex-wife's number, telling himself that Tilly probably wouldn't know anything if she answered. Since she'd gone back to work, often she was vacuuming the Mc-Graws' big new house and didn't even hear her phone.

She picked up on the second ring. "Hi." She sounded a little breathless. He pictured her with a duster in her hand standing in one of the many bedrooms. She'd been dark-haired when he'd married her all those years go. Now over fifty, she'd gone to a platinum blonde as if thinking it made her look younger.

"Hi," he said. "Busy?"

"These cowboys," she said with a sigh. Tilly usually could find something to complain about. He wondered what she'd found during the years that they had been divorced.

"Well, at least you have less to clean with Boone gone," he said.

"Ha! I just heard not only is he on his way back, but

he's bringing some…" she lowered her voice "…woman. I have to get a room ready for her."

"No kidding?" So they were headed back to White-horse, back to the ranch. He swore silently. He'd never be able to get to her at the McGraw Ranch. Even though security wasn't as bad out there as it had been following the kidnapping, it would still be impossible to break in without getting caught.

But then again, he had Tilly there, didn't he? No one would suspect anything if she brought her ex—and soon-to-be husband again—out to the ranch where she worked to see the new house.

"How did the job interview go?" she asked now, reminding him of the reason he'd given her for leaving town for a few days.

"I'll tell you all about it when I see you. I'm about to head home. I'd like to take you out to dinner when I get back."

"A date?" He could hear the pleasure in her voice and should have felt guilty for all the lies.

"Why not? You're still my Tilly girl, aren't you?"

C.J. LOOKED OUT at the passing landscape of towering mountains and deep green pines. Boone had told her it was a six-hour drive. She'd wanted to take her own car, but she knew he was right. It made sense to go with him since they were going to the same place, he knew the way and someone was after her. So it was safer being with him, at least according to him.

She hated this feeling of vulnerability and Boone McGraw only made it worse. Being around him left her feeling off balance. Before all this, she'd felt she had control of her life. She'd felt safe knowing what she would be doing the next day and the day after that. She had a plan.

Hank's death had changed all that. She'd lost her biggest supporter. She'd lost her friend and the man who'd filled in all these years as her father. Boone showing up had turned an already confusing time into… Just the freshly showered male scent of him made it hard to think. And she needed desperately to figure this all out. It's what she did for a living. She solved mysteries. She helped people, just as Hank had taught her.

But right now she felt as if she couldn't even help herself. Too many of the pieces were missing and her grief over Hank's death had her too close to tears most of the time.

She rubbed a hand over her face and told herself to quit whining. She was still strong, still determined. She'd gotten through her mother's death. But only because Hank had been there for her. Now she felt…alone. And yet not alone, she thought as she looked over at Boone.

"Thanks for last night."

He shot her a glance. "No problem." His smile warmed an already unbearably handsome face.

She felt her heart do a little tap dance against her ribs and was glad when he turned back to his driving. "I keep going over it in my head. There's no reason anyone would want to harm me."

"You were Hank's partner. Whatever he knew, the killer must assume you knew it, as well. Or realized that you were looking for the truth."

But she knew nothing. The fact that Hank hadn't told her what was going on with him hurt heart-deep. Her head ached from trying to understand what had been going on with him in the days before his death. So many secrets. Not just the stocks and bonds, but Seattle. And maybe Whitehorse as well?

"So tell me about your family," she said and turned to look at Boone, desperately needing to get her mind on something else.

BOONE GLANCED AT her in surprise. "You mean more than what you've already read about my family? I doubt there is much to tell." He knew she'd researched the kidnapping. As she'd said that first night, she didn't leave things to chance.

"I did some research, but it's not the same. You have two brothers you grew up with, Cull and Ledger. So what are they like?"

He could see that she seriously wanted to know. He suspected it was only to keep her mind off the long trip—and what she'd been through the past week—but he was happy to oblige.

"Cull's the oldest, the bossiest." He laughed. "He's great. You'll like him. He's a lot like you, actually," he said and glanced over at her. They'd left Butte behind and now traveled through the mountain pass toward the state capital.

"How so?" she asked suspiciously.

"Stubborn to a fault. Determined to a fault. Independent to a fault. But he's changed since he fell in love." He saw her turn more toward him as if he'd piqued her interest. "He and Nikki St. James, the crime writer, are engaged. She came up to the ranch to do research for a book and her digging around set some things off."

"I heard it also almost got her killed. I suspect I'm going to like her."

He chuckled and nodded. "I suspect you will."

"And Ledger?"

Boone sighed. "Ledger. He fell in love in high school with a girl named Abby. They broke up when he was in college, some misunderstanding perpetrated by her mother, and she married someone else. A bad idea on her part since her husband was abusive."

"Wade Pierce."

"Yep." He grinned. "You probably know all this."

"No, please continue."

He studied the road ahead for a moment, thinking. "But Ledger, also a bit stubborn and determined, hung in there, determined to save her."

"Sounds like someone I know," C.J. joked. "Did he?"

"He did. They're finally together again. This time I don't think anything will tear them apart."

"So you're the last single brother."

Out of the corner of his eye, he could see that she was smiling. But he wasn't about to take the bait. "Actually, my brother Tough Crandall is still single."

"Right, the one who doesn't want to be a McGraw. Oakley McGraw, the missing twin."

"Yep. Talk about stubborn. I suspect he will always be Tough Crandall. He's made it very clear that he doesn't need the McGraws or want what comes with us—lots of unwanted publicity."

"I guess I can understand that. You don't think he will come around eventually?"

"My dad does. Dad never gave up looking for the twins, never gave up believing they were still alive, just never gave up. Of course, my dad is one of those men who looks at a half-full glass and thinks it is three-quarters full. You'll meet him."

"One of those," she said with a shake of her head and a smile.

"He's never given up on finding the twins, even when we wished he would," Boone said. "For years, the kidnapping has defined us all."

"Probably why you can't get a date," she joked.

He smiled over at her. "I had a date the other night at the steakhouse."

She shook her head. "You call that a date?"

"I would have if I'd gotten up the nerve to kiss you."

C.J laughed and met his gaze. "So why didn't you?"

"I kept thinking about that gun in your purse. I didn't want to feel the barrel poking me in the ribs."

"You're smarter than you look." She turned to glance out the windshield as they passed Helena and began the climb again up another mountain pass. "Strange, the paths our lives take. Not always easy. Was it horrible growing up with the kidnapping hanging over you?"

"Not all the time. My brothers and I love horses so we spent a lot of time on the backs of them. We stayed away from the house during the bad times, especially when the anniversary of the kidnapping rolled around. There was always something in the newspaper—thanks to our Dad. That's why I have to help find Jesse Rose if she is still alive. Maybe then Dad can just enjoy his family."

"You're lucky to have such a large family, and with your brothers getting married…"

"Yes, and it's growing. One of the reasons Dad wanted the new house to be so large. He wants plenty of room there for all the family. You'll see."

She shot him a look.

"We're staying out at the ranch." He held up a hand

before she could argue. "I'm not letting you out of my sight until this is over. I know you're very capable of taking care of yourself, but if I'm right, the reason someone wants you dead is because of my family tragedy. So let me do this."

She'd opened her mouth to speak, but closed it for a moment. "Fine. Is your stepmother still behind bars?"

He laughed. "Last I heard, thank goodness. Patty, yes. Still locked up so it's safe." He shook his head at the thought of her. "I told you that she didn't just try to kill my father by poisoning for months with arsenic— we believe she did the same thing to my mother twenty-five years ago. When Patty wants something… And she wanted my father—until she got him."

"Do you think she was the kidnapper's accomplice?"

"I certainly wouldn't put it past her. But if so, her plan backfired. She didn't get my father—at least not then. She went away for nine years. The only reason she came back when she did was she needed a home for her and her baby."

"Sounds like she had another reason for returning to your ranch and just used the baby to get what she wanted."

He smiled over at her. "It certainly worked. My father raised Kitten all those years only to have Patty send the girl off to some relative. Kitten was a lot like her mother so while it was hard on my father to see her go…"

C.J. nodded. "A lot of drama?"

"Since she was little."

"So what was it like growing up on a horse ranch?" she asked as she made herself comfortable in the passenger seat.

"It was an amazing childhood, actually." He began to

tell her about learning to ride at an early age, of horse-back rides up into the Little Rockies, of swimming in the creek and racing their horses back to the corral. "Cull usually won, but there was this one time…"

Boone glanced over to see that C.J. had fallen asleep. He smiled and looked to the road ahead. He couldn't shake the feeling that his life had changed in some way he'd never planned. It unsettled him. But soon they would be on the ranch. And once Jesse Rose was found… Well, things would get back to normal. Right, normal—as if that was ever going to happen.

Chapter Fourteen

C.J. felt a hand on her shoulder and sat up quickly, suddenly awake. She couldn't believe she'd fallen asleep. But she'd had trouble sleeping since Hank's death. Last night was the best sleep she'd had in days, but she was still exhausted.

"Where are we?" she asked, looking around. The earlier mountains covered in tall pines had given way to prairie.

"Great Falls. I thought you might be hungry."

Her stomach rumbled in answer, making him smile. She really did like his smile. She wished he smiled more. He was far too serious most of the time, she thought and realized she could say the same about herself.

"Fast food? Or take our chances at that café over there?"

"Given everything that has happened to me recently, I'm up for taking a chance on the café."

"Brave woman. I like that about you," he said as he climbed out of the pickup with her right behind him.

She joined him at the table he'd selected by the window after going to the restroom to freshen up. The café smelled of coffee and bacon and what might have been chili cooking in the back and another scent that made her think of the meals her mother used to fix. Something with burger and macaroni.

As she slid into the booth, she realized she liked the feel of the place. It reminded her of the cafés she loved in Butte. Sun shone in through the window, warming their table, and she felt herself relax for the first time in days.

She had to admit that part of it was her companion. Boone was easy to be around. He made her laugh and he seemed to get her. She thought of some of the men she'd dated and groaned inwardly. Not that she'd thought a cowboy could ever turn her head. Was that what Boone had done?

"Your family knows we're coming?" she asked as she picked up the menu in front of her to chase away that last thought.

"Dad does. Not sure if he told my brothers. We discussed keeping it quiet. Just in case."

She looked up from the menu. "Just in case Hank's killer doesn't know about any of this?"

Boone shrugged. "I can only hope. Based on a train schedule and some of his doodling, I think Hank planned to meet that train tomorrow. But I don't think his killer has this information. Otherwise, why not just meet the train and stop whatever it is from happening? Why try to run you down and later break into your house?"

She shook her head. She had no idea. None of it made sense. She thought of the thumb drive. More and more she hated keeping it from him. She started to say something when the waitress interrupted.

"Know what you'd like?" the waitress asked suddenly at their table.

"What is your soup today?" C.J. asked.

"Homemade chili with a side of corn bread."

"That's what I thought. I'll have that."

"I'll have the same," Boone said and handed back his menu.

"Anything other than water to drink?"

They ordered colas and were silent as the waitress left. She felt the thumb drive in her pocket, but the moment had passed. She had to wait and see who got off that train. The mystery of who might be arriving on that train had her anxious as well as worried. But she thought that Boone was right, that Hank had planned to meet whoever was coming in from Seattle tomorrow.

"So tell me about growing up in Butte," Boone said. She knew he was asking only to distract her. But he listened as if with interest as she told him about her mother's job in Hank's building at a secondhand store, how back then there were lots of fun junk shops in town and lots of customers.

"But your favorite part was working with Hank," he said when she finished.

She smiled. "On the weekends I was like any other kid. I rode my bike with friends, played in mud puddles, snooped around in abandoned houses and made up stories. I always thought I'd write books one day."

"Really? Then you and Nikki really will hit it off."

Their chili and corn bread arrived and they dived in, both seeming to enjoy the meal as well as the quiet. They had the café to themselves since it wasn't noon yet. Other than the occasional clatter of dishes or pots and pans in the back, the only sounds were the murmurs of enjoyment from them. The chili was good. So was the corn bread, especially with fresh butter and honey.

C.J. finally pushed back her empty plate and bowl.

"How are you feeling?" Boone asked, having finished his.

"Good." The realization surprised her. For the first time in days, she felt as if she might live through this. Which made her laugh. A killer was after her and yet... She smiled over at Boone. "I'm good. Want me to drive for a while?"

THE PAIN IN his leg was worse today. Cecil hoped it hadn't gotten infected. As he drove toward Whitehorse, he tried to think about what to do next.

Tilly hadn't been able to give him much information other than Boone McGraw was returning to the ranch with a woman. That much he'd figured out on his own. The question was why?

Had they found out the truth and were now going to Travers with it? He told himself that they couldn't have. Not yet. But once they found Jesse Rose, once they started putting the pieces together like Hank Knight must have...

He thought about the night of the kidnapping. So many years ago. They'd all changed so much. Tilly had been twenty-five and pretty as a picture. Patty, the nanny, hadn't been much of a looker back then, just a mousy-looking girl. Nor had the older cook been anything to look at.

Things had definitely changed after the kidnapping. The first Mrs. McGraw, Marianne, was now in the loony bin, crazier than a mad hare. Travers McGraw had gone downhill. Now sixty, he'd recently had a heart attack and almost died. Of course, he blamed the nanny, who he'd foolishly made his second wife for trying to poison him to death. Patty had most certainly outgrown that mousy look she'd had when she was the nanny.

He shook his head. He could understand why Tilly had liked working out there. She loved minding other people's business and that ranch was a hotbed of gossip.

I'm invisible in that house, she'd once told him. *I can be standing in the same room with my duster and it's as if they don't even see me. They just go on as if I'm not there.*

Smiling in spite of the pain, he recalled how he had loved her stories about what he thought of as the rich and famous. At least in Whitehorse, Montana. Tilly was as much part of that house back then as those walls that he'd often hoped couldn't talk.

It had been on one of his visits to his wife at the old McGraw house that he'd met Harold Cline. Harold had been dating the ranch cook, a stout middle-aged woman named Frieda. He'd wondered at the time about that arrangement since Harold wasn't a bad-looking guy. So when Harold had asked him if he'd like to get a beer, he'd accepted. Actually anyone who was buying back then would get a yes from him.

At a local Whitehorse bar, the two of them had sat in a corner and shot the breeze. After the weather and how work sucked, they talked about what was going on at the ranch.

Like Tilly, Harold's girlfriend had filled Harold in on all the comings and goings. The big topic had been the first Mrs. McGraw, who'd had a set of twins six months before and was now acting strangely. Tilly had been worried about her as well, saying she didn't seem to have any interest in the twins.

"Frieda's worried that Marianne might do something to the babies," Harold had whispered after four beers. "Terrible thing. Apparently, she didn't want any more kids and now she doesn't want anything to do with the twins. Frieda's worried she might hurt them. One night the nanny caught her in the nursery holding a pillow like she was going to smother them."

He'd been shocked to hear this, not that Tilly hadn't expressed concern about Marianne McGraw, saying the woman seemed confused a lot of the time.

I sure hope nothing bad happens to them. Cute little things. Sure would be a shame, Harold had said and bought another round of beer.

Cecil couldn't remember when Harold had mentioned getting the babies out of there before something terrible happened to them.

The plan had seemed so reasonable back then. Harold knew some families who would take care of them until their mother got better. They'd been saving those babies.

But even later when it became clear that they were going to kidnap the McGraw twins for money, Cecil hadn't put up a fight. In fact, by then he'd been out of work for months, Tilly was threatening to leave him and he would have done just about anything to get his hands on some money.

Two hundred thousand dollars? he'd whispered in shock when Harold had told him how much ransom they could get.

It isn't like McGraw doesn't have it. All those fancy horses, that big house, and look at what he pays your wife and my girlfriend, Harold had said.

Actually, Tilly had gotten paid well and been well taken care of out at the ranch. That had been part of the problem. She'd had it so good out there that she'd been thinking she could do better than Cecil, but he'd kept his mouth shut and gone along with the plan. If Tilly had left him like she'd been threatening then he would need the money.

It had crossed his mind that Harold might try to cheat him out of his share. But the man couldn't pull off the kidnapping without him so he'd told himself not to worry.

The night of the kidnapping, Tilly had called to say she was sick and asked if he could bring her some cold medicine. Her timing couldn't have been more perfect.

He'd driven within a mile of the ranch near the Little Rockies. Harold had followed him in his rig. They'd hidden it in the pines, then Cecil had driven on out to the ranch with Harold hunkered down in the back. Tilly had left the side door open for him.

While he'd gone upstairs to take the cold medicine to Tilly, Harold had climbed out and hidden in the pool house. He'd already found a ladder he could use to get to the second floor window of the twins' room.

He'd given his wife a double dose to make sure Tilly was out cold. While he was waiting for her to sleep, he'd noticed a bottle of codeine cough syrup sitting there. Tilly had said Marianne McGraw had given it to her from an older prescription she'd had. Later, Marianne wouldn't remember doing that.

Once Tilly had been asleep along with everyone else in the house, he'd walked down the hall and pretended to leave. Instead, he'd ducked into the twins' room and given each of them some of the codeine cough syrup, hoping he didn't overdo it. Careful not to leave any prints on the bottle other than his wife's and the babies' mother's, he'd left it in the twins' room.

Then he'd waited in a guest room down the hall until it was time. Better to be caught there then in the twins' room. Finally it had been time. He'd checked the hallway. Empty. Not a sound in the house. He'd made his way down to the twins' room, still shocked that he was actually doing this. Both babies had been sleeping soundly.

Cecil had opened the window as Harold climbed up. He'd wrapped up the babies in their blankets with their favorite toys just in case the infants woke up. He'd handed them out and Harold had put them in a burlap bag and then descended the ladder.

He'd been thinking how they'd pulled it off when he'd heard a loud crack and had looked out the window to see that one of the ladder rungs had broken under the big man's weight. He'd thought then that it was all over, but somehow Harold had managed to hold on— and not drop the babies.

Then he'd gotten the hell out of there, scared out of his wits. Back at his vehicle, he'd driven back to where he'd left Harold's vehicle but it had already been gone. They'd planned not to meet until the ransom was paid. Cecil never saw him again, let alone his half of the ransom money.

He'd been so shaken that night that he'd just taken off, driving too fast, not even knowing where he'd been going. He'd lost control of his car miles from Whitehorse and spent the next week in the hospital in a coma.

It wasn't until recently that he'd learned what had happened to Harold and the ransom money. It had given him little satisfaction to find out from the news that Harold was dead and the money found with him in his shallow grave.

The only good news was that no one knew who had helped Harold from inside the house. But then Tilly had told him about Hank Knight, convinced that the PI knew not only what had happened to Jesse Rose, but who the second kidnapper had been.

Now he looked at the highway ahead, telling himself he might still be able to get away with it. As long as Boone and that female private investigator didn't find Jesse Rose, he should be in the clear. But as he drove, he couldn't help but worry that they knew something he didn't. He could be driving back to Whitehorse— right into a trap.

Chapter Fifteen

C.J. found herself smiling as she drove. She listened to Boone's breathing as he slept. He looked so content, not anxious like he did when he was awake. She felt she'd gotten to glimpse something few people had seen. A peaceful Boone McGraw.

The highway took them from Great Falls up to the Hi-Line and across the top part of the state. They were just outside of Whitehorse when Boone stirred.

He sat up, looking surprised that he'd let himself fall asleep. All semblances of peace and serenity left his handsome face as he glanced out the window and saw where they were.

"You need to turn up here at the next road," he said. "You okay driving? If you pull over I can—"

"I'm fine. Nice nap?"

He looked embarrassed. "I didn't realize that I'd fallen sleep, let alone that I was conked out that long. Thanks for driving. I guess I was more tired than I thought."

She merely smiled and seeing the turnoff ahead, slowed. "We aren't going into town?"

"I thought we'd go straight to the ranch."

"I'd feel better staying at a motel—"

"Not a chance. Since I'm not letting you out of my sight, you'll be much safer on the ranch than in a motel in town." He glanced in his side mirror as if, like her, he wondered if whoever was after her might be somewhere behind them.

"I don't think we've been followed," she said. "I've been watching."

He leveled his gaze at her as she turned onto the dirt road. "I keep forgetting you do this for a living."

She said nothing for a half mile. "What will your family think, me showing up on their doorstep with my suitcase in hand?"

"I'll carry your suitcase," he said.

"You know what I mean."

"They'll think…" For a moment he seemed to consider what they would think. He swore under his breath. "My brothers will give you a hard time. They'll think you and I have more than a professional relationship."

"But you'll make it clear that's all it is, right?"

"Of course. You need to turn up here. See that sign reading No Buffalo? Hang a right there." He glanced straight ahead. "This was all too complicated to explain on the phone. But don't worry. The new house is large with numerous guest rooms. While I've been gone, a designer has been putting the finishing touches on it. My father will be delighted to have you."

"So you all live in the main house?"

"I have a place on the ranch, a cabin, where I usually stay. But until this is over, I'll be sleeping at the house in a room next to yours."

If he thought that made her feel safe, he was sadly mistaken.

Ahead, the house came into view. She stared, a little

awestruck. It was beautiful. Boone had mentioned it was new. She'd read about the explosion and fire that had burned down the original house.

She felt anxious about meeting his family and braced herself. So much felt like it was on the line right now. She thought about the thumb drive in her pocket, feeling guilty for keeping it from Boone, from his family.

But only until tomorrow, she told herself. Whatever happened at the train, she would show it to Boone.

As THEY PULLED into the ranch yard, Cull and Ledger were coming up from the barn. Boone saw their interest in who was driving his pickup and swore again under his breath. The last thing he needed was them giving him a hard time about C.J.

Also he'd hoped to talk to his father first. Even better would be to tell everyone at the same time to save repeating himself. But he could tell by the inquisitive looks on his brothers' faces that they were more than curious about the woman behind the wheel of his pickup.

"Looks like you're going to get to meet my brothers right away," he said as she handed him the keys. He opened his door, hopped out and called a hello to them. Not that his brothers noticed him. They were staring at C.J.

Cull lifted a brow as he and Ledger joined them. "Hired yourself a chauffeur?"

"This is C.J. West. She's a private investigator."

Cull shook her hand. "I'm his older smarter, more handsome brother, Cull."

"And this is Ledger," Boone said, wishing his brothers could behave for once.

As C.J. shook his younger brother's hand, Cull said, "I hope you've brought good news."

Just then their father came out on the porch.

"Can we take this inside? I'll tell you everything I know," Boone said with a sigh. "But C.J. and I will be staying at least overnight."

"I'll help you with your bags," Ledger said. "Go on in. I know Dad is anxious to hear what you found out."

"So am I," Cull said.

Boone led C.J. up to the house, introduced her to his father and the three of them entered the new house.

The old one had been huge and quite opulent. This one was more practical. It had a nice big eat-in kitchen, a large dining room and living room, a master suite for their father and a ranch office. The other bedrooms were divided between two wings off the north and south ends of the house on the same level to provide privacy for anyone staying in them.

His father had gotten it into his head that his sons and their wives would be staying over a lot so he would be able to spend even more time with his future grandchildren.

The interior designer his father had hired had been given only one requirement. *Marianne loves sunny colors*, Travers had told her. *We need this house to feel like sunshine.*

Boone had to admit, as he stepped into the house, the designer had done her job well. She'd been finishing when he'd left for Butte. The house looked inviting and at the same time homey. It never had with Patty in command. He was anxious to ask his father what had been going on while he'd been gone, with Patty's upcoming trial, her threat to write a tell-all book and a rumor that more arrests would be made in his father's poisoning case.

"Do you mind if I freshen up while you bring your father up to speed?" C.J. asked as Ledger brought in their bags. He could tell she wanted to give him and his father and brothers time alone and he appreciated that.

"Take the last room on the south wing," his father told her. "And please let us know if there is anything you need or want. Boone—"

"You can put my bag in the room next to hers," Boone said, making his brothers as well as his father lift a brow.

C.J. didn't seem to notice as Ledger steered her toward one of the bedroom wings, leaving the three of them alone.

"Why don't we step into the office?" his father suggested.

They'd barely gotten seated when Ledger joined them. Like the old office, there was a rock fireplace with a blaze going in it and comfortable chairs around it along with a large oak desk.

Boone told them what had happened since he'd last seen them.

"Hank Knight is dead?" Cull said. "And you say C.J. was his partner in the investigation business?"

"She's a licensed private investigator and worked with him. But they were much closer than that. Hank helped her single mother raise her. C.J. and Hank were very close. It's one reason she is determined to find his killer."

Cull was shaking his head.

"What does the C.J. stand for?" Ledger asked.

"Calamity Jane. She said her father was a huge fan of Westerns."

"And he's deceased?"

Boone nodded. "Died when she was two."

"So you think this person who's made attempts on her life—and yours—is somehow connected to the kidnapping and Jesse Rose?" his father asked.

"It seems that way. All we know is that Hank Knight didn't share any of it with C.J., something highly unusual, according to her. And he'd flown to Seattle, also something unusual since he apparently hated to fly. He appeared to be planning another trip before he was killed. That, I believe, was to Whitehorse. We think he planned to meet the train from Seattle tomorrow in Whitehorse at 2:45 p.m."

"Who is coming in on the train?" Travers asked.

Boone shook his head. "We have no idea. But we plan to be there."

"What if no one gets off from Seattle?" Cull asked.

"Then my theory is wrong and then I don't know." Boone raked a hand through his thick dark hair, his Stetson resting on his knee. "It's possible that none of this has to do with Jesse Rose."

"Then what?" Ledger asked.

He shrugged. "But someone wants to keep C.J. from finding out the truth about her partner's murder. If his inquiries about Jesse Rose and the kidnapping are what got him killed…"

"I want to meet the train with you tomorrow," his father said.

"I'm not sure that's a good idea. I think it would be better if C.J. and I go alone. Whoever is getting off that train is expecting to meet Hank Knight. If there's a crowd," he said, looking pointedly at his brothers, "it might scare them away."

"You're hoping Jesse Rose gets off the train," Cull said. "Would you recognize her?"

"I think so."

"And if it is someone else, someone…dangerous?" Travers asked.

"I can handle myself, and don't forget—I will have a card-carrying, gun-toting private investigator with me."

C.J. PUT HER suitcase on a bench in the last room at the end of the hall where Ledger had led her. The room was lovely, bright and airy with a large sliding glass door that looked out on the mountainside beyond. She could see where it appeared a swimming pool was going in to the right. To the left were corrals and several large barns.

Opening the doors, she stepped out on the patio. Three horses watched her from a nearby corral. She smiled and walked over to them.

She was stroking one of the horse's neck when she heard someone come up behind her. She didn't turn around, didn't need to. She knew it was Boone. That connection that had been growing between them felt stronger than ever.

"You like horses." He sounded surprised. "We could go for a ride. It's a beautiful afternoon and tomorrow it's supposed to snow. We should take advantage of this weather."

She could tell that he wanted to go for a ride. "Why not?"

"I'll saddle us up a couple of horses. Come on." She followed him into the cool of the barn and watched while he expertly saddled the horses. "I gave you a very gentle one."

"I appreciate that." She smiled as he offered her a foot up. She placed her shoe in his cupped hands and let him lift her. Swinging her leg over, she settled in the saddle. It had been a while since she'd ridden a horse, but it felt good. She took the reins and watched Boone. He looked completely at home in the saddle.

They rode out into the afternoon sunlight. It was so much warmer here than it had been in Butte. She breathed in the fresh air as they rode slowly across a pasture.

"Those are the Little Rockies," Boone said, pointing to the dark line of mountains in the distance. "The story goes that Lewis and Clark originally thought they were the Rocky Mountains. When they realized their mistake, they renamed them the Little Rockies."

C.J. saw some cabins back in a stand of trees. "Is that where you usually stay?"

He nodded. "But see that land on the hillside over there? That's my section. Someday I'm going to build a house on it with a view of the mountains."

"When you get married. Is that what your brothers are doing, building on their land?" She pointed to a spot where some land had been excavated.

"That's my brother Cull's. He and Nikki will start their house in the spring. Ledger and Abby will be building about a half mile farther from there. We all wanted to be close—but not too close."

"So you'll always stay on the ranch," she said, not looking at him.

"That's what I've always planned."

She looked over at him because of something she heard in his tone. "Unless?"

"Unless I fall in love with someone who doesn't want this life."

"You'd go where she wanted?" It surprised her that he thought a woman could get this cowboy off the ranch.

"For the right woman, I would."

They rode in silence as the sun slid farther to the west before they turned back.

BACK AT THE RANCH, Cull came out to say that their father wanted to talk to C.J.

"You go ahead," Boone told her. "I'll take care of the horses and join you in a minute."

"You told them that I don't know anything, right?" she said to him.

He nodded. "But you knew Hank Knight."

"I thought I did."

"It's all right," Boone said. "My father understands."

She followed Cull back into the house. Travers McGraw was waiting for her in his office. He rose to his feet when she entered and she saw that he wasn't alone.

"This is Nikki St. James, the true crime writer who is doing the book on the kidnapping."

C.J. shook hands with Nikki, recalling what Boone had told her about the woman. She'd thought at the time that she would probably like the writer. The woman was pretty with long dark hair and wide blue eyes.

Travers asked C.J. to tell them more about her and her relationship with Hank. She told them about growing up in Butte and the impact Hank had on her life.

"I wish I could tell you more," C.J. said after she'd

told them what she knew about Hank's inquiry about Jesse Rose and the kidnapping.

"You said Hank always shared his other cases?" Nikki asked. "Had he ever been involved with adoptions?"

"No."

"Do you know if he knew a woman named Pearl Cavanaugh? She was a member of the Whitehorse Sewing Circle."

She shook her head. She'd thought she'd known everything about Hank. That he could have lived a secret life, or worse, that he was involved in the McGraw kidnapping, seemed inconceivable.

Boone came into the room and took a seat. He gave her a reassuring smile.

"How old are you?" Cull asked. He'd been sitting quietly in a corner, listening. She had almost forgotten he was there. Unlike Boone. Her nerve endings had tingled as he'd walked into the room. She'd never been more aware of a man.

"Twenty-eight," she said, wondering why he was asking.

"So you would have been three at the time of the kidnapping," Boone said and looked at his father. "She would have been too young to know if Hank was involved back then."

"He couldn't have been involved in the kidnapping," C.J. argued. "You didn't know him. He wouldn't…" She felt her eyes burn with tears. "He spent his life *helping* people. He didn't steal babies from their beds."

"I wasn't implying that," Nikki said quickly. "One of the kidnappers who was involved was told that the babies weren't safe. We think that's what gave Harold

Cline the idea of kidnapping them. It could also be the reason that someone in that house helped him. At least one of them could have thought they were saving the twins."

C.J. felt her stomach roil. If Hank had thought he was saving the babies… "If he was involved, why would he call your lawyer and ask questions about Jesse Rose and the stuffed toy horse that was taken with her?"

She saw Travers and Boone share a look before Nikki said, "He could have been worried about this new information that was released regarding the kidnapping. If Jesse Rose still had the stuffed toy horse and she heard about it or her adoptive parents did…"

"Wouldn't they have contacted you?" C.J. asked.

"The parents might be afraid of losing their daughter, getting into trouble with the law… There are a lot of reasons they wouldn't want to come forward, especially if they knew who she was when they received her," Travers said.

"As for Jesse Rose, she might not even know that she was adopted," Nikki said. "Even if she saw the digitally enhanced photos in the newspaper, she might not think anything of it."

"But if she had a toy horse with a pink ribbon tied around its neck, she might start asking questions," Boone said. "If the horse gave the six-month-old baby comfort, the adoptive parents might have kept it."

"Or they might not have known that the stuffed toy horse came from the McGraw house," Nikki said. "They could have thought it was a gift from whoever had taken the baby to save her."

"Once it hit the news, though…" Boone looked to C.J.

She felt sick at the thought of all this. That Hank might have been involved twenty-five years ago… She revolted at the idea. Not the Hank she thought she'd known. She reminded herself that he'd kept whatever was going on from her. Because of shame? Or to protect her because he knew it was dangerous?

That thought gave her a little hope. While it looked bad, there was still the chance that Hank was innocent. After all, he was a PI. He could be working for someone who was neck deep in this and was looking for a way out.

"I guess we'll find out tomorrow, depending on who gets off that train at the Whitehorse depot," Boone said. "Until then all we can do is speculate. You must have seen the digitally enhanced photos in the newspaper and on television. Or looked them up on the internet. Did you ever see anyone who resembled Jesse Rose with Hank?"

"No," she said with a shake of her head and suppressed a shudder at the thought of the thumb drive with the young woman's photo on it. She hated lying and promised herself that after tomorrow, she would show it to Boone and his family. She hated keeping secrets from him. But she also couldn't betray Hank.

If Jesse Rose got off that train, she'd recognize her.

Chapter Sixteen

C.J. said she'd like to lie down for a while. Boone took that opportunity to go into town before dinner. "Don't worry, I'll be back in plenty of time," he told his father.

He drove straight to the sheriff's department and asked to see Patty, his former nanny and stepmother. When she'd been his nanny, she'd had straight brown hair, appeared shy and reserved.

When she'd returned to the ranch nine years later with a baby in her arms, she'd changed in more ways than her bleached hair color, from everything that Boone had heard. All he knew was that she'd certainly conned his father. Travers had married her to help her raise the baby, father unknown. Patty had been hell on wheels for those years as his stepmother. She'd made all their lives miserable.

Boone was just glad to have her out of their lives.

The dispatcher started to explain the visiting hours schedule when Sheriff McCall Crawford came out.

"I need to see Patty," he said, "and I'm not going to be able to make visiting hours for a while."

"Probably just as well since she posted bail and will be released later this evening," the sheriff said.

"What? How?"

McCall shook her head. "She came up with the bail and got a judge to grant it. It's out of my hands."

Boone pulled off his Stetson to rake a hand through his hair. "Then I really need to talk to her before she's released."

The sheriff hesitated for only a moment. "Just keep it short, okay?"

He nodded and let her lead him to the visiting room. He'd barely sat down when Patty slid into the seat on the other side of the glass. She smiled at him before picking up the phone.

The smile was enough to set him off, but he reined it in. He came here hoping for information. Ticking her off wouldn't get him anything except maybe a little satisfaction.

"You're looking good," he said into the phone.

She smiled at that. "You McGraws are such charming liars. Heard you'd been out of town. Go somewhere fun?"

"Butte. Went to see a PI who had information on the kidnapping."

"Really?" Her expression hadn't changed. "So you got it all solved, do you?"

"Not quite. Where is my mother's diary?"

She shook her head. *"Diary?"*

"I know you have it."

"You're wrong. Everyone thinks I'm responsible for whatever was going on in that house twenty-five years ago. Well, I wasn't the only drama."

"We know about Frieda and her love affair that set off the kidnapping."

Patty smiled. "That was just the tip of the iceberg. Tilly ever confess anything to you?"

Tilly? Their housekeeper?

"I believe Tilly had taken cold medicine the night of the kidnapping and was knocked out and had to be awakened."

Patty just smiled.

"Are you trying to tell me it isn't true?" When she said nothing, he lost his cool. "Dammit, Patty, I know you poisoned my mother twenty-five years ago and then did the same thing with my father over the past year. I know you, remember? I saw how you treat people."

She leaned forward and lowered her voice. "Boone, I'm a bitch, but I'm not a killer. Nor did I poison anyone."

He studied her, surprised that a part of him believed her. Was it possible she might be telling the truth?

"Then who was poisoning my father?"

"Anyone with access to that house. Your former ranch manager, Blake Ryan. Your family attorney, Jim Waters." She shrugged. "They ate at the house all the time."

"What was their motive?"

She looked away for a moment. "Maybe they thought they'd get me and the ranch if Travers was gone."

"Where would they get an idea like that, I wonder?"

Patty swung back around. "Not from me."

"Frieda is dead, thanks to you. Or are you going to tell me that you had nothing to do with that, either?"

"I didn't."

He narrowed his gaze at her. "You had a lot to lose if she talked."

"But not as much as the person who helped with the kidnapping. Yes, I kept Frieda in line with what I knew about her boyfriend. Like I said, I was a bitch but I had nothing to do with killing her."

"Sounds like you're innocent of everything."

"I didn't say that. I've made my share of mistakes. My biggest regret is your father. Believe it or not, I loved him. But I always felt like I was living in your mother's shadow—because I was. He never loved me the way he did her and I knew it."

With Patty in a talkative mood, he had to ask. "Who is Kitten's father?"

She laughed. "Who knows? That's not true. It was nobody. A one-night stand. A handsome guy at a bar when I was feeling vulnerable."

"Not Jim or Blake or my father?"

She shook her head.

"Jim and Blake both think they're her father."

Patty shrugged.

"Again, I wonder where they got that idea?"

She smiled. "Like I said, I'm not innocent of everything." Sighing, she looked him in the eye. "What do you want from me, Boone? I'm about to blow this place and I doubt we'll be talking again for a while, if ever."

"The truth would be nice."

"I guess you'll have to wait for my tell-all book," she said with a sad smile and replaced her phone as a deputy came into the room.

C.J. SAT AROUND the big table in the dining room and listened to stories about the boys growing up. It felt good to laugh. She especially liked the stories about Boone.

"He was five when he tried to ride one of the calves," Cull was saying. "He hung on all right. Straight across the pasture. We thought we'd probably never see him again. He was hootin' and hollerin'." They all laughed.

"Came back looking like he'd been dragged through the mud, as I recall," Ledger said. "Told everyone he'd ridden a bull."

C.J. loved the sound of their laughter. It was clear that they all loved each other. She felt the warmth and the camaraderie. And for a while, she forgot what she was doing there with them. Forgot about the thumb drive she kept in her pocket. Forgot that Hank was dead. And worse, that someone might be getting off the train tomorrow who would forever change the way she felt about the man she'd loved as a father.

By the time she'd gone to bed, all she wanted was the oblivion of sleep. She'd thought her thoughts would keep her awake. But the moment her head touched the pillow she was out. In her dreams, though, she kept seeing Jesse Rose's face. The woman was trying to tell her something, something about Hank, but C.J. couldn't hear her because of the noise from the train.

BOONE STAYED UP late talking with his father and brothers. It felt good to be back at the ranch. He'd needed that horseback ride earlier. It was the only place he felt at home.

He couldn't help thinking about C.J.—and what he'd told her on the horseback ride. Would he really leave the ranch for a woman? Not just any woman, but her?

Unable to sleep he went outside. It was a clear, cold night but he needed the fresh air. He loved it here, loved the dark purple of the Little Rockies on the horizon, and the prairie where thousands of buffalo once roamed.

He thought of Butte and C.J. Would she leave it for a man? For him?

Shaking his head, he couldn't believe the path his thoughts had taken. He hadn't even kissed the woman. But at dinner tonight, he also couldn't keep his eyes off her. She was so beautiful. He thought of her with that ragtag bunch of half-homeless people at the funeral. She'd called them her and Hank's family. He doubted he'd ever met anyone with such a big heart.

Or anyone more stubborn.

"I know that look."

He turned to see Cull come outside.

"Something bothering you?"

Boone let out a laugh. "Seriously? I'm terrified that I'm wrong about this whole thing. Who knows if there will even be someone on the train tomorrow and now I've got Dad's hopes up and—"

"What's really got you out here wandering around in the dark?" Cull asked, cutting him off.

"I just told you."

His brother shook his head. "Like I said, I know that look. You think I didn't wander around in the dark after meeting Nikki?" Cull let out a laugh. "I used to go out in the barn and talk to myself. I thought I was losing my mind. How could I fall for a damned true crime writer—one who turned our house upside down for a story?"

Boone chuckled. "You've got it all wrong."

"Just keep telling yourself that. A private investigator from *Butte*? Wondering how you got to this point in your life, aren't you?" He held up his hands. "Don't bother lying. I saw you out here and thought I could dispense some sage advice. Take it from me. I've been there. So just go for it. Seriously. Anyone with eyes can see how crazy you are about her. Stop kidding yourself. You've fallen."

Boone shook his head. "You should get some sleep, big brother. You're talking out your—"

"Yep, just keep telling yourself that," Cull said as he laughed and headed in the direction of his cabin.

Boone watched him go. "Just go for it? Right. So much for sage advice, big brother."

Stopping just outside the sheriff's department midmorning, Patricia "Patty" Owen McGraw breathed in the fresh air and looked toward the deep blue sky overhead. A Chinook had come through and melted all the snow, but she'd heard a couple of deputies talking about a white Christmas. A storm was supposed to blow in by this afternoon.

She'd completely forgotten about Christmas. Her only thought had been freedom. And now here she was. Free. At least for a while.

"Are you all right?" asked the deep male voice next to her in a tone that told her he didn't really care. Probably never had.

"I am now," she said without looking at the former McGraw ranch manager. Blake Ryan wasn't one of her favorite people right now. Hell, no one was.

"You realize it's temporary," he said. "Only until your trial. If you take off, you lose—"

"I know what I lose," she snapped and took another deep breath. Having Blake pick her up from jail had been a mistake. He hadn't wanted to do it. She'd had to almost beg and when that failed, she'd had to resort to blackmail. It seemed no one wanted to get on the wrong side of Travers McGraw.

You betrayed Travers when you slept with his nanny twenty-five years ago—not to mention his wife much more recently, she'd snapped on the phone earlier. *He knows about us, so come pick me up. I need a ride and you need me to keep at least some of the things about you out of my book.*

"This money they advanced you on this tell-all book," Blake said now, as he opened the car door.

"What about it?" She couldn't help the irritation in her voice. It was none of his business. She owed him nothing.

"Do you have to give it back if you don't write the book?"

"Why wouldn't I write it?"

He shot her a look and cleared his voice. "Patricia, you can't tell *everything.*" She suspected Travers had set up some sort of retirement plan for the ranch manager and still contributed to it. Everyone had their reasons for distancing themselves from her, but they would all pay when the book came out. Or when this went to trial.

She glanced out the side window. "I told the publisher it was a tell-all book that dished the dirt. All the dirt. You wouldn't want me to have lied, would you?" She smiled to herself as she felt his gaze on her before he turned back to his driving.

"It wouldn't be the first time you lied," he finally said.

She burst out laughing as she turned back to him. "I wondered if you'd have the guts to call me on it. And you did. What is it you're afraid of, Blake? How about I write that you were an amazing lover?"

"I don't think that's funny."

"I wasn't trying to be funny. I meant what I said, I'm telling it all. Anyway," she said with a shake of her head as bitterness rose like bile in her stomach. "What do I have to lose? Do I have to mention that I asked for your help and you couldn't be bothered?"

"You know the position I'm in."

"Unlike the one I'm in?"

"Patricia, give me a break. I don't have the kind of money you need to get out of this."

"But I sure found out who my friends and lovers were, didn't I?" She bit at her lower lip as silence filled the truck. "You're in this just as deep as I am."

"Where do you want to go?" he finally asked. "You want a drink? Something to eat? We could swing by Joe's In-n-Out for a quick lunch."

His offer was like a knife to her heart. He didn't want to be seen with her, hoped to get rid of her as quickly as possible. She studied him for a moment, glad she didn't have a knife because it would be in Blake's chest right now. Why did she always fall in love with weak men?

"Just drop me at the Great Northern Hotel." Had she thought earlier that he would have wanted to take her to his place? Would she have gone if he had asked her?

He drove around the block and pulled up at the entrance to the GN, as it was called locally. As she opened her door to get out, he said, "I wish you wouldn't do this."

She glanced back at him. "Spend a night in a motel room alone?"

"You know what I mean."

She laughed and forced a smile. "You mean what I

tell during my trial? Or the book? I'm going to give you a whole chapter, Blake," she said and slammed the door. She didn't look back as she fought the burn of tears.

"How in Hades did Patty make bail?" Boone demanded as he stormed into his father's office. "I just heard. Tell me you didn't—"

"I didn't."

"Did you know?"

His father shook his head. He pushed away the papers in front of him and sat back in his chair. "She must have sold the book she's been threatening to write about the kidnapping. Her tell-all book. She tried to get me to buy her off. I don't care what she writes."

Boone swore. "Well, if anyone knows the truth about what happened that night, I'm betting it was Patty." He frowned. "But that kind of truth won't set her free."

"Maybe she knows more than she has ever told about someone else being in the house that night," Travers said.

"Is that what you're hoping?" he asked.

"Truthfully? I just want Jesse Rose found. As far as the other kidnapper…"

"You don't want justice?"

"Justice." Travers chuckled. "There can never be justice. Too much was lost." He got a glazed look in his eyes.

Boone studied his boots for a moment. "How *is* Mom?"

"Better. She wants to see Oakley."

He looked up in surprise. "You told her about Tough Crandall?"

"He's her son."

"Are you sure about that?" He ground his teeth at the thought of the arrogant cowboy who'd paid them a visit to set them straight. Tough Crandall had outed the man pretending to be Oakley.

But Tough had refused to take a DNA test to prove that he was the lost twin. In fact, Tough wanted nothing to do with the McGraws—any of them.

"Has Tough agreed to see Mother?"

"Not yet, but he will."

Boone shook his head. His father had lived in a fantasy world for twenty-five years, first believing the twins were alive and would come home one day. And now he thought that cowboy who'd known for years that he was the missing twin—and kept it from his own grieving birth father—would find it in his heart to visit his birth mother?

"Dad—"

"Boone, he just needs time."

He told himself that he didn't want to argue the point with his father. He didn't have time anyway. He and C.J. had to meet the train. He'd had trouble getting to sleep last night and had been anxious all morning. Cull's little talk with him hadn't helped.

Now he tried to concentrate on what had to be done. He just hoped that whoever was on that train knew something about Jesse Rose's whereabouts. That was if she was still alive. That thought was the fear that had dogged him since his father had asked him to talk to PI Hank Knight.

Oakley had been found—kind of—not that it was the happy reunion his father had hoped for. But that didn't mean that Jesse Rose would be found. Twenty-five years was a long time. Anything could have happened.

C.J. FOUGHT TO still her nerves as they drove into Whitehorse. The afternoon wind sent a tumbleweed cartwheeling across the road in front of them as they reached the outskirts of town.

"This is Whitehorse? And you made fun of Butte?" C.J. joked as she took in the small Western town.

"Easy," he said and grinned. "You're in the true heart of Montana."

She scoffed good-naturedly at that as he pulled up to a small building that had Whitehorse printed on the side. She recalled that he'd said it was unmanned. Tickets were bought online. There was only one car parked next to the depot but no sign of anyone.

Across the tracks was apparently the main drag. She saw a hotel called the Great Northern, several bars, a restaurant and a hardware store. Like a lot of towns, Whitehorse had sprung up beside the railroad as tracks were laid across the state.

Looking down the tracks, though, she saw nothing in the distance. They got out into the waning winter sunlight. The air smelled of an impending snowstorm. C.J. shivered although it wasn't that cold as they went to stand on the platform in front of the depot. The train was due to arrive soon, but they were the only ones waiting.

She could tell that Boone was as anxious and worried as she was. Looking down the tracks for the light of the locomotive, she tried to keep her emotions in check. If they were right, Hank had been planning to meet this train.

"What if a dozen people get off the train?" C.J. asked, merely needing to make conversation because she knew exactly what Jesse Rose looked like.

"Not likely,'" he said with a laugh. "This will probably surprise you, but like I told you, not many people get off here."

"That is a surprise," she said.

He smiled over at her. "This area of Montana would grow on you. If you gave it a chance."

She met his gaze. "You think?" She thought about what he'd said the day before. That he'd leave for the right woman. But no woman who'd seen him on his ranch would ever take him from what he loved. No woman who loved him, anyway.

"Ever thought about a change of scenery?"

"Whatever are you suggesting, Mr. McGraw?"

He shrugged as if embarrassed.

What *had* he been suggesting? Whatever it was, he seemed to wish he hadn't brought it up. "You know, if you ever got out this way in the future."

Little chance of that, she thought as snowflakes began to fall. In the distance, she thought she heard the sound of a train.

BOONE COULDN'T BELIEVE what he'd just said to her. What *had* he been suggesting? Whatever it was, it wasn't like him. Like he could take Cull's advice. Like he ever would. And yet he'd realized this morning that no matter who got off that train today, C.J. would be leaving.

He'd take her back to Butte and that would be it. That thought had made him ache. C.J. had gotten to him, no doubt about that. She was funny and smart. He loved the tough exterior she put up. But he could see the vulnerability just below the surface. It made him want to protect her and he knew the kind of trouble that could get him into. Look at his brothers.

But now, as he waited for the train, he couldn't help looking at her as if memorizing everything about her. Her cheeks were flushed from the cold. Her eyes were bright. He watched her stick out her tongue to catch a snowflake as if not even realizing she'd done it.

"We could wait inside," he suggested, seeing her shiver.

Hugging herself, she shook her head. "I think I heard the train."

He could guess what she was hoping. That whoever was on this train would know who might have wanted Hank Knight dead. C.J. wouldn't rest until she found her partner's killer.

He hoped he was around when that happened. C.J. might just find out that she did need someone. Even him. While he loved her independence, he'd learned it was okay to lean on family occasionally. He got the feeling that it had only been her and Hank against the world for too long, and now with her partner gone…

As much as he fought with his brothers and knocked heads with his father, Boone was damned glad he had them in his life. He couldn't imagine how alone C.J. must feel. He felt another stab of that need to protect her.

Not that there was any reaching out to her. She'd rebuffed any attempt to offer comfort. She was determined to go it alone and had only grudgingly put up with him because she had no choice. But she had let him put his arm around her at the funeral. She'd even leaned into him. For a few minutes.

Snowflakes whirled around them. C.J. had her face turned up to the snow, her eyes closed. He saw her shiver again and couldn't help himself. He stepped to her and pulled her close.

She opened her beautiful brown eyes and looked at him. He felt his heart bump against his ribs. He wanted this woman. The thought terrified him. And yet he wrapped her tighter in his arms and drew her into him as the snow spun around them.

Chapter Seventeen

C.J. looked up into Boone's blue eyes as he pulled her against him. She forgot the falling snow, the cold and the worry and pain that had seeped into her bones over the past week. In his arms, she felt warm and safe.

All her instincts told her to pull away, but she didn't move.

Her gaze locked with his and she felt her heart quicken. Slowly, he bent his head until his lips were only a breath away from her own. She couldn't breathe. Didn't dare. She thought she would die if he didn't kiss her.

His lips brushed over hers. She let out a sigh of relief and joy and pleasure. He pulled her tighter against him, taking her mouth with his own. She melted into him and the kiss, heart pounding, desire sparking along her nerve endings like a string of lit dynamite.

The sound of the train whistle on the edge of town made them both jump, bringing them back to reality with a thud. As they stepped apart, C.J. braced herself as the light on the front of the locomotive came into view.

The train puffed into town through the falling, whirling snow. Boone stood next to her as the noisy train slowed and finally came to a stop after numerous cars had gone past. Boone hadn't said a word after the kiss. Nor had she. But she did wonder if he regretted it.

She touched the tip of her tongue to her upper lip and smiled to herself. Not that it would ever happen again, she was sure. Neither of them was ready for…for whatever that had been.

A door opened on one of the coach cars. A conductor put out a yellow footstool and then began to help a passenger off. C.J. held her breath but let it out on a frosty puff as an elderly woman was helped off, followed by an elderly man. They walked toward their vehicle parked beside the depot where they'd apparently left it before their trip.

C.J. felt her heart drop. She shot Boone a look as the locomotive engine started up and the conductor picked up the stool and stepped back on to close the door as the train began to move again.

"Boone?"

The train began to slowly pull away. She wanted to scream. She wanted Boone to take her in his arms again. Tears blurred her eyes.

"It's all right," he said, touching her arm. "They still have to unload the sleeping car."

She blinked. The train hadn't left. She heard it grind to a stop again after going only a short way. This time a door opened on a sleeping compartment car next to the platform. Another conductor stepped off with a stool and reached back in to bring out a suitcase. He set the case on the cold concrete and then reached back in again—this time to help a young woman off the train.

C.J.'s hand went to her mouth as the dark-haired young woman from Hank's thumb drive stepped off and looked in their direction.

Boone made a sound, as if equally startled by the intensity of the woman's green eyes. She was beautiful, slender and graceful-looking in a way that C.J. feared she would never be. Her heart felt as if it might burst. She knew she was looking at Jesse Rose McGraw— and all that it meant.

Oh, Hank, what were you involved in?

She looked over at Boone, gripped by a wave of guilt for withholding the thumb drive. She could see him struggling, as if asking himself if this woman could be the sister he hadn't laid eyes on since she was six months old.

C.J. felt her chest constrict as she touched his shoulder. He looked over at her and she nodded. The train pulled out and was gone as quickly as it had come, leaving the three of them standing in the falling snow.

It was Jesse Rose McGraw all grown up. C.J. stared at the woman through the falling snow, her heart hammering with both relief and fear. She couldn't keep kidding herself. Hank had been involved in all this up to his ears.

"Excuse me," Boone said as they approached the young woman. "Were you expecting to meet Hank Knight here?"

Tears filled the young woman's eyes as she looked past them for a moment, before settling her gaze on C.J. "Hank…" Her voice broke. "He's gone, isn't he?"

C.J. nodded, not sure how the woman had heard about Hank's death, but glad they weren't going to have to give her the news. "I'm so sorry."

"You must be Calamity Jane," the young woman said through her tears as she stepped to C.J. and threw her arms around her. "Uncle Hank told me so much about you."

Uncle Hank? C.J. shot a surprised look over Jesse Rose's shoulder at Boone. He looked as shocked as she felt.

"But I'm surprised *you're* here," the young woman said as she pulled back to look at C.J. "He said it would either be him or…" Her gaze went to Boone. "Or someone from the McGraw family."

C.J. saw her wipe at her tears as she turned to Boone. Her face lit as she smiled. "You must be one of my brothers?"

"Boone McGraw." He sounded dumbstruck but at the same time overjoyed. "And you're…"

The young woman held out her hand. "Jesse Rose Sanderson."

"Jesse Rose?" he repeated in obvious astonishment as he took her gloved hand in his.

She smiled sadly. "Uncle Hank told me that he tried to talk my mother into changing my name, but I guess when she whispered the name to me the first time she held me, my eyes lit up. She didn't have the heart to change it."

Boone shook his head. "So you know… We definitely need to talk, but we don't have to do it out here in the snowstorm." He ushered them toward the large SUV that he and C.J. had brought into town from the ranch.

C.J. climbed in the back so Jesse Rose could be up front with her brother. As she did, Jesse Rose reached back to clasp her hand.

"Calamity Jane," the young woman said with a laugh. "You're exactly as Uncle Hank described you. But I know you prefer C.J. Sorry. I've always loved your name and wanted to meet the girl who'd stolen my uncle's heart." Jesse Rose's hand was warm in hers. C.J. wondered if she could feel her trembling. Hank had told Jesse Rose all about her?

"I was so hoping Uncle Hank would be meeting the train, but he'd warned me that he might not be able to make it. Was he very sick at the end?"

C.J. shook her head, completely confused. *Sick?*

"I hope he didn't suffer."

"No," she said quickly. Everyone who'd seen the accident said he'd been killed instantly. "He didn't suffer." She felt as if she'd fallen down a rabbit hole.

"Good," Jesse Rose said. "He looked fine when he was out in Seattle but my mother said cancer can do that. She said then that he wouldn't be with us long."

Cancer? C.J. couldn't believe what she was hearing. Was it true? And yet as she sat there staring at the falling snow outside, she knew it was. Hank's sudden decision to retire. It had been so unlike him. He'd loved what he did. She'd tried to talk him out of it but he'd made all kinds of excuses. She'd finally stopped pushing him, seeing that he'd been determined. And yet, she'd also seen how sad he'd been about the decision. Now it made sense.

But why hadn't he told her? She tried to remember if she'd ever seen him looking sick and realized there had been a couple of times when she'd stopped by his office and caught him unaware. She'd just thought he was tired, that the job had taken a toll on him. She'd never dreamed... Cancer.

It explained so much. Why he'd be so set on retiring and closing down his office. Why he'd flown to Seattle without telling her and why he'd warned Jesse Rose that he might not be meeting the train. That one of the McGraw brothers would meet the train. Clearly, he'd planned on going, otherwise he would have let someone at the McGraw ranch know. But then he hadn't planned on getting run down in the street, had he?

Jesse Rose let go of C.J.'s hand as Boone climbed behind the wheel. "I'm just so glad that Uncle Hank told me about my family out here."

"So how long have you known?" Boone asked as he started the SUV. C.J. could tell that he was hoping this wouldn't be another case of a child who didn't want to know her McGraw family like Tough Crandall.

But C.J. suspected the woman wouldn't be here right now if she didn't want to get to know her birth family.

"Known I was adopted? Or known that I had more family?" Jesse Rose asked.

Boone shifted into Reverse. "Both."

"I found out I was adopted when I was seventeen. I was looking for my birth certificate…" She shrugged. "I found it and it said I was born to my parents, but I also found a letter from a woman named Pearl Cavanaugh. Did you know her?"

"I knew who she was," Boone said.

"I only learned recently, though, about the circumstances of my adoption. Uncle Hank told me—over the protests of my mother. He said it was time I met my birth family."

"What about your father?" C.J. had to ask.

"My father died when I was twelve. My mother was apparently the only one who knew that I'd been kidnapped, but according to Uncle Hank, she had wanted a child so much, she would have kidnapped one herself if she hadn't gotten me."

BOONE GLANCED IN the rearview mirror at C.J. as he drove through the underpass and down a block before pulling in front of the Whitehorse Café. He couldn't imagine what was going through her head right now. His was still swimming. But he was more worried about her. This had to have caught her flatfooted.

He'd pictured meeting the train and Jesse Rose stepping off, but he'd never really believed it was going to happen. And then for her to already know about not only Hank's death but her own kidnapping and illegal adoption... It blew his mind. At least Hank had taken care of that.

Why, though, had he kept it all from not only the rest of the world, including the McGraws, but he'd kept it from C.J.? Didn't he realize how much this was going to hurt her? Not to mention Jesse Rose knew all about C.J. but C.J. knew nothing about Jesse Rose all these years? Clearly Hank was involved in this. How much, though?

As he parked in front of the café, Boone said, "I thought we could have something warm to drink before we go out to the ranch."

Inside, they took a table at the back. Because of the hour, the café was empty. Fortunately, Abby, his brother Ledger's fiancée, wasn't working. The waitress who took their order said hello to Boone and merely smiled at the two women he was with.

"I feel as if I've always known you," Jesse Rose said to C.J. "I've heard so much about you from Uncle Hank for years. He said that he just knew the two of us would hit it off because we are so much alike. He promised that one day we would meet."

"I'm sorry to seem so surprised but Hank never told me anything about you," C.J. said.

Jesse Rose frowned. "I guess I understand under the circumstances. I always wondered why Uncle Hank wouldn't let me come out and visit. I thought it was just my mother's doing. She and Uncle Hank…well, they didn't get along. But I adored him and he… I don't have to tell you how special he was." Tears filled her green eyes. "I'm so sorry he's gone."

"He had cancer," C.J. said as if seeing Boone's confusion. "He'd told her that he might not be able to meet the train. Apparently, he knew he didn't have long."

"Oh, wow, I'm so sorry," Boone said to C.J. Just another thing Hank had kept from her.

"You never suspected you were adopted until you found the letter?" C.J. asked.

Jesse Rose hesitated before she said, "Not really. Don't most kids think they must have been adopted if they aren't that much like their parents or siblings? I didn't have siblings." She shrugged.

"So you aren't like your parents?" Boone asked.

Jesse laughed. "My father was blond and blue-eyed and so is my mother. She always told me that my dark hair came from my father's side of the family." She sobered. "Do you think there is any chance that there's a mistake and I'm not Jesse Rose McGraw?"

"We won't know for sure until we do a DNA test, if you're agreeable, but you look just like our mother when she was your age," Boone said.

Jesse Rose brightened. "How strange and yet wonderful to find out that I might have siblings. I used to dream of having a brother or sister. I was so anxious on the train. That was the longest twenty hours of my life, but I'm like Uncle Hank. I hate to fly. Not that there was any way to fly into Whitehorse except by private plane."

"I'm sure Hank told you, but it isn't just siblings you have, but a twin," Boone said.

She nodded excitedly. "I can't wait to meet him. It's so strange. I've always felt like I was missing a part of myself. I know that sounds crazy."

"Not at all. I've heard that about twins, even fraternal twins."

"Will he be at the ranch when we get there?" When Jesse Rose saw them exchange a look, she asked, "What?"

"No, but he lives around here. His name is Tough Crandall. He ranches in the next county. It's just that he's known he was Oakley McGraw for years but he wants nothing to do with the notoriety that might come from it," Boone said.

"The kidnapping case was fairly well-known," C.J. added. "I hope you aren't worried about that part." Boone couldn't bear for Travers not to at least get to meet his only daughter.

Jesse Rose shook her head. "But if I was kidnapped and my mother knew…" She looked up, those green eyes bright with worry. "My mother wouldn't go to jail, would she?"

"We would do everything possible to keep that from happening. We don't know what your mother was told. Oakley's mother believed she was saving him. Your mother might have, as well."

"Still, I don't understand how my mother could take someone's child," Jesse Rose said.

Chapter Eighteen

All the way out to the ranch, C.J. could see that Jesse Rose was struggling with the news of her uncle's death. It was clear that they were very close even though they hardly saw each other.

She also seemed nervous, not that C.J. could blame her. She was about to meet a family she'd never known, come back to a home she'd only lived in for six months as a baby, face a father who had missed her for twenty-five years.

"Did Hank tell you how you happened to be adopted by your mother?" C.J. finally had to ask.

"No, but he said he would explain everything." Tears welled in her eyes again. "I still can't believe he's gone."

"There's something you should know," C.J. said. "Hank didn't die of cancer. He was killed in a hit-and-run accident," she said. "One of the kidnappers is still at large and we think he might have…" She reached for Jesse Rose's hand and squeezed it. "I didn't know about the cancer. He kept a lot from me."

"I'm so sorry he kept his family from you," Jesse Rose asked. "He *adored* you. He told us such wonderful stories about you. You were like a daughter to him."

Jesse Rose's words filled C.J.'s heart to near bursting. "How often did he visit you?"

"Just once or twice a year. He said he was too busy to come more than that. I always asked to come visit him but he made excuses. Mother said it was because of the way he lived, like a pauper."

"I'm afraid there might be more to the story," Boone said.

Jesse Rose chuckled. "That Hank was rich." She nodded at her brother's surprise. "His family was very wealthy, but he never wanted anything to do with the money. He wanted to find his own way in life without them telling him what to do. I guess my grandparents almost disowned him when he became a private investigator and moved to Butte, Montana."

"That explains a lot," Boone said and glanced in the rearview mirror back at C.J.

She smiled at him, also glad there was at least one thing she didn't have to worry about. The stocks and bonds Hank had left her hadn't been appropriated by ill-gotten means.

"This is beautiful," Jesse Rose said as she looked out at the country.

It was nothing like Butte, C.J. thought. Butte sat in a bowl surrounded by mountains. This part of Montana was rolling prairie. The only mountains she could see were the Little Rockies on the horizon. She thought about what Boone had said about the country growing on her. Maybe. Look how Boone McGraw had grown on her.

Boone drove up the lane to the ranch house, white wooden fences on each side of the narrow road. Yesterday C.J. had been driving and too anxious to pay much attention. Now she took it all in. The ranch reminded her of every horse movie she'd ever seen as a girl. Miles of pasture fenced in by a white-painted wooden fence that made the place look as if it should be in Kentucky—not the backwoods of Montana.

In the front seat, Jesse Rose let out a pleased sound at the sight of a half dozen horses running beside the SUV on the other side of the fence, their tails waving in the wind.

"I love horses. It's one reason I've always wanted to come to Montana. But Uncle Hank…" Tears filled her eyes again. She wiped them. "I always knew he was hiding something from us, but I just assumed it was his lifestyle."

Boone pulled up in front of the large ranch house and cut the engine. "Hope you're ready to meet the family, because they are more than ready to meet you."

The family had come spilling out the door, clearly unable to hold back. C.J. stood back to watch as Travers came down the steps. He took one look at Jesse Rose and pulled her into a hug. It was a beautiful sight, all of the McGraws and future McGraws welcoming Jesse Rose.

And Jesse Rose seemed smitten with all of them as they quickly ushered her inside.

"Hey," Boone said, suddenly next to her. "You all right?"

She wiped at her eyes and nodded, unable to speak.

"I'm sorry about Hank," he said as he got Jesse Rose's suitcase from the back and they stepped out of the falling snow and onto the porch.

"Sounds like the killer did him a favor since everyone said he died instantly. I just wish…"

"I know." He put his arm around her and she leaned

into his strong, hard body. He smelled good, felt good. She thought she could have stayed right there forever.

But from inside the house, his father called to him. "Champagne!"

JUST OUTSIDE OF WHITEHORSE, Cecil's cell phone rang, making him jump. He saw that it was Tilly. Now what?

"Hey," he said, trying to sound upbeat.

"You can't believe what is happening here," Tilly whispered.

His stomach roiled. Tilly sounded like she might bust if she didn't tell someone.

"Jesse Rose. She's been found. She came in on the train today and Boone and the female private investigator just brought her out to the ranch. Everyone is so excited."

Not everyone. "Must have been a shock to Jesse Rose."

"Didn't sound like it. Apparently she knew—that's why she came out on the train to meet her family. I have no idea how long she's known. Travers is beside himself." He heard her admiration for her boss in her voice and growled under his breath. "Where are you?"

"I'm headed back home," he said as he saw the outskirts of Whitehorse. But he needed time to think.

In fact, he'd asked her not to mention that they were back together. He knew what Travers McGraw thought of him. A lot of people thought he was a loser.

"There is going to be a huge celebration out here tonight," Tilly was saying. "The twins have been found. Bless the Lord."

Yes, he thought, his leg aching.

"When Boone called, did he say who the other kidnapper was?" He held his breath.

"I didn't get to hear all of the conversation," Tilly said, sounding so excited she was breathing hard. "But some letters came today from that private investigator I told you about. And a package from the second Mrs. McGraw."

He heard the distaste in his ex-wife's tone. "A package from Patty? You sure it's not a bomb?"

"Very funny. No, it feels like a book. It's addressed to Mr. McGraw."

A book? He brushed that away. It was the letters that he was worried about. "Who are the letters to?"

"There's one for Jesse Rose, one for that young female private eye, C.J. West, that Boone brought back with him and one for Mr. McGraw."

"Travers?" This was it. His worst fear was coming true. He looked at Whitehorse ahead. He could just keep driving to North Dakota and beyond, but they would eventually find him. Or maybe there was a chance… "So you haven't given anyone the letters yet?" he asked, praying she hadn't.

"No, everyone is too excited to see Jesse Rose," Tilly said.

"Don't give them the letters! Tilly, are you listening to me?"

"Yes, but why wouldn't I—"

"You can't give them the letters." He racked his brain as to what to do. "Burn them."

"I can't do that!"

"Then hold on to them until I get there. Can you do that?" His mind was whirling. If the McGraws knew the part he'd played in the kidnapping, then he would have heard by now. Tilly would have heard. So the little female PI hadn't found out anything.

Instead, Hank had written letters, letters that would incriminate them both. He swore under his breath. "Tilly, just do as I ask, please."

"I don't understand why you would want me to—"

"Tilly, if you love me, if you've ever loved me, I'm begging you, hide the letters. I'm on my way out there. I will explain everything when I get there."

"SOMETHING WRONG?" BOONE ASKED, making Tilly jump. She had her back to him as she was talking on the phone. She hadn't heard over the commotion in the other room.

He was still in shock. In his wildest dreams, he'd hoped Jesse Rose would get off that train. But he'd never imagined that she would already know about him and the rest of the McGraws—let alone know about C.J.

Uncle Hank? He'd seen C.J.'s expression. She'd been poleaxed by the news. What they didn't know was how Hank's sister had come to have Jesse Rose. Had Hank been involved in the kidnapping?

From everything he'd learned about the man after talking to people in Butte—including C.J.—he found it hard to believe. But the man had known that Jesse Rose had been kidnapped and he hadn't come forward. Until now, Boone thought. Hank had finally come forward after twenty-five years. Because he knew he was dying?

Travers had insisted they have champagne so he'd come into the kitchen hoping to find their new cook, but had found Tilly instead. When he'd heard the shrill rise of her voice on the phone, he'd been worried something might have happened.

But now she quickly stuffed whatever she'd been holding into her large purse along with her phone before she turned. She put on a big smile, making him all the more concerned that she was hiding something.

"If there is anything I can do…" he said seeing that she appeared to be trembling.

"Oh, you are so sweet. Your whole family. I…I feel so fortunate to work here. Your father… He's been so nice to me all these years, and letting me come back to work the way he did…" She sounded close to tears.

"Tilly," he said, stepping to her to take her shoulders in his hands. "You are family to us. That's why you can tell me if something is wrong."

She nodded, tears in her eyes. "It was Cecil on the phone…" She looked at the floor and, taking a deep breath, let it out before she continued. "He doesn't want anyone to know that we're thinking about getting back together."

Boone smiled. "Well, that's good news, isn't it?"

"Yes, of course. Cecil is just worried that people will talk or worse, you know."

He did know. He remembered years ago when Tilly and Cecil had gotten a divorce. Cecil had never been one to work and Tilly had put up with it for years and had finally had enough. Everyone had thought she should have kicked him out a lot sooner. Those same people would probably think she was a fool for taking him back.

"If you're happy, then I'm happy for you," he said. "I just wanted to check and see what room we might put Jesse Rose in."

"Oh, let me show her." Tilly started to head toward the living room, but quickly turned back to grab her purse. "I'll just put this away first."

"I'M SURE YOU all have a lot of questions," Jesse Rose said after glasses of champagne were raised to celebrate her return. "I have a lot myself. But I am so happy to learn about all of you. I always wanted siblings. I can't believe this." She smiled as she looked around the room, her gaze lighting on C.J. for a long moment. "I especially always wanted a sister."

C.J. smiled, happy for Jesse Rose, but feeling like she didn't belong here. Once it came out about Hank... Boone took her barely touched champagne glass and set it aside. His fingers brushed hers as he did, making her start. Their gazes locked for a moment.

"You okay?" he whispered.

She smiled and nodded, but she felt anything but okay and Boone seemed to sense it. He took her hand and led her down a hallway to a sunroom off the south side of the house. "You should be back there with your family," she protested when he let the door close behind them.

"I can see that you're not okay," he said, stepping to her to lift her chin with his warm fingers. "Tell me what's bothering you?"

"I shouldn't be here. This is family—"

"You're with me."

Her pulse leaped at the look in his eyes.

"I want you here. I... I want you."

Before she could move, he pulled her to him. The kiss on the train platform had stirred emotions and desires in her. But it was nothing like this kiss. C.J. couldn't remember ever feeling such swift, powerful emotions course through her. Desire was like a fire inside her that had been banked for too long. Boone deepened the kiss, sending her reeling with needs that she'd kept bottled up. She leaned into him, wanting...

There was a sound outside the door.

He pulled back, his gaze on hers, the promise in those blue eyes fanning the flames.

"Boone!" His brother Cull stuck his head in.

"Oh, there you are." Cull looked embarrassed. "Sorry. Dad needs you."

"Go," C.J. said as she tried to catch her breath. "I'm just going to step outside for a moment. It's hot in here."

Cull was grinning at his brother as they both left.

C.J. grabbed her coat and stepped outside, practically fanning herself with the freezing-cold evening air. Twilight had fallen over the ranch, gilding it and the fresh snow in a pale silver. Cooling down, she pulled on her coat as she looked to the Little Rockies. She thought about what Boone had said about this part of Montana growing on her. It had. Just as Boone McGraw had.

But it was his words just moments ago that still had the fires burning in her. *I want you here. I want you.* She'd heard how hard those words were for him to say.

Her heart was still pounding at the memory of the kiss, to say nothing of the promise she'd seen in his blue eyes, when she heard a noise behind her.

Chapter Nineteen

Before she could turn, C.J. was grabbed from behind. She felt the cold barrel end of a gun pressed to her temple.

"Listen to me," the man whispered against her ear. "Do what I say or you die and so does everyone else in that house. You understand?"

She nodded and he jerked her backward as he half dragged her to the closest barn. She noticed that he was limping badly. This was the man who'd broken into her house. The same one Boone had seen at Hank's funeral. The same one who'd killed Hank and tried to run her and Boone down in Butte?

Once inside the barn, he said, "Call your boyfriend."

"What?" She'd been thinking about her self-defense training. The problem was that the man was large and strong and he'd caught her off guard. And now there was a gun to her temple. Something in the man's tone also warned her that he was deadly serious—and nervous as hell. "I don't have a boyfriend."

"Boone McGraw. I saw the two of you. Call him. Then hand me the phone."

"No." She wasn't going to ask Boone to come out here to face a man with a gun because she'd fallen in love with him. She'd rather die than—

"Listen to me. If you do this, no one will get hurt. If I have to haul you inside the house with this gun to your head, a whole lot of people are going to die. My wife is inside that house and she has some letters I need. Once I have those, you can both go back to your lives. No one gets hurt. Otherwise…"

She thought of Boone's family. She couldn't chance that the man was telling the truth about more people being hurt. Also this would buy time and give her a chance to get out of this.

"You're the one who broke into my house," she said as she got a glimpse of the man with the scar on his face and the black baseball cap covering his graying hair. "You were at Hank's funeral."

He grunted. "Make the call." He held her tighter, the barrel of the gun pressing hard against her temple. She'd had self-defense training for her job. Hank had insisted. But he'd also warned her about acting rash.

Some of these people are all hopped up on God only knows what, he'd told her. *Best to bide your time, try to talk your way out of the situation and if all else fails, use your training.*

She doubted there would be any talking her way out of this. She could feel the man's nerves vibrating through his body. He was too jumpy. In the state he was in, he might pull the trigger accidentally. But that meant there was a good chance of him making a mistake and giving her an opening to escape. She had to count on that. If she got the chance, she would do what she had to do to keep him from killing both her and Boone.

"Okay." Pulling out her phone, she made the call with trembling fingers.

He snatched the phone away from her before she

could say a word. "Boone? Just listen if you don't want your girlfriend to die. I have a gun to her head. I need you to find Tilly. She has some letters. Tell her to give them to you and then come outside. Once I see that you have the letters, I will let your girlfriend go."

BOONE LISTENED. Someone had C.J.? Had a gun to her head over some…letters? He recalled earlier when he'd startled Tilly. She said she'd been on the phone with her ex-husband, but had said what he'd overheard had something to do with them getting back together.

He now realized it had been a lie. He excused himself and went looking for Tilly. He thought about taking one of his father's guns, but he didn't want to call attention to himself by going into the gun room where all the guns and ammunition was locked up.

And if anyone in the family knew where he was going, they would want to come with him. He couldn't chance what the man might do. The man on the phone had sounded scared. And maybe unstable. Surely he didn't believe he was going to get away with this, whatever it was.

He found Tilly in one of the bedrooms. "Tilly?"

She'd been pacing and now jumped at the sound of her name. The woman was literally wringing her hands.

"You have some letters?" he said, not having time to find out what was wrong with her right now.

Her eyes widened. "You know about the letters?"

"I was told to get them from you."

She nodded, looking like she might burst into tears. "He told me to keep them. I—"

"It's fine. Just give them to me."

Tilly moved to a table next to the bed where she'd

apparently come to clean, picked up her large bag and dug into it, pulling out one business-size envelope after another until there were three on the bed. She handed them to him.

"I just did what he asked me to do," she said.

Boone nodded as he took the letters, noting the names on them and the return address. They were all from Hank Knight. "Who asked you to keep the letters a secret, Tilly?"

"Cecil." She looked confused. "My ex-husband. Isn't he the one who wants the letters?"

C.J. COULD FEEL the man getting more impatient by the moment. He kept looking toward the house and muttering under his breath as he held her tightly, the gun to her head.

"This is about some letters?" she asked.

"As if you don't know. Your PI friend sent them."

"Hank?"

"One to you, one to Jesse Rose, one to Travers McGraw."

"What's in them?" she asked. But she already knew. The answers they all desperately needed.

"Don't you wish you knew? Once they're destroyed, it will finally be over."

She doubted that, but she didn't think telling him would do either of them any good. "The kidnapping," she said with a sigh. "You're afraid there is something in them that incriminates you." She felt her pulse jump. "You think Hank knew who was behind the kidnapping. That's why you killed him." Anger filled her. "And you thought I might discover the truth. Why else would you try to run me down in Butte? You were the kidnapper's accomplice. Now you have a gun to my head? Are you crazy?"

"Crazy like a fox. Without proof there is nothing anyone can do. I got away with it for twenty-five years. If your partner hadn't stirred things back up…"

She could tell that the man was unhinged. Fear made her heart pound. And now Boone was on his way.

The back door of the house opened and Boone stepped out. He held up what looked like three business-size envelopes.

The man pushed C.J. out of the barn door far enough so Boone could see her. Even from the distance, she could see his jaw tighten as he saw the gun pointed at her head. He started toward them in long strides.

Since hearing of Hank's death, all she'd thought about was finding his killer. Now his killer was right here, but all she could think about was Boone. *I've fallen in love with this man. I can't let this man kill him.*

"Cecil Marks?" Boone called, stopping a few yards short of the barn door. "Let her go and you can have your letters."

"BRING THE LETTERS into the barn," Cecil called back.

Boone shook his head. "Not until you let her go."

"Bring in the letters or I'm going to shoot her and then you!" Cecil was losing it. C.J. could feel him coming apart, his body shaking as if all this had finally gotten to him. "I have nothing to lose at this point. I've already killed two people. You think I won't kill two more? Bring them now or so help me—"

Boone started toward the barn.

C.J. told herself that maybe the man would take the

letters and run off. Maybe the best thing was to just hand them over—

"Cecil!"

They all looked toward the house as an older blonde woman came out into the snow. C.J. felt the barrel of the gun move a few inches against her head as Cecil saw her.

"Tilly? Go back. Everything is going to be all right. But you have to go back into the house." Cecil's voice broke.

"I can't let you do this!" Tilly cried and kept coming toward them.

"No, go back!" He was shaking hard now.

C.J. realized she was watching a man come apart at the seams. Boone must have seen it, too.

"Tilly, don't make me do this!" Cecil cried as he dragged C.J. back a step.

She knew there was no longer any time. If she didn't act now...

Preparing herself for the worst, she kicked back at the man's bad leg and let all her weight fall forward, becoming dead weight in the man's single arm holding her. At the same time, she saw Boone rush them.

Cecil let out a scream of pain and began to fall forward with her. He had to let go of her as she fell. She didn't feel the cold barrel of the gun against her temple anymore, she thought, an instant before she heard the deafening sound of the gun's report.

As she dropped to the ground, she saw Boone barrel into the man. The two went flying backward. From the ground, she saw Boone on top of Cecil struggling for the gun. The sound of the gun's first report still ringing in her ears, she started to get up when the gun went off again.

This time it was Tilly who screamed at the entrance to the barn. C.J. turned to see the woman's chest blossom red before she dropped to the ground.

Cecil let out a cry as he saw Tilly fall. Boone wrenched the gun from the man's hand and slammed him down hard to the barn floor. C.J. could hear voices and people running from the house.

The next moment, she was in Boone's arms. Her brothers had Cecil. She'd seen Nikki on the phone to the sheriff and a sobbing Cecil Marks was being restrained as he tried to get to his wife.

From the barn floor, Travers McGraw picked up the three letters Boone had dropped.

Chapter Twenty

"The sheriff just brought these by," Boone said when he found C.J. in the sunroom.

C.J. took the envelope from him and just held it for a long moment. She was still shaken by everything that had happened. Cecil was in jail. She'd heard that he'd completely broken down and confessed everything. Tilly was dead, having died on the way to the hospital.

A minute didn't go by that C.J. wasn't reminded how easily it could have been one of them in the morgue right now. That Boone could have been killed... It gave her waking nightmares.

"If you want to be alone when you open it..." Boone said.

"No." She met his gaze and smiled before patting the cushion on the couch next to her. "I suspect this is about the kidnapping. Has your father opened his letter yet? Or Jesse Rose?"

"They're reading theirs now," he said as he joined her.

Carefully she opened the flap and took out the letter.

Dear C.J.,
If you're reading this, I am no longer with you.

I didn't want you to worry about me, that's why I didn't tell you. I'm sorry. I figured you would have enough to deal with once I was gone without knowing that I was dying. I had an amazing life. I don't regret any of it. But you, C.J., you were the light of my life. I can't imagine what it would have been like without you in it from the time you came charging into my office, looked around and said, "What a mess!" You were five.

She laughed as tears welled. Boone, who'd been reading along with her, handed her a tissue. She wiped her eyes and continued reading.

I hope that by the time you read this, you'll have met Jesse Rose. Isn't she wonderful? And that you will see that she makes it home to her birth family, the McGraws.

I've confessed my part in all this to Travers McGraw in the letter I wrote him. But I wanted you to know, as well. Years ago, Pearl Cavanaugh contacted me. She had a child that desperately needed a home. It wasn't the first time I'd helped with adoptions from the women of the Whitehorse Sewing Circle. I never asked where the babies came from. I just trusted that I was helping the infant—and the desperate family that wanted a child.

At the time my sister had been trying to have a baby and after numerous miscarriages had been told it would never happen. The moment I laid eyes on the little girl who was brought to me, I fell in love with Jesse Rose. I knew who she was.

It was in all the news. But I also knew from Pearl that it was felt that the infant wasn't safe in the McGraw house.

I should have done the right thing. But at the time, the right thing felt like not returning her. When I handed Jesse Rose to my sister… Well, I've never felt such emotion. No little girl could have been more loved.

Maybe it was knowing I was dying. Or maybe it was seeing Travers McGraw on television pleading for information about his daughter. I called the lawyer to make sure the baby I'd given my sister really was Jesse Rose McGraw. Then I couldn't keep it from Jesse Rose and the McGraw family any longer. I flew to Seattle and told Jesse Rose and my sister what had to be done.

It was the hardest thing I'd ever done—short of keeping all this from you, C.J. Truthfully, I was a coward. I couldn't bear to see your expression when you heard what I'd done all those years ago. I hope you can forgive me.

I also hope you and Jesse Rose will meet. She's always wanted a sister and you two are the joys of my life.

I will miss you so much.

Hank

Tears were streaming down C.J.'s face as she finished the letter. Boone pulled her into his chest, rubbing her back as she cried.

"I know what he did was wrong, but I miss him," she said between sobs.

"I know."

When she finally pulled herself together, she straightened. "There was nothing in the letter about Cecil Marks. What if Hank knew nothing about his part in the kidnapping? What if—"

"If Cecil was free and clear and would never have been caught if he hadn't panicked?" Boone shook his head. "Apparently Tilly had told him that Hank had called our lawyer and knew something about Jesse Rose and the kidnapping. Cecil had believed it was true."

"So if he hadn't confessed…"

"We would never have known the part he played in the kidnapping."

She nodded, shocked at the irony.

"Maybe there is something in my father's letter," Boone said. "But it doesn't sound like Hank knew who the kidnapper's accomplice inside the house was."

"I need to go find Jesse Rose," C.J. said, getting to her feet. "If her letter is anything like mine…"

BOONE THOUGHT OF his father. Anxious to find out what had been in his letter, he found Travers in his office. The letter he'd received was lying open on the desk. His father looked up as he came in.

"Are you all right?" Boone asked.

"Yes." The older man nodded. There were tears in his eyes. "It's good to know what happened. Jesse Rose was raised by loving parents. That's all that matters. And now she is home. She wants to stay out here on the ranch. She has a degree in business. I think she can be an asset to the ranch and take some of the load off my shoulders. What do you think?"

Boone chuckled. "I think you're an amazing man. You are so forgiving."

His father shrugged. "If I have learned anything it's that holding a grudge is harder on you than on the person who wronged you. I don't have time for regrets. I just want to spend the rest of my life enjoying my family and it's almost Christmas. The doctors say that your mother can start coming home for visits after the first of year. If those go well… So tell me about C.J."

"What do you want to know?" Boone asked, startled by the change of topic.

"When you're going to ask her to marry you," his father said with a laugh as he leaned back in his chair.

"I barely know the woman."

"I guess you'd better take care of that, then."

C.J. FOUND JESSE ROSE in her room. The door was open so she tapped on it and stepped in to hand her a clean tissue. Jesse Rose laughed, seeing that C.J. was still sniffling, too. They hugged and sat down on the edge of the bed.

"Hank hoped we'd be friends," Jesse Rose said.

"How can we not be?" she said. "We're the only two people who really knew Hank. It's strange, though, the way he brought us together."

"Even stranger the way he brought you and Boone together," Jesse Rose said with a teasing smile.

"You can't think he had a hand in that."

The other woman shrugged and winked. "If Hank could have, he would have. You two are perfect for each other."

"I wouldn't say that exactly." C.J. felt herself blushing. "He's stubborn and bossy and impossible. On top of that, he's a cowboy."

Jesse Rose laughed. "It is so obvious that the two

of you are crazy about each other. And every woman wants a cowboy."

"Not every woman," C.J. said with a laugh. "Anyway, I live in Butte and he…he lives here," she said, taking in the ranch with a wave of her hand.

"You don't want to stay on this amazing ranch? I'm going to. I've already talked to Travers…to my dad about it," Jesse Rose said. "It's going to take a little getting used to, calling him Dad and having four grown brothers—one a twin I still have to meet. But I love it here. I know this sounds crazy, but I feel as if this is really where I've always belonged."

C.J. laughed. "It is."

"I know, but after growing up in Seattle…" She shook her head. "I feel like I've come home."

"How is your mom taking it?"

"She's just glad she isn't going to prison."

"You sound angry with her."

Jesse Rose nodded slowly. "I guess I am a little. But Hank knew, too, and I can't be angry with him. I'm just so glad he told me the truth. Maybe my mom will come around. Travers—Dad has asked her to come out for a visit. Maybe she will."

BOONE LOOKED UP to see Jesse Rose and C.J. come into the living room. He was so thankful that C.J. had agreed to at least stay through Christmas.

"We were just discussing everything that has happened," Boone said as the two joined the rest of the family. "Nikki is finishing up her book now that we all know what happened the night of the kidnapping."

C.J. sat down next to Boone. "I still can't believe

Cecil Marks thought Hank knew about the part he'd played."

"Apparently Tilly had told him she'd overheard us talking and that Hank knew who the accomplice was," Travers said. "Unfortunately, she got it wrong. Otherwise, we would have never known it was our housekeeper's ex-husband who worked with Howard Cline to kidnap the twins. Finally Marianne will now be cleared of any wrongdoing."

"Tilly was always listening to what was going on with all of us," Cull said. "She really did get caught in the crossfire this time, though."

Nikki elbowed him. "That's awful."

"Well, you know what I mean. It cost her her life."

"At least Cecil confessed to everything," Nikki said. "Now I can finally finish my book."

"So Cecil was never considered a suspect?" C.J. asked.

"Surely he was questioned the night of the kidnapping," Boone said.

"He was—once he regained consciousness," Nikki said. "He was in a car wreck on the other side of the county and ended up in a coma in the hospital the night of the kidnapping."

"Didn't anyone think that was suspicious?" C.J. asked.

"That was the problem. No one knew exactly what time the twins had been taken," Nikki said. "As it turns out, the twins had been missing for almost an hour before Patty was awakened and went in to check on them. By then, Cecil had stopped at a bar or two and gotten into a wreck. That was a pretty good alibi. Nor was there anything incriminating in his car. No one even knew he'd been out to the ranch that night since apparently Tilly was too doped up to mention it at the time and didn't think it important later I guess."

"Tilly never suspected him?" Cull asked in disbelief.

Nikki shook her head. "She'd taken cold medicine and then he'd given her even more. She was completely out of it."

"At least now we know who put the codeine cough syrup in the twins' room to make our mother look guilty," Ledger said.

"Seems like the perfect crime," Travers said. "But *someone* knew Cecil was in the house that night." Travers had been sitting quietly until then. Everyone turned to look at him. "When the letters came, there was also a package delivered. The sheriff found it in Tilly's purse where she'd apparently put it as Cecil had asked her."

"From Hank?" C.J. asked.

Travers shook his head. "From Patty. It's your mother's diary," he said to his sons. "Marianne saw Cecil coming out of the twins' room that night. That's why she went in. Unfortunately, she failed to tell anyone because of the altered state she was in from being poisoned with arsenic. When the twins were kidnapped, she apparently didn't recall seeing him. But she wrote it in her diary. Because of the poison in her system, it's possible she didn't remember."

"Patty returned the diary?" Boone asked sounding shocked. "Why would she do that?"

"There was only a short note inside. It said, 'Sorry, Patricia.' It seems she's had it this whole time, planning to use it against us."

"Except for that page she put under my door to make Marianne look guilty," Nikki said.

"Yes," Travers agreed.

"But wait," C.J. said. "Who was poisoning your mother?"

The family all looked at one another. It was finally Nikki who spoke. "We don't know. Probably Patty, but there are two other suspects—the former ranch manager, Blake Ryan, and our former family attorney, Jim Waters. Both were in love with Patty and would have done anything for her."

"Let's hope once Patty goes to trial that it all comes out," Cull said. "I suspect all three will be found guilty."

Travers got to his feet. "All I care about is that Cecil's confession clears your mother. Not that I ever believed she was in on the kidnapping. Even if Patty had been poisoning her and making her forgetful and confused, she wouldn't have hurt her babies."

"What will happen to Cecil?" Ledger asked.

"He'll probably get life. Kidnapping and deliberate homicide." Travers shook his head. "For twenty-five years he thought Harold Cline had double-crossed him, when all the time Harold was dead and buried. The man also must have lived being terrified that the truth would come out. So when Nikki began investigating the kidnapping for her book and we released more information…"

"Cecil killed Frieda to keep her from talking, although I doubt she knew anything about who had helped Harold," Nikki said. "Once Tilly told her ex about the call from Hank…"

"Speaking of the upcoming trial, Jim Waters called," Cull said. "He swears he's being framed for the poisonings. He was practically begging for you to help him, Dad."

Travers sighed. "Jim got himself into the mess he's in—he's going to have to get himself out. I would imagine the truth will come out one way or another. Blake Ryan hasn't gotten off free, either. He's being investigated for co-conspiracy with Patty and Jim Waters in the poisonings."

"If all three of them were in on it, one of them will turn on the others," Boone said.

"Jim and Blake both thought they would have Patty and the ranch once you were out of the way, Dad," Cull said.

"So who is the father of Patty's daughter Kitten?" Ledger asked.

"Patty told me it was just some one-night stand," Boone said. "If you can believe Patty." The former nanny, turned second McGraw wife, had always had trouble with the truth, he added.

"You do realize that Patty will probably get off with no more than a few years in prison for what she did to this family," Cull said.

"Probably," Travers agreed. "It's impossible to prove that she was behind the poisoning of your mother all those years ago. But I think a jury will have a hard time believing that she wasn't behind my arsenic poisoning in one way or another."

"Well, it's finally over," Ledger said.

"Except for Patty's tell-all book," Cull said.

"Haven't you heard? Because of the hype around Nikki's book about what really happened, the other publisher decided they weren't interested in Patty's," Travers said and smiled. "Explains why she returned the diary. But apparently she got to keep the advance to pay her lawyer."

A log popped in the fireplace and as darkness descended on the ranch, Boone put his arm around C.J. and looked at the Christmas tree, bright with lights and ornaments.

Ledger's fiancée, Abby, and Jesse Rose came in from the kitchen with plates of sandwiches. They were both laughing about something Jesse Rose had said.

"I don't think I ever believed in happy endings until this moment," Boone said and smiled at his father.

"All that matters is that the twins were found. They've both had good lives. That's all I could have hoped for," Travers said and smiled. "That's all I *did* hope for."

Epilogue

A year later, the family all gathered in the living room on Christmas Eve to celebrate. And they had a lot to celebrate, Travers McGraw thought as he looked at his burgeoning family.

He watched his oldest son, Cull, pour the champagne—and the nonalcoholic sparkling grape juice.

"So much has happened," Travers began, his voice breaking with emotion as he raised his glass in a toast. "I have my family back and so much more." He laughed and looked at the women who'd joined the family in the past year—all of them pregnant. "I never thought I'd live to see my first grandchild born, let alone four."

The room erupted in laughter. Cull and Nikki had started it by getting married and pregnant right after their wedding, then Ledger and Abby, then Boone and C.J.

"We have so much to be thankful for this holiday," he said and looked to his daughter, Jesse Rose. She'd moved in and was now working with the horse business right alongside her father. Travers had extended offers to her adoptive mother to come visit over the past year, but she hadn't come out to the ranch yet.

So much had happened but at least now the kidnapping was behind them. And Marianne would be coming home soon to stay. She'd come for a few visits, but the doctor said they needed to take it slowly. Finding out that she'd had nothing to do with the kidnapping had been huge in her recovery. That and seeing both of her once-lost babies now grown.

"You said Tough has been going by to see Mother?" Cull asked.

Travers nodded and smiled. "He said it's gone well. She knew him right away."

"Unlike Vance Elliot," Cull said. "He fooled us for a while. I was starting to believe he really was our brother."

"Vance got his head turned by the idea of cashing in on becoming Oakley," Travers said. "He knew it was wrong."

"I heard that you paid for Vance's lawyer," Cull commented, clearly not approving.

"Yes, I did," his father said. "I saw something in him. In fact, when he gets out of jail, I've offered him a job."

"Dad, do you think that's a good idea?" Ledger asked.

"I do. He's had a rough life. I like to think that showing someone like him kindness can change him."

"Count the silverware," Cull said, but he patted his father's shoulder. "You always see the good in a person. I guess it's something to aspire to."

Boone laughed. "Nothing wrong with being a skeptic. It balances things out." C.J. poked him in the ribs.

Travers laughed. "I'd like to toast Nikki. If it hadn't been for her... Once she started asking questions, the truth started coming out. Thank you," he said, raising his glass. "And congratulations. I heard your book made the *New York Times* bestseller list the first week out."

They all raised their glasses.

"And to Jesse Rose," Travers said. "It is so wonderful to have you home."

BOONE LOOKED AT his beautiful wife. It was true what they said about being pregnant. C.J. glowed. He couldn't believe how quickly this past year had gone. Mostly he couldn't believe that not only had he gotten up the courage to ask C.J. to marry him, but that she'd accepted.

After Christmas last year, he'd driven her back to Butte. They'd talked a lot on the way home, but mostly about the kidnapping and Jesse Rose's return. C.J. had still been dealing with Hank's death and all the secrets he'd kept from her.

Back in Butte, he'd stayed to help C.J. clean out Hank's office and close it for good. When he couldn't think of any other excuse not to return to the ranch, he'd finally realized that he couldn't live without this woman.

He'd asked her out to dinner, gotten down on one knee and proposed.

To his shock, she'd said yes.

He'd been even more shocked when she'd wanted to return to the ranch and give up her PI business in Butte.

It wouldn't be the same without Hank and I've fallen in love with your family, she'd said.

Just my family?

She'd laughed and thrown her arms around him. *I never thought I'd fall in love with a cowboy. But, Boone McGraw, you're the kind of cowboy who grows on a girl. Take me home, cowboy.*

THE LIGHTS ON the Christmas tree twinkled, the air rich with the smell of freshly baked gingerbread cookies and pine. C.J. breathed it all in, feeling as if she needed to pinch herself as she stood looking at this wonderful family scene. She wished Hank could see this. Maybe he could.

She felt Boone come up behind her. He encircled her with his arms. She leaned back against him and closed her eyes as his hands dropped to her swollen stomach, making her smile.

"Happy?" he whispered.

"Very." She opened her eyes and turned in his arms. "I've never had a family like this before."

"Well, you do now. I think Hank would be happy for you."

She nodded. "I was just thinking of him. It's all he ever wanted for me." But it was more than she had ever dreamed possible. When Boone had gotten down on one knee and asked her to marry him it had been the happiest day of her life.

C.J. had thought she couldn't give up her private investigator business. The truth was she wanted a family of her own far more. And now they were expecting. She couldn't wait.

What made it even more fun was that her two sisters-in-law were also expecting and Abby was pregnant with twin girls while she and Nikki were having boys. With all three families building on the ranch and not that far apart, their kids would all grow up together here.

She couldn't imagine anything more wonderful. Jesse Rose was as excited as anyone. All this family and soon all these babies.

Don't worry about me, Jesse Rose had said. *One of*

*these days I'll find me a cowboy and settle down my-
self. But I'm never leaving Montana.*

"I feel like all of this is a dream," C.J. said now to
her husband. "If it is, don't wake me up."

Boone laughed. "Merry Christmas, sweetheart, and
many more to come," he said and leaned down to kiss
her as the doorbell rang.

"Enough of that!" Cull called from where he and
Nikki had gone into the kitchen to check on dinner.
"Someone answer the door!"

"I've got it!" Boone gave her another quick kiss before
heading to the door.

To Boone's surprise Tough Crandall was standing on
the doorstep.

"I was invited," Tough said, taking off his Stetson.

Boone studied his brother. There was no doubt that
this cowboy was Oakley McGraw. But he was determined not to be one of them. *Good luck with that*, Boone
thought.

"Of course you were invited," he said to his brother.
"It's Christmas and like it or not, we're family." Tough
didn't have any other family since both his adoptive
parents had passed away. Nor did the stubborn cowboy want to be a McGraw, he'd said. But Travers had
been visiting him on and off and had obviously somehow talked him into spending Christmas with them.

"Help me with the presents I have out in my truck?"

Boone laughed. "You got it." Together they went out
and brought in all the gifts. "Hey, everyone, Tough's
here," Boone announced as they came back inside.

His brother actually smiled as he wiped his feet and
stepped in.

Say what you will about the McGraws, they were the kind of family that grew on you—whether you liked it or not.

Travers smiled and held out his hand to Tough. "Glad you could make it, son. I don't believe you've met everyone," he said after a moment. He began to introduce each of the family and new additions as he went around the room.

When he got to Jesse Rose, he hesitated. Tough was looking at his twin sister wide-eyed. For the past year, Jesse Rose had been dying to meet her twin, but Tough had been dragging his feet.

"This is... Jesse Rose," their father said.

Tough shook her hand. Their eyes locked and the cowboy seemed to be at a loss for words. "I had no idea," he said, his voice breaking.

She laughed, smiling as she asked, "No idea what?"

"That I would feel...such a connection."

"We're *twins*. Plus we share quite a history, wouldn't you say?"

He nodded. "It's the first time I've really felt like I was a part of this family."

"Well, now that you have," Travers said, "you're just in time for dinner. After that we're going to be opening presents."

"And singing Christmas carols," Jesse Rose said. "It's going to be our new tradition."

"I can see where we're going to have a lot more new traditions," Travers said, putting his arm around Tough and Jesse. "But you might change your mind about the carols when you hear my sons sing."

"Not all of them are tone-deaf," Tough said and grinned.

Boone listened to the good-natured ribbing during dinner. Later Jesse Rose brought out her guitar and began to play "Silent Night." C.J. came to stand by him. He pulled her close, his eyes misting over as he counted his blessings and his family began to sing.

* * * * *

MATCHMAKING WITH A MISSION

This one is for George "Clem" Clementson. A man who understands the power of love and friendship.

Chapter One

He'd known where she was for almost two weeks. He'd been watching her house, watching her. He just hadn't felt a need to do anything about it.

Until now. Fate had forced his hand. He didn't have much time left. He had to use it wisely. Take care of all those loose ends in his life.

As he pried at the flimsy lock on the side window he thought about how he had loved her. Idolized her. Thought she was the most beautiful woman he'd ever seen.

Unfortunately she hadn't felt the same way about him.

The lock snapped with a soft pop. He froze, listening even though he knew she wouldn't have heard it. Usually by this time of the night she'd finished off enough cheap wine that she would be dead to the world.

Dead to the world. He liked that. He'd been dead to the world thanks to her.

He'd planned this for so long and yet he felt uneasy, a little thrown by the fact that he'd had to break in tonight. All the other nights, she'd forgotten to lock up. Why tonight, of all nights, did she have to remember to lock the damn doors?

A few days ago he'd waited in the overgrown shrubs outside, watching her shadow move behind the sheer curtains in the living room to turn off the television before she stumbled down the hall to bed.

When he'd been sure she'd passed out, he'd slipped inside the house, wanting to take a look around, to know the layout of the house. Not good to bump into something and wake her up on the night he planned to finally finish it.

So he'd poked around, looking into her things, seeing how she'd been doing since he'd last seen her. He'd made a point of testing to see just how deep a sleeper she was. He couldn't have her screaming her head off when the time came, now could he?

For some reason tonight, though, she'd locked the doors. He tried not to let that worry him. But he was superstitious about crap like that. It was her fault. She'd put all that hocus-pocus stuff in his head, her and her horoscopes, palm readings and psychic phone calls. She wouldn't cross the street without checking to make sure her stars were aligned.

Except when she was drunk. Then she threw caution to the wind. He hated to think he was a lot like her that way. Except he didn't have to be drunk.

So, as much as he hated it, he was leery as he hoisted himself up and over the windowsill to drop into the bathroom tub. He landed with a thud and froze to listen.

Maybe she'd remembered to lock the front door because her horoscope told her that she should be more careful today. Or she could have spotted him watching the house, he supposed. But wouldn't it also be possible, given the connection between them, that she'd sensed he was here?

He liked the latter explanation the best. That would mean that she had occasionally thought of him, wondered what had happened to him.

A shell-shaped night-light next to the sink made the bathroom glow pink. She'd done the whole place in a tropical motif. The shower curtain was plastic with huge palm trees. What the hell had she been thinking? As far as he could tell, she'd been landlocked all her life and never even seen an ocean, let alone a real palm tree.

He wasn't sure why, but it made him even more angry with her, this pretending she lived in a beach house. Did she also pretend he'd never existed?

The shower curtain made a soft swishing sound as he brushed against it. Again he froze and listened. A breeze wafted in with the smell of the river.

He thought he heard a noise from the bedroom. The creak of bedsprings as she rolled over. Or got up to come find out what the noise had been in the bathroom. Had she bought herself a gun?

He waited behind the shower curtain, hidden by the fake palms. *I'm right here. Right here. Just waiting for you.*

It surprised him how nervous he was about seeing her again. He'd anticipated this moment for so long he'd expected to be excited. But as he drew the switchblade from his pocket, his fingers were slick with sweat. He wiped them on his jeans and blamed the hot, humid night.

It reminded him of other hot nights, lying in bed, afraid he wouldn't live until morning. The only thing that had kept him going was imagining this day, the day he found her and made her pay for what she'd done to him.

He wanted her to know that kind of fear before this night was over. He glanced at his watch in the glow of the shell night-light. He had plenty of time before her husband came home.

She'd married some guy who worked the graveyard shift as a night watchman. The irony of that didn't escape him as he got tired of waiting in the bathtub and peered around the edge of the shower curtain.

No movement out in the hall. No sound coming from the vicinity of the bedroom. Gently he slid the curtain aside to step out onto the mermaid-shaped shag rug.

He felt hatred bubble up as he noticed she'd bought herself a pretty new mirror since he was here just a few days ago. The mirror was framed in seashells, and it was all he could do not to smash it on the tile floor.

It wasn't the mirror. Or even the stupid seashore stuff. It was that she'd done just fine without him. Better than fine once she'd dumped him.

The realization was like acid inside him. It ate away at the hope that she'd missed him. That she'd been sorry she'd left him.

He thought of the seven-year-old boy he'd been. He could smell the dust her car tires had thrown up as she'd torn across the dirt lot of the filling station. He'd run out of the restroom, thinking she hadn't realized he wasn't in the car, and had called after her. Running, tears streaming down his dirt-streaked face, until he'd stumbled and fallen and lain bawling his heart out as her car had grown smaller and smaller on the two-lane highway in the middle of nowhere.

The memory jarred him into motion. Stepping through the bathroom doorway, he stopped to wait for his eyes to adjust. Her bedroom door was closed. That was odd. It had been open when he'd been here a few nights before.

Worry knifed through him. The hallway was lit by another shell night-light. The cramped space smelled of stale beer and old cigarette smoke.

He inched down the hall, anticipation thrumming in his veins. At the door, he stopped, suddenly worried what he would do if for some reason she'd locked it.

His hand shook as he reached out and took the knob in his damp fingers. He closed his eyes, knowing it couldn't end here, with him locked out of her room, and that it would end very badly if he had to break down the door. She would be able to call the police before he could get to her. He should have cut the phone lines, he realized now.

The knob turned in his hand.

He slumped against the doorjamb for a moment, his relief so intense it made him light-headed. He was sweating hard now, his T-shirt sticking to his skin, and yet he felt a chill as he looked into her bedroom.

The bed was one of those California kings he'd heard about—and damned near as big as the bedroom. He could make out a small form under the covers. Another one of those stupid shell night-lights glowed from a corner of the room.

He stepped in. The only sound was her drunken snores. She was curled on her side, her back to him on the edge of the bed farthest from him. All he could see was the back of her head on the pillow. Her hair was darker than he remembered it. He realized she probably dyed it because she could be getting gray by now.

It finally struck him: he was going to come face-to-face

with the mother who had abandoned him at a gas station twenty-four years ago.

A memory blindsided him. A memory so sweet it made his teeth ache. The two of them sitting on the couch watching her favorite soap opera. A commercial came on for hair color. Him telling her she would look beautiful no matter what color her hair was, even gray. And her smiling over at him, tears in her eyes as she kissed his cheek and pulled him into her arms for a hug.

She'd held him so tightly he couldn't breathe. But he hadn't complained. It was the last time he remembered her touching him.

He crept around the perimeter of the bed, feeling as if he were floating. It all felt so surreal now that he was finally here, finally ready.

She stirred and he froze. She let out a sigh and drifted off again. He edged closer until he was standing over her.

He couldn't see her face. Not the way he wanted to. He knew he was going to have to turn on the lamp beside her bed. He wanted to look into her eyes—and have her look into his. He wanted her to know.

As he turned on the lamp, his fingers brushed the stack of old magazines next to the bed. The magazines toppled over, hitting the floor with a whoosh that startled him as much as the brightness of the lamp as it came on.

She jerked up in bed onto one elbow, blinking against the brightness of the light.

He could see that for a moment she thought he was her husband. She'd aged. It shouldn't have shocked him. But she'd been only twenty-three when she'd left him at that filling station in Montana. She wasn't even fifty, and yet she looked a lot older.

He'd always wondered if she'd grieved over what she'd done. Her life's road map was etched unkindly in her face, but he knew that the very worst she'd had wasn't even close to what he'd been through.

She blinked, that moment of mistakenly taking him for her husband turning to confusion, then fear. Her mouth started to open as she clutched the sheet to her throat.

"Don't scream," he said and touched the knife in his hand, the blade leaping out to catch the light. "Don't you dare scream."

Surprisingly, she didn't. Only a small sound came out of her as her eyes met his and he saw the recognition.

That should have given him some satisfaction.

She knew him even after all these years.

He used to have this dream that she would fall to her knees and beg his forgiveness. He'd always wanted to believe that she'd come back for him but it had been too late. He'd thought about her searching for him for years, her life as miserable as his had been because of what she'd done.

The dream popped like a soap bubble when she opened her mouth again. "So you found me." Her voice was rough from years of cigarettes and late-night boozing, bad men and barrooms.

"So what now?" she asked with a shake of her head. Her eyes flicked to the switchblade in his hand and something came over her face. A hardness that he now remembered from when he was a boy.

What he saw in her eyes was not the remorse he'd hoped for. No sorrow. No guilt. Not even fear anymore.

Her gaze was challenging. As if telling him he didn't have what it would take to kill her.

"You think I haven't always known that you'd turn up one day?" she said as she sat up in the bed and reached for her cigarettes and lighter on the nightstand. She lit a cigarette and took a deep drag.

He stared at her. He'd often wondered if that day at the gas station she'd looked in her rearview mirror. Now he knew that answer. She hadn't looked back. Not even a glance. He guessed he'd always known that.

"Don't you want to know what happened to me?" A seven-year-old boy abandoned like that. He wanted to tell her about the man who'd picked him up and eventually dumped him just the way she had. Dumped him at a place with an innocuous name: Harper House.

He and the others, though, they'd called it Hell House.

Her eyes narrowed at the question, cigarette smoke curling around her. "What? You want to swap horror stories?" She let out a laugh that turned into a cough. "I could tell you stories that would make your hair curl."

She must have seen his hurt. "Hoping for a heart-warming reunion, were you?" She flicked another glance at the knife. "Or were you thinking you could get money out of me?" She let out another laugh. "Sorry, but you're going to be disappointed on both counts."

He shook his head. What had he expected from a woman who'd abandoned her only child the way she had? "Just tell me *why*."

She blew out a cloud of smoke. "*Why?* That's it? That's all you want to know?" She gave a drunken nod of her head. "Because I knew you were going to turn out just like your father. And—you know what?—I was right. I should have gotten rid of you like he wanted me to before you were even born."

He'd wanted to make her suffer, but in the end it had all gone too quickly. Still, he'd thought that once she was dead he would feel some release, some measure of peace. Instead he felt empty and angry, just as he had for years.

He'd just finished her when he heard someone coming in the front door of the house. The husband coming home early.

It often amazed him the way things happened—as if they were meant to be. He waited until the husband came down the hall. Killing him was too easy.

Taking the credit cards and checkbooks, along with what cash he found in the house, proved a little more satisfying.

As he climbed out her bathroom window after smashing the shell-framed mirror to sand, he walked to his pickup parked down the block and told himself he wouldn't find the peace he'd spent his life searching for until everyone who'd hurt him was dead.

He didn't need to check the map. He knew the way to Whitehorse, Montana. Unlike his mother, he'd spent more time there than what it took to put five dollars worth of gas into the tank and drive away.

He'd spent the worst years of his life just outside of that town. And now he was going back for the first and last reunion of Harper House. It would end where it started.

But first there were a couple of stops he needed to make along the way. There couldn't be any loose ends.

He checked to make sure he had the switchblade he'd

cleaned on her tropical-print sheets and told himself it had been destined to end this way.

Still, as he drove away it nagged at him. What kind of mother just drove off and left her son beside the road? He eased his pain with the thought that the babies must have been switched at the hospital. His real mother was out there somewhere. She'd spent her life looking for him, feeling that something was missing.

He felt a little better as he drove west toward Montana. By the time he reached the border he'd convinced himself that he'd been stolen from his real parents—a mother who loved him and a father who would never have run out on him.

He *had* to believe that. He couldn't accept that he'd killed his own mother. Otherwise, it might be true what she'd said about him being like his father.

Chapter Two

McKenna Bailey rode her horse out across the rolling prairie, leaving behind Old Town Whitehorse. The grass was tall and green, the sky a crystalline blue with small white clouds floating along on the afternoon breeze.

She breathed in the warm air, wondering how she could have stayed away from here as long as she had.

The ride south toward the Missouri Breaks was one she knew well. Even before she was able to sit alone in a saddle she'd ridden hugging the saddle horn, in front of her older sister, Eve.

Lately she'd felt antsy and unsure about what she wanted to do with her life. So she'd come home to the one place that always filled her with a sense of peace. But since she'd been home she'd realized this was where she belonged—not opening her own veterinarian clinic as she'd planned since she was twelve because she loved animals. Especially horses.

On impulse, she angled her horse to the east and watched the structures rise up out of the horizon ahead, an idea taking shape.

The barn came into sight first, a large weathered building with a cupola on top and a rusted weather vane in the shape of a horse. As she drew closer she heard the eerie moaning sound of the weather vane as it rotated restlessly in the breeze. It was a sound she remembered from when she used to sneak over here as a young girl.

As she rode closer, the house came into view. The old Harper place. She felt a rush of adrenaline she'd never been able to explain. Something about the house had always drawn her—even against her father's strict orders that she and her sisters stay far away from the place.

Chester Bailey had said the property was dangerous. Something about it being in disrepair, old septic tanks and uncovered abandoned wells. Things horses and kids could get hurt in.

McKenna had never gone too close, stopping at the weathered jack fence to look at the house. The structure was three stories, a large old ranch house with a dormer window at each end. An old wooden staircase angled down from the third floor at the back. A wide screened-in porch ran the width of the house in the front.

Her gaze just naturally went to the third-floor window where she'd seen the boy. She'd been six. He'd looked a couple years older. She had never forgotten him. He'd disappeared almost at once, and an old woman had come out and run her off.

As she stared up at the window now, sunlight glinting off the dirty glass, she wondered what had happened to that sad-looking boy.

Whoever had lived there moved shortly after that, and the house had been occupied by Ellis Harper, an ornery old man who threatened anyone who came near. He kept a shotgun loaded with buckshot by the backdoor.

McKenna had heard stories about the house. Some of the kids at the one-room school she'd attended in Old Town Whitehorse had whispered that Ellis Harper stole young children and kept them locked up in the house. Why else wouldn't he let anyone come around? For years there'd been stories of ghosts and strange noises coming from the house.

McKenna didn't believe in ghosts. Even if she had, she doubted it would have changed the way she felt about this place. She'd ridden over here even when Ellis Harper had been alive, but she'd never gone farther than the fence. Too many times she'd seen his dark silhouette through the screen door, the shotgun in his hands.

As she sat on her horse at the fence as she'd done as a child, she realized she'd always been so captivated by the house and its occupants that she'd never noticed the land around it.

The breeze rustled the new leaves on the copse of cottonwoods that snaked along the sides of the creek and through the rolling grasslands. Good pastureland and, unless she was mistaken, about forty acres worth. There were several old outbuildings a good ways from the house, and then the big old barn and a half dozen old pieces of farm machinery rusting in the tall weeds.

While the idea had come to her in a flash, she knew it had been in the back of her mind for years. She had always been meant to buy Harper House and the land around it.

She just hadn't known until that moment what she planned to do with it.

NATE DEMPSEY SENSED someone watching the house and looked out in surprise to see a woman astride a paint horse just on the other side of the fence. He quickly stepped back from the filthy second-floor window, although he doubted she could have seen him. Only a little of the June sun pierced the dirty glass to glow on the dust-coated floor at his feet as he waited a few heartbeats before he looked out again.

The place was so isolated he hadn't expected to see another soul. Like the front yard, the dirt road in was waist-high with weeds. When he'd broken the lock on the back door, he'd had to kick aside a pile of rotten leaves that had blown in last fall.

As he sneaked a look, he saw that she was still there, staring at the house in a way that unnerved him. He shielded his eyes from the glare of the sun off the dirty window and studied her, taking in her head of long blond hair that feathered out in the breeze from under her Western straw hat.

She wore a tan canvas jacket, jeans and boots. But it was the way she sat astride the brown-and-white horse that nudged the memory.

He felt a chill as he realized he'd seen her before. In that very spot. She'd just been a kid then. A kid on a pretty paint horse. Not this one—the markings were different. Anyway, it couldn't have been the same horse, not considering the last time he had seen her had been more than twenty years ago. That horse would be dead by now.

His mind argued it probably wasn't even the same girl. But he knew better. It was the way she sat on the horse, so at home in a saddle and secure in her world on the other side of that fence.

To the boy he'd been, she and her horse had represented freedom, a freedom he knew he would never have—even after he escaped this house.

Nate saw her shift in the saddle, and for a moment he feared she planned to dismount and come toward the house. With Ellis Harper in his grave, there would be little to keep her away.

To his relief, she reined her horse around and rode back the way she'd come.

As he watched her ride off he thought about the way she'd stared at the house—today and years ago. While the smartest thing she could do was stay clear of this house, he had a feeling she'd be back.

Finding out her name should prove easy since he figured she must live close by. As for her interest in Harper House… He would just have to make sure it didn't become a problem.

"I THOUGHT WE'D already discussed this?"

McKenna Bailey looked up from the real estate section of the newspaper the next morning as her sister Eve set down a platter of pancakes.

"You don't need to buy a place," Eve Bailey said as she pulled up a chair and helped herself to a half dozen of the small pancakes she'd made. "You can live in this one and use as much of the land as you need for this horse ranch you want to start."

McKenna watched her older sister slather the cakes with butter before drowning them with chokecherry syrup. "Are you nervous about getting married next month?" she asked, motioning at Eve's plate.

Eve looked up, a forkful of pancakes on the way to her mouth. "No, I'm just *hungry*."

"Right," McKenna said. "Like the way you've suddenly started holding your fork with your *left* hand?"

Eve looked down at the fork, then at the engagement ring on her left hand and smiled. "It *is* beautiful, isn't it?"

McKenna nodded, smiling at her older sister across the table, the same table they'd shared since they were kids.

"I am doing the right thing, aren't I, marrying Carter?" Eve asked with a groan as she pushed her plate away.

"You love Carter and he loves you," McKenna said. "Be happy. And *eat*."

"You'd tell me if you thought I was making a mistake?"

McKenna nodded, smiling. Carter Jackson had broken her sister's heart back in high school when he'd married someone else. That marriage had been a disaster, ending in divorce. McKenna had no doubt that Carter loved her sister as much as Eve loved him. For months the poor man had been trying to win Eve back; finally at Christmas he'd asked her to marry him. The Fourth of July wedding was just weeks away now.

Eve pulled her plate back in front of her and picked up her fork. "I really *am* hungry."

McKenna laughed and went back to studying the real estate section of the *Milk River Examiner*. But none of the houses interested her. There was only one place she wanted, and even though she'd heard the owner had died recently, she didn't see it listed. Maybe it was too soon.

"I'm serious," Eve said between bites. "Just live in this house. With Mom and Loren living in Florida, it's just going to be sitting empty."

McKenna looked around the familiar kitchen. So many memories. "Dad doesn't want the house?"

Eve shook her head. "He's moved in with Susie, and they're running her Hi-Line Café. He seems…happy."

"Do you know if anyone has bought the old Harper place?" McKenna asked.

"You can't be serious." Eve was staring at her, her mouth open. "Harper House?"

"Did you leave me any pancakes?" their younger sister, Faith, asked as she padded into the room in a pair of pajama bottoms and a T-shirt and plopped down at her chair. "What about Harper House?"

Eve shoved the platter of pancakes toward Faith without a word and gave McKenna a warning look.

"Is anyone going to answer me?" Faith asked as she picked up a pancake in her fingers, rolled it up and took a bite. She looked from Eve to McKenna and back. "Are you guys fighting?"

"No," Eve said quickly. "I was just telling McKenna that she could have this house," she said with a warning shake of her head at McKenna. There was a rule: no fighting, especially when Faith was around.

The youngest of the three girls, Faith had taken their parents' divorce hard and their mother's marriage to Loren Jackson even harder. Because of that, both Eve and McKenna had tried to shelter their younger sister. Which meant not upsetting her this morning with any problems between the two of them.

"It would be nice if someone lived here and took care of the place," Eve said.

"Not me," Faith said and helped herself to another pancake.

"It's our *family* ranch," Eve said.

"That's why I want a place of my own close to here," McKenna said.

Faith shot her a surprised look. "Are you really staying around here?" Since high school graduation she and

Faith had come home only for holidays and summer vacation from college.

"I think I'm ready to settle down, and this area is home," McKenna said.

Faith groaned. "Well, I'm not coming back here to live," she said, getting up to pad over to the kitchen counter to pour herself a cup of coffee.

"I don't want to see this house fall into neglect, either," McKenna told Eve. "But I want my own place. This house is…"

"Mom's and Dad's," Faith said as she came back to the table with her coffee, tears in her eyes. "And now, with Mom and Dad divorced and her married to Loren and living in Florida, it just feels too weird being here."

McKenna knew that Eve had come over this morning from her house down the road to cook breakfast in an attempt to make things more normal for her and Faith. Especially Faith.

"Where are you and Carter going to live after you're married?" McKenna asked Eve.

"My house." Eve had moved into what used to be their grandmother's house when Grandma Nina Mae Cross had gone into the rest home. "We're going to run cattle on the ranch, as always. It's what put us all through college. It's our heritage."

Faith shot McKenna a look that she knew only too well. *Here goes Eve, off on one of her legacy speeches.*

The ranch had always been intended for the three of them. Since Eve had returned she'd been running the place and sending both McKenna and Faith a share of the profits.

"So what happens to this house?" Faith asked, clearly trying to cut Eve off before she got started.

"I guess if the two of you don't want it, the house will just sit empty," Eve said, giving McKenna one of her meaningful big-sister looks.

"That's awful," Faith said. "Someone should live here."

McKenna watched her little sister run a hand along the worn tabletop and smiled. She didn't know what it was about this part of Montana, but it always seemed to bring them back. She'd watched friends leave for college, swearing they were glad to be leaving, only to return here to raise their children.

It was a simpler way of life. A community with strong values and people who knew and looked after their neighbors.

She, too, had left, convinced there was nothing here for her, but here she was. And, like Eve, McKenna figured the day would come when Faith would return and want the house, since she seemed to be the most attached to it.

"If you want your own house, you could build on the ranch," Eve suggested. "There's a nice spot to the east…." Her voice trailed off as if she realized she was wasting her breath. McKenna had already made up her mind.

"Did I hear you mention Harper House?" Faith asked as if finally coming full awake. "My friend who works for the county said it's going to be auctioned off."

"When?" McKenna asked.

"This Saturday, I think."

McKenna couldn't help her rush of excitement. This was obviously meant to be.

Faith laughed. "You *always* liked that place. I remember when you used to sneak over there even though Dad told us not to." She grinned. "I used to follow you."

"You used to ride over there?" Eve asked with a shake of her head. "Do you have any idea how dangerous that was?"

"We never believed that story about old wells on the place," Faith said. "I think Dad didn't want us around the people who lived there. They weren't friendly at all. But they sure had a lot of kids."

Eve shot a look at her youngest sister that McKenna recognized. It was Eve's can-you-really-be-that-naive? look.

"Harper House was a place for troubled boys," Eve said. "That's why Dad didn't want you riding over there. I can't believe you did it anyway," she said to McKenna. "Do you have any idea what could have happened to you?"

"Why didn't Dad just tell us that?" Faith asked, frowning.

"Because he knew the two of you," Eve said as she rose to take her plate to the sink. "You'd have gone over there just to see if the boys were really dangerous."

"Well," McKenna said with a sigh, "it's just an old, empty house now that Ellis Harper has died. But there's forty acres with a creek, trees, a barn and some outbuildings. It's exactly what I'm looking for and it's adjacent to our ranch land to the east."

Eve shook her head, worry in her gaze. "I think you're making a mistake, but I know how you are once you've made up your mind."

"I'm just like you," McKenna said with a grin.

Eve nodded. "That's what worries me."

Chapter Three

McKenna called her Realtor friend right after breakfast to find out what she knew about Harper House.

"You heard about the auction? Minimum bid is what is owed in back taxes, but I don't expect it to go much higher than that given the condition of the house. It's really a white elephant. Why don't you let me show you some houses that don't need so much work?"

"Don't try to talk me out of it," McKenna said with a laugh. It amazed her that April sold anything the way she always tried to discourage buyers. "If the price doesn't go too high, I intend to buy it."

She had worked all through college, saving the money her parents and Eve had sent her. She also had money from a savings account her grandma Nina Mae Cross had started for her when she was adopted into the family.

"With auctions, you just never know," April said. "But I can't imagine there would be that many people interested in the place. The property isn't bad, though. The fences are in pretty good shape, and it does border your family ranch, so that is definitely a plus. The barn needs a new roof. But you might want to just tear down the house and build something smaller on the land."

McKenna couldn't imagine doing that. Something about that house had always interested her. She had just hung up when her cell phone rang.

"Have I got *good* news for you," a female voice said.

She was about to hang up, thinking it was someone trying to sell her something, when she recognized the voice. *"Arlene?"*

"Who else?" Arlene Evans let out one of her braying laughs. She was a gangly, raw-boned ranch woman who'd had her share of problems over the last year or so, including her husband leaving her alone with two grown children still living at home and her oldest daughter in the state mental hospital.

McKenna had signed up for Arlene's rural online dating service at a weak moment—following a wedding and some champagne. She now regretted it greatly.

It wasn't a man she needed but the courage to do what she'd always wanted: start a horse ranch. She'd loved paint horses from the first time she'd seen one. Descended from horses introduced by the Spanish conquistadors, paints were part of the herds of wild horses that once roamed these very plains.

With paints becoming popular with cowboys for cattle work, McKenna believed she could make a good living raising them. *If* she could get the Harper property for the right price at the auction Saturday. It was all she could think about.

"I've found you just the man," Arlene gushed. "He's perfect for you. I hear wedding bells already."

"Slow down," McKenna said, wishing she'd read the small print to see how she could get out of this.

"He's handsome, a hard worker, loves horses and long walks and…did I mention he's handsome?" Arlene laughed again, making McKenna wince. "He's going to be out of the cell phone service area until Saturday night, so he'll meet you at Northern Lights restaurant at seven. You're going to thank me for this."

McKenna groaned inwardly. There was no backing out at this late date, especially since calling him sounded like it was out of the question. But suddenly she was more than a little afraid to find out who Arlene Evans thought was her perfect man.

She only half listened to Arlene rattle on about the man as she thought of the auction and her plans for the future: a man was the last thing on her mind.

It wasn't until after she'd hung up that she realized she hadn't caught her date's name. Great. She thought about calling Arlene back but didn't want to put herself through another twenty minutes of hearing about how perfect this guy was for her.

In a town the size of Whitehorse, spotting the man should be easy enough at the restaurant Saturday evening.

McKenna quickly forgot about her date. The house would be open for viewing before the auction, but she couldn't wait. She had to take another look at the place, and this might be her only chance to spend a little time there alone.

ARLENE EVANS GLANCED away from her computer screen to see her daughter Charlotte sprawled on the couch.

Just moments before that Arlene had been feeling pretty good. Her internet rural dating service had taken off. Several of the matches she'd made had led to the altar. She'd always known she had a knack for this, even if she'd failed miserably with her own children.

For years she'd tried to find someone for her oldest daughter, Violet—with no luck at all. A lot of that was Violet's doing, she had to admit now. Violet was crazy—and dangerous—so no wonder no man had wanted to take that on.

Now Violet was locked up in a mental institution— hopefully never to be released, if Arlene had anything to do with it.

Bo, Arlene's only son, had been engaged to Maddie Cavanaugh. The two had been all wrong for each other from the beginning. Unfortunately, since the breakup, though, Bo hadn't shown any interest in finding himself a good woman to spend the rest of his life with. In fact, when Arlene had offered to line him up with one of her clients, he'd told her it would be over his dead body. It broke her heart, since Bo had always been her favorite.

And then there was Charlotte, the daughter that Arlene had thought would never have any trouble finding a husband.

Arlene scowled as she studied her youngest child— and Charlotte's huge protruding belly. For months Arlene had been trying to find out who had fathered the baby now growing inside her daughter. The baby was due next month, and Arlene was no closer to discovering the name of the father than she'd been when she'd found out about the pregnancy.

Charlotte took perverse pleasure in keeping it a secret. *If* her daughter even knew, Arlene thought with a silent curse. Other mothers considered their children blessings. Arlene had come to see hers as a curse.

Not for the first time, Arlene saw a silver SUV drive past. She couldn't see the driver, not with the glint of the June sun on the darkened side window, but she had the impression it was a woman behind the wheel.

Arlene frowned, trying to remember how many other times she'd seen the vehicle. Strange, since not much traffic ever came down this road. She put it out of her mind. She had a lot more important things to worry about.

When she turned back to her computer, she was surprised to see that she had a potential new client. She completely forgot about the silver SUV as she clicked on the man's email and felt a small thrill that had nothing to do with success or money.

Since my wife died, I find myself deeply needing the company of an interesting woman. I want someone who would like to travel the world with me. Someone who wants to share my final years.

Travel the world. What woman wouldn't want to do that with an attractive older man? A man only a little older than Arlene herself.

She emailed Hank Monroe back, promising to find him the perfect woman and set up a time to meet.

BEHIND HARPER HOUSE, Nate Dempsey leaned on his shovel to rest for a moment and listened to the sound of the wind in the trees. A hot, dry wind that made his skin ache. The years must have distorted his memory. He'd been so sure he was digging in the right place.

But the land looked different than he remembered, and it had been a long time ago.

He began to dig again, turning over one shovelful of dirt after another, trying to gauge how deep the body would have been buried.

As he dug, he tried not to think about that hot summer night. Not the sounds he'd heard. Nor the fear he'd felt knowing he could be next. What he hadn't known was who they were burying out back. He didn't know that until the next morning. Until it was too late.

The heat bore down on him. He stopped digging for a moment to look up at the blue wind-scoured sky overhead and catch his breath. Standing there, it was impossible not to think of the past. Had a day gone by that he hadn't remembered this place?

He'd spent years looking over his shoulder, knowing whose face he would see that instant before he felt the blade. But now he was no longer that skinny, scared boy. Nor was he a man willing to run from his past any longer. It would end here.

He began to dig again. Had it really been twenty-one years since he'd left this godforsaken place? Coming back here, it felt as if it had only been yesterday.

His shovel hit something that made the blade ring. He shuddered at the sound as he looked down, expecting to see bones. Just a rock. No body buried here.

He stopped again, this time the skin on the back of his neck prickling. As he had earlier, he felt someone was watching him. Carrying the shovel with him, he strode back to the house and stripped off his shirt to use it to wipe the sweat from his eyes.

For a moment he stood at the back door, surveying the land behind the house, the tall, old cottonwoods that followed the creek bed, the weather-beaten barn and outbuildings, the rolling grassy hillsides.

He couldn't see anyone, but that didn't mean Roy Vaughn wasn't there. He was the man Nate had to fear now, just as he had as a boy.

Stepping inside, he turned on the faucet at the old

kitchen sink, letting the water run until it came up icy cold, all the time watching out the window. He could almost convince himself he'd only imagined that someone was watching him.

Discarding his shirt, he scooped up handfuls of water, drinking them down greedily. Johnny's remains were out there somewhere. With all his heart he wished it wasn't true. That Johnny had run away, just as he'd been told. But he knew better. Johnny would have come back for him if he'd gotten away. Johnny wouldn't have left him at Harper House. Not when Johnny had known how dangerous the place was for Nate.

As he turned off the faucet and wiped his wet hands on his jeans, he gazed out the back window again.

Ellis Harper hadn't let anyone near the house in years. That meant no one else would have had a chance to dig up the body and hide it, right? He'd come as soon as he'd learned of Harper's death. But had he come too late?

Bare-chested, he went back out and began to dig again in a different spot, the heat growing more intense. He dug down deep enough, turning over a final shovelful of dirt, and looked down into the hole seeing nothing but more earth.

This was the area where he'd thought they'd buried the body. He'd stake his life on it. Hell, he *was* staking his life on it.

There was just one problem.

The body was gone. If it had ever been here.

CRICKETS CHIRPED IN the tall grass as McKenna dismounted, loosely tied her horse and slipped between the logs of the jack fence.

The grass brushed her jeans, making a swishing

sound as she moved through it toward the house. She listened for the sound of a rattlesnake, telling herself not only was she trespassing but her father could have been right about the dangers—including snakes.

A stiff breeze at the edge of the house banged a loose shutter and whipped her hair into her face. She stopped to look around for a moment, feeling as if she was being watched. But there was no vehicle parked in the drive. No sign that anyone had been here in a very long time.

She tried the screen door on the front porch first. The door groaned open. The wind caught it, jerked the handle from her fingers and slammed the door against the wall.

McKenna thought she heard an accompanying thud from inside the house, as if someone had bumped into something. She froze, imagining Ellis Harper coming out with a shotgun. But Ellis was dead. And she didn't believe in ghosts, right? *"Hello?"*

No answer.

"Hello?" she called a little louder.

Another thud, this one deeper in the house. She stepped to the front door, knocked and, receiving no answer, cupped her hands to peer through the window next to the door.

The house was empty except for dust. That's why the recent footprints caught her attention. The tracks were male-size boot soles. Someone from the county would have been out to check the house before the auction, she told herself.

The tracks led into the kitchen at the back. What she saw leaning by the back door made her reconsider going inside. A shovel, fresh dirt caked on it, stood against the wall. Next to it was a plaid shirt where someone had dropped it on the floor.

Her horse whinnied over at the fence. Another horse whinnied back, the sound coming from behind the house.

Someone was here.

Not someone from the county, who would have driven out and parked in front. Someone who'd come by horseback. Someone who didn't want to be seen? Just like her?

Ellis Harper's funeral had been earlier this week. Anyone who read the paper would know the house was empty.

But why would that person be digging?

She retreated as quietly as possible across the porch and down the steps. As she angled back toward where she'd left her horse, she glanced behind the house.

There appeared to be several areas on the hillside where the earth had been freshly turned. She hadn't noticed it earlier; all her attention had been on the house. As she reached the fence and quickly slipped through, her horse whinnied again. The mare's whinny was answered, drawing McKenna's gaze to the hillside beyond the barn in time to see a rider on a gray Appaloosa horse.

From this distance she could see that the rider was a man. He was shirtless, no doubt because he'd left his plaid shirt in the house where he'd discarded it along with the shovel.

She caught only a glimpse of him, his head covered by a Western straw hat, as he topped the hill and disappeared as if in a hurry to get away.

She wondered who he was. Obviously someone who wasn't supposed to be here—just like herself. She hadn't gotten a good enough look at him and knew she wouldn't be able to recognize him if she saw him again, but she would his horse. It was a spotted Appaloosa, the ugliest coloring she'd ever seen—and that was saying a lot.

As she swung up into her saddle, she couldn't help but wonder what the man had been digging for—and if he'd found it.

ARLENE CALLED HANK MONROE to confirm their appointment to sign him up for her rural dating service before she headed into Whitehorse. The first thing that had struck her was his voice. It was deep and soft and sent a small thrill through her. Had any man's voice ever done that before? Not that she could remember—but then, she was no spring chicken anymore.

She knew she was setting herself up for disappointment. The man couldn't be as good as he sounded either in his email or on the phone.

"I'm looking forward to meeting you," he'd said. "I have to confess, I've never done anything like this before. You know, dating online. The way my generation did it was gazes across a crowded room. I'm a little nervous."

She'd assured him there was nothing to it.

But Arlene was nervous herself when she reached the Hi-Line Café where they'd agreed to meet.

The moment she walked in and spotted Hank Monroe sitting at one of the booths her heart began to pound wildly. Never in her life had she experienced such a reaction.

She'd been pregnant with Violet when she married Floyd Evans. It had been the result of a one-night stand.

She'd said she was on the Pill so he wouldn't take her right home. Floyd had been good-looking and popular, and she'd thought she could fall in love with him—and him with her if he'd give her a chance.

She'd also erroneously thought that she wouldn't get pregnant.

She'd been wrong on all counts.

But when she'd discovered she was pregnant, Floyd had seemed as good a bet as anyone. He had a farm down in Old Town Whitehorse and, while reluctant, he had agreed at the urging of his parents to stand up and accept his responsibilities.

She'd known she was no looker. It was one reason she'd learned to cook at an early age. She'd realized she needed more to offer than other girls. She'd thought her cooking and cleaning would make Floyd fall in love with her. She'd still dreamed of the happily-ever-after romance she hadn't found with Floyd or any other boy.

She'd been only seventeen when she and Floyd had married. He'd been twenty-eight. Now, at fifty-one, Arlene had long ago given up on love, let alone romance.

Hank Monroe looked up just then. He wasn't handsome, not by anyone's standards, but there was something about him that had her pulse pounding as she made her way to his booth.

"Arlene?" he asked hopefully as he got to his big feet.

She could only nod and smile. "You must be Hank."

He nodded with a laugh that resembled a donkey's bray. She laughed then, too, and they exchanged a look that made Arlene feel seventeen again.

"I like your laugh," he said and grinned.

By the time she had him signed up for her dating service she had a date with him for Saturday night and was on her way to buy herself something special to wear.

She couldn't remember the last time she'd been this excited. But at the back of her mind she heard her mother's nagging voice warning her that this feeling wouldn't last. It couldn't. Because Arlene didn't deserve to be happy.

HAD VIOLET EVANS known what her mother was feeling at that moment, she would have joined her deceased grandmother in warning Arlene not to count on a future—let alone a happy one.

If Violet had her way, her mother wouldn't be around long. And from what the doctors were saying at the mental hospital, it looked as if Violet was going to get her way.

And not even Arlene—who'd seen through Violet's ruse—could stop her. In fact, Arlene Evans might be the only person alive who knew how sick—and dangerous— her daughter really was.

But while Violet hadn't fooled her mother, she *had* fooled her doctors. As Violet sat next to the window and looked over the hospital grounds, she could almost taste freedom. It wouldn't be long now. She'd played her role perfectly. All those case histories of psychosis had given her the script. Now she was nearing the final act, the one that would get her released.

It didn't surprise her that her mother was fighting her release. Arlene knew what Violet was capable of and, worse, had an inkling of what she *would* do once she got out of this place. Violet's great sin, she believed, was that she'd shamed her mother by not being marriageable.

She'd been born unattractive and hadn't grown out of it. Even her mother—who Violet resembled—had snagged a man. Arlene's endless attempts at marrying her off had only made matters worse. Violet hated her for it. Hated that she'd taken after her mother, unlike her two siblings.

"Violet? Is everything all right?"

She turned to find her doctor watching her closely, a slight frown on his face.

"I was just thinking about some of the awful things my mother said I did," she covered quickly as she realized he'd seen her true feelings when he'd walked up on her.

She really had to be more careful.

He sat down beside her. He was a small man with small hands. "Does that make you angry?"

"Only with myself," she said piously. She'd worked so hard to hide what was really going on inside her. She would have to remember not to think about her mother.

"I am getting better, aren't I, Dr. Armond?" she asked pleadingly.

"Yes, Violet. I am very pleased with your prognosis. Very pleased. In fact, that was one reason I came to find you." He paused and smiled. "I'm recommending your release."

Violet's heart leaped. "Oh, Dr. Armond. Are you sure I'm ready?"

"Yes, Violet. I'll recommend some outpatient visits, of course, but there is no reason you can't be an active member of society again. I'd hoped you would be excited."

"Oh, I am. I can't wait. To think that I have my whole life ahead of me…" Her eyes brimmed with tears and he covered her hand with his.

"I'm so glad to hear that because I've set your release for next month."

Next month? She'd been planning on getting out sooner than that. What was wrong with the stupid old quack?

She was careful not to let her disappointment or her anger show. She tried to calm herself. What was another thirty days here? Nothing compared to what she'd been through. But it still felt like a lifetime, she was so anxious to get out.

"I wanted you to have enough time to prepare for re-entering that world," he was saying. "I think it would be unhealthy for you to return to your mother's home given the way she feels, don't you?"

"Yes."

"I thought you could prepare by working here in the hospital office. You'll also need income. I'll help you put together a résumé for when you're released."

The imbecile. She wasn't going to need a job when she got out. "That is so kind of you," she said. "How can I ever thank you?" She could think of several ways she'd like to thank him, all of them involving his pain.

"You being well and getting on with your life will be thanks enough," he said as he removed his hand from hers and rose to leave. "I want you to be a survivor, Violet."

She nodded and smiled. "I intend to be." She couldn't say the same for her mother and the others who had made her life a living hell.

She tried not to shudder at the thought of the mediocre life she would have on the outside if it was up to these doctors. Some dismal job, a cramped apartment, several cats and nothing to look forward to at night but television and a frozen cheesecake.

A woman as smart as she was? Not a chance. She'd

been foolish in the past. She'd let them catch her. She wouldn't make that mistake again.

She thought about her mother's face when she saw her oldest daughter again. Payback was a bitch, she thought with a secret smile as she looked out the window.

Thirty days. And counting.

Chapter Four

The auction was held in front of the Harper House on a bright blue-sky June day. Someone had mowed part of the weeds in the front yard the night before. The air smelled of fresh-mown grass and dust from the county road out front.

As McKenna mounted the steps to the open front door, she saw that the footprints she'd seen yesterday evening in the thick layer of dust had been trampled by the half dozen people who'd traipsed through the house this morning.

April had been right. The house needed work. But that wasn't what surprised McKenna. She'd always been enthralled by the house. She'd just assumed she would feel the same once inside. The interior had a dark, cold feel even with the warm sun shining through the dirty windows, and she found herself shivering as she walked through the rooms.

She noticed the shovel and shirt she'd seen by the back door yesterday were gone. On the third floor, when she looked out a small back window, she couldn't see the places where the man had dug. They'd apparently been covered with cut weeds. Had she not caught the man in the act yesterday, she would never have guessed anyone had been digging on the hillside.

It still made her wonder what he might have been looking for, but she turned her attention to the house as she wandered from room to room, trying to imagine herself living here. It was hard given the condition of the house. It would take days just to clean, let alone paint. She knew exactly what her sister Eve would say.

Raze the house and start over.

McKenna had heard several such comments from the other people who had gathered for the auction.

"There's a nice building spot upon the hill once the house is gone," she'd heard one man say.

But the rooms were spacious, and she told herself once the house was cleaned up, painted and furnished she could be happy here. Anyway, the house was the reason she'd always wanted the place, wasn't it?

At one fifty-five she gathered with the others in the front yard as the auctioneer climbed the porch steps and cleared his throat to quiet the small crowd.

McKenna glanced at the group around her, surprised that some of the people who'd toured the house earlier had left. Just curiosity seekers. She recognized only one elderly man and his wife, Edgar and Ethel Winthrop. The couple lived about two miles to the north. McKenna was surprised they'd stayed, since she doubted they would be bidding on the place.

She didn't recognize any of the others waiting. Three of the men appeared to be in their early thirties; the fourth man, in his forties, was on a cell phone. She figured he was here bidding for an investor and turned her attention to the other three men.

One, clearly a local rancher, wore a Mint Bar cap,

a worn canvas coat and work boots, and had a tooth-pick sticking out the side of his mouth. The second was dressed in a dinosaur T-shirt, jeans and athletic shoes. The third man wore jeans, cowboy boots, a Western shirt and a gray Stetson.

As the auctioneer described the property and the county auction requirements, she saw another man, one she hadn't noticed before. He'd parked on the county road some distance from the proceedings and now stood, his arms crossed over his chest as he leaned against the front of his pickup truck, his battered Western straw hat pulled low against the sun.

He'd obviously just come to watch. He was dressed in work boots, jeans and a white T-shirt that called attention to his tanned, muscular arms. There was a toolbox in the back of his truck and a construction logo of some kind on the cab, but she couldn't make out the name from where she stood.

"If everyone's ready, let's begin," the auctioneer said, drawing her attention back to the front.

The cowboy glanced over at her as the auctioneer began the bidding. He was good-looking enough to make her do a double take.

"I can't believe anyone would buy that house," Ethel Winthrop whispered behind McKenna.

"Not everyone cares about a house's history, Ethel," her husband whispered back.

"Who would like to start the bidding?" the auctioneer inquired.

When no one responded, the auctioneer started the bid high and had to drop the price when there were no takers.

McKenna waited as the man on the cell phone bid

along with dinosaur-shirt man and the local rancher. The cowboy hadn't bid either, she noticed, apparently waiting as she was. Or maybe he'd just come to watch.

As the price rose, the man on the cell phone quit bidding and left. It had come down between the rancher and dino-shirt man when the cowboy jumped in. McKenna feared the men were going to drive the price up too high for her.

The rancher quit. It was down to the cowboy and the dino-shirt man when McKenna finally bid.

The cowboy shot her a look and raised her bid.

She bid two more times, dino-shirt dropping out, so it was just her and the cowboy. One look into his dark eyes and she realized he was enjoying himself—at her expense.

"The young woman has the bid," the auctioneer said after they'd gone back and forth.

Time seemed to stop, and then the cowboy tipped his hat, his dark eyes flashing. "It's the lady's."

McKenna couldn't believe it.

The auctioneer closed the bidding. Edgar Winthrop stepped up to congratulate her and ask her what she planned to do with the house as the remainder of the small group dispersed.

"I'm going to live here," she said and saw his wife's expression.

"Not alone, I hope," she said.

"Ethel," the husband said in a warning tone.

"Edgar, she should know about that house," the elderly woman insisted. "If she moves in and then finds out…"

The husband took his wife's arm. "You'll have to excuse my wife. All houses have a history, Ethel." He smiled at McKenna. "I wouldn't concern yourself with local gossip. What's past is past, right?"

McKenna smiled, too excited to care about the house's history. Anyway, she figured the woman was referring to the troubled boys who'd lived on the place when she was a girl. They couldn't have been any worse than she and her sisters.

"Congratulations, I'm sure it will make you a fine home," Edgar said.

"I'm sure it will, too," she agreed.

He tugged at his wife's elbow, but Ethel grabbed McKenna's sleeve. "If you need us, we live up that way as the crow flies." She pointed north.

"Thank you," McKenna said as Edgar Winthrop took his wife's hand and led her toward their car.

"You remember what I said," Ethel called over her shoulder.

"I will, thank you." She turned, looking for the cowboy who'd given up the bid to her, but he'd apparently left right away.

As she moved up to the porch to take care of the paperwork, she noticed the man who'd parked on the road and watched from a distance also leaving. While she couldn't see his face in the shadow of his Western straw hat, she had the impression he was upset.

If Nate Dempsey had been superstitious, he would have gotten the hell out of Whitehorse the moment he'd seen the blonde cowgirl again.

When he'd seen her in the small crowd that had gathered for the auction, he'd hoped she was here out of curiosity and nothing more. Ultimately he'd hoped that no one would bid on Harper House or that the minimum bid would be too high and that the house would remain empty just long enough for him to finish what he'd come here to do.

But that hope had been shot to hell the moment the young blonde began to bid. He'd seen her interest in the house when she'd come around the place before.

When she kept bidding, he knew she was determined to have Harper House.

When the dust settled, the bidding done, the blonde had the house. McKenna Bailey. He'd discovered he'd been right about her living nearby. Her family owned the ranch adjacent to the property. The Bailey girls, as they were known in these parts, had a reputation for being rough-and-tumble cowgirls with a streak of independence that ran as deep as their mule-headedness.

McKenna Bailey had proven that today.

Not the kind of woman who would be easily intimidated.

But as he drove away from Harper House he knew he had to find a way to make sure McKenna Bailey didn't get in his way. He'd waited so long to end this, and now she had unknowingly put herself in the middle of more trouble than she could imagine.

He cursed the way his luck was going as he raced north toward the small Western town, ruing the day he'd ever laid eyes on Whitehorse, Montana—and McKenna Bailey.

BY THAT EVENING McKenna was actually in the mood for a date—even a blind one—as she walked into Northern Lights restaurant. She was still floating on air from the excitement of her purchase earlier that afternoon, although she hadn't had much time to look the place over after signing all the papers.

She couldn't wait to take her horse out and ride her property.

Northern Lights restaurant had been opened just before Christmas by McKenna's friend Laci Cavanaugh and her fiancé, Bridger Duvall. It was *the* place to eat in Whitehorse. The fact that her date had chosen it gave McKenna hope.

She was instantly disappointed, though, when she was told by a young waitress she didn't know that Laci wasn't working tonight and that Bridger was swamped back in the kitchen.

"Are you dining alone?" the waitress asked.

She certainly hoped not. As she glanced around the restaurant, she spotted a lone male sitting off in one corner. He raised his head and got to his feet when he saw her.

He was the good-looking cowboy who'd bid against her at the auction earlier that day. Just her luck. And his.

"Small world, huh?" he said with an ironic smile.

This was her *date*? She remembered the way he'd tipped his hat to her when he quit bidding. She was pretty sure that had been anger she'd seen in his dark eyes.

"You look like you could use a drink. I know I could." He motioned to the waitress before turning back to McKenna. "What'll you have? Hell, you probably want champagne to celebrate, don't you? Give us a bottle of your best."

The waitress took off before McKenna could stop her. The last thing she wanted to do was have dinner with this man, let alone celebrate with him.

He held out his hand. "Flynn Garrett."

His hand swallowed hers. "McKenna—"

"Bailey," he finished for her. "Yeah, I know." His smile broadened as he seemed to take her in. "The woman who bought herself a house and forty acres today. No hard feelings. You won fair and square. So let's celebrate."

He pulled out a chair for her and waited.

She tried to think of a good reason to break the date, but then the champagne arrived and she found herself taking a seat as the cork was popped and Flynn made a show of pouring them each a glass.

"To you, Miss Bailey," he said, tapping his glass against hers.

His dark eyes never left hers as he took a sip. "Hmm, not bad," he said, although she was almost positive he would have rather had another beer like the one he'd been nursing when she'd arrived.

She tried to relax. Blind dates were nerve-racking enough without her ending up having dinner with the man she'd outbid. A very handsome man, she might add.

"You're a tough woman to beat at her own game," he said, his gaze hard to read. She'd put her money on him still being angry. She'd bet he was the kind of man who didn't like to lose.

"If it makes you feel any better, you drove the bid up so high I have very little money left for improvements."

He appeared shocked. "You aren't considering doing anything with that house?"

"Yes. Why?" She watched the way he nervously took a drink of his champagne. "What had *you* planned to do with it?"

"Burn it down."

Now it was her turn to be shocked. "You aren't serious."

"I just wanted the land. The house is in such bad shape…" He frowned. "Sorry, I'm sure you don't want to hear that."

"It needs work, I'll admit, but structurally—"

"You planning to do the work yourself?"

She bristled. "I'll have you know I'm capable of doing just about anything I set my mind to."

He nodded slowly, eyeing her with an intensity that made her a little nervous. "I bet you are."

The waitress brought the menus and he disappeared behind his. McKenna told herself that he was still angry with her for outbidding him and that he wouldn't have bid so high if he hadn't wanted the house as well as the land. What he said about the condition of the house was just sour grapes.

"How are the steaks here?" he asked over the top of his menu. His eyes were almost black. "You look like a woman who could handle a steak." He put down his menu as the waitress appeared and grinned at McKenna. "Am I wrong?"

She ordered a rib eye, rare, which made him chuckle. He ordered the largest T-bone the restaurant served, also rare.

"So tell me about McKenna Bailey," he said, leaning forward to rest his forearms on the table, those dark eyes intent on her again.

"And bore you to tears?"

He shook his head. "There is nothing boring about you, and we both know it. Why Whitehorse? Come on, I really want to know."

"I was born and raised here."

His eyebrow shot up. "No kidding."

"Well, that's somewhat true," she amended with a smile. "I was adopted when I was born. My adopted family lives in Old Town Whitehorse. That's where I grew up."

"You're adopted?" That seemed to interest him.

"I didn't find out until recently."

"No one told you?"

She shook her head. "If you knew my adoptive mother, that would make sense to you. She said the moment she laid eyes on my sisters and me we were hers and nobody else's, and that's why she didn't tell us. Lila Bailey Jackson is a very strong, determined woman."

"Like her daughter." He took a sip of his champagne, then frowned. "Lila Bailey *Jackson*?"

"She recently married Loren Jackson. It's a long story, but apparently they were in love for years."

"Jackson," he repeated softly. "Like the sheriff?" He refilled her glass. She hadn't realized she'd emptied it already. Nerves.

"The sheriff is Loren's son and my sister Eve's fiancé. It's a small town," she added with a laugh and realized she was starting to enjoy herself. And why shouldn't she? She did have something to celebrate, and her date was just as handsome as Arlene had said.

She hadn't dated all that much, too busy between school and a job working for a local veterinarian in Bozeman while she'd attended Montana State University. It felt good to be in the company of an attractive cowboy.

"So tell me about you."

He shrugged. "Not much to tell. Raised on a ranch, like you."

Had she told him she was raised on a ranch? She couldn't remember.

"I've worked all over, wrangling and doing odd jobs. Once you turn thirty you can't help but think about planting roots. Not too deep, though," he quickly amended. "I like being a free spirit. When I leave here I'm thinking of going to South America. Like Butch Cassidy and the Sundance Kid. You know, they robbed a train up here right before they went to South America."

Allegedly. But she didn't tell him that. She knew Flynn Garrett's type. He liked to think of himself as an outlaw. He'd used his looks to get him through life, always taking the path of least resistance. She'd dated a few boys like him in college. They were fun. At least for a while.

"So why did you bid on the old Harper place?" she asked and took a drink of her champagne. She might as well celebrate because she'd just bought herself a house and forty acres.

He shrugged in answer. "I like competition."

She eyed him over the rim of her champagne glass. Yeah? But he wasn't as good at losing as he was at pretending, she thought. The question was: had he wanted Harper House or did he just not want anyone else to have it?

"What will you do now?" she asked.

"I don't know. You've forced me to change my plans." He smiled at her as if he thought he could con her into thinking she owed him. Not likely.

"Sorry," she said with a grin, "but I've always wanted that place."

"Really? Why?"

She shook her head. "I wish I knew."

Flynn seemed lost in thought for a long moment, and she wondered if he understood the pull of Harper House more than he was admitting.

She felt a kinship with him because of the house. It was odd. She'd just met him earlier today and yet it was as if she'd known him a lot longer. Which made this date a little sad, since she didn't think she would be going out with him again.

Flynn poured them both more champagne, emptying the bottle. "Don't worry about me," he said as if there hadn't been a lag in the conversation. "I'm a man who always lands on his feet, one way or another. Meanwhile, I'm having dinner with a beautiful, fascinating woman." His expression was so intense she was glad that the waitress appeared with their salads.

The conversation turned to horses during dinner and that awkward moment passed. McKenna realized that he'd either guessed about her love of horses or someone had told him. But then, that would mean that he'd asked around about her. Arlene. How had McKenna forgotten that Arlene had set this up?

She recalled how Arlene had been so confident this man would be perfect for her. She really should cancel her membership in Arlene's dating service first thing in the morning. If only she'd read the contract more closely.

The evening passed quickly, and suddenly they were at that uncomfortable end of the date where he walked her out to her pickup and she feared he would kiss her.

And feared he wouldn't.

His kiss was nice. Soft, sweet, tentative. What surprised her was that she sensed a vulnerability in him when he kissed her that he'd kept well hidden in the time she'd been around him. Flynn Garrett didn't have it all together as much as he wanted everyone to believe.

He drew back from the kiss, and she was surprised to see regret in his gaze. As he turned and walked away, she could only assume she wouldn't be seeing him again.

Chapter Five

The ringing of her cell phone wrenched McKenna out of a terrifying dream in which she was running for her life.

She jerked up in the bed, her heart pounding, her nightshirt stuck to her skin with sweat.

"Hello?"

"McKenna, I wanted to catch you before you took off this morning."

She glanced at the clock. It wasn't even six o'clock. *"Arlene?"* If she was calling to see how McKenna's date had gone—

"I didn't want you to feel bad about what happened last night. These things happen, although I *was* surprised. He seemed like such a nice young man. And he was so interested in you I couldn't imagine why he'd cancel."

"What?" She was still caught in the dream; danger hunkered in the room like dense fog, making everything seem surreal.

"I just feel bad because I couldn't get hold of you to tell you. I tried your cell. You must have had it turned off. And when I called the restaurant to give you a heads-up—"

"Arlene, what are you talking about?"

"Your date last night. I just hate that he stood you up, but I have someone else who I think—"

"Wait a minute." McKenna sat up straighter and rubbed her free hand over her face as she tried to make sense of what Arlene was saying. "I wasn't stood up."

"You mean he changed his mind and met you at the restaurant after all?" Arlene let out a relieved laugh. "Good, I wasn't wrong about him. I told you Nate Dempsey was perfect for you. I'm so glad he showed up. I do wish he'd let me know, though. If he'd read the dating service agreement, he'd have—"

"Nate Dempsey?" McKenna repeated.

"Your *date*." Arlene laughed. "It must have been some night if you don't remember his name."

Arlene was mixed up. McKenna regretted the day she'd signed up for the online dating service.

"Arlene, my date was with *Flynn Garrett*. Not anyone named Nate Dempsey."

Silence. An anomaly for Arlene.

McKenna felt her first sense of unease. "My date *was* with Flynn, right?"

"I've never heard of a Flynn Garrett," Arlene said at last. *"Who* did you have dinner with last night?" she asked, sounding horrified.

It was too early in the morning for this. "Arlene, I have to go." McKenna hung up and replayed the scene at the restaurant. She'd just assumed that Flynn was her date. Now that she thought about it, he'd never mentioned the online dating service—and neither had she.

She felt a little foolish. But, then again, no harm had been done. She'd enjoyed dinner and Flynn Garrett.

Unfortunately, she couldn't help but wonder who this Nate Dempsey was. And why he'd canceled his date with her at the last minute. Arlene said he'd been "so interested" in her?

Not that it mattered, she thought as she gave up on returning to sleep and headed for the shower in an attempt to throw off the remnants of the nightmare she'd been having before Arlene's phone call. Her legs felt weak as if she really had been running for her life. The dream emerged again. She had a flash of Harper House. It had been dark in the dream. She'd been running away from the house, she thought with a chill, because someone had been chasing her.

Turning on the shower, she climbed under the spray, determined to forget the nightmare. She had a big day ahead of her. Once she had the house cleaned she could start painting. She was anxious to get her horses on the property and get moved in.

Her sister Faith was still asleep, and Eve was over at her own house this morning as McKenna left. She drove through Old Town Whitehorse—what was left of it, which was only a few buildings.

Old Town was the first settlement of Whitehorse. It had been nearer the Missouri River, in the country McKenna had grown up in. But when the railroad came through in the 1800s, most of the town migrated five miles north, taking the name with it.

The original settlement of Whitehorse was now little more than a ghost town except for a handful of buildings, including the community center and the one-room schoolhouse, in the area now referred to as Old Town.

The Baileys had been one of the first families, along with the Cavanaughs and the Jacksons, to settle in the original Whitehorse. That was one reason McKenna had wanted to buy closer to her family's ranch. This was where her history was. By buying the Harper property she would be continuing a tradition around Old Town.

She was thinking about that—and the roots she would be putting down—when she parked her truck across the street from the hardware store. As she got out of her pickup, she heard the train pull in.

The tracks were just across a small town park. Today it was the Amtrak passenger train coming through, the only line in the state that provided service as far west as Seattle or east to Chicago.

As the train slowed to a stop to pick up several waiting passengers, McKenna heard a horse whinny and turned to see a truck and horse trailer a few vehicles ahead of hers. Nothing unusual about seeing horses in trailers on the main street in this part of Montana.

What caught her eye was the horse sticking his head out the side of the trailer. It was a spotted Appaloosa, and even before she walked over to get a closer look she knew she'd seen this horse before—and where.

"I wouldn't do that if I were you," said a deep male voice behind her. "Old Blue is pretty temperamental."

She pulled her hand back from the horse's neck and turned. From behind her, the Appaloosa nuzzled her shoulder and snuffled her hair.

"That's odd—he usually doesn't take to strangers," the man said with a shake of his head and a wry smile. He rested his hands on his jean-clad hips and eyed her from under the brim of his straw hat.

"I have a way with horses," she said after her initial shock had passed at recognizing him as well as the horse.

"I can see that." He was the man she'd seen parked on the road at the auction, the one who'd been standing back, leaning against his pickup, watching from a distance.

She'd taken him for a construction worker when she'd seen him at the auction because of the logo on his truck, she recalled. The night before that, when she'd seen him ride over the hill behind Harper House on this Appaloosa, she'd taken him for a trespasser like herself.

Now she was more than a little curious about his interest in her house and why he'd been digging the evening before the auction on what was now her property.

"The first time I saw this horse I knew I would recognize him if I ever saw him again." She chuckled. "Imagine my surprise at seeing him again. And *you*."

"I guess it's a small world," he said, smiling back at her.

"Not *that* small." She glanced at the Montana license plate on the back of his pickup. Park County. He was a long way from home. Taking a step back, she craned her neck to see the logo on the side of his truck.

Dempsey Construction.

No wonder she'd thought he worked construction.

Dempsey?

Her gaze shot back to the man. "*Nate* Dempsey?" She couldn't believe this. *This* was the man Arlene thought would be perfect for her?

He wasn't nearly as good-looking as Flynn Garrett, although he was nicely built, tall with slim hips and muscular broad shoulders. His eyes were a warm, rich brown, and his hair that curled at the nape of his neck under his Western straw hat was a darker blond than her own.

Lantern-jawed, his features were rugged and rough, like a man who'd been in his share of fistfights. But when he smiled, well, there was something about him that made her heart beat a little faster.

"I'm McKenna Bailey," she said. "The woman you stood up last night."

At least he had the good grace to look sheepish. "I can explain about that."

She cocked her head and crossed her arms over her chest. "This ought to be good."

NATE CURSED HIMSELF for making the date. At the time he'd thought it necessary to find out how much of a threat McKenna Bailey might be, and Arlene Evans had been a wealth of information about McKenna and the Baileys.

But after he'd seen McKenna at the auction yesterday the date hadn't been necessary. In fact, he'd felt the date would be dangerous. He hadn't wanted her to know who he was. Let alone what he was doing in Whitehorse.

Now, though, he saw that standing her up had been a mistake.

McKenna Bailey was everything he'd heard she was—and more. She was trouble in a pair of slim-fitting jeans and boots. And if he wasn't careful, she would get him killed.

"I didn't stand you up," he said. "Not exactly," he added quickly. "I called Arlene and told her I couldn't make it because I was running so late, then I realized after I hung up that you would already be at the restaurant. So I dropped everything and hurried into town, but then I saw you having dinner with some other man…" He shrugged, amazed how easily lying came back to him.

"I thought he *was* my date," she said, looking a little less angry.

"I can see where you could mix us up, especially if his name was Nate Dempsey, too."

She flushed. "I forgot to get a name from Arlene when she told me about the date. I just assumed since this other man was at the restaurant alone..." She groaned, realizing she was digging herself in deeper.

He smiled at her, letting her off the hook even though he enjoyed seeing her flustered. He doubted that happened often. "I'm the one who's sorry. Apparently we just weren't meant to have dinner last night."

"Apparently," she said and glanced toward his horse trailer and old Blue, his horse. "So now you're leaving town?"

"What gave you that idea?" he asked.

"Your license plates." She narrowed those oh-so-blue eyes of hers at him. "You're not from around here, but you look familiar."

"I just have that kind of face," he said, feeling the heat of her gaze.

She was still eyeing him. "So what brings you to Whitehorse?"

He smiled. "You sound like a cop."

"Have you been interrogated by a lot of cops?"

He laughed, shaking his head at her. "I thought I explained about dinner."

"You did," she said, nodding in agreement. "Now I'm just wondering what you were digging for the other evening out at the old Harper place."

So she *had* seen him riding away. *"Digging?"*

Her hands went to her hips, her eyes narrowed again. "Shovel. Dirt. Red-and-blue-plaid shirt. Appaloosa horse. That horse," she said, turning to point at Blue.

"I admit I was out there riding the property, but I'm

afraid I didn't do any digging," he said. What was one more lie?

She frowned, seeming not so sure now. "Well, *someone* was there digging. I wonder who it was?"

He shrugged. "When I rode the perimeter of the property I noticed that the fences are in good shape. Better shape than I thought they'd be in."

"If you were interested in the property, then why didn't you bid?"

"I was just looking for a cheap place to board my horse while I'm in town. Truthfully, I really didn't think anyone would bid on the house and I thought…" He smiled. He did have a great smile.

"You thought you could leave your horse out there for free," she finished for him.

"Not just my horse. I saw a spot on that creek in the cottonwoods that would have been perfect to pitch my tent."

She glanced at his rig and he could almost read her mind. Neither the truck nor the horse trailer came cheap. "You don't look exactly destitute."

He shook his head. "I have some business in town, but I'm trying to make it feel more like a vacation. I've always preferred the outdoors and like to camp." He shrugged.

"I'm sorry I ruined your plans," McKenna said, thinking how she'd also messed up Flynn Garrett's plans. She, apparently, was just that kind of woman.

"So what are you planning to do with the place?" Nate Dempsey asked.

"Live there."

"You aren't serious."

She bristled.

"Sorry. I saw the state the house is in. I'm sure it would be cheaper to start fresh with a new house."

She really was getting tired of hearing this. "It's going to take a lot of work, but I'm not afraid of hard work," she said, annoyed. Why was it that everyone was so negative about the place? "I happen to like old houses. There's plenty of room and it's quiet."

"Well, it's isolated enough," he agreed.

She'd heard enough. He must have sensed that he'd made her angry again.

"Look, I'm sorry. We really have gotten off on the wrong foot. Let me make it up to you."

"That's not necessary."

"No, give me a chance. I'm pretty good with a hammer."

She would hope so, given the logo on his truck. "I'm afraid I can't afford to hire anyone right now," she said, taken aback. She'd expected him to ask her to dinner again. Apparently he'd changed his mind about wanting a date with her.

"I wasn't looking for a job. Actually, I'm taking some time off, but I thought maybe we could make a trade. As I said, I was looking for a place to board my horse while I'm here. I just thought maybe we could trade horse boarding for some part-time construction work. After all, I do owe you after last night."

"You don't owe me anything. I ended up with a very nice date last night. In fact, he was great."

Nate arched a brow. "Great, huh? Well, that *would* be hard to top. But was there any electricity involved?"

"I beg your pardon?"

"Did he offer to check your wiring?"

She had to smile. "As a matter of fact…no."

"I didn't think so."

She felt herself weaken. She definitely could use his expertise and she had plenty of room to board his horse. So what was the problem?

"Just think about my offer." He gave her a smile. What was it about that smile?

"I'll give it some thought." She took a step backward. "You're sure we've never met before?" she asked again.

"I'm sure. I would have remembered."

NATE REMEMBERED ONLY too well. And he figured it was just a matter of time before McKenna remembered, too. By then, he hoped, he'd be long gone.

"Nice horse," she said, giving Blue another pat before starting across the street.

He still couldn't believe Blue had taken a liking to her. She really *was* good with horses. He thought about her date last night and wondered who the man had been. He'd lied about seeing her with the man. Arlene had filled him in when she'd called this morning to offer to set him up with someone else.

A sliver of worry burrowed under his skin as he watched McKenna cross the street and considered what to do next. He had to find a way to spend more time at Harper House. As he climbed into his truck he looked in her direction again. She was standing in front of the hardware store, her blond hair floating around her shoulders, her Western hat brim low, so low he couldn't see those incredible blue eyes, but he could feel them on him.

Had she remembered where she'd seen him before? He would never forget the first time he'd seen her, sitting on her horse outside the fence at Harper House all those years ago. Had he known then that their paths would cross? Or had he only dreamed they would?

But not like this. Not with him lying to her.

He told himself he couldn't concern himself with anything but finishing what he'd come to Whitehorse to do. He couldn't let anyone get in his way. Not even McKenna Bailey. Especially McKenna Bailey.

Why the hell did she have to buy that house?

He shook his head as he started the engine and pulled away. As he drove down the main street he had that feeling again of being watched. Hadn't he figured he wasn't the only one who'd come back to Whitehorse after hearing of Ellis Harper's death? He was counting on company. What better place to settle old scores than Harper House, where it had all begun?

THE HOUSE FELT even colder than before when McKenna unlocked the door and stepped inside. A weak June sun shone in the dirty windows. She climbed the stairs to the third floor and looked out to the spot where she had ridden as a young girl. She could imagine herself sitting astride her horse, staring up at the house.

This is where the boy she'd seen had been standing, looking out at her. She shivered, unable to shake the eerie feeling that came over her as she looked out.

Turning away from the window, she moved to the middle of the room and tried to visualize what it would look like cleaned up, painted, blinds on the windows.

It was going to take a lot of work, she thought, looking up at the bare lightbulb hanging down. She really did need someone to look at the wiring.

Nate Dempsey had graciously offered to help. Why hadn't she accepted? She had plenty of space to board his horse, and trading for help around here would have been ideal.

But she knew why she'd hesitated. That nagging feeling that he wanted something from her. Something more than a place to board his horse. Or camp. What if he'd lied and he was the one who'd been digging on the hillside behind the house? But digging for what?

It made no sense for anyone to be digging out there. What could there possibly have been buried behind the house?

It wasn't as if there was buried treasure out there. Ellis Harper hadn't had two nickels to scrape together. Or had he? He wouldn't be the first old-timer to hide money in the yard. He might not even have remembered he'd done it.

McKenna thought of her grandmother Nina Mae Cross, who had Alzheimer's. If she'd buried any money, she wouldn't remember doing it either.

Other than seeing Nate Dempsey ride away from Harper House and having him standing her up for a date, she wasn't sure what it was about him that made her leery of him. He seemed normal enough, and she did like his horse. And his smile was killer.

There was something about him that drew her to him, which made no sense, since Flynn Garrett was much better-looking and she hadn't felt anything but mild interest. Even his kiss hadn't set off a firecracker, let alone a Roman candle.

But Nate Dempsey... All he had to do was smile and it was the Fourth of July. She just wished she could remember where she'd seen him before. It would drive her crazy until she recalled.

She glanced around the room, realizing that her earlier enthusiasm for the house had waned some—and that worried her since so many people seemed to think she was crazy to try to save this house. She knew that her older sister, Eve, thought she'd acted impulsively.

Maybe she had. But even as a girl, sitting astride her horse and looking at the house from a distance, she'd had the feeling that the house needed her, that it called to her.

Well, what it was saying right now was that she'd made a mistake. Not that the property alone wasn't worth what she'd paid for the place. But she was beginning to fear that razing the house *was* the smartest thing to do.

It wasn't something she wanted to hear as she skirted the ancient square of linoleum that covered the center of the wood-plank floor like a rug. Stubbornness alone would make her try to save this house.

She noticed that the wood around the linoleum was in fair shape. Her first job would be to tear out the floor covering to expose the wood, she thought as she bent down to lift a corner of the linoleum.

One of the boards stuck to the underside. The board lifted a few inches, and she thought she saw something in the space beneath it. Sitting down on the floor, she shoved the floor covering back with her feet and pried the board the rest of the way up.

In the space between the floor joists was what had clearly been a child's secret hiding compartment. There were several old metal children's toys, rusted with age, a handful of marbles and a piece of rolled-up once-white paper.

She wiped away the cobwebs and plucked the faded

paper from between the boards, letting the board and linoleum drop back down as she scooted out of the way.

Unrolling the paper, she thought she'd find a child's artwork. Instead it was an old announcement about Whitehorse Days, a June rodeo event held every year at the local fairgrounds. This one was dated twenty-one years ago.

Disappointed that's all it was, she turned the paper over. And froze.

Her pulse roared in her ears as she realized with horror what she had in her hands.

Chapter Six

The sheet of paper gripped in her fingers was stained dark with blood—bloody thumbprints and what appeared to be more than a half dozen names. Next to each small bloody thumbprint was a name and an age. All of them were children twelve and under.

But it was the wording at the top of the page, written in an older child's shaky print, that horrified her.

Under the threat of death we make a blood oath to avenge those who harmed us in this house if it is the last thing we ever do. We vow to return at a set time to finish what needs to be done—or suffer the consequences.

It sounded like something kids might write. But the bloody prints on it and the names and ages gave her chills.

She glanced around the room. What *had* happened in this house? Shivering, she scanned the list of names.

Roy Vaughn

Lucky Thomas

Steven Cross

Bobby French

Andrew Charles

Denny Jones

Lyle Weston

She didn't recognize any of the names and was

thankful for that. Seven names on the list. What had happened to these boys?

McKenna hadn't thought too much about it when Eve had told her that Harper House had been a home for troubled boys. It hadn't mattered. Now she wasn't so sure.

Under the threat of death? Suffer the consequences? Surely they were being overdramatic. Kids were like that. And yet, as she stared down at the paper, her hand trembled.

The boys had made a blood oath to avenge the people who'd hurt them. They'd spilled their own blood to make the vow.

The paper was dated twenty-one years ago. The boys who'd signed it were too young to do anything at the time. But they would all be in their late twenties to early thirties by now. If they really had planned to do something to the people they felt had mistreated them, wouldn't they have done it by now? Wouldn't she have heard about it?

Still, she felt the need to show this to someone. Her soon-to-be brother-in-law, the sheriff. Not her sisters. It would only upset them, just as it had her.

Carefully she rolled up the sheet and rose on quaking legs from the floor to put it in her large shoulder bag.

As she turned, she let out a shriek. A man she'd never seen before stood in the doorway. He was massive, his clothing worn, his expression amused.

"Did I frighten you?" he asked, knowing full well he had and seeming to enjoy her discomfort. "I called up from below. I guess you didn't hear me." He glanced toward her shoulder bag she was still holding after she'd stuck the paper inside. How long had he been standing there watching her?

"Can I help you?" she asked. Her voice quaked, giving away her fear at being alone here in the house with him. Why hadn't she heard him drive up?

"I was told in town that you needed some help out here," he said, glancing past her to the window. "I'm handy with tools." His gaze came back to her and she saw that odd amusement in his eyes.

"I'm sorry, but you were misinformed. I'm planning on doing the work myself," she said. "But thanks for the offer Mr…"

"Turner," he said. "Hal Turner."

The name was a lie. His gaze challenged her to call him on it. Just as it challenged her to shake his hand as he outstretched it toward her.

His slightly damp paw of a hand swallowed hers. She did her best not to grimace. "McKenna Bailey."

"I know who you are," he said as she broke contact and fought the urge to wipe her hand on her jeans.

He knew who she was? But she didn't know who *he* was. She took a step toward the door, but he was blocking her way.

"I work cheap," he said, not moving.

He knew he was scaring her. He seemed to be enjoying it. She tested the weight of her shoulder bag, the only weapon at her disposal. The purse, if swung hard enough, might surprise him but little more.

She had a fleeting crazy thought: if she'd agreed to let Nate Dempsey board his horse out here, he'd be here now.

The sound of a vehicle coming up her road made her

almost sag with relief. The man heard it, too, and she saw his expression change.

"Well, if you're sure you don't need any help..." He turned and stepped back through the doorway.

She listened to his heavy footfalls on the stairs and tried to calm down. The man had frightened her more than she wanted to admit.

Stepping to the window, she saw a pickup pull up in the yard and felt such a sense of relief she had to grab hold of the window frame to keep her knees from buckling.

Nate Dempsey's truck came to a stop next to her pickup. She saw with surprise that there were only two vehicles in the yard—her pickup and Nate's. How had the man who called himself Hal Turner gotten out here? And where was he now?

She watched Nate Dempsey emerge from the cab of his truck and stop to stare up at the house, his expression hidden in the shadow of his straw hat's brim.

The house suddenly felt ice-cold as she rushed to the north-side window. The backyard was empty. So was the hillside behind it. Was it possible the man had never left the house?

McKenna ran back to the front of the house to tap on the window. Nate looked up, shading his eyes. She waved, wanting him to know where she was just in case the man was still in the house. Waiting for her.

She ran downstairs, not stopping until she was through the front door and halfway down the porch steps.

THE MINUTE NATE saw McKenna's face he knew something was wrong. She came rushing out of the house and down the porch steps. Her cheeks were flushed, her blue eyes wide and wild.

"Hey! You all right?"

"Sure." She tried to brush it off, but he saw the way she glanced around the yard, then looked over her shoulder back at the house as if she was being chased. "It's just that there was this man here…"

"Is he still in the house?" Nate asked, suddenly on alert.

"I don't know. Did you see anyone leave?"

"No. I'll make sure he's gone," he said as she hugged herself. She didn't seem to hear him. He touched her arm; it was ice-cold. "Just wait here."

He mounted the steps of the porch. He could feel the gun in his shoulder holster, snug against his side, as he opened the front door and listened for a moment before stepping inside.

The house seemed unusually quiet. He glanced back at McKenna. She was right where he'd left her. It took him only a few minutes to search the house since he knew all its hiding places. He started upstairs, working his way down. There was only one place he dreaded looking in.

The basement.

He hadn't been down there in more than twenty years, but he could remember it as if it were yesterday. The smell, the feel of the cold dampness around him, the furtive sounds that made his skin crawl.

At the door to the basement he hesitated, his hand inches from the knob. Funny how fears, no matter how irrational, linger into adulthood.

He opened the basement door. The smell alone was enough to transport him back. He was seven again, a skinny, scared kid locked in the basement for a punishment he didn't deserve.

He took a breath and reached around the edge of the doorjamb for the light switch.

MCKENNA HAD WAITED. Then, feeling vulnerable outside and worried about Nate, she'd cautiously climbed the porch steps and slipped back inside the house.

She saw him standing at the top of the stairs to the basement as if listening. She started to tell him where the light switch was, since it wasn't easy to find. But the words never left her lips as she watched him reach around the doorjamb and flip on the light as if he'd done it dozens of times.

Startled, for a moment she couldn't catch her breath. How had he known where the light switch was?

She realized even though he hadn't bid on the house, he'd probably toured it before the auction like everyone else. He would have remembered the location of the light switch just as she had.

She let out a ragged breath. Her heart was pounding and she knew she wasn't thinking clearly and hadn't been since she'd turned around to find that man standing in the bedroom doorway upstairs.

She listened to Nate descend the steps slowly, almost tentatively, and tried not to read any more into what she'd seen than she already had. There had been no Nate Dempsey on the list of names she'd found under the floorboards.

When he came back up a few moments later, moving a little quicker as he ascended the steps, she was waiting for him.

"I thought I told you to wait outside," he said, sound-

ing irritated and upset, although she doubted it was
with her. He apologized at once. "Sorry. I just wanted
to make sure he wasn't still in the house."

She watched him switch off the light, then close the
basement door. "Did you find anything?"

He shook his head, still seeming upset. "So tell me
what happened."

She told him what she knew, which wasn't much.
"He was large and unkempt."

"Homeless, you think?"

"Maybe. He said he'd heard I needed help with the
house."

"Where would he have heard that?" Nate asked.

"Anywhere in town. News travels fast around Whitehorse. When I told him I didn't need any help, he kept
at me. I tried to step past him, but he was blocking the
door."

Nate swore. "When you're here alone, you really
should lock your door."

"I've never locked my doors in my life in this part
of Montana."

"Well, maybe you'd better start. So did this guy tell you
what his name was or give you any idea what he wanted?"

"Just work, I assume. He said his name was Hal
Turner, but I think he was lying." She couldn't miss
Nate's reaction to the name. "Do you know him?"

"I used to know a Hal Turner, that's all."

That *wasn't* all. "Maybe it's the same guy."

Nate was shaking his head. "The Hal Turner I knew
is dead."

That would explain his startled reaction, she told
herself.

Nate seemed anxious and upset again. "You shouldn't stay out here alone. It's not safe."

"You think he'll come back?" She hated the catch she heard in her voice.

"If he thinks you're here alone, he will. A woman alone this far from another house—you're a sitting duck."

"What would you have me do? This is going to be my home. I refuse to be run off. I'll get some pepper spray. I'll lock the doors. I'll be more careful."

He took off his Western straw hat and wiped his shirtsleeve over his face. She noticed he was sweating, while she was freezing.

"Think about my offer. Right now I'm staying at a motel in town, but I'd rather be camped somewhere. I could pitch my tent down by the creek. You wouldn't know I was there—unless you needed me." He held up a hand before she could say anything. "Just think about it. I'll check the barn and outbuildings to make sure he's not hiding out there." He didn't wait for a response.

She stood at the back screen door, hugging herself as she watched him cut across the yard, toward the barn. In all the years she'd lived up here she'd never been afraid. Until now.

But she wasn't going to let one incident like this make her frightened. She would take more precautions. Once she was moved in she didn't expect any trouble.

Not that she didn't realize how close she'd come. What would she have done if Nate hadn't stopped by? She hated to think what would have happened.

Why had he come by? she wondered, frowning. She hadn't even thought to ask.

WHEN NATE RETURNED to the house, he noticed the change in McKenna. She was acting skittish, and he realized she was probably picking up on his reaction. But what she'd told him had frightened him more than he wanted to admit.

At first he'd thought the man had been just some homeless poor soul passing through town, probably looking for work or a free meal, who'd come on a little too strong and had frightened her.

Until she'd said the man had called himself Hal Turner. Nate hadn't heard that name in years. But he would never forget it. Hal Turner hadn't just been one of the first boys to live in Harper House, he had become a hero to the boys who came later.

It was Hal Turner who'd started the first revenge pact among the boys. Allegedly he'd grown up and come back to Whitehorse as part of that original pact to kill the first Harper House attendants: Norman and Alma Cherry. At least that was the story. Hal Turner had allegedly made the murders look like a murder/suicide and gotten away with it.

Coincidence that someone showed up now using that name?

Not in a million years.

The man who'd called himself Hal Turner hadn't come looking for work. Nor had it been about McKenna. No, the man had been sending a message. And the message was for Nate.

"Are you all right?" he asked McKenna, worried that he'd done something to give himself away. Or, maybe worse, that she remembered where she'd seen him before.

She nodded, looking scared again.

"Look," he said. "I understand if you don't want me staying out here. Forget I said anything about it. Same with boarding my horse or me helping with the house. I tend to come on too strong sometimes."

"No, I appreciate the offer. It's just that I can't ask you to—"

"You're not *asking*. The truth is, I'm picky about where I leave Blue. He's temperamental with most people, and after seeing how he took to you I just thought…"

He saw her consider. The horse, he thought, was his ticket.

"Let me give it some thought," she said. "I do appreciate the offer. I don't know what I would have done if you hadn't shown up when you did."

"No problem."

"Thank you." She brushed a lock of blond hair back from her face, and he could tell the man who'd been here earlier had made her feel vulnerable—something new for McKenna Bailey.

"Are you having second thoughts about the house?" he asked.

"*No.*" She softened the abrupt answer with a smile. "The house apparently has a past, one that the locals think precludes anyone living here—maybe especially me."

"What kind of past?" he asked, although he knew only too well.

"It was some kind of boys' ranch for troubled youth years ago," she said. "I think the boys might have been abused."

"What makes you think that?" He warned himself to be careful. He was on shaky ground.

"Just things I've heard," she said noncommittally. "You don't seem surprised by that."

He shrugged. "I heard some rumors."

"You don't think they're true?"

He caught the hint of hopefulness. She wanted him to tell her nothing horrible had happened in this house. He wished he could. Not even he could lie that well.

"It was a long time ago, right?" he said and narrowed his gaze at her, only half kidding when he asked, "You're not worried that the house might be haunted, are you?"

"I don't believe in any of that nonsense. I just feel badly for the boys."

He wondered if she would if she knew some of them. It wasn't just ghosts that came back to haunt a place.

"I wish I could find out if any of them survived what happened to them here," she said wistfully. "It would make me feel better."

He doubted that a whole lot. "I can't see that it could make any difference when it comes to this house. You can't change the past."

"I suppose not," she agreed.

He studied her. The house was getting to her. "You can always unload it if you change your mind about living here."

"Is that what you would do?" she asked, her gaze intent on him again.

"It's not *my* house."

She turned to the window, staring out as if she could see the boys out there in the yard, before she turned to him abruptly. "You never said why you stopped out when you did."

He could see that she was still guarded with him. He said the first thing that came to his mind. He'd come out here hoping she wouldn't be around so he could look the place over again in the daylight. Digging was out of the question—except at night, when no one was around.

"I nearly forgot," he said, winging it. "Everyone in town is talking about something called Whitehorse Days? I suppose you've been?"

"Whitehorse Days?" she repeated, her face seeming paler than before, the light dusting of freckles popping out like stars on a clear night.

He knew then that she'd found the blood oath that Roy Vaughn had made everyone sign. He had wondered if it still existed. He swore silently. The damned thing had everyone's names on it. Well, almost everyone's.

"I heard it's a fun time," he said, rattled by the realization. No wonder she had looked so spooked.

"If you like cotton candy and carnival rides and farm animals and baked-goods contests."

"Do you like that sort of thing?"

She seemed surprised. She let out a small laugh. "Actually, I do."

He knew she was waiting for him to ask her out. Hell, he almost did. What was he thinking? Instead he turned at the sound of a vehicle pulling up in the drive. "Appears you have company. I saw some wiring coming into the house that looked kind of funky. I was just going to take a quick look. Wouldn't want the place to catch fire and burn down." No, wouldn't want that.

He ducked out the back door, surprised how much making a date with her to Whitehorse Days appealed to him. But what would have been the point? He'd either be finished here and long gone by then...

...or he'd be dead.

Chapter Seven

McKenna looked out to see a pickup she recognized pull into the drive. Eve was behind the wheel, Faith in the passenger seat. McKenna had never been so happy to see her sisters.

She felt off balance. First the man who'd called himself Hal Turner and then Nate Dempsey almost asking her for a date. Or had she just imagined that?

Worse, she was seriously considering taking him up on his offer—not just a trade for work on the house but his staying out by the creek that meandered through the property. Until she moved in, at least. Someone to watch the place.

Glancing back through the house, she caught a glimpse of Nate. He appeared to be doing just what he'd said—checking the wiring to the house. She felt a wave of gratitude that was quickly replaced with concern.

Maybe he was just who he seemed to be—a nice man who wanted to help her. Why did that alone make her suspicious of him?

Because he wanted more. She could feel it, and her instincts told her what he wanted had something to do with this house. And yet she was about to invite him to camp by the creek? Had she lost her mind?

Maybe, she thought as she turned and walked through the house to meet her sisters. Or maybe what bothered her was that she couldn't remember where she'd seen him before.

"Boy, are you a welcome sight!" she called from the porch as her sisters climbed out of the pickup carrying cleaning supplies.

"Are you all right?" Eve asked as McKenna came down the porch steps to help carry the supplies.

"Great. I'm just glad to see you," she said.

"We figured you could use all the help you could get," Faith was saying.

"You have company?" Eve was studying Nate's pickup as if memorizing the license plate number.

"Not company exactly," McKenna said as Nate Dempsey rounded the outside corner of the house.

He gave her a nod as he saw that she had guests. "It's going to need a little work, but there's nothing to worry about for now. Catch you later," he said as he climbed into his pickup.

"Just a minute!" McKenna called to him. "I need to tell him something," she said to her sisters before hurrying over to his pickup.

He had his window down and looked surprised but glad she'd come over.

"I just wanted to tell you," she said, a little breathless, more from her concern about what she was about to do than the short run. "I'd like to take you up on your offer. For a while."

"You're sure?" he asked, his expression serious.

"Yes. I'd appreciate it. If you can get the shower to work downstairs, by the kitchen, you can use that bathroom."

He smiled. "I'd planned to use the outhouse behind the barn and bathe in the creek."

"That won't be necessary. Bring your horse and you're welcome to stay in the house if you like until I get moved in."

"No. I'd just as soon camp by the creek. But I might take you up on the use of the shower. Thanks."

"Thank *you*," McKenna said and stepped back from the pickup as he cranked up the engine.

"What was that about?" Eve asked as McKenna joined her again.

"Nate's a contractor."

Eve watched him drive away. "I didn't know you were going to hire a contractor."

"I'm not. He's interested in trading his services for boarding his horse out here." She left out the part about him camping in her backyard.

"Are you going to do it?" Eve asked, sounding surprised.

"Yeah," McKenna said. "I could use the help and I like his horse."

Eve raised a brow. "His horse? How did you meet this man? Not through Arlene's internet dating service, I hope."

McKenna laughed as if that was the craziest thing she'd ever heard. "If Arlene had found him, she'd be convinced he was perfect for me. Don't you want to hear about my date last night with the cowboy who bid against me for the house?"

"Seriously?" Faith cried.

"Seriously. He is handsome as all get-out, too. He bought champagne so we could celebrate me beating him. We had a steak dinner and he even kissed me good night." McKenna knew she was going on too much in her effort to divert interest away from Nate Dempsey.

Eve was eyeing her suspiciously. Her older sister knew her too well. "So let's see this place you bought," she said, glancing skeptically at the house.

"I want to know more about the cowboy hunk you had a date with last night," Faith said.

"His name's Flynn Garrett and he loves horses."

"He sounds perfect for you," Faith said as they headed for the house.

Not really, McKenna thought as she glanced down the road. All she could see was the dust Nate Dempsey's pickup had churned up into the warm summer air.

"The house is certainly big enough," Faith said as she stepped into the shadow of the house.

"Three stories," McKenna agreed, glancing upward.

"Isn't it scary out here alone?" Faith asked.

Recently? Yes. "It won't be once I get moved in." Not to mention Nate Dempsey would be camped down by the creek. At least for a while.

"It's pretty scary-looking in the daylight," Faith said. "I can't imagine staying out here at night."

Would everyone please just stop it!

Eve shot their younger sister a warning look. "I'm sure it will be fine once McKenna gets her horses out here. And, anyway, we're just a few miles down the road."

McKenna gave her older sister a grateful smile. She needed to hear that right now. Eve had lived alone. True, her house had been broken into and a crazy woman had almost killed her…

Pushing those thoughts aside, she and Eve climbed the porch steps after Faith, who was already letting the screen door slam behind her in her rush to see the house.

"I should warn you—it's still a mess in there," Mc-Kenna called after her.

"You sure you're all right?" Eve whispered, grabbing her arm to detain her for a moment.

McKenna realized that Faith's question about being scared out here had her hugging herself tightly. "It's just cold in the house, that's all."

Eve nodded skeptically as they followed Faith inside the house. Eve stopped at once, looking back over her shoulder at McKenna as if even more worried.

As McKenna was hit by a wall of heat, she understood why. The house was scorching hot, the sun blinding as it bore through the dusty windows, and no breath of air moved inside the four walls.

"I can't tell you how much I appreciate your help cleaning this place," McKenna said, changing the subject. "I'm hoping to start painting upstairs tomorrow so I can get moved in."

"I guess we'll start upstairs, then," Eve said. "It's good Ellis Harper's cousin Anita Samuelson hired someone to clean out all the junk before you bought the place. I heard Ellis was a terrible pack rat. Every inch of this house was filled."

McKenna thought about the secreted paper she'd discovered under the floorboards, but she wasn't about to mention it to Eve or Faith. They were worried enough about her living in this place. And, anyway, hadn't she convinced herself there was nothing to it after all these years?

NATE DEMPSEY KNEW the moment he opened his motel room door that he wasn't alone. It was something he'd learned at a young age, an awareness of his surroundings that had saved his life on more than one occasion.

He stepped in, moving quickly to the side to avoid being framed in the doorway and made into an easy target. At the same time he drew the gun from his shoulder holster. The movement was practiced and smooth. If he'd ever needed the gun, it was in Whitehorse, he thought, ironically a town with almost no crime.

"Easy," said a voice from the shadows. "No need for that."

Nate recognized the slightly amused voice as Lucky Thomas stepped from behind the bathroom door.

Two things struck Nate in that instant. Lucky had changed little from the good-looking kid he'd been. And Nate had seen Lucky recently—at the auction. Only he hadn't recognized him because he'd never gotten a clear view of him. But even after twenty-one years the way the man moved had seemed familiar.

It hadn't registered that the man at the auction might be Lucky Thomas. Probably because this was the last place Nate had expected to see him.

"What the hell are you doing here?" Nate demanded as he holstered his weapon.

"Nice to see you, too," Lucky said, clasping Nate's hand to pull him into a hug. "It's been too long."

Nate nodded as he stepped back to look at Lucky. Nate had been seven, Lucky nine, when they'd met at Harper House.

"*You're* awfully jumpy," Lucky said. "And packin' heat, too."

Nate swore. "What *are* you doing here?"

"Isn't it obvious?" Lucky said. "I heard about Ellis

Harper dying. I knew you'd come up here. I figured you'd need someone to watch your back."

Did Lucky know that Roy Vaughn was in town? Or had he just assumed Roy would come back because of that stupid oath they'd taken?

Nate shook his head. He'd never expected to see Lucky again after the state had come and taken them away in separate cars.

"Twenty-one years," Lucky said as if thinking the same thing. He dropped into a chair at the small round table next to the closed drapes, pulled a flask from his jacket pocket and offered it to Nate.

Nate shook his head as he pulled out the other chair, drawing it back so he could stretch out his long legs.

"Just being here brings it all back, doesn't it?"

"Yeah," Nate agreed. Not that the nightmares had ever gone very far away.

"Can you believe old man Harper hung in all these years?" Lucky asked.

"Why the hell did you bid on Harper House?"

Lucky laughed. "I got a little carried away."

"What would you have done if you'd won the bid?" Nate had to ask.

Lucky shrugged. "I had this crazy idea that I could buy the place and burn that hellhole down. I guess I can still do that, only it won't be my house I'm burning down," he added with a laugh.

Nate said nothing, fearing that Lucky meant what he said about planning to burn down the house. It was a strange feeling knowing someone so well for such a short period of time. He still felt he knew him.

But how was that possible? He hadn't seen Lucky in years, didn't know what had happened to him. If they hadn't both come back because of Ellis Harper's death, they probably would never have crossed paths again.

Hell, Nate didn't even know Lucky's real name. From the day the scrawny, good-looking kid had arrived at Harper House he'd said to call him Lucky Thomas, as if it was an inside joke that only he could appreciate.

"I could have bought the house, you know," Lucky said. "I have the money." He shrugged. "So tell me you're not here because of the pact."

Nate shook his head. "That was just kids pretending to be tough."

"Right. You just keep telling yourself that, but don't expect me to believe it. Roy Vaughn seemed pretty serious the night he made us all sign it. Well, almost all of us." He grinned at Nate. "They'll all be afraid not to come."

"Is that why you're here?" Nate asked.

Lucky laughed. "To fulfill my…obligations? That's it. But you," he said, studying Nate, "I figure you've got bigger fish to fry than killing some mean old people. I heard Frank Merkel and Rosemarie Blackmore are still kicking. Hard to believe. I thought they were ancient when we were boys. Apparently no one has tipped them over yet. So what can I do to help?"

Nate watched Lucky take another drink from the flask, then screw the lid back on and put it into his jacket pocket again. "Go home."

Lucky laughed. "You don't even know where my home *is*."

"No, I don't. Just so long as it's away from White-horse—and Harper House."

"Here's the way I figure it," Lucky said. "Whatever you have planned, it's dangerous or you wouldn't be packin'. Add to that the fact that you're doing nothing to hide. In fact, just the opposite. It's almost as if you're looking for trouble."

Lucky knew him better than even Nate had thought.

"I, on the other hand, don't really want to stick my neck out," Lucky said with a grin. "So I'm sneaking into your motel room and planning to sneak right back out."

"Good. Sneak right back out of town. This doesn't concern you."

Lucky laughed. "Everything about Harper House concerns me." He seemed to search Nate's face. "I can't believe you're still looking for Johnny."

Nate remembered the feeling he'd had that he was being watched while digging for Johnny's body. He'd thought it was Roy Vaughn. But maybe it had been Lucky.

"And not just Johnny. If the gun is any indication, you're still looking for Roy Vaughn."

"Like I said, this doesn't concern you. I know what I'm doing." Right now Nate wouldn't put money on that, but he didn't want to talk about Johnny. Even after all these years it still hurt too much.

"So you think Roy Vaughn will come back," Lucky said.

"He already has," Nate said. Only he was calling himself Hal Turner and making no secret out of why he was in town.

Chapter Eight

By late afternoon McKenna's sisters had left, after helping her clean, promising to come back the next morning to paint.

She waited until they'd driven away before she locked the front door and went to the back of the house. Stepping out, she surveyed the yard for tracks.

It still bothered her. Where had the man who called himself Hal Turner gone? Or, more to the point, how had he gotten out here? Harper House was a long way from town, and no one had seen him leave.

It made her uneasy even though she knew that Nate had searched all the outbuildings as well as the house. Since then, she'd made a point of locking the doors.

Out back, the ground close to the house was still damp from a rain earlier in the week. She could make out boot prints in the soft soil where Nate Dempsey had checked the wiring coming into the house. Along with his tracks were a set of others, these larger and made by cheap work boots.

She shuddered, her blood running cold as she saw where the man had stood beneath the back windows. There were handprints on the glass where he had wiped the dust to peer inside.

Nearby were Nate's Western boot tracks. Nate had to have seen where the man had looked in the window. No wonder he'd been so worried about her staying out here alone.

Inside the house, she locked the back door and stood for a moment leaning against it. Her heart was racing. She'd never felt afraid in all the years she'd lived in this isolated country.

But today she was running scared. The man had frightened her. As had the document the boys had signed with bloody fingerprints. She shuddered at the memory, although common sense told her that nothing had come of it.

She was just thankful that she'd had the good sense to ask Nate Dempsey to stay by the creek. It was still a good way from the house, but if she needed him, she could reach him a lot faster than getting anyone out here from Old Town or Whitehorse.

She reminded herself that Nate Dempsey wouldn't always be around. If she was going to live here, she had to come to grips with the house's past and the remoteness of the property. She refused to live in fear.

She started for the front door, when she realized she'd left her shoulder bag with the paper the boys had signed upstairs on the third floor. She'd dropped it after the man had left, to wave down at Nate in the front yard.

Climbing the stairs, she quickly retrieved her bag. While she'd pretty much convinced herself there was nothing to the document she'd found, she still wanted to show it to Sheriff Carter Jackson.

As she turned to go back downstairs, she caught sight of movement behind her. She let out a yelp before she realized it had only been a cat.

A black cat. Good thing she wasn't superstitious. But how had it gotten into the house?

On seeing her, the cat turned and raced down the stairs. She followed. The moment she opened the front door the cat took off across the porch to disappear in the higher weeds along the side of the house.

It must have been Ellis Harper's cat. She'd have to pick up some cat food in town for it. Or maybe it was Ethel Winthrop's up the road. Just the thought of Ethel reminded her of the woman's warning about buying this house.

ARLENE EVANS COULDN'T have been more excited to have a new client for her rural online dating service—and one her age, to boot. Not only that, Hank Monroe seemed to think Arlene was the cat's pajamas—an expression her mother had used but one that fit.

Hank Monroe was something, that was for sure. It still amazed her how much respect he seemed to have for her as a woman—and as a businesswoman.

"This online rural dating thing you started, why, it's brilliant," Hank had said when they'd talked earlier on the phone.

He'd called to say he'd made reservations for dinner at Northern Lights restaurant at seven and that he'd pick her up at six so they could take a ride beforehand.

Her ex-husband, Floyd, hadn't been the least bit impressed when she'd started the business. Nor had he ever taken her out to dinner at such a nice restaurant. Floyd always said it was cheaper to eat at home.

After dinner they were going to the movie. There was only one showing in Whitehorse at the old-time theater, and she didn't even care what was showing. She felt like a girl again, all starry-eyed and giggly.

Hank hadn't suggested that she make popcorn to sneak into the show to save money, the way Floyd would have. She was betting Hank Monroe wouldn't be cheap about beverages or candy at the movie, either.

But even if Hank Monroe had been flat broke, she would have liked him. He made her laugh. He made her forget that most of her life had been dismal at best. He made her feel special.

Arlene knew she shouldn't be thinking this way, but Hank Monroe gave her something she hadn't had for a long, long time. Hope. Hope for the future—something she sorely needed given her disappointing offspring. Charlotte got more pregnant each day, her body grotesquely swollen, her once-pretty blond hair drab and lanky. Bo was either in front of the television or in his room, the stereo blaring.

Eventually Hank would want to meet her children.

Arlene Evans dreaded that day and planned to put it off as long as possible. She still held out hope that Charlotte would come to her senses and give the baby she was carrying up for adoption. Or at least give up the name of the married man who'd fathered the baby so he could be held responsible for child support if the fool girl decided to keep the infant once it was born.

Charlotte hadn't taken any interest in the baby books Arlene had bought for her. Half the time Arlene suspected her youngest daughter ignored the pregnancy, refusing to think about the fact that it was inevitably going to end in a baby.

Not that Arlene didn't know who would end up raising the baby if Charlotte insisted on keeping it. While it would be her first grandbaby, Arlene wasn't sure she was up to the task of raising another child. Look how her other children had turned out.

Nor did she have the time or patience for her own grown children—let alone a baby. It frightened her to think of what would happen to the infant under Charlotte's care. The girl wasn't even able to take care of herself.

That's why spending time with Hank Monroe was such a godsend. For a while Arlene could forget about her real life.

Unfortunately real life became realer by the day. Charlotte would be having her baby in less than a month. There was talk of Violet getting out of the mental institution. Bo was making no move toward leaving the nest.

Arlene had lived long enough to know that even a hint of happiness from her would attract disaster like a lightning rod in a storm.

It was only a matter of time before disaster struck. But in the meantime Arlene Evans was going to enjoy this fleeting feeling of being happy for the first time in her life.

NATE HADN'T RETURNED as far as McKenna knew, and she hated the worried feeling that gave her. She looked out the back window as she came downstairs, wondering where he'd gone—and if he'd even be back. He seemed a man who spurned ties. Or maybe he just wanted to keep his distance from her. Why did she care one way or the other?

She didn't know the man, wasn't sure she entirely trusted him…and yet she felt drawn to him. Just as she had at Harper House, she reminded herself. So why, since he seemed to have no real interest in her, was he planning to stay behind her house?

Because he was just a nice guy.

Or because his real interest was in her house?

Unable to stop herself, she went downstairs and stepped outside to see if he'd come back while she'd been upstairs working. It would be just like him to settle in back there without letting her know he'd returned.

But there was no pickup by the barn. No tent that she could see pitched beside the creek under the big cottonwoods.

As she started to go back into the house, she saw something that stopped her. That was odd. It almost looked as if someone had been digging up the hillside again. They'd clearly tried to cover it up, but the wind had blown off the weeds covering the spot.

She felt a chill. Who was doing this? Nate? Or someone else? Well, once he was staying back here, that should put an end to the digging, right? Maybe she should do some digging herself and see exactly what was back there.

Suddenly she didn't want to work any more today. She was feeling antsy and out of sorts and hated the reason why. It had bugged her all afternoon. Earlier she'd thought Nate was going to ask her out. But he hadn't.

He had made no effort to ask her out since he'd stood her up for their one and apparently only date. She told herself she didn't want to go out with him anyway, but still it bothered her that he hadn't even tried to make up for their date that never happened.

Because he wasn't interested in her. He was inter-

ested in her property. For a place to camp and board
his horse. Nothing more.

She locked up the house and headed for her pickup
feeling lost. It was too early to go to the ranch house.
Faith probably would be in town with friends. McKenna
hated the thought of wandering around her family's
empty ranch house thinking about Nate Dempsey and
this darned house.

As she climbed into her truck, she remembered the
black cat she'd seen. Maybe it did belong to Ethel Winthrop up the road. McKenna knew she was only using
the cat as an excuse to visit the elderly couple.

What she really wanted to do was ask about Harper
House. Ethel had indicated at the auction that she knew
things about the house, things McKenna needed to
know.

Maybe it was time she knew what those things were.

A few miles up the road to the north, McKenna
pulled into the Winthrop ranch and cut the pickup's
engine. The breeze as she opened her truck door smelled
of the thick stand of cottonwoods that ran along the
creek behind the ranch house. The same creek that cut
through her property.

Cows milled in a rich green pasture that ran as far
as the eye could see. Only the blue-gray outline of the
Little Rocky Mountains broke the long line of the horizon. The mountains and the badlands in the distance
that marked the Missouri River gorge.

Ethel answered the door at McKenna's knock with
a look of confusion. "Yes?"

"Hi, we met the other day. I'm McKenna Bailey. I
bought the house down the road."

Ethel frowned, and McKenna was beginning to

worry that this trip had been a waste of time when Ethel's husband, Edgar, came out of the kitchen.

"Who's here, Ethel?" he asked.

"I don't know," the elderly woman said vaguely.

"Why, it's the woman who bought Harper House," Edgar said. His wife started as if prodded with a cattle prod.

"You!" she said and stepped back, eyes widening with fear. "Have you heard the noises yet?"

"Ethel, let our guest come inside," Edgar said. "It's hot out there."

McKenna stepped into the cool, dim house. "Actually, I came about a cat I saw. Do you have a black cat?"

Ethel crossed herself. "There's no black cats on this ranch."

"Then it must have belonged to Ellis Harper," McKenna said quickly. "I'll see that it gets fed. But I *am* interested in knowing more about Harper House."

"A little late for that," Ethel said with a shake of her head.

"Ethel, didn't I see that you made some iced tea earlier?" her husband asked pointedly.

Ethel, distracted by the mention of the tea, padded off toward the kitchen.

"Won't you sit down?" he offered McKenna as he drew her into the living room. "You'll have to excuse my wife. She's been upset ever since you bought the house, worried about you living there alone."

"I haven't actually moved in yet," McKenna said as she took a seat on the flowered couch, moving one of a dozen pillows all adorned with yarn cross-stitch cat images.

"My wife likes cats," he said unnecessarily. "Just not black ones. She's superstitious that way."

McKenna smiled.

"You sure you want to go digging into the past?" he asked, glancing toward the kitchen.

McKenna could hear the clink of glasses, then the refrigerator open and close.

"Yes, I'm sure," she said, not sure at all. She owned the house. What did it matter now? Unless there was cause for concern because of the bloody document she'd found. Otherwise there was nothing to be done about the way the boys had been treated—or mistreated—at Harper House so many years ago.

Ethel called from the kitchen and Edgar rose to go help her. They both returned a few moments later with him carrying the tray. Ethel wrung her hands, winding them in the front of her apron as she looked nervously at McKenna.

"You sit there, Ethel," he said, directing his wife into a rocker as he put the tray on the coffee table and poured her a glass of iced tea, then another for McKenna before pouring one for himself.

The glass was cold and wet—and she wondered if she would ever be warm again.

"Did he tell you about the first Harper who owned the house?" Ethel demanded.

"I haven't told her anything," he said patiently. "I was waiting until you could join us. As you know how it works around these parts, the house keeps the name of whoever lived there first, so it's always been known as the Harper House."

Ethel hadn't touched her iced tea. "The first Harper?

His wife died, and he died of a broken heart right after that. The house is unlucky."

Edgar sighed. "I think she's interested in the house's more recent history."

McKenna took a drink of her tea. It was cold and bitter.

"Those poor children who lived in that house?" Ethel touched the tiny cross she wore around her neck. "It was just horrible. When the wind blew out of the east we could hear them at night. The cries were unbearable."

"I called the sheriff a few times, but when he drove out, he'd never find anything amiss."

"Didn't look very hard, did he?" Ethel leaned toward McKenna conspiratorially. "He was like a lot of people who weren't concerned about what happened to those boys. Rough bunch. Most people were afraid of them and glad the people who ran Harper House kept the boys on the place."

"Didn't the boys tell the sheriff what was going on out there?" McKenna asked.

Edgar shook his head. "I would imagine they were afraid to say anything, swore everything was fine, poor things. A mismatched bunch they were, too. Orphans, strays, boys nobody wanted. It was a blessing when the state closed down the place."

McKenna felt sick. "When was that?"

Edgar gave that some thought. "Place ran from the seventies to sometime in the late eighties. Closed in 1987."

Twenty-one years ago, McKenna thought with a shudder.

"After that, Ellis Harper, a shirttail relative of the

first Harper, came back and lived alone in the house until he died," Edgar said.

"The place drove him insane," Ethel said. "The ghosts of those boys. I stopped by to see him one day. He told me he'd seen two of them boys in the backyard. That old mutt he had kept barking and barking from the back steps as if he saw them, too, up on that hill-side. But there wasn't anybody out there." She shook her head ruefully.

Edgar chuckled. "Hard to say what Ellis saw. He drank. That's what killed him," he said as if that explained seeing ghosts in the backyard.

"Did he ever mention any of the boys by name?" McKenna asked.

Ethel shook her head. "He just said 'them two' like they were the ones who haunted him. It gave me the shivers the way he said it, sounded as if he was half-afraid of them."

"Any chance Ellis might have buried money in the backyard?" she asked, trying out one theory.

Edgar chuckled.

"That's ridiculous," Ethel said. "If there is anything buried in that backyard, it's those boys."

McKenna couldn't suppress a shudder even though Edgar signaled with a shake of his head not to believe Ethel. "What *did* happen to the boys?"

"After the state closed the place, they took them," he said. "The younger ones were probably adopted. The older ones…" He shrugged. "The state saw that they were taken care of, I assume."

"Couldn't have come to any good, not after what they'd been through," Ethel said.

McKenna shared the woman's fear. "Would you recognize any of them if you saw them?"

Both Edgar and Ethel shook their heads. "Never got a good look at any of them, and after all these years…" Edgar sighed. "I wouldn't worry about them. They're men now. They either put their pasts behind them or they didn't."

"Well, thank you for the tea and the information," she said, putting her glass down on the coffee table to leave even though she'd barely touched her tea.

"That house is evil. You'd be wise to strike a match to it," Ethel said.

"I don't believe houses are evil—just people," McKenna said.

Ethel gave her a we'll-see-about-that look as McKenna left. She was still disturbed by what she'd learned about the house but somewhat relieved. If the state had stepped in, the boys would have been saved and could have gone on to lead normal lives—she hoped. At any rate, the boys had apparently put Harper House and the blood oath and their plans for revenge behind them.

It was near dark by the time she reached the road to her house. She would make a point of bringing what she needed tomorrow so she could start staying in the house. She wasn't going to let anyone scare her off her own property. Especially ghosts.

But as she started to drive by her new house she remembered that she'd forgotten her paint samples upstairs in the third-floor bedroom. How foolish of her not to have gotten the paint samples at the same time she'd grabbed her purse. She'd also apparently left the light on when she'd gone back up to get her shoulder bag.

Or maybe Nate had turned on the light.

As she pulled into the drive, though, she was disappointed to see that Nate's pickup was nowhere in sight. Was it possible he'd changed his mind about staying out here? She tried to remember turning on the light upstairs.

Earlier, with everyone in the house working, she'd felt safe and excited. She'd thrown off her worry about the house being a mistake for a while. Cleaned, the rooms had taken on new life. She couldn't wait to see paint on the walls—starting with that front bedroom on the third floor. That would be her office.

She'd picked a nice sunny yellow to cover the drab faded blue in the room. A boy's room, she thought as she got out of her pickup.

The house loomed up out of the darkness, a black silhouette of jagged corners and cornices—except for the dim yellow light coming from the third-floor bedroom.

She hesitated for a moment, overwhelmed by everything the Winthrops had told her, finding the bloody document, being frightened by the man who'd called himself Hal Turner.

Reassuring herself that he was long gone—just like all the bad things that had happened here—she headed for the house, keys in hand, trying to remember if she'd locked the front door or not.

She hated being afraid. In order to live out here by herself and raise horses, she had to overcome these fears.

But she knew it wasn't ghosts that made her fingers tremble as she unlocked the front door and reached for the light switch. It was a fear that whatever horrors had happened in this house would act like a magnet to attract new evil as they did in those scary movies she'd watched with her sister Faith.

As she climbed the stairs to the third floor she told herself that kind of thinking was crazier than believing in ghosts. Dormant evil attracting evil. *Really.*

When she reached the third floor, the glow of the light spilled across the hardwood floor of the landing. She hesitated, positive she hadn't left the light on.

Taking a step toward the room, she started, her hand going to her mouth as she saw someone standing at the dormer-side window. Her breath caught in her throat and it was all she could do not to cry out.

But it wasn't a man next to the window. It was her sister Faith's jacket that she'd hung on what was left of the curtain rod.

The paint samples were on the windowsill where she'd left them. She hurried over and picked them up, hating how anxious she was to leave. *Once I have new locks and am moved in it will feel different. Once I have my horses out here, it'll be all right.*

As she turned out the light and started down the stairs, she heard a soft thump downstairs.

She froze, one foot balancing on a step, her hand gripping the wood railing. Listening, she heard the wind in the cottonwoods and the soft scrape of what had to be a limb against the side of the house.

Once she lived here she would get use to the house's noises, she told herself as she let out the breath she'd been holding and continued on down the stairs.

She tried not to hurry, telling herself this wasn't like her, turning on lights as she went and turning them off behind her. Down the stairs, through the living room,

locking the door behind her as she crossed the porch
and dropped down the stairs.

She didn't scare easily. But after the day she'd had—
She tried to reassure herself. Her family ranch was only
a few miles down the road. This was her country, her
land. There was nothing to fear.

Something hit her the minute she reached the last
porch step. What felt like a hand slammed into her back,
and she went sprawling into the weeds, the air knocked
from her.

For a moment she was too surprised to do anything
more than gasp for breath. Then she was up, scrambling to her feet, running as fast as she could toward
her pickup. She didn't dare look behind her. She knew
it was the man who'd called himself Hal Turner. She
knew he was right behind her, breathing down her neck,
and that any moment he was going to grab her and—

She reached the pickup, flung open the door and
dived inside, slamming the door behind her and hitting
the locks. She was shaking all over as she looked out the
windshield. Darkness cloaked the house and trees, deep
shadows stretching across the yard. A breeze stirred the
cottonwoods in a flicker of light and dark.

Where was he?

She fumbled the key into the ignition. The engine
roared. She snapped on the headlights, bracing herself
for when he came at her again. In her imagination she
could see him coming at the truck with something to
shatter the side window and grab her before she could—

Her mind raced as she shifted the pickup into First,
wanting only to get out of there. She was trembling with
fear—and confusion. Someone had pushed her down.

She'd felt the hand in the middle of her back. A hard shove that had sent her sprawling.

But if the person had meant to harm her, why hadn't he come after her?

She hadn't imagined being pushed. She hadn't. But where had he gone. And why—

Suddenly her pickup cab was filled with the glare of a set of headlights as a vehicle came rushing toward her.

Chapter Nine

As his headlights splashed over McKenna's pickup, Nate Dempsey watched her kill her engine. He saw her hurrying to get the pickup going again, only to back into one of the fence posts.

He slowed, wondering what the hell was going on. Stopping his truck and horse trailer in the beams of her headlights, he climbed out, leaving his engine running, and walked cautiously through the glare of her headlights toward her.

When he reached the side of the pickup, he could see her face behind the wheel. It looked stark white, her blue eyes round as tumbleweeds. Both hands were gripping the wheel, and it seemed to take her a few moments before she recognized him. What had happened?

As he tapped on her side window, it came partway down and he caught a whiff of her perfume. It mingled with another smell he recognized at once. Fear.

"Are you all right?" he asked, seeing that she wasn't. Worse, she seemed afraid of him.

Her eyes flooded with tears, her voice breaking as she stared at him. "Someone was here. He...struck me."

"Are you hurt?"

She shook her head. "I don't know where he went."

His gaze went to the house. "I'll make sure he's gone."

"No," she cried. "He's dangerous."

If her attacker was who Nate believed it to be, the man was more than dangerous. He was a cold-blooded killer. "Lock your doors. Honk if you need me. I'll be right back."

He turned and left before she could argue further. Once out of the sweeping glow of the pickup's headlights, he pulled the gun from his shoulder holster and moved cautiously toward the house.

First he checked the area around the house, then made sure the doors were locked before he holstered the gun again and went back to her.

He was glad to see that she'd done what he'd told her to do. As he neared her pickup, she put her window down partway again, as if not sure who she had to fear.

"Feeling better?" he asked. He could see that she was. There were no more tears and she seemed to have steadied herself. He wasn't surprised given what he knew about her.

"Did you see him?"

Nate shook his head. "I'm sure he took off when he saw me coming up the road. You think it was the same man who was here earlier?"

"I don't know." She seemed confused, definitely upset. "You didn't see any sign of anyone?"

He shook his head, studying her. "What did he do?"

"He...he pushed me." She looked uncertain.

"He *pushed* you?" It dawned on him that she'd been half-afraid it had been him. That was why she'd reacted so oddly to him earlier.

"I know it sounds crazy, but someone *pushed* me. He knocked me down."

"But other than that, he didn't do anything to you?"

"No. He pushed me and then I guess he left." She shook her head as if realizing her story didn't make a lot of sense. Why would someone just push her and take off?

"All that matters is that you're okay."

She nodded. She wasn't okay. He could see that.

Apparently this had just been another message for him. "Well, it won't be a problem after tonight. I'll be here. But maybe you should consider staying at your family's ranch until I catch him."

She was shaking her head before he even finished talking. "I won't let him run me out of my own home."

An admirable attitude that he feared would get her killed. Except Roy Vaughn didn't have a score to settle with this woman. He was after Nate. Fooling with McKenna Bailey was just Roy Vaughn's way of letting Nate know he was in town—and was coming for him.

The problem was McKenna Bailey had inadvertently put herself right in the middle.

"If you're determined, then I'll just have to make sure no one bothers you," Nate said. "Were you working late?"

"No. I'd been over to the neighbors' and was headed back to the ranch when I remembered I'd left my paint samples in the house." She glanced toward the front yard. "I dropped them when—"

"I'll get them," he said. "I have a flashlight in my rig." He started for his truck when he heard her get out of hers. Turning, he watched her walk back toward the house, her own flashlight beam bobbing through the darkness as she moved.

He waited as she shone the light on the front of the house, then on the ground. He joined her even though he could see that she'd already found what she was looking for.

He walked her back to her truck. "Do you want me to follow you as far as your ranch?"

"No, it's not necessary. I'm fine now." As she climbed behind the wheel, he saw her hesitate. "I was afraid you'd changed your mind about staying out here."

He shook his head. "I'm sorry I was so late. I decided to have dinner in town. I thought you might still be here working, so I brought you something." He walked over to his pickup and came back with the foil-wrapped package. "It's just a piece of peach pie."

She peeked under the foil, seeming touched by his thoughtfulness, making him feel even more guilty. "Mmm, it smells wonderful. I think I forgot to eat today." She looked up at him. "Thank you."

"You're welcome."

"How did you know my favorite pie is peach?"

He smiled. "I guess I just got lucky. Well, see you in the morning."

"Wait, I forgot to give you a key to the house." She reached into the glove box for one of the extras she'd had made. "That will open the back door. This one's for the front. Be careful. That man might not have gone far."

"Don't worry." He took the keys, stepped away from her open window and, giving her a nod, walked to his truck.

Nate could feel her watching him all the way, as if she suspected he was the last man she should be trusting. Or it could have been his conscience that dogged him all the way back to his pickup—if he still had a conscience.

BEFORE GOING TO BED, Arlene Evans checked her email, hoping to see something more from Hank Monroe.

What she saw almost gave her heart failure. She hadn't completely forgotten about her young, handsome new client Jud Corbett. Originally she'd planned to pair him with her daughter Charlotte. That obviously wasn't happening right now given that Charlotte was almost eight months pregnant and not at her best.

So Arlene had set Jud up with a few local young women, feeling as though it was such a waste. A good-looking, eligible man like Jud. Jud's father, Grayson Corbett, had just bought a huge ranch down by the Missouri Breaks.

While Jud was the only one she'd seen so far, Arlene had heard there were four other brothers. She hoped they were as handsome and as eligible as Jud.

She was still hoping that her daughter Charlotte would come to her senses, give up the baby, get her shape back and hook up with Jud Corbett when she read the email from Jud and let out a shriek.

She read it a second time, telling herself this had to be a bad dream. According to the email, Jud had seen a woman on Arlene's rural Meet-A-Mate online service who he was very interested in meeting.

That was how the service worked, true enough.

But it was the name of the young woman whom Jud was requesting that sent Arlene into a tizzy.

Not only was the woman in question not a member of the online dating service, she wasn't even in town.

And Arlene certainly wouldn't have put up the profile of her son Bo's former fiancée, Maddie Cavanaugh.

How had this happened? And now Jud was anxious to date the woman. Not only was Maddie Cavanaugh all wrong for him, Maddie was also Arlene's least favorite person in the world. She wasn't good enough for Jud Corbett!

Who had put Maddie's profile up on her internet site? Arlene wanted to know. Was this supposed to be a joke? And how had Maddie's photo and information gotten up on the site without Arlene's permission? No one had that kind of access except for—

"Bo!" she bellowed as she stormed down the hallway to her son's room. *"Bo!"* She counted to ten before she threw open his door.

Storming in, she shut off his blaring stereo and glared at her son. He was lying sprawled on the bed, looking bored, as usual, and annoyed that she'd turned off his horrible music.

Bo was still handsome even though he had been letting himself go since his breakup with Maddie Cavanaugh. With him, Arlene still held out hope that he would meet the right woman and settle down.

"Did you put your former fiancée's profile and photo on my internet dating service?" she demanded.

His smirk said it all.

"Why would you do such a thing knowing how I feel about Maddie Cavanaugh?"

"I thought you'd want to see her married off so she leaves me alone."

He had a point, although, as far as she knew, Maddie

didn't want any more to do with Bo than he did with her. Maybe a whole lot less.

Arlene shook her head. If she didn't have a meeting with Hank Monroe, this little incident would have ruined her whole week.

"Leave my matchmaking business alone," she ordered. "Tomorrow I'll fix it so you won't be able to pull something like this again." Had she once hoped that she could interest her son in her business? That they could work together? What had she been thinking?

"Why don't you get out of this room and find yourself a nice young woman?" she snapped.

"What would I want with a nice young woman?" he asked with a leer.

She cuffed him on the side of the head.

"Hey, what was that about?" he whined, sounding hurt.

It was her lot in life, Arlene thought as she left his room, the loud music in her wake.

But she was determined not to let anything spoil her good mood. She was going to see Hank Monroe tonight. Not even her horrible children were going to spoil this.

She'd just email Jud and tell him that Maddie Cavanaugh's profile was a mistake, that the girl didn't live here anymore, and then she'd find him someone else he could date until Charlotte came to her senses.

Still, it worried her. Jud had sounded way too interested in Maddie. Not that there was much chance Maddie would ever come back to Whitehorse for more than a visit.

But just in case, Arlene swore she would go to hell in a handbasket before she'd let Maddie Cavanaugh have Jud Corbett. She was saving him for Charlotte. One way or the other.

AFTER A NIGHT riddled with bad dreams, McKenna awoke, determined to put an end to her fears about the house—and Nate Dempsey.

She told herself she should be grateful that he showed up when he did and it was time to stop second-guessing herself. But even as she thought it, she wondered if he'd spent the night digging up on the hillside behind the house—even though he said he hadn't the other time.

Skipping breakfast, since she'd eaten the peach pie Nate had brought her last night—and felt guilty the whole time for mistrusting his motives—she drove into Whitehorse to the sheriff's department.

Sheriff Carter Jackson would become her brother-in-law next month on the Fourth of July. Independence Day. McKenna had pointed that out to Eve, who'd only laughed.

"I like the idea of fireworks on our anniversary every year," Eve had said, getting that faraway look in her eyes.

McKenna had known Carter Jackson all her life, so she didn't feel strange showing up at his office with the paper she'd discovered under her floorboards. Carter would no doubt think she was overreacting for bringing it to him. But after a sleepless night worrying, she felt she had to show it to him.

"McKenna," he said, sounding happy to see her. But then, he'd been happy ever since Christmas when her sister had accepted his marriage proposal.

She gave him a hug, then took the chair he offered her.

"So what can I do for you?" he asked, leaning back in his chair. "Tell me Eve didn't send you here with last-minute changes regarding the wedding."

"No, it's about the old Harper House."

"I heard you bought the place."

From his tone she could tell that her sister had shared her concerns with him. McKenna wished those concerns were unfounded. She opened her mouth to tell him about the man who'd pushed her last night, but in the light of day, she wasn't so sure anyone had pushed her. It made no sense. Why would the man hang around just to push her down and then take off? That was something a kid would do.

And, anyway, Nate would be staying on the property for a while. So the problem, if there even was one, was solved. And this way, word wouldn't somehow get back to her sister Eve. The last thing she needed was Eve worrying about her just weeks before big sis's wedding.

What concerned McKenna was what she'd found under the floorboards at the house. Even after twenty-one years, if there was any chance the people who'd worked there were in danger...

"I found something in the house that is...disturbing," she said as she removed the paper from her purse and carefully unrolled it to hand the sheet to him.

Carter frowned as he peered down at the blood-stained document. "What is this?"

"From what I can tell, it's a contract, a blood oath to take revenge against the people who hurt them."

"Where did you find this?"

"Under the floorboards in the house. I found out that it was once a home for troubled boys. Given the date of the Whitehorse Days event on the back, I can only assume those are the names of the boys who lived there twenty-one years ago."

"I heard rumors about the place when I was growing

up," Carter said, studying the paper a moment before handing it back.

"So you don't think I should be concerned about it?" she asked him, knowing that was exactly what she wanted to hear.

He shook his head. "You know kids. At the time I'm sure they were angry and wanted to feel they had power over their lives. But, like you said, it's been twenty-one years. If they haven't acted on it by now…"

"They were too young to act on it back then, though. Now they'd be men in their late twenties to mid thirties," she said, wondering why she didn't just agree with him and leave it at that. "They would finally be old enough to make good on their threats." Not to mention consequences if not carried out.

"But why wait twenty-one years? They've been plenty old enough for years."

A question she'd asked herself. So why couldn't she just let it go? "I was wondering if you could find out what happened to these boys and the people who worked there."

He looked as if he thought that was a bad idea.

"I know it's an unusual request. But I would feel better if I knew for certain there was nothing to it."

Carter hesitated, then smiled. "Sure. Why not? If it will relieve your mind. I need you to keep your big sister sane. I'm worried she's going to get cold feet. You know Eve. She could just take off on horseback and we'd never see her again."

McKenna laughed. "Don't worry. She's not going anywhere. She loves you. She wouldn't miss that wedding for anything." At least McKenna hoped that was true.

Carter seemed to relax a little. "There is just one thing that would make her wedding day perfect," he said wistfully.

McKenna knew exactly what he was going to say. Her sister had looked nothing like either of their parents, Chester and Lila Bailey, or her sisters. From the time Eve was little she'd somehow known she was adopted even though their mother had denied it. As far as Lila Bailey had been concerned, Eve, McKenna and Faith were her children in every possible way— even if all three were adopted. Adopted through rather strange channels.

Eve had only recently discovered the truth about her adoption. While McKenna had no interest in her birth parents, Eve seemed unable to move on until she knew.

Unfortunately, since the adoptions hadn't exactly been legal, only one person apparently might know the truth about Eve's—and her brother Bridger Duvall's—birth mother. That person was Pearl Cavanaugh, who now lived in the nursing home following a stroke that had left her unable to speak.

"Knowing who her birth mother was and who she is would certainly make Eve happy," Carter said.

McKenna scoffed. "Eve *is* happy. And we all know who she is, and so does she. Knowing who her birth parents are won't change the woman Eve has become. How is Pearl doing, by the way?"

"Better. I understand she can say a few words. Bridger visits her every day. I think he's grown quite fond of her and vice versa." Carter shook his head as if surprised by that since the two were definitely at cross purposes.

"What would happen if it all came out about the illegal adoptions?" McKenna asked. "The women responsible wouldn't have to go to prison, would they?"

"I certainly would hope not given that they're all up in years. But I doubt that would ever happen," he said. "I don't think Pearl is ever going to divulge any information about the babies—let alone the names of the others involved in the illegal adoption ring. Nina Mae Cross has Alzheimer's, so she would never stand trial."

"I hope Pearl takes it to her grave with her," McKenna said more adamantly than she'd intended. "I don't want to know. I figure my birth mother had her reasons for giving me up. If anything, I'm thankful."

Carter nodded. "I wish Eve felt that way."

A silence fell between them for a moment, then McKenna asked, "Would you mind making a copy of the paper I found? I'd like to keep it for now."

"No problem. I just don't want you taking it too seriously, all right?"

She nodded and waited while he went to make a copy.

"Off the top of my head, I know of at least two people who worked at Harper House," he said when he returned. "Rosemarie Blackmore and Frank Merkel. Both are still alive—so, see, there's nothing to what you found. But I'll look into what happened to the boys who lived there if it will make you feel better."

She took the document he handed her back, rolled it up and put it in her purse, relieved. "Thank you." She tried to settle down. She'd done everything she could. Now she would just wait until she heard from Carter.

There would be no point in her going by to talk to Rosemarie or Frank. What would she say anyway? That their lives might be in danger after twenty-one years? Crazy.

As crazy as worrying Carter—and ultimately her sisters—by telling the sheriff about last night.

If the sheriff thought there was any chance Frank and Rosemarie were in danger, he'd warn them. Why scare a couple of nice elderly people over nothing?

It *was* nothing. Just like that incident at the house last night. And now with Nate Dempsey staying out there, she had nothing to worry about but getting moved into her house.

AT THE NURSING home on the edge of Whitehorse, Pearl Cavanaugh looked up to see Bridger Duvall come into her room.

She closed her eyes as she listened to him pull up a chair next to her wheelchair.

"How are you today, Pearl?" he asked, just as he had every morning for months.

She opened her eyes with a sigh, pretending she wasn't glad to see him. While she used to dread his visits, she had to admit that she now looked forward to them and regretted the day when he would no longer come by.

That day would be when she told him the truth about his birth parents. His and Eve's, since the two were fraternal twins.

"It's a beautiful day out," he said. "Wouldn't you like to go outside?" He stood, waiting.

She gave a nod and he smiled down at her. "I thought you'd enjoy that." He went around behind her to push the wheelchair down the hall.

All of the nurses knew him and said hello, along with

the doctors. Pearl liked hearing them compliment him on the restaurant he'd opened with her granddaughter, Laci. Northern Lights was doing well, from what she'd heard. That pleased her.

She hadn't been as pleased about Laci's engagement to Bridger. She'd originally worried about Bridger's motivations for getting close to her granddaughter. She'd prayed his reason wasn't the same one as why he'd come to Whitehorse and why he visited Pearl's nursing home every day.

Since then, though, she'd seen the two of them together. No two people had been so perfectly made for each other. Just the sight of them together made her smile. At least she thought she was smiling. Since the stroke, she couldn't be sure.

"We set a wedding date," Bridger said after circling the nursing home block and stopping to sneak her a flower from the ones growing in the beds out front.

She fingered the flower stem.

"We're getting married next Christmas," he said.

Her head came up, her eyes widening in surprise. She tried to form the words that were in her head, but nothing intelligible came out, to her growing frustration. At first not being able to speak had been a blessing in disguise. She couldn't have told Bridger what he wanted even if she was so inclined—or if he caught her in a weak moment.

But now she would give anything to get her speech back.

"Why such a long engagement?" he asked as if he could understand her gibberish.

She nodded weakly.

"Laci has her heart set on you being there." He knelt

down in front of the wheelchair and took both her hands in his. "She wants you and her grandfather to be there to give her away. She has this dream that you'll be able to walk down the aisle with your husband, Titus."

Tears welled in Pearl's eyes. She swallowed around the lump in her throat and squeezed his hand. She and Titus had raised her two grandchildren after their father was killed and their mother disappeared.

"Thank you." The words came out slowly, awkwardly, but he beamed at her progress.

"I am so glad you're getting better. I knew a stroke couldn't hold you down."

She looked into his dark eyes, worried that she wouldn't live long enough to see Laci married.

"I don't want you to get better just so one day you'll be able to tell me about my birth mother. You have to know that I have grown to care a great deal for you. It's Eve I'm worried about now. She's getting married next month. Carter wants a half dozen children at least," he said with a laugh. "I know why Eve isn't as sure about children."

Pearl nodded slowly. She *did* understand. For months she'd had nothing but time on her hands. Way too much time to think—and soul-search. She'd often wondered if she hadn't had the stroke, if she would have told Bridger and Eve what they wanted to know. She'd always sworn she would take what she knew about the Whitehorse Sewing Circle's more secret activities to her grave.

She and the others had placed so many babies over the years. She knew what they had done was illegal in the eyes of the law, but she didn't believe in laws that made it difficult for those who wanted children not to be able to have them, no matter their age, their income, their abilities. Love for the child was the only criterion she could see. She would still stand behind everything she had done—even if it meant going to prison.

She'd always believed it was best if the adopted children didn't know about their birth parents. The stroke and getting to know Bridger Duvall had changed everything, she realized. She now knew the frustration of being unable to have something she desperately wanted or needed.

She also knew that she wouldn't have kept records of the information about each baby's birth parents unless she'd thought she might need it one day.

That day was near. She was able to say more words and had been practicing writing. Soon she would be able to tell Bridger what he wanted—and thus tell Eve Bailey, as well.

Eve's wedding was next month. Bridger had already informed her that he would come by to pick her up so she didn't have to miss it since he and Laci were catering the affair and he also didn't want her to miss the food.

Pearl knew what Bridger wanted for Eve's wedding day. It was why she'd been doing so much soul-searching lately. She'd seen how haunted both Bridger and Eve had been by their need to know who they were. She thanked God she hadn't died, the information dying with her. She alone knew the codes to the birth parents.

She'd done that to protect the others in the White-horse Sewing Circle.

And now she questioned whether she had the right

to keep such a secret. But what would the truth do to those involved? Bring them the peace they so desperately sought? Or, in some cases, destroy their lives?

Chapter Ten

As McKenna came out of the sheriff's department, she was surprised to see Flynn Garrett driving by. He slowed to a stop in the middle of the street and rolled down his window.

"Hello," he said, sounding genuinely glad to see her. "I had a great time the other night."

"Me, too."

He seemed to study her for a long moment. "Home ownership seems to agree with you."

She smiled and nodded, although that wasn't the case.

He glanced toward the sheriff's department. "Is everything all right?"

She knew he'd seen her coming out of the office and must wonder why. "My future brother-in-law is the sheriff."

"That's good," he said. "But why do I get the feeling there's more? You looked like you'd lost your best friend when you came out of there."

Tears blurred her eyes. She bit her lip and glanced away.

"Hey," he said. "Whatever it is, you can tell me."

She nodded and swallowed. This was so unlike her.

She'd been through so much lately. Her emotions were right on the edge.

"Is there someplace you have to be?" she asked. "I could use a cup of coffee."

"You got it," he said. "Hop in."

He took her to the only coffee shop in town. It was empty this late in the morning in a town like Whitehorse. He ordered them two black coffees and they sat at a table by the window.

"Okay, tell me what's going on," he said, not touching his coffee.

"Promise you won't think I'm crazy?"

He laughed. "Too late for that. I already think you're crazy for buying that house."

She told him about the man who'd come by supposedly looking for work and about being pushed down last night.

Flynn looked skeptical. "So you think this man hung around to push you off your porch?"

"See, I told you it sounds crazy."

"Did you get a look at him?"

She shook her head.

"Pretty odd. Unless, of course, it was a ghost."

"I don't believe in ghosts—and, believe me, the hand I felt on my back was no ghost's. That's not all." She opened her shoulder bag, took out the piece of rolled-up paper and handed it to him, desperately seeking another opinion.

His eyes widened as he unrolled it.

"Apparently it's a kind of contract. I found it under a floorboard in the house. I'm pretty sure the names on it belong to the boys who lived there when it was a home for troubled youth."

He let out a low whistle. "So what do you make of it?" he asked as he handed the paper back.

"That's just it. I don't know."

"What did your future brother-in-law say when you showed it to him?"

As she put the paper back in her shoulder bag, she glanced up at him, only a little surprised he'd figured out why she'd gone to Carter. "You think I was wrong to show it to him?"

"Not at all. Quite frankly it gives me the creeps."

She let out a relieved sigh. "I can't tell you how glad I am that someone else feels that way. It really upset me when I found it." She cupped her coffee mug in her hands and stared down into the dark brew as she breathed in the rich scent, more calm than she'd been in days.

"Your future brother-in-law wasn't worried about it?"

She shook her head. "It *has* been twenty-one years. If the boys were going to do something, wouldn't they have done it?"

Flynn shrugged. "Makes sense, I guess."

"The sheriff is going to see if any of the people who worked at Harper House—"

"Got whacked?"

She grimaced at his frankness. "There are several people who were employed there who are still alive and living here in Whitehorse, so I'm sure there is nothing to it. Just hurt and angry kids finding a little power in the idea of retribution, just like Carter said."

"Yeah. You did the right thing showing it to the sheriff, though."

Just as she'd done the right thing telling Flynn Garrett about it, she thought as she felt a sense of relief. He was easy to talk to and didn't confuse her the way Nate Dempsey did. With Flynn, she knew exactly what he wanted from her. Typical male.

But Nate Dempsey? She didn't even think he was attracted to her. He'd certainly never acted as if he was. And he *had* stood her up for their date. Nor had he bothered to ask her out again.

"So what are you doing tonight?" Flynn asked, making her realize she'd been lost in thought. About Nate. "I could go for another one of those steaks at that restaurant. What do you say?"

She had to laugh. Here she was thinking about Nate when a very handsome cowboy was asking her to dinner. "Yes, but I have to get out to the house and get some painting done first. I'm running late as it is."

"No problem. I could pick you up out there if that would save you time."

Why not? She could bathe at the house since the upstairs bath had running water. She would be glad when the shower was fixed downstairs. All she had to do was pick up a change of clothes at the ranch.

"That would be great," she said, wondering if she'd agreed to having Flynn pick her up at the house because she wanted Nate Dempsey to see that other men were interested in dating her.

Sick, she thought. She'd never thrown herself at any man and she certainly wasn't going to start now. Nor was she going to use Flynn to try to make Nate jealous.

"You know, it would be easier for you if I just met you at the restaurant like last time."

"Not a chance. I'll pick you up at the house. It's not a problem. Really. This time it's a real date," he said with a meaningful look.

She smiled, wondering about the look—and him being so agreeable to picking her up at the house he'd lost in the bidding auction.

Flynn Garrett was the type of man who might think buying a woman two steaks and a bottle of champagne warranted staying over at her house after a "real" date.

He was going to be disappointed if that was the case.

SHERIFF CARTER JACKSON hadn't wanted to worry McKenna. He was sure there was nothing to the paper she'd found under her floorboards at the house.

Yet at the same time it was the kind of thing that wasn't easily brushed off as of no consequence.

He made a few calls to people he thought might have known someone who worked out at Harper House during the time the boys had been incarcerated there.

The fact that Frank Merkel and Rosemarie Blackmore were still alive pretty much proved that the boys hadn't followed through with their threat.

Finding the boys proved harder. Some had apparently been adopted and thus had different surnames. Others just appeared to have dropped off the radar. He suspected some had died; some might have gone to prison.

He hadn't found anyone else he knew who'd worked at Harper House, either, when he looked up to see his fiancée in his office doorway. It never failed. Every time he saw Eve Bailey she took his breath away. He couldn't believe the woman had agreed to marry him. Falling in love with her was the only smart thing he'd ever done.

"Hey," he said, unable to hold back a grin. "What a surprise."

"Are you busy? If I'm interrupting something important—"

"Are you kidding? Nothing is more important than you," he said, coming around his desk to give her a kiss. He motioned to a chair and took one opposite her. "What's up?"

He just assumed it would be something about the wedding since it was only a few weeks away now.

"I have a favor to ask," Eve said.

Eve Bailey wasn't the kind of woman who asked for help if she could prevent it.

"It's about my sister."

He knew which sister at once. Eve had been concerned about McKenna buying the old Harper place. Carter doubted McKenna had shown her sister what she'd found in the house, which was just as well since he knew it would only upset Eve and he was trying desperately to keep that from happening in the days before the wedding.

"Faith?" he asked, even though he knew better.

"No, McKenna." Eve took a breath and let it out slowly. "I know you think I shouldn't be worried about her and that house. But now there is a man who is hanging around out there. When I was at the house yesterday I could tell that McKenna was upset about something. That man was there."

Carter frowned. "Someone I know?"

She shook her head. "He was driving a black pickup with Dempsey Construction on the side. She said his name was Nate."

He nodded. "You want me to see what I can find out about him?"

"Would you mind?" She sounded so relieved he couldn't help but lean across the space between them and kiss her.

"Not to worry. I'll get right on it. If there is something amiss, I'll take care of it."

Eve blessed him with a smile and he walked her to the door. He'd promised himself and her that they wouldn't make love until they were married, but it was getting more difficult with each passing day.

"I can't wait to be your wife," she whispered as she brushed against him.

He groaned. "You're a vixen," he whispered.

She laughed. "You're the one who said we had to wait."

"Yeah."

"You could change your mind."

He shook his head. "No, I want to do this right. We have the rest of our lives as husband and wife—and, believe you me, I intend to make up for lost time."

She laughed and kissed him. "I can hardly wait. You won't forget about checking on this Nate Dempsey guy. I took down his plate number, if that helps." She handed him a slip of paper with a license plate from Park County.

Carter studied his bride-to-be with admiration and a little concern. "You're really worried about this guy."

She nodded. "It's just a feeling."

"Then I'll see what I can find out right away."

McKenna had planned to pick up paint and supplies and head for the house. The last place she'd intended to go was Frank Merkel's on the edge of town.

But after showing Flynn Garrett the document she'd found, she felt even more worried. Flynn had taken it seriously, although she suspected the sheriff had played down his concern.

A small dust devil whirled through the yard as she parked and sat for a moment trying to talk herself out of this. What was she going to say, anyway?

She saw the curtain in the front room move and decided since she'd driven out this far...

Climbing out of the truck, she heard a dog bark in the backyard, then a deep male voice yell at the canine to shut up.

Before she even reached the front door, it swung open and a large, dark-haired and bearded man filled the doorway. He wore faded overalls and a flannel shirt with holes in the elbows, and his feet were bare.

"Frank Merkel?" McKenna said, questioning the impulse to come out here.

"Yeah?" He had a broad, flat face that looked as if it had been slammed in a door and flat, dark eyes that stared blankly at her.

This had seemed like a good idea a few minutes and miles ago. "I'm McKenna Bailey."

His eyes narrowed.

He looked past her to her pickup, then shifted his gaze back to her face. "What do you want?" His tone was even less friendly than his expression.

"I just bought the old Harper House—"

"You have the wrong person." He started to close the door.

"Wait. I heard you used to work there. I wanted to warn you."

"Warn me?" he demanded through the crack between door and jamb.

All she could see now was one of his eyes. "I found something in the house, a piece of paper that the boys wrote on. I think you might be in danger."

Her words echoed off the closed door as he slammed it. In the backyard, the dog began to bark again.

She didn't have the wrong person. She'd seen his change of expression when she'd mentioned Harper House. She stood for a moment, thinking he might come back. Then, admitting this had been a mistake, she walked back through the patch of weeds to her pickup.

Angry with Frank Merkel for dismissing her concerns so rudely and furious with herself for thinking talking to him was a good idea in the first place, she started the engine and checked her watch. She needed to get out to the house. Her sisters would be there soon to help paint. She needed the help, and they would both be understandably angry if she wasn't there when they arrived.

But she had one more stop to make and then she would put this whole blood-oath thing behind her.

As McKenna pulled up in the driveway of the small clapboard house at the end of the Whitehorse street, she saw a small white-haired woman out watering her flower beds.

The woman looked up as McKenna got out of her truck and walked up the narrow sidewalk. The street was quiet except for the groan of a lawn mower a block away and the coo of a dove on a telephone wire overhead.

That was something McKenna had missed living in a larger city: the sound of birds instead of traffic. In Whitehorse, if four cars went by, you could bet something was going on.

Rosemarie Blackmore gave her the once-over and returned to watering her flowers. Ever since McKenna had purchased the old Harper House she'd felt as if people were treating her strangely. She suspected Rosemarie knew why she was here and wanted none of it—much like Frank Merkel.

But, damn it all, she had to try. She'd never forgive herself if something happened to them and she hadn't even tried to warn them. As the new owner of Harper House, she felt responsible.

"Mrs. Blackmore?"

Rosemarie flicked a look at her but said nothing.

"I need to talk to you about Harper House," McKenna said, getting right to the heart of it. "If you could just spare me a minute. It's important."

Rosemarie made a displeased face, but she shut off the water, wiped her hands on the apron she was wearing and said, "Well, come on in, then."

McKenna followed her inside. Rosemarie Blackmore looked like a grandmother, from the countless knickknacks everywhere to the crocheted doilies and the knitting bag beside her chair with a half-finished afghan spilling out of it. Across from it was a worn leather chair with a stack of hunting magazines next to it—no doubt just as it had been when her husband was alive.

"I'm McKenna Bailey," she said once they were standing in the cluttered living room. "I just bought the old Harper House."

"I know who you are," the older woman said impatiently.

"I understand you used to work at what was known as Harper House when it was a home for troubled boys."

"It's no *secret*. I used to cook out there." A large yellow tomcat came strutting into the room. He wound his way around Rosemarie's legs and purred loudly. As the elderly woman stooped to pick up the cat, she motioned McKenna into a chair, then took one herself, the large cat on her lap as she waited for the next question with impatient politeness.

"When did you work there?"

Rosemarie shrugged. "A few months in the early eighties, I believe. Why do you care about this anyway?"

"I heard that some of the boys might have been mistreated."

She snorted. "So you're one of those people who thinks they should have been pampered. Let me tell you something—those boys were hellions. I lived in fear every minute I was in that house."

"I had no idea they were that bad," McKenna said.

"Bad? They were evil. The whole lot of them were destined to become hardened criminals."

"But they were so *young*," McKenna said.

Rosemarie snorted again. "Their characters were already forged by the time they ended up at Harper House." She hugged the cat closer as if chilled.

"Can you tell me who else worked there?"

"Why?" she asked suspiciously.

"I'm trying to find one of the boys," McKenna said.

"I can't imagine why."

"Would you know any of them or how to contact them?"

She shoved the cat off her lap. He skulked away, meowing loudly. "No, I wouldn't." She rose to her feet. "I stayed in the kitchen, did my job, then got the devil out of there. They were a rowdy bunch of boys. It wasn't my place to say how they should be raised. They were boys nobody wanted and there was a reason for it."

"But you *did* hear things."

"I didn't hear anything. I didn't see anything."

"You never heard from any of them?"

Rosemarie's eyes widened. "Why would I?"

"I just thought there might have been one who appreciated your cooking, one you might have gotten close to." McKenna knew she was clutching at straws, but she couldn't help thinking of the boy she'd seen in the third-floor window that day so many years ago.

Clearly agitated, Rosemarie shook her head. "I didn't want to see any of them ever again and I hope I don't. They were like wild dogs. I saw the way they looked at me each day when I left." She cringed. "Now, if you'll excuse me, I have things to do. Leo will be wanting his lunch."

It wasn't near lunchtime, and her husband, Leo, had been dead for four years. But McKenna didn't argue. She rose, thanking Rosemarie for her time.

"There is one other thing," McKenna said, unable to leave without at least warning the woman. "I found something in the house. A note the boys wrote," she said, playing it down. "They sounded angry and made some threats…"

Rosemarie was visibly agitated now. "You really should go."

"I just thought you should be warned. I doubt there is anything to worry about, but if any of them should come by—"

"I don't see why you want that house," Rosemarie said. "Makes no sense."

Makes no sense to anyone in this town, McKenna thought. And lately it hadn't been making a lot of sense to her either.

"Please, just take care of yourself," McKenna said as she left, Rosemarie closing the door firmly behind her.

McKenna was mentally kicking herself for upsetting Rosemarie as she started to climb into her truck when Nate Dempsey pulled up.

"Hey," he said as if surprised to see her. "I thought you'd be painting like crazy by now."

Why did she get the feeling he'd been looking for her? "I should be. I decided to talk to a couple of people who used to work at Harper House."

"Why?" he asked, sounding worried.

"I want to know more about the place."

"Do you think that's a good idea? You might not like what you find out. Unless you've already found out something that has you upset."

Did he know about the paper she'd found? But then, how could he? And why hadn't she shown it to him? After all, he was staying out at the place. If she trusted him...

"I'm headed for the house now. My sisters are coming over to help me paint."

He nodded. "I came in to pick up a couple of plumbing parts. By the time you get to the house I'll have your shower working for you."

"Thank you. Let me know what I owe you for parts..."

He waved that off as he drove away, leaving her standing in the street. She couldn't help but feel that he was upset with her. She reminded herself that he thought she was crazy for buying Harper House. No wonder he thought she was wrong to go around digging up its past.

As she turned toward her pickup, she glanced back at Rosemarie Blackmore's small white house.

The tiny gray-haired woman was standing in the front window. She was staring after Nate Dempsey.

McKenna saw the expression on the woman's face and felt her knees go weak.

Rosemarie Blackmore looked as if she'd seen a ghost.

Chapter Eleven

Her sisters were waiting for her when McKenna reached the house. She noticed that Nate's pickup was nowhere to be seen—just Eve's parked out front.

"Sorry. I got hung up," she said as she quickly began to unload the paint she'd purchased and the supplies.

"We just got here," Faith said, even though Eve was giving McKenna a questioning eye.

"Nate was leaving as we came in," Eve said.

"I guess he got my shower fixed, then," she said as she headed into the house with a gallon of paint dangling from each hand. "I'm going to have to quit early. I have a date with Flynn tonight."

"Flynn?" Eve and Faith echoed behind her, making her smile.

"He's the one I had dinner with Saturday night after the auction. We're having dinner again tonight." She grinned at them as she stopped to open the door.

"Flynn?" she heard Eve say again behind her. "How many men is she seeing?"

Faith giggled. "She's just having fun."

"Fun? You call this fun?" Eve said as she and Faith followed McKenna into the house.

They painted throughout the rest of the morning.

Eve had brought a picnic basket. They ate sandwiches on the porch and discussed how the work was going. Well, since all of the rooms upstairs were painted except for the trim, and they would have that done by midafternoon and quit for the day so McKenna could get ready for her date.

"So tell us about Flynn," Eve said.

McKenna smiled over at her sister. "You worry too much."

"Right."

"He's picking me up here, so if you're that curious, you can stay and meet him," McKenna said.

"So you aren't serious about him if you'd let us meet him," Eve said and took a bite of her sandwich.

"I'm not serious about anyone," McKenna protested. "I'm going to be too busy getting my business going to worry about a man."

Eve nodded, her gaze saying she didn't believe it for a minute. "So tell me about this Nate who's helping with your house."

McKenna shrugged. "There isn't much to tell. He needed a place to board his horse, so we traded services."

"He sure didn't stick around long once he saw us," Eve commented.

"I'm sure he had things to do," McKenna said, wondering where he'd gone—and why he did seem to make himself scarce when her sisters were around.

NATE DROVE HIS pickup down the dusty, rough road, keeping his eyes peeled on his rearview mirror for any sign of another vehicle.

He was certain he hadn't been followed, but for days

he'd felt as if he was being watched. It surprised him that Roy Vaughn hadn't made his move. But, then again, Vaughn had always loved playing cat and mouse—just as long as he got to be the cat.

Nate couldn't be sure that the man who called himself Hal Turner was indeed Roy Vaughn. But Vaughn had been a big kid, a bully, and he'd liked to think of himself as the next legendary Hal Turner.

That was why for years Nate had found himself looking over his shoulder, expecting at any moment to feel the burning prick of a knife blade in his back. He remembered only too well the switchblade that Roy Vaughn had kept under his mattress. It took a dark soul to like killing up close and personal with a blade.

So what was Vaughn waiting for? That's what bothered Nate as he drove. That and the fact that he hadn't seen Lucky.

"I'm not afraid of Roy," Lucky had said.

"You should be."

Lucky had only shrugged. "Maybe I'm enough like him that he's always left me alone."

Lucky had always liked to think himself tougher than he was. But, thinking back, for some reason Roy Vaughn *had* left Lucky alone. Maybe it was because Vaughn had had Nate and Johnny to pick on.

The road wound through a narrow canyon in the Bear Paw Mountains. Pine trees grew lush green against towering vertical slabs of sandstone. Not far up the road, the canyon opened some to end in a jumble of rock. A box canyon. A dead end.

Nate slowed the pickup, on alert. He'd seen the tracks in the road where someone had been up here right after the rain. But that could have been anyone. He'd seen no sign of another living soul. Not unusual in this part of the country. Montana had an average population of 6.2 people per square mile—except up here, where it was more like 0.3 people.

In this part of the state there were more cows than people. Hell, cows outnumbered people in Montana three to one.

Nate stopped the pickup at the end of the road and sat for a moment, window down, just listening. This is where they'd found Roy Vaughn the one and only time he'd escaped from Harper House. Nate would never forget the look on Vaughn's face. He'd been holed up in some rocks at the back of the canyon. The fool hadn't realized it was a box canyon—no way out.

Mostly Vaughn hadn't realized that Harper House was the same way. No way out back then. Except maybe death.

Nate always wondered if Vaughn hadn't wished for that very thing when he saw the Harper House's old Suburban drive up and knew he was trapped. Worse than trapped. Caught.

Shoving away the memory, Nate cautiously got out. The ground had dried since the rain. Heat beat down from a sun positioned overhead. The ponderosa pines glistened, a silky green. There was no breath of air down in here. No sound. The stillness would get to anyone, Nate told himself as he pulled his weapon from his holster and walked toward the back of the canyon wall. To the place where they'd found Vaughn hunkered down.

He'd looked like a wild animal. His eyes glowing in the blare of the flashlight beam. Everyone had known he would head for the mountains if he ever got away. He missed the mountains the most, he used to say.

It had taken four of them to restrain Vaughn. He'd fought like the animal he appeared to be. But that wasn't what haunted Nate to this day. It was the sound Vaughn had made. A high-pitched keening sound. The sound Nate suspected someone made when they were being tortured—right before they were killed.

As he neared the rocks, he felt his pulse quicken. His senses intensified; he thought he could feel Vaughn's presence here. He peered into the shadows of the rocks, the gun in his hand, the hair standing up on the back of his neck.

He'd thought just by coming back to Harper House he would have drawn Vaughn out by now. Instead Roy Vaughn was toying with him. Or maybe he was waiting to see if Nate found Johnny's body, all the time knowing that wasn't going to happen because he'd moved it.

Either way, Nate knew he'd been a fool to think that Vaughn would make it easy for him.

But he also couldn't keep looking over his shoulder for the rest of his life. Vaughn was in town. Nate was convinced he was the man McKenna had seen. It would end where it had started. But apparently on Vaughn's terms.

Or maybe it would end in this canyon, right here, right now. Vaughn would know that Nate would search him out. Hell, he could be watching Nate from some of the rocks higher up the canyon wall and laughing his ass off that Nate had been so stupid as to come here alone.

Even armed, Nate knew he would be no match for the Roy Vaughn he'd known. The kid had been a bull, strong and tough. Nate hated to imagine what he was like as a grown man with years of cruelty behind him.

But unfortunately—or maybe fortunately—Vaughn wasn't hiding in the canyon. At least not today.

Which meant he could be anywhere. Even at Harper House.

McKENNA DIDN'T SEE Nate all afternoon. After lunch, some of their friends came by, including the sheriff and a couple of deputies.

She saw Eve and the sheriff, their heads together, discussing something that looked serious. But a few moments later she saw Eve give Carter a kiss and tried to relax. This wedding had to go off as planned. McKenna was the maid of honor and felt responsible for seeing that nothing went wrong.

At one point the sheriff pulled McKenna aside.

"I did some checking on people who used to work out here." He seemed to hesitate. "Quite a few of them *are* deceased, but the only ones with foul play indicated were the Cherrys."

McKenna nodded. She'd grown up on the edge of Old Town Whitehorse, so she knew the story of Norman and Alma Cherry only too well. Norman had allegedly taken his wife down to the root cellar in the middle of the night, put a bullet in her head, then one in his own. No one had ever known why.

"Is it possible they were the first?" McKenna asked.

Carter shook his head. "That was more than thirty years ago. The paper you found was dated only twenty-one years ago."

She had a terrible thought. "Unless this death pact wasn't something new to Harper House. The Winthrops told me it's been operating over thirty years. Maybe these boys got the idea from others who had lived there before them."

"Let's not jump to conclusions," he said. "I'm still doing some checking."

"Who else is deceased?"

Carter handed her a list of the names.

She scanned it and froze. "Hal Turner?"

"Killed in a hunting accident."

McKenna fought to breathe. "A man stopped by here the other day. He said his name was Hal Turner."

"Obviously not the same Hal Turner," Carter said and then seemed to notice how shaken she was. "Am I missing something here?"

"What if the man I saw was one of the boys using the name of someone who used to work there?"

"McKenna, you're starting to worry me now. I think you're letting this get to you. Hal Turner didn't work there. He was one of the first guys who lived there." He took the list from her. "All of these deaths were ruled an accident, okay?"

She nodded numbly. It was too much of a coincidence that the man had used that name. She'd known he was lying at the time. Now she knew Hal Turner had been one of the boys who'd lived in the house. "What about the names on the list that I found?"

"Three of them are deceased," Carter said. "Lyle Weston, Steven Cross and Andrew Charles. Bobby French is serving time in prison in Oregon. The others I haven't been able to find. But, as I told you, some of them were adopted, so their names would have been changed when they were still juveniles."

She nodded. That left only three names on the list:

Roy Vaughn, Lucky Thomas and Denny Jones. She felt some relief that the others were accounted for.

"By the way, I see you have someone staying out back," the sheriff said.

She cringed. So like Carter to have noticed even though Nate's tent wasn't visible from the house. The only way Carter could have noticed was if he had looked around the property.

"Nate Dempsey," she said, trying to sound as casual as possible. "He's trading work for boarding his horse. I told him he could camp out there to make it easier for him to work on the house."

"What do you know about him?" Carter asked.

"He fixed my shower and made some other repairs that will make it possible for me to move in soon," she said maybe a little too cheerfully.

"How long is he staying?"

Good question. "Just until I move into the house," she said, thinking that was probably true. As much as he apparently liked his solitude, she couldn't see him hanging around after that. Unless he was the one who'd been digging in her yard—and hadn't found what he was looking for.

She expected Carter to interrogate her further and was surprised when he didn't.

By late afternoon the painting was done. Tomorrow, if it didn't rain, the furniture would be brought in.

She'd painted her office a sunny yellow. The bedroom she'd painted a pale lilac like the trees just outside her window. The other rooms were varying shades of warm, rich color.

"Too girlie," one of the off-duty deputies said about

the color she'd chosen for her bedroom. "Didn't they have a nice tan?" he only half joked.

"White's good, too," said Deputy Nicolas Giovanni.

"A little colorphobic, are you, Nicolas?" Eve teased. "Are you trying to tell me that Laney is painting all the walls in your new house white?"

"I suggested it," Nicolas said with a grin.

"And he lived to tell about it," Carter added. "We've got to go. You have everything under control out here?"

McKenna nodded and thanked them all. After the men left, she noticed that Nate's pickup was still gone. What did he do when he wasn't here? She had no idea. He'd said he had business in Whitehorse. None of her business.

The men all left promising to help with the furniture move. After they'd gone, Eve said she had to go, as well.

"What? You aren't going to stay and meet Flynn?" McKenna asked.

"No reason to," Eve said. "You aren't serious about him."

"Well, I'd like to meet him if he's as handsome as she says," Faith joked.

As McKenna watched her sisters leave, she thought how she'd never been able to fool Eve even when they were young. Eve knew her too well.

SHERIFF CARTER JACKSON had just walked into his house when he got the call.

"You were asking about people who used to work out there at the old Harper place?"

"Yes." He recognized the woman's voice as that of Mabel Brooks, an eightysomething ranch woman who raised sheep on her place outside of town. He didn't bother to question how she'd heard he'd been asking around.

"I remember the first couple who worked out there," Mabel was saying. "Cherry was their name. Both dead. Then there was Lloyd Frasier. Also dead."

Carter listened, jotting down the new names going back to when Harper House had begun taking in troubled boys. All of the former workers were deceased. Heart attacks, car wrecks, ranch and hunting accidents. Except for the Cherrys' murder/suicide.

The longer he listened, the more concerned he became. A lot of bad luck had befallen anyone who'd worked at the place, apparently.

Still, he thought as he hung up, Frank Merkel and Rosemarie Blackmore were fine. Could it be a coincidence so many of the people had died? Could be their ages, he reminded himself. The place had sprung up more than thirty years before. The youngest of people who worked there had to be over fifty now, many much older than that.

He realized he hadn't heard back on his request for information on Nate Dempsey, and now that he knew the man was staying on McKenna's property…

He called, this time ringing the chief of police in Paradise at home. The joke about small-town sheriffs and chiefs of police was that more people knew their home phone number than that of their office.

"You're inquiring about Nate Dempsey?" the chief asked, sounding amused. "May I ask why?"

"With all the construction fraud nowadays, I was just checking to make sure there wasn't a problem with him working on a house up here."

"He picked up a hammer again? He must be doing some moonlighting on his vacation, then," the chief said.

Huh? "Are you saying he isn't employed in construction? He's driving a truck with Dempsey Construction on the side."

"He *was* in the construction business with his brother. That must be his brother's pickup he's driving. But Nate hasn't worked construction for almost ten years now."

Chapter Twelve

After everyone was gone, McKenna felt restless. She finally walked up the creek to where Nate Dempsey had pitched his tent. She saw his Appaloosa on the other side of the fence, grazing in the summer sun, but no sign of Nate. His horse trailer was parked next to the barn, his pickup gone.

Blue came over to the fence to give her a nuzzle. She rubbed the horse's neck and thought about peeking into Nate's tent. *For what?* she asked herself. *What is it you need to know before you trust the man?*

At the sound of a vehicle coming up the road she turned to see a black pickup headed this way. The last thing she wanted to do was get caught out here by his tent, but it was too late to escape unnoticed.

Nate drove up the drive past the house to park next to the barn.

She could only watch him as he got out and strode toward her. It wasn't until he was almost to her that she could see his face in the shadow of his Western straw hat brim. He didn't look happy.

"That horse can be temperamental," he snapped.

"Yeah, I can see that," she said, giving Blue one last

pat before she moved away from the fence. "He seems to be settled in fine. What about you?"

"As you can see, I have everything I need."

Apparently.

"How did the painting go?" he asked as if trying to make conversation, although clearly something else was on his mind. "I thought your sisters would still be here with you."

"They just left. We got the upstairs done. They're coming back tomorrow with a load of my furniture."

"You're going to move in before you finish all the painting?" He sounded more than surprised.

"It will make it easier to get the work done if I'm staying here. We plugged in the old fridge in the kitchen. It works. So I'll bring some food out. My new stove should be delivered soon. I'll be fine."

He nodded but didn't look happy about it.

"And you'll be here if there's any trouble, right?"

She hated the fear that seemed to close her throat at the thought that he'd hightail it the moment she moved in.

"I'll be here," he said, not sounding in the least happy about that, either.

"Great." She wanted to ask him what he was really doing here. Not for a place to board his horse. He'd said he was here on business. He just hadn't mentioned for how long.

She glanced at her watch, telling herself that once she was settled in the house maybe it would be best if he left. She would always wonder what it was that he really wanted. He still hadn't asked her out, although she'd expected him to mention Whitehorse Days again. He hadn't, though.

"Well, I need to get ready for my…" She bit her tongue, but it was too late. "Date." She groaned inwardly. Why had she mentioned her date? Was she expecting some kind of reaction from him? Say, something akin to jealousy? Well, if she was, she was sadly disappointed.

He said nothing as she took a couple steps backward. She turned and walked toward the house as quickly as she could, mentally kicking herself the entire way.

FLYNN GARRETT WAS nothing if not prompt. As he climbed out of his truck, she saw him glance up at the house and shake his head.

"Want to see what we've done upstairs?" she asked.

"A waste of paint," he said but smiled as he did. "Maybe some other time. I have us a reservation for seven and we'll be late if we don't leave now. Rain check on the tour?"

"Sure." Although she was disappointed. But she understood on some level that he didn't want to see the house he'd tried to buy himself.

They ordered steaks again. No champagne this time. Conversation seemed harder this time, and McKenna wondered if she'd made a mistake by having Flynn pick her up at the house. He'd been overly quiet ever since, as if brooding.

"I did something crazy today," she said.

He looked up expectantly from his dessert.

"I went by the homes of the two people who used to work at Harper House and warned them they might be in danger."

He put down his fork. "You're kidding? I thought the sheriff told you there was nothing to worry about."

"Yes, but I felt I had to."

"And?"

"Neither appreciated my concern. Both pretty much threw me out."

"Ingrates," he said. "You do realize that you may have just put yourself in jeopardy, though, don't you? I mean, if you're right and these guys are coming back after twenty-one years, seeking vengeance, they probably wouldn't appreciate you butting in."

She hadn't thought of that. "More than likely all I did was scare a couple of old people for no reason. I'm beginning to think that I'm dead wrong about this."

"Interesting turn of phrase." He smiled. It was nothing like Nate's smile. "I wouldn't worry about it. If you're right, by buying Harper House you've already put yourself in jeopardy. You probably didn't make it any worse today."

"Thanks," she said with a laugh. "I knew you'd make me feel better."

"Sorry." He frowned. "I just wish I'd known you were considering doing that. I would have tried to talk you out of it."

She nodded, knowing he wouldn't have been able to, but no reason to tell him how stubborn she could be. "Fortunately, I don't think there is anything to it. After all these years, what are the chances?"

"Well, you gave it your best shot," he said.

Yes, hadn't she? She frowned as she remembered Rosemarie's expression as she'd watched Nate drive away. No doubt it was from being frightened by the news McKenna had brought her. Or maybe she'd mistakenly thought Nate was one of the boys, grown now.

She reminded herself again that his name hadn't been on the list. That she and Rosemarie Blackmore were both a little crazy.

"I have to tell you," Flynn said, drawing her attention back to their date. "When I picked you up at the house this evening I was thinking about what you found there. The paper. Quite frankly, I'm not sure you're safe there. Maybe you should stay at your family's ranch until you're sure there's nothing to all this."

She thought about mentioning the man she had living on the creek behind the house but thought better of it. The fewer people who knew about her arrangement, the better.

"Maybe," she agreed, then changed the subject, and in a few minutes Flynn was telling her funny stories about the ranches he'd worked on, his worries about her apparently forgotten.

IT WAS DARK by the time Flynn dropped her off at the house. He left the engine running.

"I have an early day tomorrow," he said as he got out and walked her to the door.

This time when he kissed her McKenna knew it was their last date—and she realized she was fine with that.

She watched him drive away, wondering if Nate was camped on the creek. Or if he'd gone into town. Or maybe even left. And told herself the only reason she cared was that she wanted him around for a while. Just until she got completely moved in. Until she was sure the strange man wouldn't be back. Or that there re ally was nothing to the contract she'd found under the floorboards.

But the truth was she wanted him around. She had no idea what it was about him that drew her to him. These feelings made no sense, especially since he obviously didn't share them.

She pulled her pickup keys from her shoulder bag. There was really no reason to go into the house since she was still staying down at her family's ranch until her furniture was moved in tomorrow.

But she was here and the night was young. She might as well take a look at the upstairs, admire the work they'd done and think about where she'd put the furniture when it arrived.

Unlocking the door, she reached in and turned on a light before stepping inside. The wood floors gleamed. She couldn't wait to finish the painting. The house already had a different feel to it, didn't it?

She glanced through to the kitchen and the window that looked out on the backyard—and the creek. She could see a flickering light through the branches on the cottonwoods along the creek. A campfire. Nate. Her pulse took off, heart beating a little faster. He was here.

Climbing the steps to the top floor, she turned on a light and surveyed the painted rooms, talking herself out of walking back up the creek on some pretense to see him. The floors up here glistened in the light, the paint smell still strong even though she'd opened all the windows.

The faint breeze wafting in smelled of cottonwoods and summer nights. She stepped to it, breathing in the memories of her childhood summers. What kind of memories did the boys have who used to live here?

The thought startled her, just as did the creak of the stairs behind her. She spun around to find Nate Dempsey standing in the doorway.

NATE TRIED TO still the pounding in his pulse. He'd followed her up here with one thing in mind. But seeing her standing there...in this room...the summer smells coming through the open window—all of it took him back to a place he had never wanted to go again.

"You scared me," she snapped, a hand going to her heart, those blue eyes wide and frightened.

"I'm sorry. I didn't mean to startle you. I saw a light..." He was sick of the lying. "Are you all right?"

She nodded.

"I saw someone leaving the house," he said, trying not to let her see how upset he was.

"My *date*."

He couldn't miss her sarcasm. "I thought he'd take you back to your family ranch and you'd come over in the morning with your sisters. I didn't realize you'd be back here tonight."

"It *is* my house. I came back for my pickup."

He chewed on his cheek for a moment. She hadn't just come back for her truck. He suspected she'd come back to check up on him. And she wasn't just scared, she was angry. Angry with him.

"If I've done something to make you mad at me—"

"Other than scare me half to death?"

He sighed. "I apologize. I called up the stairs. I'm sorry you didn't hear me." Another lie.

She let out a long breath. "It's not you. It's me. I'm just tired." Lying seemed to be catching.

"So I take it your date didn't go well?" He hated how much that appealed to him.

"The date was fine. It's just been a long day and you scared me, that's all."

"Okay." He pretended to start back downstairs but hesitated as if as an afterthought. "Mind if I ask who that was you were with tonight?"

She touched her tongue to her lower lip, then seemed to make up her mind. Damn, but the woman had a fine mouth.

"Flynn Garrett."

Lucky was going by the name Flynn Garrett? Or maybe that was his *real* name, for all Nate knew. But why hadn't Lucky mentioned this? It took all of his self-control to keep from letting her see how upset he was.

"Flynn's the man I had dinner with the other night who I thought was my date." She frowned. "I thought you saw us together?"

A lie that had come back on him. When was he going to learn? "It was dark out front. I didn't recognize him. You're still seeing him?"

She cut her eyes to him.

"I'm not jealous, if that's what you're thinking."

"Why would I think that?"

"You can see anyone you want. It's just that…wasn't he at the auction? Didn't he bid against you?"

"What are you trying to say?" she asked, hands going to her hips, blue eyes firing.

"Nothing. I'm not trying to say anything. Just forget you even saw me tonight. I wouldn't want to ruin your *date*."

Since the first time he'd laid eyes on McKenna Bailey as a grown woman he'd done his damnedest not to notice just how much of a woman she'd become. But it had been getting next to impossible for some time now.

The thought of her with Lucky was enough to make him homicidal. Nate couldn't believe he was letting this woman work him up like this. What the hell was wrong with him?

And what the hell was Lucky up to?

Before Nate could descend the stairs, she grabbed his arm and spun him around to face her. "You have something to say, so let's hear it."

McKENNA WASN'T ABOUT to let him get away that easily. He was angry and upset, and she wasn't going to just let him walk away until she knew what was going on with him. This had been coming for a long time between them, a tension building, and tonight was the night.

"Okay," he said slowly, squaring off against her. He seemed to choose his words carefully, although she could see that he was as angry as she'd been. "All I'm saying is that the guy might have ulterior motives, that's all. He bid against you on the house. He might think there's another way to get the house that would cost him even less if he plays his cards right."

As if she hadn't thought of that herself. "Unlike you," she said.

"I'm not after your *house*."

"Oh, yeah? Then what *are* you after? I know you aren't out here out of the goodness of your heart—or for a place to board your horse. So why don't you be honest with me? Tell me the truth for once."

He took a step toward her, closing what little distance there'd been between them, his brown eyes blazing. Suddenly there wasn't enough air in the room.

"You want honesty?" he asked, his voice deep and low and fired with passion. "You sure you can take it?"

She felt a hitch in her chest, but she held her ground.

"I *am* jealous, all right?" He was within inches of her now, his gaze locked with hers. "Ever since I first saw you, you've been a thorn in my side. I wanted you. I *wanted* to ride off with you. I still *want* you—and you're the last thing I need right now."

Before she could move or breathe or speak, his warm palm cupped her jaw and his mouth was on hers.

The kiss was even more unexpected in its effect on her. His free arm encircled her waist to drag her to him as he tipped her head back and deepened the kiss. She felt her toes curl, her face flush, her heart threaten to burst from her chest.

This was some kiss, and yet she suspected Nate Dempsey was just getting started.

She leaned into him, swallowed up in his embrace, in the feel of his mouth on hers, the taste of him. *She'd* wanted this. As crazy as it seemed, she'd dreamed of this from the day she'd first laid eyes on Nate Dempsey on the street in Whitehorse.

And just when she was being completely honest with herself about what she wanted from Nate Dempsey, he let her go.

"Any more questions?" he asked, his voice sounding rougher than sandpaper.

She shook her head, not trusting her voice. She was shaking all over and close to tears.

"I think that's enough honesty for one night, don't you?" he said.

No! she thought. She couldn't stand to let him walk

away. Not now. Her body cried out for him even as her mind warned her not to be a fool.

"Good night, McKenna. If you need me, you know where to find me."

With that, he turned and left, leaving her emotionally wasted, her body still tingling from his kiss and, worse, wanting more.

She stood for a long while listening to the thud of her heart before she went downstairs. She'd known he would be gone, but she'd half hoped he would come back.

Downstairs, she wandered through the house, telling herself she hadn't made a mistake. About this house. About Nate Dempsey.

But as she locked up and left, she feared she had on both counts.

NATE WAITED UNTIL McKenna left before he went to look for Lucky. He found him at the local bar. At a glance, he could see that Lucky had had more than a few beers.

"We need to talk," Nate said, not bothering to take a stool.

Lucky grinned over at him. "Wondered how long it would be before you found out."

"Let's take this outside. *Now.*"

Lucky shoved away the half-empty bottle of beer sitting in front of him and slid off his stool. "Let's do it." He staggered a little as Nate let him lead the way outside.

The main street that ran through Whitehorse was nearly deserted except for the pickups parked in front of the bars. The night was dark and cool. A few streets over, a semi truck shifted down as it slowed to turn south off the Hi-Line highway.

"What the hell do you think you're doing going out with McKenna Bailey?" Nate demanded.

Lucky laughed. "Whoa, buddy. Look, McKenna and I had dinner together. When we ran into each other again I thought what the heck. But that was it. No chemistry, you know?"

Nate thought about the chemistry he felt around McKenna. "I don't want you seeing her again. It's too dangerous."

Lucky held up his hands. "You're telling me? Just picking her up at that house…it gave me the creeps."

"You sure you're up to what we had planned for tomorrow?" he asked.

Lucky straightened. "I'm sober as a judge."

Right.

"Hey, buddy," he said, laying a hand on Nate's shoulder. "You were my only friend at Harper House. I haven't forgotten that." His face seemed to cloud. "I just wish you could let this go, man. I really wish you could. I don't want anything bad to happen to you."

Nate nodded. "I appreciate that. So tomorrow morning, right?"

"Yeah," Lucky said, removing his hand and smiling ruefully. "Give me a couple hours. I'll do what I can."

Chapter Thirteen

The next morning when McKenna reached the house, she wasn't surprised to see that Nate's truck and horse trailer were gone.

And still her heart fell. Of course he would leave. He'd opened up to her last night. He'd told her how he felt and that she was the last thing he needed. And now he was gone.

She unlocked the front door to the house, hating the horrible ache she felt. What was it about this man? She was too smart to fall for someone like him. The man couldn't be any more unavailable. Was that the appeal?

Her furniture would be arriving this afternoon. Eve had called to say she had a wedding gown fitting so she and Faith wouldn't be out until afternoon to help.

Suddenly McKenna felt overwhelmed and had more doubts about her impetuousness in buying this house and starting a horse ranch. Had she been a fool to think that she could do this on her own? Let alone overcome this house's past?

At the sound of a vehicle, she saw Nate's pickup and horse trailer turn into the driveway. She hated the way her heart soared at just the sight of him. He hadn't left.

She frowned as she saw that he had two horses in the trailer. She hurried out to meet him. "Is that *my* horse?"

"I certainly hope so. Otherwise I'm going to be arrested and hanged as a horse thief." He looked shy and uncertain this morning. His hair sticking out from his Western straw hat looked damp, as if he'd only recently come from a shower. She caught the fresh scent of him and felt an ache that went beyond wanting.

"Look," he was saying. "I hope you don't mind me taking it upon myself, but you've been working so hard on this place. I thought you might want to ride the property and remember maybe why you bought this place. It certainly couldn't have been because of the house."

She started to correct him but stopped herself. His offer couldn't have come at a better time. How did he know this was exactly what she needed? "Want to tell me how you knew which horse was mine?"

"I'm good, but I'm not so good that I just drove by your ranch and said, 'Hey, I bet McKenna Bailey rides that paint.'" He smiled, his eyes warming her like the summer day. "I asked your sister Faith, told her what I had in mind, and she helped me load your mare in my trailer along with your saddle and tack."

Apparently Nate wasn't the only one who knew she needed her horse today. The thought of riding around the property instead of working on the house was more than a welcome one. She'd been so busy she hadn't ridden her horse in days. And riding with Nate...well, she couldn't have asked for anything better right now.

"Thank you," she said. A little voice at the back of her mind questioned his motive for the gesture, but she ignored it, refusing to look a gift horse in the mouth. Especially this particular one. "This was very thoughtful of you."

NATE SAID NOTHING, feeling the sting of guilt. Thoughtful was the last thing he was.

They saddled up and rode through the tall green grass undulating in the breeze. It was one of those days when the sky was as blue as McKenna's eyes. White clouds drifted along on the summer-scented breeze.

Nate loved days like this. He remembered hiding in the grass, staring up at such a sky and praying that someday he would escape Harper House. But his dream had been to learn to ride a horse and go riding with the girl he'd seen on the paint horse.

He glanced over at McKenna. As beautiful as the woman and the day were, it wasn't quite the dream he'd hoped for. In his dream he hadn't been doing it to get her away from the house for his own selfish reasons.

He pushed the thought away as they rode over a rise, the house disappearing behind them. They followed the edge of the creek to her property line, then angled toward a stand of juniper at the far corner.

In the distance he could make out the rough breaks of the Missouri River as it cut across this wild part of Montana. He was surprised how pretty this country was. He'd remembered it as stark, as stark as his heart had been when he'd finally escaped Harper House.

"If you tell anyone what happened here, no one will believe you," he'd been told by the people who'd run the place. "No one will want to adopt a child like that. They'll put you in a mental hospital behind bars, and you will never see daylight again."

At eight, he'd believed it. He'd known how powerless he was as a child. People believed adults, and he'd seen what these adults were capable of, as well as the other kids. He wasn't about to say a word.

"It's beautiful, isn't it?" McKenna said as she reined in her horse and sat looking out across the land.

"Yes." He wished he was seeing it for the first time. But in a way he was—through her eyes.

The breeze played at wisps of her blond hair that hung from beneath her straw hat. The hat was pushed back, exposing her sun-kissed face, the skin lightly freckled and glowing. She couldn't have been more beautiful. Or more unattainable.

He looked away, torn by a desire to have this woman that ran deeper than her roots in this untamed country.

"This would be a great spot to build a house," he said. From here, he couldn't see Harper House. From here, he could believe it no longer existed. Here, he could believe dreams came true.

"I *have* a house," she said, frowning over at him.

He wished he hadn't spoken and broken the spell. As she spurred her horse and took off down the slope toward a spot where the creek pooled, he caught a whiff of her perfume. It threatened to drop him to his knees.

By the time he caught up to her, she had already dismounted and was pulling off her boots.

He swung down from his horse and watched as she kicked aside her boots, stripped off her socks and rolled up her jeans to wade into the clear, flowing water.

She let out a squeal that made him laugh. "Aren't you going to join me?"

He knew the water would be ice-cold this time of

year, but he couldn't resist the challenge he heard in her voice any more than he could resist the woman herself.

Shaking his head at his own foolhardiness, he tugged off his boots and socks and, rolling up his pant legs, waded in. "It's freezing cold!"

She laughed, a wonderful sound, and for a moment it could have been one of his boyhood dreams. They were kids on a summer day, playing in the creek. She splashed him, and he let out a shocked roar as the icy water took his breath away. He lunged for her as she splashed him again.

And time stopped. Their eyes locked across the frozen space. The suspended water droplets flashed in the summer sun and turned to jewels. Her laughter rode the breeze. And there it was: this connection between them that he'd fought ever since seeing the woman she'd become sitting astride that paint horse on the other side of the fence.

As he looked into her eyes he saw that she had felt it all those years ago, as well. Just as she felt it now.

Stunned at this realization, he couldn't help but feel all of this had been written in the stars years before they were to meet. As Lucky would say, it was fate.

He reached for her. Wet, her hand slipped his grip and she stumbled backward toward the deep pool. As she started to fall back into the deep water, he grabbed her again, but he only succeeded in going in with her.

The cold water took his breath away. Just as she did.

They both gasped as they surfaced. Her laughter filled the air and he pulled her into his arms.

Wet hair clung to her cheek. He brushed it back, his gaze going to her mouth an instant before his lips. The kiss was soft, tentative at first.

She wrapped her arms around his shoulders, gazing up at him, those blue eyes as challenging as they'd been only moments before.

He kissed her again, telling himself this was meant to be. And damned if it didn't feel that way.

"I'm freezing," she whispered against his lips.

He carried her over to the sunny green grass along the bank. Her fingers trembled as she tried to unbutton her shirt. He covered her hands with his and slowly unbuttoned the top button, then another. His gaze went to hers. She was watching him, those blue eyes no longer cool. Instead they burned like a hot, bright flame.

He freed the rest of the buttons to expose a pale lavender lace bra that did nothing to hide her hard, erect nipples.

His own desire was a pounding heat in his veins. He looked from her full, round breasts to her face as he slipped off her shirt and bent to touch his tongue to the dark nipple pressed tight against the lace fabric.

She moaned in response and reached to unbutton his shirt.

He stopped her. "You don't know me."

"Don't I?" she said.

Their gazes locked for a long moment, then he let go of her hands. She knew that boy he'd been. The one who still dreamed.

McKenna worked open the buttons on his shirt to spread the fabric aside. His chest was tanned and smooth, his abs hard and muscled, his shoulders broad and strong.

But as she rose on her knees to push the shirt from his shoulders, her finger brushed a scar. "My God," she breathed and leaned past him to stare at the network of scars laced across his back. "Who did this to you?"

He reached for his shirt.

"No." She moved back to face him, bending down to kiss his lips. He didn't yield at first.

She wrapped her arms around him, drawing him down on the grassy sun-drenched bank. She didn't question this need for this man. She'd never been this brazen. But then, she'd never felt this strongly about any man.

He drew back from her kiss, his eyes searching hers. Then slowly, his gaze still locked with hers, he began to unbutton her soaking wet jeans and free her from them. His fingertip trailed along the edge of her lace panties for a moment, his eyes taking her in as if memorizing every inch of her.

She'd always been shy with men. She'd only known two others intimately, one her high school sweetheart, the other a man she'd dated through most of college.

Neither had made her feel like this. But both of them had been "safe," men she'd known a long time. Nate Dempsey was neither. She didn't know him. Nor could she explain why he frightened her more than she wanted to admit. Just as she couldn't explain why she wanted him so fiercely.

As she began to unbutton his jeans, he reached behind her and unhooked her bra. She groaned as he freed her breasts and took one hard nipple in his mouth. Her body tingled at his touch, goose bumps rippling over her bare skin.

He worked off her panties as she did the same with his jeans and shorts, and then they were both naked on the grassy creek bank, the breeze whispering in the trees over them, new leaves flickering, the light playing on their bodies as they made love. Once with a fever, then slowly, as if they might never get another chance.

"DO YOU WANT to tell me about it?" she asked as they lay spent on the creek bank. He'd left her only long enough to hang their clothing on a limb to dry in the sun. The horses grazed nearby to the murmur of the creek.

"No," Nate said and softened his words with a rueful smile. "It happened a long time ago."

She chewed thoughtfully, then asked where he'd learned to ride a horse.

He was thankful she hadn't pushed, as well as grateful that she'd brought up a pleasant memory. He told her about the ranch where he'd grown up in Paradise Valley along the Yellowstone River by Livingston.

"My adoptive family raised cattle and horses—quarter horses," he told her. "My adoptive father taught me how to ride. I fell in love with it immediately and I've had a horse ever since."

"What was your mother like?" she asked, not looking at him as she twisted a few strands of green grass in her fingers.

He knew what she was asking. "My birth mother couldn't care for me. She was alone, and her choice in boyfriends left something to be desired." While avoiding the whole truth, he didn't lie to her. He couldn't. Not now. "I never knew my father. All I had of him was his name. I kept his name. Dempsey. It was all I had of my father. My adoptive parents understood. My birth mother had a lot of boyfriends, but she never remarried, even when she had my little brother years later. My adoptive mother was the most loving, generous woman

I've ever known. She loved to bake. There were always cookies and pies and homemade ice cream. My adoptive parents more than made up for anything that had happened to me before they took me into their family."

"You must have made them proud," she said, finally meeting his gaze.

"I hope so." He glanced away, unable to shake the feeling that she knew. Not just why he was in Whitehorse but what he'd come here to do. "McKenna, don't move into the house. Not yet."

"Is that what this was about?" she demanded, sitting up abruptly.

"No, making love to you has nothing to do with—"

"Save your breath. I know it's never been about me. It's always been about whatever has you on this property."

"You're wrong. You have to understand it's about that man who came by—"

She was on her feet. "I thought you said he was gone."

"He'll be back."

"And you know that how? No, don't," she said, holding up her hands before he could speak. "I'm moving in. I don't need you to stay and *protect* me, if that's what you're worried about. I know that's not why you're here."

"Wait. I—"

"We should get back," she said, walking over to retrieve her clothing from the tree.

He rose, knowing that anything he said would be wrong. Too many people had told her that buying Harper House was a mistake. But it was her own doubts, he thought, that had her back up. She was determined to stick this out come hell or high water.

If he told her the truth—that the man who called himself Hal Turner was, he believed, in fact Roy Vaughn and a killer—then she would go to her future brother-in-law, the sheriff. And that would scare Vaughn away.

Nate couldn't let that happen. Once Roy Vaughn was dead...

But he knew it would be too late for him and Mc-Kenna. All the lies would come to the surface. And all the truths.

He avoided her gaze, wondering if he could feel any more guilty. He should never have let this happen.

As he dressed, his back to her, he cursed himself for forgetting what was at stake. And, more to the point, the danger.

Vaughn would be back. He could be watching them right now. If he thought for a moment that Nate cared for this woman...

Nate knew he'd have to fix this. In his attempt to keep McKenna safe, he'd only made matters worse.

He turned to look at her. She'd dressed and was now pulling on her boots, her eyes cast down. Did she regret what they'd done? How could she not?

What if she knew that while they'd been making love Lucky had been digging on the hillside behind her house for a body? And that this whole ride wasn't thoughtful but deceitful—just like Nate Dempsey himself.

Even if he told her how he felt about her...

He shoved that thought away. Any way he looked at it, this was going to have a bad end.

McKenna said nothing on the ride back to the house. Nor did Nate. What was there to say, anyway?

"If it's all right with you and Blue, I'll go ahead and keep my horse here, too," McKenna said as they unsaddled their horses. If anything, her words were a little cool. She acted as if she knew the score. They'd both gotten carried away. It had been consensual. No harm done. He should be grateful she was taking it so well. Instead he felt like hell and it was all he could do not to tell her how wrong she was.

"It was a nice break from working on the house," she said. "Thank you again."

He watched her turn and walk toward the house, head up, shoulders squared and back ramrod straight. He cursed himself for hurting her.

"My pleasure," he whispered to himself as he watched her walk away. How much longer could he take being this close to her? He wanted her as desperately as he had back in the hills beside the creek. But then, he would always want this woman, he thought as she disappeared inside Harper House.

What he had to concentrate on was keeping her alive.

Chapter Fourteen

Nate had left shortly after their return from their horseback ride, and her sisters had arrived with a horse trailer full of her furniture.

Between painting and overseeing the placement of her things, the rest of the day passed in a haze. But not for one moment was Nate Dempsey far from her thoughts.

A mistake, her sister Eve would have told her. And there were moments McKenna would have agreed. But she couldn't regret making love with him. Nate had opened up to her. Had she glimpsed the man she believed in her heart him to be?

He was such a mystery to her, and not for a moment was she foolish enough to think he wasn't hiding something from her. Holding back. She thought of the scars on his back. He'd implied that they had been the result of one of his birth mother's boyfriends. Not that it mattered who'd done it.

She thought about the boys who'd lived here at Harper House. Had they been just as cruelly treated?

"Are you all right?" Eve asked at her elbow.

McKenna came out of her thoughts with a start. "Fine."

"You seem a little flushed."

"I told you—I went on a horseback ride this morning. I guess I got too much sun."

Eve didn't look convinced. "Where is your hired man?"

"Nate? He's not my hired man."

Her sister was eyeing her intently. "Just be careful, okay? I don't want to see you get hurt."

McKenna started to deny that was a possibility but decided to save her breath. She nodded and felt tears burn her eyes. "Might be too late for that."

"I DIDN'T FIND a thing," Lucky said when Nate finally caught up with him late in the afternoon at the cabin he was staying in on Nelson Reservoir, outside of town. "I'm telling you there's nothing out there to find."

Nate walked over to the window to stare out at the water. He'd been upset since his horseback ride with McKenna. He hadn't been able to stop thinking about her. Or worrying about her safety.

He'd hoped that Lucky would find something. That he could quit sneaking around. Quit lying.

"Nate, come on, what if he left just like Roy said he did?"

"Johnny would have come back for me. He wouldn't have left me there," Nate said. He had to believe that. "He was my *brother*."

"Maybe for some reason he couldn't come back for you before the state showed up."

"He would have found me somehow over the years."

"Not if he couldn't face you. Not if—"

Nate turned to look at him.

"Not if he ran out on you," Lucky finished. "Look, I know you don't want to hear this, but Johnny's body *isn't* out there. I dug in the area where you thought you saw Roy Vaughn bury someone that night. There's no body there."

"Then Vaughn got to it first."

"How is that possible? You were here within hours of hearing about Ellis Harper's death. You see any place where someone had been digging?"

Nate said nothing. Lucky was right. He couldn't explain what had happened to Johnny's body—just that he knew he was dead, that Johnny hadn't run away, that he had been buried late that night behind Harper House.

"I gotta tell you, I think you're wrong about Roy coming back, too," Lucky said. "After all this time, he's forgotten about the past. Hell, he could be dead."

"He's alive. A man calling himself Hal Turner turned up at Harper House."

"Hal Turner?"

"This man fits Roy's description—big, mean-looking."

Lucky laughed. "It's been more than twenty years. You're telling me that you can tell from that description that he's Roy? The last time you saw Roy Vaughn, he was *twelve*."

"I'm telling you it's Vaughn. It has to be Vaughn."

Lucky shook his head. "If it's Vaughn and he's so hell-bent on revenge, then why are Frank Merkel and Rosemarie Blackmore still kickin'? And why aren't you dead? You've been making yourself a fine target ever since you hit town."

"You remember Vaughn. He liked to play games with our heads. He scared McKenna Bailey by showing up there twice, once pretending he was looking for a job, the second time by pushing her down as she was leaving the house."

Lucky blinked. "Giving her a push? Does that sound like *Roy* to you? He would just as soon cut her throat. Buddy, I think you're losing it here."

Nate hated to think how close Lucky was to the truth. "It has to end here. I'm not giving up on finding Johnny's body." Or taking down Roy Vaughn once and for all.

"Okay," he said, holding up his hands. "Then I'm with you."

"No, you've done enough. I don't want you involved. I never wanted you involved. Vaughn doesn't have anything against you." He started for the door, then stopped to look back at Lucky. "Let me handle this."

Lucky shook his head. "I don't know how you can do it, being out there. All the time I was digging behind the house I was looking over my shoulder—and it wasn't Roy Vaughn I was feeling behind me. It was all those memories, man."

"You *know* why I have to stay out there."

"Yeah? I'm telling you, you aren't going to find Johnny buried behind Harper House. He's tipping margaritas down in Florida with some hot woman in a bikini."

Nate wished that was the case. He could forgive Johnny for leaving. For running for his life. He wished with all his heart that's exactly what Johnny had done.

"It doesn't have to be this way. We can leave. Roy isn't coming back. None of them are coming back. It's over, don't you see? Even if you're right and Johnny *is* dead, nothing will bring him back. Roy ain't worth going to prison for the rest of your life."

Nate had no intention of going to prison. Vaughn would disappear. Just as Johnny had. "It won't be over for me until I find Johnny and his killer."

Lucky shook his head. "That's why I'm here."

"Thanks, but I'd feel better if you weren't around."

"No such luck, buddy. If you're determined to go through with this, then I am, too."

AFTER EVERYONE LEFT, McKenna finished unpacking a few more boxes. She knew she was just stalling, hoping to see Nate.

There was nothing stopping her from staying in the house tonight. She wouldn't need Nate Dempsey to protect her. When had she suddenly needed a man to protect her anyway?

When you bought this house.

It wasn't the house, she repeated silently to herself. *No, it's the house's past.*

She could always sell the place and buy something else. She could send Nate packing.

But she knew she wouldn't do either.

"Why do you have to be so stubborn?" she asked aloud, her voice echoing in the room.

She wondered if her fight for this house was now more about stubbornness than the house itself.

And Nate Dempsey?

She knew how that would end. Heck, it probably already had. A man like him, one who'd built such a wall around himself, he would run as fast as he could after this. If his horse trailer wasn't still parked out back and his horse still in the pasture, she would have assumed he was already long gone.

At the sound of a vehicle, she went to the window. A truck slowed and turned in, the headlights sweeping across the house. She ducked back until the lights passed the window before she looked out. Nate. Her heart took off at a gallop even as she tried to rein it in. *Don't go falling for this man.*

She watched him drive by, not slowing even though he had to see the lights on in the house and her pickup parked outside. She waited until she heard the truck engine die, knowing he wouldn't come to the house.

He didn't.

Disgusted with herself for even thinking that he would, she turned off the light and headed for her pickup, knowing she wouldn't get a wink of sleep here tonight. She'd deal with all this tomorrow. She wasn't in the habit of wanting unavailable men. She wasn't even in the habit of dating. She hadn't met anyone who interested her enough to date more than once for a long time now.

As for wantonly wanting a man as she had this morning on the bank of the creek…well, this was new territory and she felt completely inept at it.

It wasn't until she reached the truck that she realized something was wrong.

The yard light was out. Darkness and silence bathed the property, the nearby cottonwoods black against the sky. One tree cast a long, inky shadow over the pickup.

McKenna glanced toward the house as she fumbled her keys from her pocket. The night felt too quiet. Definitely too dark. This house far too isolated, even with her knowing that Nate was just down by the creek. It seemed too far away right now. A distance neither of them was willing to cross.

She started to open the pickup's door when her ankles were grabbed by someone hiding under her pickup. As her feet were jerked out from under her, she fell backward so fast she didn't have time to break her fall. Her back slammed into the ground, the air knocked from her. Before she could move, she heard him come clambering out from under the truck.

Instinctively she kicked at him as she fought to breathe, to scream, as she crab-walked furiously backward in an attempt to escape. But there was no getting away, no making a sound before his big hands grappled her to the ground and locked on her throat.

He bent over her, so close she could smell him and make out the coarse features of the man who called himself Hal Turner.

"Stupid bitch," he said as he tightened his grip on her throat. "You should have cleared out when you had a chance."

NATE TOLD HIMSELF that going up to the house would be the worst thing he could do. The moment he saw McKenna he'd want her in his arms. He'd made that mistake earlier today. A man head over heels with a woman made mistakes.

He needed his mind on Roy Vaughn because he was betting that Roy's was on him. Worse, Nate worried that he'd already blown it. By morning McKenna Bailey would want him off her property. He was surprised she hadn't come out tonight to evict him.

Maybe she was pretending that what happened between them hadn't mattered. That she did this sort of thing all the time. But he knew better. She wasn't that kind of woman. She must be as upset about their lovemaking as he was. He just prayed it wasn't the worst mistake she would ever make. Because Vaughn had already been using her to get to Nate. If Vaughn thought that Nate cared anything about her...

He glanced toward the house before crawling into

his tent. The lights were out. She'd probably left. He hadn't heard her drive away. Maybe she'd left as soon as he'd come in. Or maybe she was staying the night here.

Angry with himself, he lay on his back on his sleeping bag and listened to the night. Listened for the man who'd haunted his nightmares for years. He'd been so sure he would find Johnny's body. But then what? Without DNA tests, how could he even prove it was Johnny? And as for proof that Vaughn had killed him…

He swore. Why kid himself? He hadn't come here looking for justice. He'd planned to kill Vaughn in cold blood. He wanted revenge. Retribution. To hell with justice.

He also wanted to give his brother a proper burial. If he ever found his body.

Vaughn would know that he wasn't up here looking for evidence to convict Johnny's killer. He'd know that Nate was gunning for him. Is that why he hadn't shown?

Nate wasn't leaving here until Johnny's killer was dead. It surprised him that Lucky had tried to talk him into leaving without finishing this. Lucky wouldn't have been here if he hadn't known Nate, known exactly why he was here and what it would take to make him leave without what he'd come for.

The only thing Nate hadn't planned on was McKenna Bailey. He swore softly. Had he thought making love to her this morning would free him of the hold she had on him?

Well, that sure as hell hadn't happened. Just the thought that he'd never be with McKenna Bailey again was killing him. He wished he'd never come back to this godforsaken place. Maybe Lucky was right. Maybe if he could just let it go—

He closed his eyes and quickly opened them again. If

he closed his eyes, he feared he would hear the sounds he'd heard that night. The night Johnny disappeared. And the horrible silence that had followed. The silence had drawn him, then eight years old, to the back window under the eave.

He had leaned against the wall, afraid to look out as he'd heard the heavy tread of footsteps coming up the basement stairs, the thump of the back door, then the singing sound of the shovel blade digging into the rocks and soil in the backyard.

He had stood on tiptoe, turning to wipe the grime from the glass with shaking fingers before peering out into the darkness. He'd heard the wind. The tired scrape of a tree limb against the side of the house. The glass had trembled in its frame, and he'd shivered as the cold night air had crept in through the cracks.

At first he didn't see them, the fearful dark figures that moved in the night. But as the clouds had parted and the moon peered down on the hillside behind the house, he'd seen the hunched figures carrying something all wrapped up as if in a blanket.

He had buried his head under the covers as another ring of a shovel blade had filled the late-night air. He'd known one of the boys was dead. He'd just never dreamed it was Johnny, his own brother.

Inside the tent now, he heard the first scream.

THE HANDS ON her throat loosened. McKenna got out one scream before the man closed his large hands around her neck again. She struggled to fight him off, but he was too heavy, too powerful. She swung wildly at him. But he only shook off her blows as if they were nothing more than pesky gnats.

She couldn't breathe. He was squeezing her throat, and the weight of him on her... All the time he was talking, but his words made no sense and he seemed to be distracted, as if he thought any moment Nate would appear to save her.

She stopped flailing at him. Air. She had to get air. Tiny black spots appeared on the edges of her vision. She had to get him off her or she was going to die.

Her hand dropped to the ground along the edge of the gravel driveway. Her fingers searched the grass and weeds, closing around something cold and heavy. A piece of rusted iron from the old iron fence. She grabbed it tightly in her fist, feeling as if she was about to pass out, and drove it into him.

He let out a bellow of surprise and pain. His hands released her to reach for the rusted iron now protruding from his chest. With one angry swipe, he jerked the rusted iron out and threw it into the darkness.

McKenna groped for something else to use for a weapon, realizing there would be nothing to stop him from killing her now.

She grabbed a small rock, swung it as hard as she could in the vicinity of the man's head as he reached again with both hands for her throat. A loud *whap* filled the air, then his startled angry cry.

Gulping air, she swung again, this time connecting with his forearm as he tried to grasp her arms. He howled with pain and lurched backward. She sat up, brandishing the rock gripped in her hand and scrambling away from him as she tried to get her feet under her.

She was woozy from lack of oxygen and disoriented. She sucked in more air, gasping, her throat on fire. He was getting to his feet, shaking his head like an angry bull and swearing.

She hurled the rock at him, hitting him in the chest. He let out a bellow as she clambered to her feet. He was between her and the pickup, so she turned and ran—not toward the house, because she knew she'd never be able to get inside and lock the door behind her before he caught up to her.

Instead she ran around the side of the house, headed for the creek and Nate, praying he would hear her cries for help, praying he hadn't gone for a horseback ride. She needed him as she'd never needed a man before.

She ran, screaming Nate's name, her legs aching, the breath in her lungs burning. She could hear the man behind her yelling something she couldn't make out. All she knew was that he was gaining on her.

His fingers dug into her shoulder and he pulled her down the way a lion takes down its prey.

She hit the ground hard.

"Scream, bitch, scream!" he yelled into her face.

Her chest heaved, her panic accelerating as she fought to catch her breath. She couldn't scream. She couldn't breathe again with him on top of her.

He slapped her, making her head snap to the side. Out of the corner of her eye she saw him ball up his fist and rear back to slug her. "I said scream."

She closed her eyes, anticipating the blow, knowing that it would be over soon. A boom filled the air, making her recoil as hot, wet spray splattered over her.

Her eyes flew open an instant before the man straddling her fell forward, his heavy, bloody body slumped across her, pinning her to the ground. A new surge of panic filled her as she felt his warm blood soaking into her clothing. She couldn't breathe, the weight of the man crushing her, the smell of his blood filling her nostrils.

"Get him off," she cried, shoving at the dead weight as Nate appeared, a gun gripped in both his hands, the barrel leveled at the man on top of her. "Get him off!"

Nate raised a foot, put his boot heel against the man's body and shoved, all the time keeping the gun on the man. The body flopped over into the weeds next to her with a soft thud—and a groan.

As she scrambled to her feet, she saw the cold fury on Nate's face as he crouched to put the gun to the man's temple.

"You sorry bastard," Nate said, bending over him.

She saw him saying something else to the man, but she wasn't close enough to hear. The man's eyes widened, though, and a terrible high-pitched laugh emanated from his mouth along with a stream of blood.

McKenna looked away, still trying to catch her breath, her throat in agony, her body trembling. When she looked back, the man on the ground was trying to say something.

He coughed, blood gurgling from his mouth, and spoke, his words coming out as if he was taking his last breath. She only caught a couple of words, but she saw Nate's expression.

Then the man's eyes rolled back in his head and he fell silent, leaving his last words floating in the night air.

McKenna stared, too stunned to move, to speak, as she watched Nate hurriedly check for a pulse. Apparently finding none, he holstered his gun and let out a string of curses.

"He said your name." Her words quaked like her body. "He *knew* you."

Chapter Fifteen

Nate froze, his back to her.

"I heard him," McKenna said, her voice rising. "He said *Dempsey*. And it was you he was calling for when..." Her voice broke. "He wanted me to scream so *you* would come."

Nate closed his eyes for a moment. Hadn't he known it was just a matter of time?

"Who *are* you?" she asked behind him, sounding afraid—only this time of him.

He turned slowly to face her. They were only feet apart. A sliver of moon and a handful of stars illuminating the darkness around them. Her face was ghostly white and she was trembling, her shirt and jacket soaked dark with blood, her cheek scratched and her hands filthy and bleeding.

He wanted nothing more than to take her in his arms and hold her. To tell her everything was going to be all right. But he was tired of lying. And things were far from all right. "I'm a cop."

She shook her head and took a step back. "A cop who just happens to know a killer?"

None of that mattered. "Are you all right?" His voice sounded strange even to him. He'd gone from fear to a cold, steely rage that had always frightened him. He could see that his calmness at having just killed a man was scaring her as much as what she'd overheard.

"I asked you who you are," she snapped.

"I told you who I am," he said, stepping past her and heading toward his tent. There would be no comforting her right now. Nor was this the time to talk. Not that she would listen to what he had to tell her now anymore than she would later.

"Where do you think you're going?" she yelled after him.

"To call the sheriff," he said and kept walking. He wanted to comfort her, but he knew better than to even try. He could hear her behind him.

"You *knew* that man," she said to his back as she followed him at a distance to the tent.

He reached in and picked up his cell phone where he'd put it earlier, pressed 911 and only then did he turn to look at her.

"He said your *name*," she repeated.

"There's been a shooting at the old Harper place," he said into the phone when the operator answered. "A man's been killed. We need the sheriff." He looked at her in the sliver of moon that had broken free of the clouds and disconnected before the dispatcher could ask him any questions.

As he snapped the phone shut, he reached into his tent and grabbed his jacket, tossing it to her. He felt as shaken as she looked now that it was over.

He could see the bruises already forming on her neck—just as he'd seen that the bullet hole wasn't the only wound in the dead man's chest. She'd fought back and it had saved her life. He tried not to let himself think about what would have happened if he hadn't been here. But then she'd never have been attacked if he hadn't come back here.

"Tell me the truth," she said, glaring at him in the dim light as she angrily put on his jacket and crossed her arms over her chest.

The truth. What was that? "I think we should wait until the sheriff gets here. Here." He dragged his camp stool over to the ring of rocks he used for a fire pit. She didn't move. He could see that only stubbornness was holding her up. "Sit down before you fall down."

ALL THE FIGHT went out of her. Her legs seemed to crumble under her. Nate lunged for her, catching her around the waist to keep her from falling as he lowered her gently to the camp chair.

"The sheriff will be here soon," he said as he busied himself making a fire in the circle of rocks next to her.

She watched him, dazed and spent. A cop? He'd let her believe he owned a construction company. And a few minutes ago he'd acted like anything but a cop as he'd put his gun to that man's head. What had he whispered to him?

At first she'd thought Nate was scared for *her*. Angry for *her*. But after she'd heard the man say Nate's name and seen Nate's reaction when the man died, she'd known it had never been about her. Not Nate being at Harper House, nor this man showing up when he had.

Glancing back toward the house, she could make out the dark shape of the man lying dead in the weeds. She began to shake harder, soaked with the cold wetness of the man's blood beneath the jacket Nate had given her.

"You can't get out of those clothes until after the sheriff gets here," Nate said. "But the fire should help."

Why was he acting as if he cared? She stared down into the flames. As she listened to the crackle of the dry wood and watched the smoke rise into the night air, she tried not to relive the terror. Or look at Nate. Hadn't she known there was more to him being here?

Her eyes burned with tears. She squeezed them shut, but still the hot tears leaked out and ran down her cheeks. She heard Nate move to her, crouch in front of her, felt the rough pads of his thumbs as he brushed at her tears. She tried to pull away but couldn't.

His arms came around her. She buried her face in his chest as in the distance she heard the wail of a siren growing closer and closer.

IT WAS LATE by the time the coroner and the ambulance pulled away from Harper House. The sheriff had taken their statements.

"This is the same man you said called himself Hal Turner?" Carter asked McKenna.

She only nodded since they'd already been over this a half dozen times.

"And you didn't think to tell me that he had tried to attack you?" the sheriff demanded.

"He didn't *attack* me. He pushed me. At least I think it was him. To tell you the truth, I thought I'd imagined it."

She'd told Carter everything she could remember from the moment the man grabbed her from under the pickup and knocked her down to stabbing him with the piece of rusty iron from the fence to running for her life only to be caught and almost killed before Nate shot the man.

The only thing she hadn't told him was her suspicions or what the man had said right before he died. She told herself she wasn't covering for Nate. She wouldn't do that. She knew she wasn't thinking clearly after everything she'd been through. She'd convinced herself that she couldn't be sure that the man had said Nate's name.

Dempsey.

She couldn't be sure she'd heard correctly since the rest of what the man had said made no sense. She could have misunderstood. Just as she'd misunderstood the man's motives last night? If she was right and he'd wanted her to scream so Nate would come...then the man must have had a death wish.

She had to talk to Nate alone. She wanted to know what was going on. Nate and the man *had* known each other. But what did that mean?

There was also a good chance that when Nate gave his statement he'd told the sheriff things he hadn't confided in her, since they'd given their statements separately.

Carter finally had one of the deputies drive her to the ranch so she could get a shower and change clothing. She was exhausted, but she knew she wouldn't be able to sleep. McKenna felt sick to her stomach. That was the first man she'd ever seen killed. She remembered the dead weight of him on her and shuddered.

Nate had been taken down to the sheriff's department for more questioning. Was it true Nate was a cop?

McKENNA HADN'T EXPECTED to get a wink of sleep even as exhausted as she'd been. So she was surprised when she'd awakened late the next morning.

She showered again, letting the water beat down on

her until it ran cold, wishing she could wash away the memory of last night.

Humans are amazingly resilient. Except for a few aches and pains, she didn't feel any different. How was that possible when a man had tried to kill her, would have if Nate hadn't killed him? She tried not to think about how close she'd come to dying.

Even though the day was warm, she dressed in jeans and a long-sleeved shirt. Eve had thrown Nate's jacket he'd lent McKenna into the washer and dryer along with her own clothing. As she retrieved it, she was glad to see there were no bloodstains when each article of clothing came out of the dryer.

"Where do you think you're going?" Eve asked from the doorway. "After what you're been through, you should be in bed."

"I can't sleep and I can't just sit here. I have to know what's going on. I'm driving in to talk to Carter." McKenna didn't mention that she was also going to find Nate.

Both Eve and Faith had gotten up when the deputy had brought her home late last night. No doubt Carter had called to inform them of what had happened. And yet they'd both quizzed her, one sitting on the closed toilet while the other perched on the edge of the tub as she took her shower.

"Carter isn't going to tell you anything if the killing is still under investigation," Eve said.

"The man died right in front of me." Right on top of her.

"After he tried to *kill* you. How's your throat, by the way?"

McKenna touched a finger to the bruises. "Sore, but I'll live."

Eve shook her head. "I don't want you going back to that house."

She knew better than to argue with her older sister right now. Eve had been terrified last night to hear about what had happened. Being older, and with the folks gone from the ranch, Eve felt responsible for her sisters' safety. It didn't matter that both Faith and McKenna were plenty old enough to take care of themselves. At least under normal circumstances.

"I'm just going into town. I'll be back as soon as I find out what's going on."

Eve eyed her. "Anita Samuelson called this morning. She said she has some photographs you had inquired about? She said she'd drop them off."

McKenna nodded. She'd completely forgotten she'd called the woman for the photos of Harper House. It seemed like a lifetime ago. Back when she'd been excited about the house.

"Are you sure you're all right?" Eve asked.

"I'm fine." It wasn't true and they both knew it. A person didn't get over something like this after a few hours sleep. Eve would have been even more worried if she'd known what had *really* kept McKenna awake.

SHERIFF CARTER JACKSON didn't seem at all surprised when McKenna walked into his office. He got to his feet and hurried around to offer her a chair.

"How are you?" he asked.

"Fine," she said automatically.

"I'm surprised Eve let you out of the house," he said, taking his chair again behind his desk.

"She knew she'd have to hog-tie me to keep me from coming to town to see you," McKenna said. "I need to know what you found out about the man."

Carter leaned back in his chair. "The investigation is ongoing at this p—"

"Eve told me you'd say that. Carter, please, I have to know."

He seemed to study her for a long moment. Finally, with a sigh, he said, "His prints came up with a hit. He served some time at Deer Lodge. His name is Dennis Jones."

She felt her heart rate shoot up. His name was on the list she'd found under the floorboards of the house. "Denny Jones."

Carter nodded. "He did spend some time at Harper House. Apparently the place was never state-certified, and some pretty awful things happened to the boys."

She sat back. "What about..."

"The blood oath, as you call it? I've contacted both Frank Merkel and Rosemarie Blackmore. They're both fine."

She knew she should have been relieved. "What if this Dennis Jones isn't the only one from Harper House in town?"

"This is why I didn't want to tell you," Carter said. "Jones hadn't made contact with either Frank or Rosemarie. The truth is, he recently escaped from a mental care facility where he was being treated for schizophrenia. His doctors believe he returned to Harper House because that was the part of his life he dwelled on most."

She shook her head, feeling as if she'd stepped into a nightmare and couldn't wake up. "What about Nate?"

"What about him?"

"He isn't being held for anything, is he? If he hadn't killed the man when he did…"

"No. He's free to leave."

To leave? "Is it true that he's a cop?"

Carter eyed her strangely. "He's on personal leave from the Paradise Police Department. You didn't know that?"

She hated to admit that she'd thought he owned a construction company until last night—when she'd seen him kill a man with a .38.

McKENNA WAS ALMOST to the turnoff into Harper House when she saw Anita Samuelson's little white sedan pull into the yard ahead of her.

With a groan, McKenna turned into the driveway and parked beside the elderly woman's car.

Nate's pickup and horse trailer were parked out by the barn, but for how long? If she was right, Nate would be leaving town now. She couldn't shake the feeling that what had happened last night was why he'd stayed around. Why he'd finagled his way into staying near Harper House to begin with.

McKenna hoped to cut this short with Anita. The last thing on her mind was photographs of the house. But Anita was already getting out of her car, an old shoe box secured with a rubber band under one arm, her huge purse in the other.

"Perfect timing," Anita said as she headed for the porch. "I haven't had time to go through the photographs. I thought I would just let you see if there are any in here you can use of the house."

"Thank you," McKenna said, wishing the woman

would just leave them and let her go through them later. But clearly that wasn't Anita's plan.

"I'd ask you in, but we're in the process of painting," McKenna said quickly. "Hardly any furniture, either."

"This will do fine," the older woman said as she lowered her bulk into one of the rockers McKenna's sisters had given her for a housewarming present.

"How are you doing today?" Anita asked once she'd settled in the rocker, one large hand lying protectively over the box of photos.

McKenna shot her a look. "You heard about last night?"

"Everyone in town knows. It must have been horrible. What did the man do to you?"

McKenna was glad that the shirt she wore covered most of the bruises on her neck. "He didn't get a chance to do anything before he was killed."

"Yes, by a police officer from Paradise."

McKenna shouldn't have been surprised, but she was stunned at how news moved on the Whitehorse grapevine. "Yes. That's why I don't have long to visit. I need to speak with the sheriff again."

"Oh?" Anita asked, all ears.

"You know he's marrying my sister Eve. He just worries about me being out here alone. In case the man hadn't been acting alone."

Anita suddenly glanced around, clearly nervous now.

"I'd better have a quick look at those photographs and get back into town," McKenna said.

Anita shoved the box at her.

McKenna slipped off the rubber band and opened the lid of the box. A dank, musty smell rose up from the snapshots. She'd thought there would be old pho-

tographs of the house that she might be able to enlarge
and frame. It was an idea that had lost its luster after
everything that had happened.

Her fingers began to shake as she saw a photograph
sticking out of the box of three young boys standing in
front of the house. Her heart thundered in her ears as
she looked into their faces. She knew at once they had
to be the boys who'd once lived in Harper House. The
troubled boys that no one wanted.

For a moment she almost closed the box and handed
it back to Anita, who was rocking nervously next to
her. McKenna wasn't sure she could do this. She knew
that seeing these boys in these photographs would only
make her more invested in what had happened at this
house. *Her* house.

"If this is a bad time, you could stop by my house
one day—"

"No," McKenna said, and with her heart in her
throat, began to leaf through the photographs.

There were old photographs of the Harpers inter-
mixed with the others. Many of the photos were taken
in the front yard of Harper House. Would it ever feel
like it was hers? Or would it always belong to the boys
and the horrible memories they had of the place?

The Harpers' own photographs resembled those
of the boys. Grim faces, backs ramrod straight, eyes
narrowed. The Harpers hadn't been a cheerful bunch.

But the few photographs of the boys were heart-
breakers. It was their expressions and what she saw in
their eyes. A lack of hope.

In one shot she recognized a boy who could have
been Dennis Jones. He was large and plain faced, his
expression hurt and angry.

She turned the photo over, hoping someone had written the name of the boy on the back. The back was blank.

In each snapshot the boys ranged from six or seven up to maybe eleven. They were dressed shabbily, hair uncut, faces appearing expressionless. But it was the eyes in some that made her draw back from them. She'd never seen such cold hatred in young boys' gazes.

She couldn't bear to look at any more. She scooped up the photographs, intending to tell Anita that she was going to have to take them to Carter at the sheriff's department. She couldn't bear the pain she saw in these boys' faces. Or her fear of what they had become as adults. She thought about Dennis Jones, that crazed look she'd seen in his eyes.

But as she was putting the photographs back into the shoe box, one of the boys' faces caught her eye. She froze.

The rest of the snapshots tumbled out of her hands and onto the porch floor. She'd seen that face—and that expression—before.

Her pulse boomed in her ears. He was the boy she'd seen all those years ago in the third-floor window. Her memory had been imperfect, but seeing the photograph and having seen him as an adult, she recognized him.

Now she knew why Nate Dempsey had looked so familiar. And why she'd thought Dennis Jones had said Nate's name.

The boys had both once lived in Harper House.

DENNY JONES. NATE had been so sure the man Mc-Kenna had described—the man who called himself Hal Turner—was Vaughn. Instead it was Jones?

Nate wondered if he wasn't wrong about everything else, as well. He was still shaken after last night. It wasn't every day that he killed a man, thank God.

Even when he'd seen that it was Denny instead of Roy Vaughn, Nate had been so sure that Vaughn had put him up to this. But Denny had been lost in the past. He'd been talking as if it were more than twenty years before and they were boys and telling anything you knew could get you killed.

The irony had cut Nate to the core. Denny had been dying and yet he'd refused to tell anything—even though Nate had always suspected Denny had been one of the boys who'd helped carry Johnny's body out to be buried.

The morning he awoke to learn that Johnny was gone, Nate didn't get a chance to talk to any of the other boys. The state had come and taken them away, most in separate cars to different destinations.

When he'd joined the police force in Paradise, Nate had tried to find out what had happened to some of the boys. Roy Vaughn in particular. But he'd come up empty. Roy had dropped off the radar. Just like Denny Jones.

Recently he'd discovered that Steven Cross, Lyle Weston and Andrew Charles were dead. Bobby French was in prison. Nate had thought about paying him a visit. But Bobby had been in his bed that night at Harper House. So had Andrew Charles. The other boys had slept a floor below, in one of the large bedrooms next to the caretaker's room.

Nate rubbed his forehead. He hadn't gotten any sleep last night and it was starting to catch up with him. But how could he sleep? Right before Denny died, his mind seemed to clear and he'd said something that had rocked Nate to his core.

I saw Roy's soul leave his body. It drained off him like the blood that ran from his throat. I'm telling you the truth, Dempsey. The truth.

All McKenna had heard was the Dempsey part.

"Before he died," Nate had told the sheriff last night at Carter Jackson's office, "Jones said something about a man named Roy Vaughn." The moment Nate said it he saw the sheriff's expression.

"I got an APB this morning on Dennis Jones," Carter Jackson had told him. "Along with his escape from the mental facility, Jones was wanted for questioning in the death of one Roy Vaughn Martin."

So someone *had* adopted Roy. "He told me Vaughn's throat had been cut," Nate had said.

The sheriff had nodded. "The authorities found Jones's prints all over the murder scene, and there is an eyewitness who saw Jones leave Roy's after what sounded like an altercation. The neighbors had already called the police."

Nate had been thinking about Denny's last words. "He told me Vaughn's soul left his body just like his blood." No doubt on the way to hell. "I guess Jones was thinking his was about to do the same."

The sheriff had nodded. "Ravalli County is going to be glad to hear that Jones is dead. I would imagine it will help them tie up the loose ends in their murder cases."

"Murder *cases*?" Nate had asked.

"Roy had only recently gotten out of prison on a medical release," the sheriff had explained. "He was dying of cancer. He only had a short time to live. Are you thinking Roy got Dennis Jones out of the mental facility? If that is the case, then Jones probably did him a favor by cutting his throat."

Nate remembered the switchblade Vaughn had kept under his mattress at Harper House. Had Dennis Jones used Vaughn's own knife?

"Scares the hell out of me that he was after Mc-Kenna," the sheriff had said. "I'm glad you were there. We owe you a lot."

Nate had said nothing, having trouble fitting into the hero role the sheriff was trying to put him in.

Since leaving the sheriff's office, he'd been trying to come to grips with the fact that Roy Vaughn was dead. He knew what was bothering him: he'd wanted to be the one who killed him. Instead he'd killed the man who'd taken that privilege from him. But if Vaughn had already been dying of cancer…

It wasn't supposed to end like this.

Or maybe it was, he thought, his thoughts going to McKenna, as they often did now.

For the first time Nate noticed that the wind had kicked up. The limbs of the cottonwoods slashed back and forth, groaning and creaking. In the distance he could see the black clouds of a storm coming this way and could almost smell the rain on the wind.

He looked toward the house and saw McKenna headed toward where he stood by the creek waiting for her. He'd heard her drive in earlier along with another car.

Her blond hair blew back from under her straw hat, her face in shadow. He watched her give a wide berth to where Dennis Jones had been killed the night before. The crime-scene tape had been taken down this morning after the sheriff had closed the investigation.

Nate knew that if he hadn't been a cop, it would have taken a whole lot longer. Even if he was a cop on leave. When he'd asked for the personal leave after hearing about Ellis Harper's death, he hadn't planned to go back to Paradise, let alone to the police department. He thought he'd be a murderer, possibly on his way to Mexico. Or prison.

Now he wasn't sure what he was going to do.

As McKenna grew closer, he saw that she wore a pale blue checked shirt that brought out the same color blue in her eyes. The jeans hugged her slim body, the cowboy boots dusty from her walk out to him. He remembered every curve beneath her clothing, the pale soft skin, the tiny sprinkling of freckles, the feel and taste of her. It was all indelibly branded on his memory.

She raised her head, the wind whipping the ends of her hair, and he knew what was coming. It had been inevitable.

"I wasn't sure you'd still be here," she said, an edge to her voice.

"I wanted to see you before I left."

She raised a brow. "Were you finally going to tell me the truth about why you came here before you left?"

"No."

She nodded, anger sparking in all that blue. "I *know.* I know you used to live in Harper House. I know you were the boy who I saw in that third-floor window twenty-one years ago. I know you've been lying to me."

He hated the way she kept some distance between them. It reminded him of the way people had treated the Harper House boys when on the rare occasion they'd been taken into town. Fear, repulsion. And with her, anger. Was there regret there? Or just the anger?

"I should have told you," he said. "But then I knew what your reaction would be and I needed you to trust me so I could protect you."

"Protect me?" She shook her head angrily, raising her voice over the shriek of the wind. "You were waiting for that man to come back to kill him."

Not *that* man, but he didn't argue the point.

"You knew he'd come here," she said, eyes narrowing speculatively as she studied him. "Because of the pact you made as boys. Why wasn't your name on the list?"

"My brother and I refused to sign it," he said.

"Your *brother*? Let me guess—the one who owns a construction business in Park County?"

"The truck and construction company belong to my *younger* brother, Robert. My mother had him after she farmed my older brother, Johnny, and me out to Harper House."

McKenna stopped, all her anger spent. How could she be angry with this man who had suffered so much at this house? The wind was screaming now and battering the cottonwood branches overhead. She felt the dark clouds moving in, but her mind was on nothing but the storm going on inside her.

"The scars on your back?" she asked.

"My mother's boyfriends. You should have seen my brother Johnny's back. He got it much worse for standing up for me."

She felt tears flood her eyes and bit her lip, forced herself to look away. Her hair blew into her face. She made a swipe at it as she looked at him again. "Why didn't you just tell me?"

He shook his head. "Harper House isn't something I tell *anyone* about. Especially someone who's just bought the place and plans to live there."

She stared at him, wondering how that would be possible now. "You mentioned your older brother, Johnny. What happened to him?" she asked, recalling what he'd said about him and his older brother refusing to sign the revenge oath.

"Roy Vaughn killed him. He would have killed me, too, if the state people hadn't shown up the next morning when they did."

"Roy Vaughn?" She remembered the name from the list. She couldn't hide her shock. "You reported it, didn't you? And this Roy Vaughn went to prison."

"I told the state people, but they didn't believe me. Roy was twelve, older than most of us and bigger and stronger. He got the others to swear that my brother ran away the night before. The state never investigated. They had their hands full just trying to figure out what to do with us."

Her heart broke for him. "I'm so sorry."

He nodded, and she could tell the last thing he wanted was her sympathy.

"Your future brother-in-law told me last night that Vaughn's dead," Nate said. "It appears that Vaughn helped Dennis Jones escape from the mental facility, for whatever reason. Vaughn was dying of cancer and didn't have much time to live. Dennis apparently killed him before coming back to Harper House, presumably because the place still haunted him."

She thought about the digging behind the house and suddenly it all made sense. "You came back here to find your brother and kill the man who you believed murdered him."

He didn't answer, but she knew she was right.

"I take it you didn't find your brother's body," she said.

"No. Maybe Roy Vaughn moved it that night before the state came. I don't know."

She glanced back to where she remembered he'd been digging and frowned. The tall green grass undulated in the wind like ocean waves.

"Did you know there was a flood along the creek nine years ago?" she asked. "It washed out a part of that hillside and changed the course of the creek." She turned to point down the creek where a mound of dirt from the hillside had been deposited.

Nate swore as he stared down the creek to where she indicated, his face grim. "Would you mind if I did this alone?"

"You're going to get wet," she said, glancing up at the storm clouds, and realized how foolish that sounded. He wouldn't care about something as mundane as a rain shower.

She hesitated, wishing there was something more she could say, then she turned and ran against the wind back to the house. The sky overhead was black, the clouds ominous. She hadn't heard the weather report but suspected that a severe storm alert had gone out. In this part of Montana extremes in weather were common.

Back inside the house, she glanced out the window and saw Nate get the shovel from the barn and head down the creek. She turned away, unable to watch.

She wandered through the house. On the third floor, she stood at the window, the same one where she'd first laid eyes on Nate Dempsey. She tried not to think about what his life had been like here. Or his brother's. She prayed he would find his brother—and the peace she knew he so desperately needed.

Hugging herself, she looked around the room, seeing it through Nate's eyes. She'd told herself it was just a house made of inanimate objects that had no memory. No ability to hold on to the past. Or harbor evil.

But she knew this house would always remind her of the boys who'd lived here and suffered. It would always remind her of Nate.

How could *she* stay here?

She turned and caught movement from the front window. Moving to it, she saw a pickup pull into the driveway. She hadn't heard the engine, not with the sounds of the approaching storm. To her surprise, she recognized the truck and the man who threw open the door and raced through the wind toward the house.

What is Flynn Garrett doing here? she wondered as she headed downstairs.

Chapter Sixteen

Nate stared at the mound of dirt that the flood had deposited downstream. Grass and weeds grew lush green over the soil as if it had always been there. He hadn't even noticed it and would never have guessed part of the hillside had been washed down here.

He knew he was finally going to find his brother, and for a moment that knowledge made him incapable of action. He told himself that after all these years there might not be anything of his brother left. The flood or animals could have carried off his remains.

But Nate knew better. He told himself he was prepared for what he would find. This was no longer about revenge or justice or proving what had happened to his brother. This was now about burying Johnny. And moving on.

The earth was soft and damp here by the river as he turned his first bladeful of soil.

He thought about the woman in the house. Could McKenna Bailey move on after this? Would she keep the house? Sell the place? Hadn't she said she wanted to raise horses here? Paint horses. Like the one she'd been riding the very first time he saw her.

He stopped shoveling for a moment to look out across

the rolling green hills, to imagine paint colts running in the wind across the green pasture. He wished she'd been able to complete her dream. He would have liked to have seen that here, he thought as he began to dig again.

The wind howled through the trees over his head, the cottonwood branches thrashing back and forth, freed leaves peppering him. The storm was imminent, the sky an odd color—the color it turned when it was about to hail.

He dug faster. The first raindrops lashed down, cold and hard. The rain dropped down through the trees, shredding the leaves over his head, running off the brim of his hat, soaking him to the skin.

He dug heedless of the storm, lost in the monotonous action until the blade of his shovel hit something with a thud. He bent down. What he'd struck seemed to be caught in some sort of fabric. How was that possible after all these years? But then he remembered. The quilts from the beds where they'd slept were made of old jeans that were said to wear like iron. Perfect for rough boys.

He pulled back the edge of the rotted material and saw what he knew was the leg bone of a boy of ten.

FROM THE WINDOW McKenna watched Flynn race toward the house as rain began to pour down on him. She hurried to open the front door, surprised to see him.

"What a storm," Flynn said as he shook the rain from his jacket before stepping inside. "I haven't seen anything like this in years." He stilled as he glanced around the living room, his expression turning grave.

The wind and rain beat against the old windows, making them rattle. She could no longer see the mailbox up on the road through the pouring rain and mist. All she could think about was Nate out in it.

"So are you here alone?" Flynn asked, drawing her attention away from the storm and Nate.

She felt a stab of unease at the odd question. "What?"

"Your sisters. I thought they would be here helping you paint or something."

She shook her head and watched Flynn look around the living room, his expression still grim.

Lightning flashed, and an instant later a boom of thunder shook the house. McKenna jumped, surprised how tense she was.

"My mother was afraid of storms," Flynn said, noticing her reaction. "She always wanted me to sit with her. She would hold my hand and we would sing songs so she didn't have to listen to the thunder." He shook his head. "Funny the memories a storm brings back, huh?"

She nodded, wondering what he was doing here—and why he was making her so uneasy.

"So let's see the rest of the house," he said and headed toward the back without waiting for an answer. "It looks as if you're moving in." He started up the stairs.

She stood for a moment, then followed him. Obviously he'd just come out because he'd been worried about her after what had happened out here last night. And maybe he finally did want to see what she'd done with the house. After all, she had extended the invitation to him just the other day. She tried to relax, but the storm and worrying about Nate…

When she reached the third floor, she found Flynn standing at the window, looking toward the front of the house. "This was going to be my office," she said to his back.

"Was?" he asked, turning to face her.

"I don't think I'm staying in the house," she said and wished she hadn't said anything.

"Really?" He seemed almost amused by that. "What changed your mind?"

Nate. "Everything."

He nodded as he looked around the room. "They didn't come back," he said, his gaze lighting on her. "The boys. So much for that blood oath, huh?"

"One of them did. The one who…died out here last night."

"Yeah, I heard about that. I'm glad to see that you're all right. But wasn't he crazy or something?"

"I guess he'd been in a mental facility. Schizophrenia."

He nodded. "Well, all your worries were for nothing, it seems. I'm surprised, though, now that it's apparently over, why you aren't planning to stay. Wouldn't have anything to do with my buddy Nate Dempsey, would it?"

She felt a tremor of shock. "You know Nate?"

"Nate and I go way back. He knows me as Lucky, though. Lucky Thomas."

"You said your name was Flynn Garrett." McKenna felt as if her head was swimming.

"It is. Thomas Flynn Garrett. When Nate and I met here at Harper House, I called myself Lucky Thomas. Even at that young age I had a keen sense of irony. Lucky is the last thing I've ever been."

Lucky Thomas. She remembered his name on the list she'd found and felt her pulse begin to thrum. "You lived here?" Why hadn't he said something when she'd shown him the blood oath she'd found under the floor-boards?

"I could tell you stories about this house that would make your hair curl." He frowned. "My mother liked that expression." He must have seen her face. "Don't look so panicked," he said with a laugh. "I didn't come back to Whitehorse because of the pact. I'm here because of Nate. I knew the minute I heard Ellis Harper had finally died what Nate would do."

She watched him move around the room as he talked and wished Nate would come in soon. Flynn bumped against a mirror she'd left leaning against the wall until she decided where to put it.

As the mirror fell over, he lunged for it with a curse. The glass hit the floor and shattered, making them both jump. Flynn began to swear, backing up from the broken mirror as if it were a rattlesnake coiled to strike.

"It's all right," she said quickly. "It was just an inexpensive mirror. Really, it's no big deal."

He turned on her, his eyes wide. "Seven years of bad luck. That's a pretty big deal."

"I don't think that really happens," she said cautiously.

He seemed to pull himself back together, but she noticed he avoided going near the mirror.

He was making her more nervous by the moment. Obviously something was bothering him. Between his odd behavior and the storm and what Nate was doing behind the house right now, she was a wreck.

"If you came out to see Nate—"

"He was like a brother to me." Flynn stopped again at the window, his back to her. "We didn't know each other for long, but I never forgot him. He was my best friend.

My only friend in this house." Flynn turned to face her suddenly. "He saved my life when we were kids here. Did he tell you that? No," he said with a laugh before she could answer. "He wouldn't have mentioned me. But he told you he used to live here, didn't he?"

She nodded, unable to speak. She tried to assure herself that her fears weren't justified. Just because Flynn had been one of the boys in this house…

She glanced toward the window. The rain fell in a deluge, the wind gusts throwing it against the glass. By now Nate would have taken shelter. He couldn't still be digging. He would wait for the storm to let up before he came into the house. *If* he came to the house before he left.

"I owe Nate my life," Flynn was saying. "I would do anything to protect him. Hell, I already have. But I'm afraid it isn't going to be enough."

"I'm sure he's grateful for everything you've done for him."

Flynn laughed at that. "He doesn't even know the half of it. No one does."

Didn't he realize Nate was out back? Surely he would have seen Nate's pickup and horse trailer, unless he hadn't been able to see it through the rain.

He thought she was alone here. A shaft of icy fear raced up her spine. She was.

SHERIFF CARTER JACKSON picked up the APB that came over the wire just about the time the storm hit.

His second in command, Deputy Nick Giovanni, came in on a gust of wind and rain. "There's going to be some flooding for sure before this one's over."

"They're talking a chance for hail on the news."

Storms like these always meant more accidents on the highways. He was glad Eve and Faith were at the ranch and not out in the middle of it. He recalled the last bad storm they'd had. Eve had been trapped in it.

Shoving that unpleasant thought away, he read the APB that had come in.

"Something up?" Nick asked.

"Double-murder suspect. He's driving a pickup with out-of-state plates. They think he might be in our area." Carter handed the information to Nick, who frowned.

"I think I've seen a truck like this in front of a cabin out on Nelson Reservoir," he said.

"He's wanted for questioning in the murder of a woman and her husband in Nebraska," Carter said. "Looked like an apparent robbery/murder. One of the neighbors had seen the pickup around for several weeks. It's believed he took money and credit cards. Could be a relative. One of the woman's former husbands was named Garrett."

"Wait a minute," Nick said as he saw the photograph being distributed. "I've *seen* this guy. He was at Northern Lights restaurant with McKenna the other night. I'm sure it's the same man."

Carter swore as he tried McKenna's cell first. She must have had it off, because it went straight to voice mail. He dialed the Bailey ranch.

Eve answered the phone.

"Hey," he said. "I'm hoping McKenna is there. I need to ask her a couple more questions."

"She left to go see you," Eve said.

"You don't know where else she might have gone?" he asked.

Eve groaned. "Probably back out to that house. You're sure everything is all right?"

"It will be once we're married," he said. "Got to go. I'll call you later." He got off the line before she could quiz him more. Eve had a way of seeing through most people, especially those she knew well. She could read him like a book.

"No luck?" Nick asked.

Carter shook his head as he reached for his hat and his patrol car keys. "You go out to the cabin where you saw his pickup. I'm going to find McKenna."

NATE SLUMPED DOWN into the mud as the rain washed the dirt from the bag of bones. Johnny.

He'd known Johnny wouldn't have left him to the cruelties of Harper House. Johnny had always protected him even though Johnny had always gotten the brunt of it.

Tears streamed down his face along with the rain as he turned his face up to the storm and let out a roar of rage, the sound lost in the wind. The storm was deafening, but it was nothing like the storm raging inside him. He felt powerless. He'd come back to find his brother and avenge his death.

But there would be no vengeance. Roy Vaughn was dead. So was Dennis Jones and whoever else had helped carry Johnny's body out to what would be a shallow, restless grave.

Nate drove his fist into the mud again and again as the storm thundered around him, the wind hurling stinging rain into his face, until his knuckles were bloody and bruised.

Johnny was dead. Just as Nate had known for years.

But finding his body was more devastating than even he had imagined.

He wiped his jacket sleeve across his eyes and pushed himself to his feet again. Leaning down, he carefully pulled the bag of bones free of the mud. It was over. Roy Vaughn was dead. There would be no more looking over his shoulder. He would bury Johnny now. It was all he could do for the brother he'd loved more than life.

His fingers caught on something. He raised his hand, surprised to see that it was a thin silver chain. The end was hooked on the almost indistinguishable fabric of the old denim quilt.

He broke it loose and held the chain up to the light, letting the rain wash over the cheap chain that had tarnished from being in the ground and the small silver medallion that hung from it. This had been in with Johnny's body. Why?

He turned the medallion up to see it, wiping away the rest of the mud with his thumb, and saw with a start that it was a St. Christopher medal. His heart began to pound so erratically he didn't trust his legs. He slumped back against one of the cottonwood trunks. He'd only known one person who'd worn a St. Christopher medal.

My mother gave it to me, Nate remembered the boy saying. *It's the only thing I have from her.*

Even before Nate turned the medal over he knew what name would be there. Engraved into the silver was the word *Thomas.*

FLYNN MOVED TO the back window. "I tried to convince Nate to let the past go. I did everything I could to protect him. But he just can't let it go, can he?"

"Maybe we should go see how he is," McKenna said. "He's just out back."

"Digging?" He stepped to the back window. "He's not going to find Johnny's body way down there."

McKenna's head snapped up, her pulse a thrum in her ears. Flynn seemed to have frozen, as if his own words had finally registered.

She glanced toward the doorway, but before she could take a step Flynn turned, and she saw what seemed to leap into his hand. She heard the snick of the switchblade as the blade shot out and saw the look on Flynn's handsome face as he blocked the doorway.

"No," she said, shaking her head as she stepped back, bumping into the wall. "I don't understand."

"I'm afraid you do," Flynn said.

She stared at the blade of the knife gleaming dully in the light from the storm. She feared she understood only too well as he came toward her.

The sound of a door slamming downstairs made them both turn. She opened her mouth, but Flynn was faster. He grabbed a handful of her hair and pressed the blade of the knife to her throat.

"You do exactly as I say and no one gets hurt," he whispered into her ear.

"McKenna?" Nate called from below them.

"Answer him," Flynn whispered. "Say, 'Up here, Nate.' And nothing more."

She felt the sting of the blade as Nate called her name again. "Don't come up!" she cried out. "He's got a knife!"

Flynn laughed. "So it's like that with you and Nate?" He shook his head at the sound of Nate's frantic footfalls on the stairs. "I guess we'll do it your way, then."

NATE STOPPED IN the doorway, taking in everything in one quick flash: Lucky clutching a handful of McKenna's hair and holding a switchblade knife to her throat.

"Hello, Lucky," he said, feeling that cold calm come over him. "Or should I call you Flynn?"

"I like Flynn better since we both know that my luck has run out. You found Johnny?" He sounded surprised.

Nate nodded. "And I found this with his remains." He opened his hand and the St. Christopher medal tumbled out to dangle from the tarnished chain.

Flynn stared at it for a moment as if hypnotized, and Nate thought about rushing him but couldn't chance it. He met McKenna's gaze. She was scared but strong. He knew he could count on her when things hit the fan—which they were going to do. And soon.

"This is between you and me, Flynn," he said calmly. "Let McKenna go."

"I've tried to make up for what happened with Johnny," Flynn said, sounding close to tears.

"What *did* happen with Johnny?"

"You know how Johnny was. He wouldn't back down from Roy."

"I asked what happened the night you killed Johnny," Nate said.

"It was Roy. He made me do things." Flynn's voice trembled. "I knew he would hurt me if I didn't do what he said. I was just a *boy*," he wailed. "Didn't you ever wonder why Roy never hurt me? You had to know."

Nate knew. He'd never admitted it though, but it was one of the reasons he had hated Roy Vaughn for so many years.

"Then this one night Roy came over to my bed and told me I had to do something to prove my loyalty to him," Flynn said, pulling himself together. "If I didn't do it, he would kill you. I begged him, but Roy—" Flynn's voice broke.

"How did your St. Christopher medal end up with Johnny's body?"

"I put it there. It was all I had. I wanted to give Johnny something. Bad idea, huh?"

Nate nodded. Flynn had left a clue, one he must have realized later would come back to haunt him if Nate ever found his brother's remains. "So that's why you came up here the minute you heard Ellis Harper had died. Just like you said, you knew I'd be here looking for Johnny."

"I killed Roy for you," Flynn blurted out. "I heard he was living with his mother and her boyfriend. You should have seen Roy. He was dying of cancer and had wasted away to nothing. He cried like a baby when I killed him."

Nate felt sick. He could see the look of horror in McKenna's eyes. And the fear. She had to know just how dire this situation was. Did she also know that he would die trying to save her if it came to that?

McKenna watched Nate, afraid to do more than breathe. Flynn still had the blade to her throat. She knew he planned to kill her—just as he'd killed before.

It was Nate she didn't have a clue about. She'd seen that cold, calculated look on his face before, after he shot Dennis Jones. It frightened her even more now because she didn't have any idea what he was going to do faced with what he now knew.

"See, that's what's so crazy, Nate," Flynn was saying. "All of us spending years looking over our shoulders, worried about this bogeyman that no longer existed. It's whacked, man. Don't you see? It wasn't Roy we had to fear. It was the bogeyman inside us all. We took it with us when we left this house."

"No," Nate said.

"Bull. You came back here to kill Roy. What makes you any different from me? I tracked him down for you, man. I saved you from having to kill him."

"Only it turns out Roy wasn't responsible for Johnny's death. You were."

"How can you say that? I told you—Roy *made* me do it. You think I wanted to hurt Johnny? I knew how close you two were. I would have killed Dennis, too, but he got away. I wasn't worried, though. I knew you could handle him."

"You got Dennis out," Nate said.

Flynn nodded. "I thought I was going to need some help with Roy. But as it turned out…"

"It's over," Nate said. "The cops know everything. You can't run far or fast enough. You need to turn yourself in," Nate said.

Flynn shook his head. McKenna could feel his agitation. "You know what would happen," he said, a whine to his voice. "Prison would be like Harper House. There would be another Roy Vaughn. That's why it has to end here, in this house. I knew before I came back to Whitehorse that it would end like this. It's the only way I will ever find my peace. It's fate. *My* fate."

Something moved off to McKenna's left. Flynn didn't seem to notice as the black cat she'd seen before slipped into the room.

"Then let it end with just the two of us, like it

was when we were boys," Nate said and took a step toward them.

"The two of us," Flynn repeated. "Just like old times, huh?" He shook his head and drew McKenna closer. The knife bit into her neck. She felt the sting and saw in Nate's eyes that Flynn had drawn blood.

"Sorry, Nate, but McKenna's the only one besides you and me who knows the truth. I can't let her go."

McKenna caught something in Nate's expression. He'd seen the black cat. She recalled how Flynn had reacted when he'd broken the mirror and met Nate's gaze. Did Nate know how superstitious Flynn was?

Suddenly the black cat came into view. It stopped in the middle of the room only feet from her and Flynn. She heard the sound that came out of Flynn when he saw the cat and knew this might be her only chance.

With both hands she shoved his arm away from her throat as she threw her body into him—and they both began to fall forward. Flynn let go of her hair as he fought to regain his balance, his gaze seemingly locked on the cat as they both went down. Out of the corner of her eye, she saw Nate spring toward them.

The cat let out a shriek, which was nearly drowned out by Flynn's cry of pain as the switchblade was twisted from his fingers.

She scrambled out of Flynn's grasp. As she turned she saw Flynn get to his feet. Nate was holding the switchblade. Time seemed to stop. The two men were staring across time at each other when the cat leaped up on the windowsill off to their right, drawing Nate's attention for just a second too long.

"Nate!" McKenna screamed as Flynn lunged for the knife.

But she saw at once that it had never been Flynn's intention to try to take the knife back. Flynn threw himself onto the blade, driving it deep into himself before Nate could move.

Flynn stumbled back. Blood bloomed across his shirt and over his fingers splayed over the wound. He glanced down at the blood, then up at Nate.

"I loved you like a brother, Nate. I could never have hurt you." Flynn started to fall forward.

Nate caught him and lowered him to the floor, and McKenna watched as Flynn died in Nate's arms.

Epilogue

A few days before her sister Eve's wedding, McKenna saddled her horse and rode out toward the Breaks. She hadn't ridden her horse since that day with Nate Dempsey.

It seemed a lifetime ago.

Nor had she been back to Harper House. Eve had insisted she stay at the ranch for a while, not make any big decisions until she'd given herself some time.

Nate had gone back to Paradise. Back to the police department. He'd called a few times. Just to see how she was. She always told him she was fine.

They didn't talk about Harper House. Or Flynn.

Carter had told her Flynn's history, about him being left at seven in a gas station bathroom on the edge of Whitehorse, and warned her that kids like that often couldn't get past their childhoods.

She knew what he was saying. Forget Nate Dempsey.

If only it was that easy.

She rode toward the wild country of the Breaks. It felt good to be back in a saddle. She'd missed riding. She told herself that she wouldn't think about Nate or Harper House, but of course that was impossible.

She hadn't gone far when she turned her horse and

rode east. The barn came into view first, the horse weather vane on top moaning in the breeze. She slowed her horse as the house appeared out of the horizon.

She'd had a lot of time to think about the house—and why it had always called to her. While she wasn't superstitious, she wasn't so sure she didn't believe in fate. She'd seen Nate the first time in that house. And it had drawn her back years later.

If she hadn't bought the house, she knew her path and Nate's never would have crossed. She'd believed it was meant to be that she got the old Harper place. She still did.

But what about her happy ending? she asked herself as she rode up to the fence and sat staring at the house. She would never have it in Harper House.

While Eve had made her promise not to make any decisions until she'd given herself time, McKenna had made one she hadn't told anyone about.

Tomorrow the house would be razed. Eventually the land would heal—and maybe Nate would, too. By next spring the wild grasses would come back and all sign of Harper House would be gone.

No matter what she decided to do with the land, she couldn't let another unsuspecting soul move into that house.

She took one last look at the house and rode to the south until she reached the gate. Opening it, she rode across the pasture. Her pasture. How she had wanted to raise paint horses here. That dream was the hardest one to let go of. As Eve said, she could raise horses anywhere.

But that dream had always been connected to this place, McKenna realized. She didn't understand it, just knew it to be true. If she'd learned anything in all this, it was to trust and not question. Some things just were.

She reined in her horse at the top of the mountain, just as she and Nate had done. From this spot she couldn't see Harper House. From here the land stretched as far as the eye could see.

Her horse whinnied and moved under her. She hadn't heard the other rider. Blinded by the sun, she couldn't see him. But she recognized the horse. An Appaloosa.

Her heart leaped to her throat as Nate Dempsey rode up to join her. She stared at him, unable to utter more than a word. "How…?"

"Eve told me where to find you," he said as he looked out across the land as she had been doing only moments before.

She followed his gaze, her heart racing. For weeks she'd been trying to accept that Nate was gone. That he would never be back here. That the connection she'd felt between them hadn't existed.

"It's beautiful here," Nate said. "I never saw how beautiful until I saw it through your eyes. It would be a shame not to raise horses on this land, McKenna."

Tears welled in her eyes as she met his gaze.

"I think I mentioned that I thought here would be a great place for a house," he said. "I'm pretty good with a hammer, and you have a way with horses. I love you, McKenna. I loved you from the first time I saw you. So what do you say?"

What could she say as he dismounted and lifted her from her horse and into his arms?

His kiss was an early Fourth of July. The summer day was brighter than any she'd ever seen. And as he held her and they gazed out over the land, the future stretched before them, she knew that one day this place would be called "the old Dempsey place" and people would talk of all the paint horses that had been raised here.

McKenna knew as Nate bent to kiss her again that it would be their children and all the generations that would follow that would ultimately heal this place.

And it would be their love that would heal Nate Dempsey.

* * * * *

We hope you enjoyed reading

ROUGH RIDER AND MATCHMAKING WITH A MISSION

by *New York Times* bestselling author
B.J. DANIELS

HARLEQUIN

INTRIGUE

EDGE-OF-YOUR-SEAT INTRIGUE,
FEARLESS ROMANCE.

HIBJD1017

She prayed for sleep, but her mind kept returning to that time in the Sahara. Being part of the expedition had been such a privilege. She remembered the way they'd all felt when they'd broken through to the tomb. Satima Mahmoud—the pretty Egyptian interpreter who had so enchanted Joe Rosello—had been the first to scream when the workers found the entry.

Of course, Henry Tomlinson was called then. He'd been there to break the seal. They'd all laughed and joked about the curses that came with such finds, about the stupid movies that had been made.

Yes, people had died during other expeditions—as if they had been cursed. The Tut story was one example—and yet, by all accounts, there had been scientific explanations for everything that had happened.

Almost everything, anyway.

And their find…

There hadn't been any curses. Not written curses, at any rate.

But Henry had died. And Henry had broken the seal…

No mummy curse had gotten to them; someone had killed Henry. And that someone had gotten away with it because neither the American Department of State nor the Egyptian government had wanted the expedition caught in the crosshairs of an insurgency. Reasonably enough!

But now…

For some reason, the uneasy dreams that came with her restless sleep weren't filled with mummies, tombs, sarcophagi or canopic jars. No funerary objects whatsoever, no golden scepters, no jewelry, no treasures.

Instead, she saw the sand. The endless sand of the Sahara. And the sand was teeming, rising up from the ground, swirling in the air.

Someone was coming…

She braced, because there were rumors swirling along with the sand. Their group could fall under attack—there was unrest in the area. Good Lord, they were in the Middle East!

But she found herself walking through the sand, toward whomever or whatever was coming.

She saw someone.

The killer?

She kept walking toward him. There was more upheaval behind the man, sand billowing dark and heavy like a twister of deadly granules.

Then she saw him.

And it was Micah Fox.

She woke with a start.

And she wondered if he was going to be her salvation…

Or a greater danger to her heart, a danger she hadn't yet seen.

Don't miss
SHADOWS IN THE NIGHT,
available November 2017 wherever
Harlequin® Intrigue books and ebooks are sold.

www.Harlequin.com

INTRIGUE

EDGE-OF-YOUR-SEAT INTRIGUE, FEARLESS ROMANCE.

Save **$1.00**

on the purchase of ANY Harlequin® Intrigue book.

Available wherever books are sold, including most bookstores, supermarkets, drugstores and discount stores.

Save **$1.00**

on the purchase of any Harlequin® Intrigue book.

Coupon valid until December 31, 2017.
Redeemable at participating outlets in the U.S. and Canada only.
Not redeemable at Barnes & Noble stores. Limit one coupon per customer.

52614978

® and ™ are trademarks owned and used by the trademark owner and/or its licensee.

© 2017 Harlequin Enterprises Limited

HIBJDCOUPI017

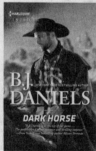  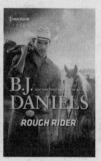